The Blue Evening Gone

Jessica Stirling

CORONET BOOKS
Hodder and Stoughton

First published in Great Britain in 1981 by Hodder and Stoughton
A division of Hodder Headline PLC
First published by Hodder and Stoughton in paperback in 1999
A Coronet Paperback

10 9 8 7 6 5

A CIP catalogue record for this title is available
from the British Library.

ISBN 978 0 340 70834 7

Printed and bound by
CPI Group (UK) Ltd, Croydon, CR0 4YY

Hodder and Stoughton
A division of Hodder Headline PLC
338 Euston Road
London NW1 3BH

For Gillian

Contents

Contents

PART ONE

Côte d'Azur

1

The Holbein Miniature

Monsieur Hugues de Rais, a pale-eyed little Breton, was known throughout Europe by a variety of uncomplimentary nicknames. In Paris he was *Le Fouet*, the Whisk, in Zurich *Le Petit-gris*, the Squirrel; grumbling Italian art dealers alluded to him as *Il Cappello Nero*, the Black Hat. In Moscow, where he had helped the Russian government out of a financial hole by discreetly transferring six million dollars' worth of treasure from the Hermitage into Mr. Andrew Mellon's capacious pocket, the ingrates damned him as a puff of wind from the bowels of a Czarist lackey – or words to that effect. In his home town of Marseilles the handful of folk who knew of his existence referred to him as *Le Fantôme* for, like a ghost, he was seldom seen in daylight and would vanish entirely for months on end. Forty years of dedicated service to the cause of art had not made Monsieur de Rais awfully popular. In his cosmopolitan circle only three women had ever confessed that they were fond of the foxy little chap – Gertrude Stein, who was notoriously perverse, Abby Aldrich Rockefeller, who had a kind word to say for everyone, and Holly Beckman King.

Holly King had been around the art market too long to be taken in by de Rais' air of gracious innocence. She knew that he often ran close to the wind and on occasions could be totally unscrupulous. On the other hand she had much sympathy for the Frenchman; he was a gutter rat from Brest,

11

she a slum kid from Lambeth, and the climb to the top had not been easy for either of them. Beneath his appetite for profit Hugues de Rais nurtured a deep and abiding love of fine art that enabled him to put up with the stuffiness and hypocrisy of the acquistive millionaires to whom he pandered. In these respects Holly King and Hugues de Rais were akin. Compatability stopped short of trust, however. Hugues de Rais operated with a deviousness that ranged from the right side of amusing to the wrong side of sinister. How he found out that Holly was registered at the Regina Hotel in the Rue de Rivoli that first week in March 1932, and that she had private business with Monsieur Lenormant of the Galerie Voltaire, were mysteries that were never solved, the first tiny strands in a web of intrigue and deceit in which Holly would eventually be enmeshed.

The invitation seemed harmlessly eccentric. Holly received the letter at breakfast on the morning of her fourth day in Paris. The note was short and formal. It suggested that it would be pleasant, and possibly rewarding, if Madame King would drop in for lunch *chez* de Rais as soon as it was convenient to her. She scanned the letter for a Paris address, found none and was forced to conclude that Monsieur de Rais intended her to call on him at his home in Marseilles, a long night's train ride from the capital. Holly knew de Rais' methods of old; the invitation was not casual, more of an urgent summons than anything. She did not mention it to Monsieur Lenormant who considered de Rais an out-and-out scoundrel and a blight on the good name of an honourable profession, but invented a plausible excuse for interrupting her business at the Galerie Voltaire and, that same evening, boarded the sleeping-car express to discover just what it was that the Phantom might have for sale.

*   *   *

Monsieur de Rais unlocked a drawer in his bureau and brought out a case no larger than the palm of his hand. Bound in scarlet morocco, the case had tiny brass hinges and a scalloped latch. Reverently de Rais placed the case on the table and moved back to his overstuffed armchair by the window.

Seating himself, he crossed his legs and lit a Caporal.

"Open it, Madame."

Holly did.

The unfaded velvet lining confirmed her initial impression that the case was of modern manufacture. The portrait within, however, was very old indeed, framed in an oval of chunky ebony with a crude tight-fitting glass spy piece. The object had been thoroughly cleaned and the face beneath the glass was perfectly clear.

De Rais spoke excellent English, buttered with soft *zee* sounds. "Do you know what it is?"

"An early English miniature."

"Take it out."

Carefully Holly extracted the miniature from the velvet bed and turned it over.

"The backing board is not detachable," said de Rais. "Stiff shell paste glued to the frame. The glass will come out, however."

"Have you taken it apart?"

"Naturally, as far as I dare to without damage."

Expertly Holly separated glass from frame and leaned forward to examine the painting in detail. Already she had an inkling as to its worth but held her tongue, giving no signs of eagerness or pleasure.

Blue smoke wreathed from de Rais' cigarette. Sunlight filtered through lace curtains. The Frenchman squinted shrewdly through his pince-nez. In fine art dealing there was no demarcation between buyer and seller. Today you were one thing, tomorrow another. Holly wondered where de Rais had unearthed the piece and how much it had cost him. No doubt he had made a thorough job of authentication. Amicable though relations were between them, Holly could not simply accept de Rais' word at face value.

"Painted on parchment on board, perhaps a playing card," she said. "Odd shape, not circular, almost oval."

"Distinctive, is it not?"

"Extremely. Beautifully executed."

13

Dark-haired, dark-eyed, quiet of manner, Holly King displayed an effortless sense of style that was more French than English. She had none of the imperious 'look at me, ain't I grand' attitude that so many English women adopted in the false belief that it made them attractive. Gravity was toned down by charm and humour. As always de Rais was impressed by the woman. His admiration for her had been increased by certain intimate information that had come his way of late. Holly King was of Russian-Jewish stock and Kennedy was her second husband. Her first husband, the father of her son, had been a young poet named Christopher Deems who had died tragically in a fire in London's Pimlico. Perhaps, de Rais thought, the woman's considerable self-control stemmed from that disastrous period in her life. She was certainly shrewd, more so than her husband. He regretted having to dupe her but, under the circumstances, there was no help for it; he was obliged to do what he was told.

"It's a court portrait but not quite as formal as one would expect," Holly said.

"A Hilliard perhaps?" de Rais teased.

"It isn't hard enough for a Hilliard. The modelling of the fabrics and features suggests the Isaac Oliver school, but the clue lies in the blue background."

"You have it?"

Holly glanced at the dealer. Why was he so eager for her identification? Did he doubt his own opinion? Not de Rais! Now she understood why he had invited her to Marseilles, to cut her off from Monsieur Lenormant's advice and sources of research. She was not dismayed by his ruse to foster uncertainty. The Kings' axiom had always been, 'Sell your successes; pay for your mistakes.' Hordes of art dealers dressed their errors and sold them unblushingly under spurious labels, tarted up with vague histories, but Holly steadfastly believed that dishonesty had a way of coming home to roost.

She was obliged to commit herself.

She said, "I think it's a Holbein."

"Bravo!" de Rais stubbed out his cigarette and got to his feet. "One of the best examples of Hans Holbein's miniature work I have ever encountered. Do you not agree, Madame King?"

14

He was pressing her, nudging her towards an offer.

"Except for gallery examples I've never seen a Holbein miniature in the flesh before," Holly said.

"Nor have I," said de Rais. "It is for the reason that they are so very scarce.

In silence the dealers stared down at the miniature.

Outside, noon traffic clacked on the cobbles of the Rue Honorat and the timbers of the old house shook slightly as a train rumbled into Gare St. Charles. The domicile had once been an annex of a Capuchin convent, but a century of progress had swallowed up the stone dwelling and smothered it in warehouses and déclassé cottages. In the shop below there was no evidence of de Rais' wealth. The fly-blown window was sparsely dressed with bric-à-brac. Even the long interior contained little of worth. Nobody, not even Madame Sempach, a whiskered Swiss widow who ran the household as if it was a cuckoo clock, knew where Hugues de Rais stored his treasures. Basically he was an entrepreneur not a shop-keeper. Most of his 'stock' lay in other people's galleries and houses while de Rais negotiated 'marriages' between sellers and buyers for a percentage of the profit.

Was he selling the Holbein on behalf of a client?

Was it a Holbein and not just a good sixteenth-century copy – and if it was a copy did de Rais know it was a copy?

Holly had to tread warily. "I take it, Monsier de Rais, that you've conducted appropriate research and that the painting is a Holbein?"

"Take comfort. It has been examined by an expert in Dresden and pronounced authentic."

"Did he provide you with a deposition to that effect?"

"It was not needed; he examined it as a favour to me."

"What was the expert's name?"

"Apologies, Madame; I cannot tell you."

"Really, Monsieur de Rais, you're not helping to allay my doubts."

"He is a forger, a faker, you see."

"Oh!"

"Who better to spot a fake than a faker?"

"I take your point," said Holly.

The domestic apartments were impeccably furnished with choice pieces acquired long before the war. Since he had reached his sixtieth year, and lost interest in the last of a string of young mistresses, secretiveness was de Rais' only vice. It was perfectly understandable; Marseilles was a rough-and-tumble seaport, an ideal location for smuggling art objects into and out of France.

"How long have you had the painting?"

"Three weeks," said de Rais.

For no good reason Holly found herself thinking of her brother Ritchie who, mercifully, had passed out of her ken years ago. More comprehensible would have been a stray thought of her eldest brother Maurice, for he had always reminded her, a little, of the Bishop of Lavour in Holbein's painting *The Ambassadors*. She glanced at the portrait, imagining that the long-dead Tudor lady bore a slight resemblance to Ruth Erbach, Ritchie's wife; a nonsense, a fantasy. The overnight train journey must have tired her.

"I take it there is a reliable provenance," Holly said.

"Naturally," said de Rais.

"May I see it?"

"Of course," said de Rais. "Before we commence to barter, however, may I enquire if you are in a position to present yourself as a potential purchaser?"

Holly said, "If you mean do I want to buy it, the answer is yes."

"The question," de Rais delicately cleared his throat, "is not whether you want to buy it, Madame, but whether you can afford to buy it."

"Afford?" What sort of value do you put on it, Monsieur de Rais?"

"Something in the nature of fifty thousand dollars, ten thousand pounds."

Holly sucked in her breath.

"That's . . ." .

"Too much for you?"

"I was going to say unrealistic; I've never heard of a miniature painting fetching anything like that price."

"Have you ever heard of a Holbein miniature, an excellent Holbein, with a history, being offered for sale at all?"

"No, but . . ."

"There are, Madame King, less than a dozen genuine Holbein miniatures in existence. To add to that tally by one – and such a one – is an achievement. I need not tell you how collectors covet rarity."

"If it can be proved that it is genuine," said Holly, "then one might possibly – only possibly – make that kind of price."

"If Pierpoint Morgan had still been alive, he would not have hesitated to pay such a sum for it," said de Rais. "I could have asked Morgan for the moon – and got it."

Holly said, "Monsieur de Rais, why are you selling this object to me? You have so many connections; a direct sale would give you more profit."

"I am out of favour with Americans," said de Rais. "My name is slightly – how do you say – in a puddle?"

"Mud."

"*Oui* – mud."

"Why?"

"I made an error. It was crass of me. I offended Mellon's agents – Knoedlers – and they spread unpleasant stories about me."

I've heard nothing. Were the stories true?"

"No, it was an error of tactics," said de Rais. "I insulted them."

"But for this kind of object, surely Knoedlers would forgive you?" said Holly.

"I tell you the truth, Madame, they would not pay me what it is worth."

"Offer it directly to Mellon, then. He isn't particularly unapproachable, is he?"

De Rais shrugged. "Mellon is after bigger fishes – Raphaels, Botticellis, van Eycks. It is said that he is building a collection to donate to a new museum in Washington."

"There are other institutions?"

"State galleries are the graveyard of art," said de Rais solemnly.

"Come now, Monsieur de Rais," said Holly. "Tell me the truth."

"I paid high for the miniature, said de Rais. "I was forced to a quick deal, to back my own judgment. I have not been in good straits recently. Besides, I never traded with a miniature before."

"What are you trying to say?"

"You have a friendship with the Ogden Hillises, do you not?"

"So that's it!"

"They will buy from you because they trust you," said de Rais. "If I go see them, they will have heard of my . . . my *contretemps* in America and they will beat me down in price. I speak the truth, Madame. I paid much money for this piece."

Holly believed him. He had probably cheated Knoedlers in some way, 'swinging' percentages perhaps, or stealing one of their clients. His deal with the Russians had become something of a legend in the antique trade, though little enough was known of the details. It was also possible that de Rais had overreached himself and that his finances needed a boost. Holly knew only too well how the popular idea of 'wealth' differed from reality. Kennedy and she were wealthy by the standards of the day, yet they were constantly pressed for cash.

"There is also the fact that the Ogden Hillises will not hang the Holbein in the bathroom," said de Rais. "They do not buy by the bushel."

"Yes, Ray's an acknowledged expert in miniatures," Holly agreed. "He'd cherish one like this."

"For such reasons, Madame King, I am inviting *you* to buy my Holbein."

"Will you guarantee its authenticity?" said Holly. "If I offer it to Ray Hillis and he spots it as a fake, or a copy, will you take it back?"

"That is not in question," said de Rais.

"What of the history of the painting?"

"The painting was brought to France by an English doctor a hundred years ago," said de Rais. "It was stolen from him."

"Stolen?"

"Stolen," said de Rais. "It has been in the possession of a provincial French family ever since."

"Now they have chosen to sell it?"

"*Non*; the family died out. The miniature was sold with other scraps to an acquantance of mine. He identified the artist, and contacted me."

"And you thought of Ray Ogden Hillis?"

"At once – and then of you."

Holly closed her eyes to shut out the Holbein and the drift of tobacco smoke. Fifty thousand dollars would stretch the Kings' resources. Tacitly de Rais had indicated that he required payment in cash. In the long run she might beat the Breton down to around forty thousand, less if she was lucky. He would expect her to haggle, would have inflated his initial asking price to accommodate 'generosity'. Even so, fifty thousand was a sizeable sum to invest in a single small work.

"When must you have an answer, Monsieur de Rais?"

"Today."

"And when do you wish payment?" said Holly.

"The moment you are satisfied that the Holbein is genuine."

"Fifty thousand dollars is your final asking price?"

"The Kings are used to high finance, no?"

"Not quite so high as this, Monsieur de Rais," said Holly. "Not for a miniature."

"Hmm!" De Rais jiggled his fingers. "Maybe we split a hair about the final price – just a little."

Holly glanced at the dealer. He was not teasing now. He stood by the great brown armchair, his hand draped on the lace 'macassar.

"I have identified the woman of the portrait," he said. "She is a famous personage. A famous artist and a famous subject; there is value in that combination, is there not?"

"There is," Holly agreed. "Who is she, Monsieur de Rais?"

"Anne of Cleves."

"Can you prove it?"

"Almost conclusively."

"Almost?"

In Monsieur de Rais' hand a photograph appeared as if by

legerdemain. He advanced to the table and set the photograph by the miniature. "The pose and apparel are different but it is the same woman, is it not?"

"Yes, the same woman," Holly unhesitatingly agreed.

"The photograph is of the Hans Holbein three-quarter length portrait that hangs in the Louvre. I have been there in person, with our miniature, to make a comparison. The Louvre portrait was painted in 1539 on commission of King Henry, before his marriage to the lady. The history of the miniature is not specific. Indeed it lists the work as *Portrait of an Unknown Noblewoman*. But then poor Anne was not long in favour with Henry."

Holly lifted her head from a comparison of photograph and miniature. "I do believe you're right."

"It is a nice beginning for the story, no?"

"A very nice beginning," Holly agreed. "Yes, Monsieur de Rais, if the provenance and final price are right, I will buy the Holbein."

"*La politique de l'immortalité*; history and hard cash," de Rais said.

"It has always been so," said Holly in French.

Monsieur de Rais carefully returned the miniature to its frame, then to the leather case. He carried the case to the bureau and locked it again. Turning, he offered Holly his arm.

"Madame Sempach has prepared luncheon for us in the dining room. Come, we will eat together and talk of money and the sad history of Anne of Cleves; the provenance of discarded queens."

Two hours later the first clause of the contract of sale had been settled and the Holbein miniature had begun to pass into Holly Beckman King's possession at a price of thirty-eight thousand dollars, seven thousand six hundred pounds.

Both seller and buyer were delighted with the deal – at the time.

* * *

The sleeping car express from Marseilles to Paris carried Holly through the darkness of Monday night and Tuesday morning. She did not sleep well. She spent most of Tuesday with Monsieur Lenormant of the Galerie Voltaire finalising the sale of a magnificent Italian cabinet in ivory, gold and red lacquer that Kennedy had bought privately from the Borestone family, whose fortunes had slumped after the Wall Street Crash three years ago.

On Tuesday evening Holly flew from Le Bourget to Croydon. She reached home in Chelsea just as her husband was finishing dinner.

Solicitously, he rose and rang the bell for Jenny, the maid. He apologised to Jenny, who was preparing to slip out for the evening, and asked her to find Madam something to eat.

"Really, Kennedy, I'm not hungry."

"You look rather tired, m'dear," Kennedy said. "A bite of supper will perk you up."

Holly took the glass of sherry her husband poured for her and sipped it thankfully. She was relieved to be home again, to share her elation and her anxiety with Kennedy. She seated herself by the fire and told him to finish dinner, intending to ease into the tale of her 'find' in Marseilles. But the pressure of the news was too much for her. She could wait no longer.

"Kennedy, I need seven thousand and six hundred pounds in the drawing account by Monday of next week."

"Thirty-eight thousand dollars! Good God! What for?"

"To buy a Holbein miniature from Hugues de Rais."

"Is it worth such a price?"

"Every penny."

"In that case," said Kennedy, "the money will be ready when you need it."

"But it's so *much*."

Kennedy rose from the table, dabbed his mouth with a napkin, came over and kissed his wife on the brow.

"I assume you already have a buyer in mind?"

"The Ogden Hillises."

"Oh God!" said Kennedy, in mock horror. "I know what that means."

Holly smiled and reached for his hand. She knew how much he disliked travel out of England but she needed his companionship and support.

"A trip to Monte, I'm afraid," she said.

*   *   *

The cynical old saying that the husband is always the last to know did not apply to Kennedy King. He understood his wife better than anyone alive, better than she understood herself. Friends and acquaintances who had not encountered Holly before marriage to Kennedy King found her dauntingly self-contained. On the surface she might appear to be nothing but a clever minx who had snared a man much older than herself to lay hands on his money – but there were anomalies in the relationship that defied obvious explanations.

Kennedy and Holly were partners in business as well as marriage. It was undeniable that she had dragged the fusty Edwardian bachelor out of his shell, undeniable that she had made him happy. One had only to watch the couple together to realise that florid old Kennedy adored his much younger wife. Kennedy ignored the prattlers and spite merchants. Neither he nor Holly made any bones about the past. Their frankness had successfully laid the ghost of her first husband – Kennedy's nephew – Christopher Deems. Since his death in 1921, Deems' reputation had grown. Grouped with Owen and Brooke, his poems were frequently anthologised and studied in schools and universities. Holly left the administration of her first husband's literary estate to Victor Lawfeld, a lawyer who took pleasure in the task. Profits were channelled directly to the Malvern Home for War Wounded. Holly made not a penny from them.

As for the rest of the Beckman family, to Kennedy's vast relief, Holly was not inclined to keep in touch with her relatives. Brother Maury was the only exception. A successful real estate dealer, Maury dined regularly at the Kings' Chelsea home. He was fond of his sister as she was of him. Holly's father, Leo Beckman, remained in Lambeth. Maury called on the old man every couple of weeks and listened to his complaints. Holly shunned her father completely, though she contributed to the 'allowance' that Maury gave Leo to keep him in beer and tobacco and to ensure that he had no need to soil his hands with work. Holly's other brother, Ritchie Beckman, whom Kennedy had never met, was, by all accounts, a thoroughly bad lot. But he had cleared off out of England long ago and nothing was known of his whereabouts.

For eight years, going on nine, since Holly had finally given in to Kennedy's pleading and agreed to become his wife, life for the Kings had been comfortably hectic. Centred on the buying and selling of antique works of art and the expansion of King's Bond Street premises in the Chalfont Arcade, Holly had also found time to transform Kennedy's house in Chelsea into an elegant, comfortable home. Though everything in the Kings' garden appeared rosy, Kennedy was never quite free from a nagging anxiety that one day Holly's loyalty would waver, her affection for him diminish and her almost compulsive fascination with antiques would no longer substitute for instincts and impulses that, he was sure, she had unwittingly suppressed for the good of her son and the progress of the business.

What was more he was growing old. He felt himself to be in danger of slipping into premature stuffiness. For instance, he had less and less inclination to race about Europe, dining, wining and dealing, or even to trot round England in pursuit of choice antiques. Cultivating the rich and influential was a job for the young and Holly had gained immeasurably in sophistication during her travels on his behalf. Kennedy experienced apprehension at the widening gap between them. He spurred himself to keep up with her, accompanying her to Paris or Lyons, to Grenoble or the Riviera when he would far rather have been at home, snug in his own routines.

Conscious of subtle changes in himself, Kennedy thought he detected even more subtle changes in Holly, a shift from enthusiasm to restlessness. It was as if maintaining the status of King & Company in the international art market had become more of a duty than a pleasure, something she continued to do because no alternative offered itself. Not that Holly complained; she, Kennedy thought, was probably unaware of how restless she had become these past couple of years. It worried him considerably. He had observed many an act of apparent madness in men and women of his acquaintance. Hadn't he gone through such a phase himself about the time of his marriage to Holly? Craving change and a solution to the uncertainties of maturity, people did strange things – bought castles in Scotland, villas in Spain, deep-sea yachts or Thames barges, took up ballooning, yoga, rhumba dancing or bridge, set off on voyages to China, Peru or the Mountains of the Moon; had love affairs by the score or found a brand new partner who, they supposed, would offer them another whirl at novelty or add purpose once more to their lives.

Kennedy had never had occasion to doubt Holly's loyalty. In almost a decade of marriage she had shown no interest in any of the many men who had flirted with her. She shrugged off their attentions or stung the more thick-skinned with sarcasm; yet Kennedy had glimpsed the dark river of passion that ran deep beneath his wife's composure and feared that one day it would sweep her away from him. How or when that dreaded day might come Kennedy, of course, could not be sure. He found it difficult to reconcile Holly's candour with the image of a cheating wife, and consoled himself, rationally, with the notion that he, not she, was the partner who lacked stability. Was he too unconsciously seeking to become a martyred old man, to replace contentment with astringent suffering, to court change for its own sake?

When the day came, however – in the Hotel Britannique on the Avenue de Monte Carlo in the early summer of 1932 – Kennedy was there to witness the beginnings of the affair and thereafter could not be sure whether he was relieved or angry that Holly had first met the man who would become her lover right under his very nose.

* * *

The Avenue de Monte Carlo with its view of the port and Great Rock of Monaco was congested with traffic. Charabancs and swaying trucks laden with produce from the Ventimiglia market vied with Alfas, Opels and sleek Renault limousines. Supercharged sports coupés and sturdy little Citroens pipped past the huge plate-glass window of the morning lounge and distracted Holly's attention from the parchment-covered notebook that served her as a business diary. She stared out at the automobiles and beyond at the pleasure craft that speckled the waters of the Mediterranean and wondered which of the raffish steam launches belonged to the Ogden Hillises or if they were still somewhere round the coast to the north, gliding along with the utter disregard for appointments, for time, that separated the very rich from those of *la haute bourgeoisie* who still had to earn their livings.

Holly had long ago shed her excitement at the prospect of meeting famous people in de luxe hotels. Such locations had become, as Kennedy put it, 'her back office'. Glittering elegance no longer impressed her.

She glanced across the glass-topped table at her husband. He was sipping coffee and puffing a panatella. He smoked too much for a man with a respiratory complaint. He too looked faintly bored. In recent years, however, Kennedy had developed such a degree of stoicism that his florid features seldom showed much emotion and Holly could never be sure what he was thinking or feeling. The Victorian inhibitions that had choked his boyhood like weeds, had re-emerged in middle-age. Idly he watched the traffic. Even in a soft cream silk shirt and striped lightweight blazer, he looked more like a gentleman-farmer than a *boulevardier*. She supposed he was happy enough.

She reached across the table and put her hand on his.

"Shan't be here too long, old duck," she said. "You'll be home by the weekend. Did you write to Chris?"

"Hmm! We've an arrangement to meet at the Oval on Saturday."

"Will you collect him at school?"

"Lord, no, he'll come up by train."

"Don't you think . . . ?"

"He's a young man, Holly. Besides it's only a three-coacher from Cambridge, not the Shanghai Express!"

"But you will take him back?"

Kennedy smiled reassuringly. "Of course I'll take him back. He's promised me a cocoa and sausage supper and I've no intention of missing that – assuming, that is, that we're not still sitting here waiting for the blessed Ogden Hillises."

"Well, we didn't specify a time. We said 'about' ten."

"And it's 'about' noon now. You know, they won't even apologise."

"Raymond will," Holly said. "He's really very courteous."

"Can you handle him?"

"Yes," said Holly. "Marion's the problem."

"I don't like her much," Kennedy admitted. "I almost wish she was more typical, less . . . less . . ."

"Clever," said Holly. "Her cleverness is disconcerting. She may pretend to be feather-headed but she's the power behind the throne. It's her money, after all."

Once Kennedy had revelled in gossip but he seemed to have lost his taste for that simple pleasure too. Holly was about to embroider her opinion of Marion Ogden Hillis's character when Kennedy grunted, "Talk of the devil."

The American couple had walked up from the landing quay at the yacht harbour, leaving servants to attend to the tiresome business of transferring luggage to a conveyance. The Hotel Britannique would have dispatched one of their bright yellow vans and a regiment of porters if the Ogden Hillises had so much as hinted at a need of them, but the couple affected a kind of modesty that was at odds with their life style. Hand in hand, they crossed the boulevard. Raymond was exceedingly tall, upright and cautious, and held his brisk sprite of a wife by the wrist as if to restrain her from leaping over the automobiles like a springbok. Though there was nothing to distinguish them from other handsome couples along the Avenue they somehow attracted attention. Heads turned as they forded the thoroughfare, mounted the broad steps of the hotel and came through the doors into the ornate foyer that connected to the lounge. Managers advanced simpering, clerks bustled, bell boys poised hopefully. Ray lingered, talking, arranging. Marion gave a graceful dismissive sweep of her arm and pivoted like a ballerina. She floated towards the Kings through shiny mirrored planes of light, while outside, at the doorway, two men emerged from a laden taxicab and began to haggle with the driver over a conglomeration of cabin trunks and kidskin valises, a piece of business that instantly developed into a shouting match.

"Howard's here, I see," said Marion in flight, then, touching down at the Kings' table, "Holly, you're beautiful. How do you do it? I swear, Kennedy, you should have your wife painted by Augustus John. Have you met him? John, I mean? Clara – do you know Clara Pendle, she of Toledo – Toledo, Ohio, I mean – Clara met John last year in some exotic spot like Eastbourne. Or was it Bath? Eastbourne, I think. You live near Eastbourne, don't you?"

"Chelsea," said Kennedy, quietly. "On Thames."

"Chelsea, yes, of course." Marion released the conversation like a helium balloon. For a split second she was vulnerable. Quickly she plucked another topic from the air to protect herself against seriousness. "Holly, let me look at you. *Wonderful* to see you. Ah, Howard's gotten things rolling, I see."

The squabble at the pavement's edge had been settled. Uniformed porters, like a column of ants, were lugging baggage into the hotel.

"I'm sure you'll appreciate Howard, Howard Crocker. What a guy. He's dying to meet you. Aren't we travelling light this time? All that cabin space going to waste. Shame! Haven't you heard of Howard? The Broadway producer? Ray invested the odd dollar in that direction. Proved worthwhile too. And Peter? Peter Freeman? So charming! So talented. And rather dangerous." Marion Ogden Hillis poured coffee from the silver pot into her cup, drank it swiftly and lit a cigarette. "There he is now, in all his glory. See what I mean, darling?"

Porters had removed the very last valise and the taxicab had departed. Pedestrians went on their way. Nobody paid the slightest attention to the man who loitered on the pavement before the hotel. He was dressed in casual flannels and open-collar shirt, his jacket neatly folded over his arm, one hand in his pocket. He was, Holly thought, the most graceful man she had ever seen. He reminded her – slightly – of David

Aspinall, her first lover, though he was not so tall and his air of self-assurance was less gauche. Even so, the resemblance was there. It engendered in Holly an unreasonable affinity, a one-sided rapport with the stranger, and a heart-lurching eagerness to meet him.

Peter Freeman was in no hurry to enter the Britannique. At first Holly thought he had paused to talk with a friend or to admire one of the many pretty girls that were to be found in Monte Carlo. She was surprised when he stooped and offered his hand, at ankle height, and she saw that the object of his attention was a dog. The ragged wharf mongrel, with mean eye and wrinkled mouth, snarled at Freeman.

"He'd best not take liberties with that brute," said Kennedy.

Oblivious to anything except the animal, Peter Freeman coaxed and cajoled the dog to him. From the safety of the lounge the Kings and Marion watched in fascination. Catching the dog's ruff, Peter put a hand on its throat and held it, staring into its eyes, smiling. They could see his lips moving as he soothed it, settling it so that aggressiveness was replaced with reluctant trust and the animal allowed itself to be petted. Peter's fingers kneaded the heavy coat around neck and throat, his face only inches from the slavering tongue and yellow teeth.

"Isn't that rather dangerous?" said Holly.

"It's Peter's idea of fun," said Marion.

Holly watched, unable to decide whether Freeman was treating the dog to a show of domination or whether his affection was genuine; perhaps a little of both.

A waiter drifted to the table.

"Well, since you're here," said Marion, "I'll have a Marguerite. Do you know what that is?"

"*Mais oui, Madame.*"

"Holly? Kennedy?"

"Cocktails before noon?" said Kennedy. "Not for me, thank you, Marion. My dear?"

Holly shook her head then, her gaze still upon Freeman, instructed the waiter to take a handful of sugar loaves to the gentleman outside. The waiter, nonplussed, would have baulked at such a crazy request if Marion had not explained, "The young man is with my party."

A minute later, to his surprise, Peter Freeman was tapped on the shoulder by a hotel waiter bearing a salver upon which perched a sweet dish glistening with sugar loaves. Aware of his audience now, Freeman glanced up at the lounge window and gestured thanks. He continued to hold the dog with both hands, though the animal struggled and snapped at him, disturbed by the presence of the waiter. Freeman's fingers gripped tightly around the mongrel's throat. He reached for a sugar loaf and crushed it against the dog's teeth, jerking as the animal flinched and flung away. He got quickly to his feet, releasing the dog, which coughed and barked and slavered then turned and loped away into the crowd of strollers, baying as if it had been whipped.

Peter Freeman shrugged. He plucked a sugar loaf from the dish, tossed it high in the air, executed a series of shuffle steps and caught the sweet neatly in his mouth. He crunched it, bowed to the lounge and ran lightly up the steps into the hotel.

For Holly all resemblance to David Aspinall was lost for ever. In wistful emptiness she found herself impressed by Freeman's individuality; his mastery of the mongrel, spoiled by her interference, had shaded into a performance, a party trick.

She waited tensely, unblinking, staring beyond Marion to the sea.

Marion chattered on. "Dancer. Brilliant. Glowing reviews. Splendid future."

The fingers that, moments before, had soothed the stray touched Holly lightly on the shoulder.

Holly turned and looked up at Peter Freeman.

"My doggie friend doesn't understand kindness," Freeman said.

"I'm sorry."

"Don't apologise. I liked the sugar, even if the dog didn't."

"Peter, allow me to introduce Kennedy King and his wife Holly."

"Hi!"

"Hi!" said Holly, though she had never before used the

Americanism. She enjoyed the light, flippant feel of the greeting and, smiling, said again, "Hi!"

"Are you the art expert?" said Peter.

"Yes, I suppose I am."

"You're not what I expected."

"What did you expect, Mr. Freeman?"

He shrugged. "A frump – and that you're not."

Before Holly could respond to the delicate compliment, Kennedy got to his feet. "If you'll excuse me, Marion, Mr. Freeman, I believe it's time I changed for lunch."

"What a splendid idea," Marion agreed. "Peter, will you accompany me?"

"Sure."

Marion delivered a tiny smirk of triumph as the young man took her arm and she steered him away from the Kings. To her amazement Holly experienced a pang of disappointment at the realisation that Peter Freeman, in all probability, was just another of Marion's possessions.

*　　*　　*

Alone in their suite, Ray and Marion Ogden Hillis were dressing for dinner.

"Not a word," Ray complained. "Not a goddamed word about the Holbein."

"She's proceeding according to form, that's all."

"The hell she is. Holly isn't like that."

"Oh, dealers are the same the world over, Ray," said Marion. "She's baiting the hook, that's all."

"I'm beginning to believe that old proverb about never buying art from the English has some truth to it," said Ray. "Didn't she mention the Holbein this afternoon? I mean, hell, you had her off in a corner; what did you talk about?"

"This and that."

"Marion!"

"Her son. Art gossip. Peter. Yes, we talked a lot about Peter."

"Didn't she even mention the miniature?"

"God, if you're so all-fired obsessed with your damned

painting why don't you tackle King about it straight after dinner?"

"When you talk art you don't do it with King; you do it with his wife – and it isn't polite to rush a lady."

"What's gotten into you, Ray?"

"Marion, we're not picking up a Pascin drawing or a Dufy sketch; we're here to buy a Holbein, Hans Holbein, the greatest, and the rarest, of all miniature painters."

"You don't have to convince me, Ray. I'm as keen to see it as you are."

"Sure you are, sure."

"When do you have to be back in Milwaukee?"

"Not until the Board meeting on the twenty-fifth."

"There you are; nine days. Be patient."

"I've always wanted a Holbein, Marion."

"I know you have, darling. Holly King knows it too. She's making you sweat, that's all."

"She isn't that devious."

"Don't be fooled by the quiet manner. I reckon she can be as devious as the next one when it suits her. Why didn't she quote us a price?"

"Because it's a secret purchase."

"And why is it a secret purchase?"

"She explained it all in her letter, Marion."

"Not to my satisfaction."

"All right, after dinner I'll ask her straight."

"No, Ray. Play it her way. Let it ride until she's ready."

"Geeze, Marion."

"She isn't the only one who can play games."

"Now what the hell does that mean?"

"You'll see, darling, you'll see."

*　　*　　*

Howard Crocker tucked the end of his napkin into the vee of his dinner jacket and, with the distracted frown that was his usual expression, hunted among the tableware for something with which to eat his soup. Patiently Peter lifted a spoon and presented it to his manager.

"Ah, uh, yes, that's it, spoon. Thank you, my boy."

Howard's relationship with Peter was that of agent, manager and friend. For all his bumbling Howard Crocker was extremely shrewd and had steered his protégé's career well. Howard was close to Kennedy's age. He had a long hang-dog sort of face and a cropped hair style that he claimed, dead pan, was a relic of his days at West Point. Howard, of course, had been no closer to military academy than the stage of New York's New Amsterdam theatre during the run of the 1918 revue *The Boys Are Marching* in which he had made a brief appearance as Digby Dogface, the worst cook in the army. Since then Howard had graduated from acting to producing, a profession that he found so demanding that he became excessively agitated if he was not constantly within range of a transatlantic telephone. Pretty girls were Howard's only distraction; he had learned no lessons from three painful, expensive marriages to chorus girls. He remained a sucker for any pert miss on the sunny side of twenty-three. Peter predicted that Howard would eventually go to his rest in Forest Lawn mourned by more pretty little gold diggers than you could find in five Ziegfeld chorus lines. Peter's penchant for ladies was of a different order, less naive, much more discreet, but with an edge of calculation that earned him a reputation as a 'heartbreaker' up and down Broadway and in the homes of the rich on the Parkway and Long Island. Peter could not understand Howard's ruinously casual approach to sexual affairs; the intensity of his need of women was too great to be light-hearted, however charming he might seem at the dinner table or in the cocktail lounge.

Howard crumbled golden brown toast into his borsch and, paying no attention to his manners, talked while he supped, rambling on about successes past and in the future. Holly judged him to be the sort of person who evades contact with the present by being mentally elsewhere but, to her surprise, she suddenly found his eyes upon her and his plummy American voice saying her name. "Mrs. King, I don't believe I've met a lady like you before. Art dealer. Man's world. Travel and competition. Quite a strain, Eh?"

"I enjoy it, Mr. Crocker."

32

"Call me Howard. Doesn't seem right for a pretty thing like you."

Holly had never been referred to as a 'pretty thing' before and would normally have spiked a boor like Howard Crocker with an icy smile and a sarcastic remark. His glance rested on Holly's breasts. She wore a dress the colour of old pewter. Its smooth lines were enhanced by scalloped frills at the shoulders.

"Competition suits me very well, Howard."

Howard Crocker was harmless. She wished she could say the same for Peter Freeman. Her fascination with the dancer was quite novel, her responses too intricate to be dismissed. His gracefulness and boyish charm made Holly covetous. She envied his happy-go-lucky air, the ease with which he impressed himself upon her, making her forget the contradictions that she had already detected in his character. No mark of fretful uncertainty blemished his confidence. In contrast to Howard, Peter Freeman was wrapped entirely in the present moment; it was impossible to be in his company and still retain thoughts of life's true realities – dyspepsia and rain, income taxes and mosquitoes, stuffy trains and cold London salerooms, the memory of Lambeth's bleak streets and the discomforts of her girlhood.

"Are you accusing Holly of being an emancipated woman?" said Marion.

"Liberated," said Howard. "Sounds better, liberated."

"Howard has never adjusted to the twentieth century," said Marion. "Howard, darling, women are no longer the mere servants of man."

"Not sure they ever were," said Ray.

"It's different in England, Howard," said Peter.

"Is it?" said Holly.

"In England, ladies have always had the upper hand."

"That's just nonsense, Peter," said Marion.

"Spent much time in England, Mr. Freeman?" Kennedy asked.

"I crossed the Pond in 'twenty-six and played some three hundred performances at the Empire."

"In *Lady Be Good*," Howard added.

"You danced with the Astaires?" asked Holly, impressed.

"Behind the Astaires," said Peter. "In the chorus."

"Peter's too modest," said Marion. "He was first understudy to Fred."

"Fred has the constitution of a bison. He never ducked a show," said Peter. "I was back in London in nineteen twenty-nine."

"In *Funny Face*?" Holly enquired.

"Solo," said Peter. "I was way down the bill in the Oman revue, *Alphabet Soup*. It only ran for a couple of months."

"But it led to better things, darling, did it not? "Marion patted the dancer's wrist proprietorially.

Peter shrugged and tactfully changed the subject.

Was it in that year that Marion had first met the dancer, Holly wondered, and had they been – or were they still – lovers? The thought depressed her, the banality and cynicism of it, warning her that Peter Freeman's charisma was just part of his stock-in-trade, an essential ingredient of the actor and, probably, unrelated to the man. He had turned from Marion and watched Holly with, she imagined, apology in his expression, a fleeting sadness that seemed to excuse his past without disowning it. Imagination! Holly told herself. But felt again the longing that had been in her since the first moment of meeting – and with it a mounting panic. It was all she could do to stop herself rising from the dinner table there and then to fetch the miniature from the Britannique's safe and press an immediate sale, pushing the little painting at Ray and letting him offer what he wished for it – all to be free of Peter, released from Monte Carlo and the dancer's magnetic attraction.

Ray would be delighted. He disliked the affectations of dealers and collectors. He was too forthright to enjoy the mystique of bargaining. Marion, though, would be sure to see a trick in such straight dealing and Holly would not give the woman the satisfaction of surrender. It was not, however, to spite Ray or to thwart Marion that Holly made no mention of the Holbein; she wanted to stay here in the Riviera, to be near Peter Freeman. For once, her secret desires were stronger than the common sense practices of good business.

Kennedy cracked a lobster claw.

Holly was relieved that her husband appeared unaware of her inner confusion. Like Howard Crocker, Kennedy's thoughts would be far from the Britannique's opulent dining room. He would be day-dreaming about the Oval cricket ground or the Royal Automobile Club where he lunched two or three times in the week with his old friend Simon Black and other men of his generation. It startled Holly to notice how old Kennedy had become; she had never really paused to study him before. In such lively company, however, he was detached, stooped a little over his plate, oblivious to the conversation.

Perhaps he was thinking of Chris, anticipating their day out together on Saturday.

She could hardly hold that against him, even though she had become impatient with her son lately, irritated by his wild enthusiasms, resentful of the world he was building for himself, a world of hobbies and obsessional ambitions that seemed to exclude her completely. What would Chris care if she . . .

If she what?

For a split second Holly clutched at doubt as if it was a straw that would save her from drowning, as if routine and inconsequentiality could buoy her up still, so far from London, so far from her home and her office, from the rain and the dank salerooms where she could ride on the millpond of habit like a green leaf prematurely broken from the bough.

"Perhaps, after dinner, Mr. Freeman would care to walk in the gardens," Holly heard herself say.

It was not as she had expected. She did not flush with shame at the utterance or feel drawn down by her candour. On the contrary, impulsiveness exhilarated her, made her feel youthful with a reawakened instinct for adventure that she had supposed as dead in her as it had become in her husband.

Marion scowled and Ray slid his eyes from Peter to Kennedy.

"I only want to ask Mr. Freeman about the famous people he's met in his career, what they're really like," said Holly with a smile.

"Just another stagedoor Jill." Howard sighed. "The world's, uh, full of them."

"Kennedy," said Holly, "will you accompany us?"

"Not," said Kennedy, "if I can muster three for bridge."

"I'll join you," said Ray. "You any good at the game?"

"Competent," said Kennedy.

"High stakes?" asked Howard.

"As high as you wish."

"Count me in."

"Marion will make a fourth," said Ray.

"I thought I might walk . . ." Marion protested.

"You've heard all Peter's tales before, darling," Ray said.

"Marion? " said Kennedy. "Bridge?"

"Oh, very well."

"Perhaps you'd prefer to play cards too, Mr. Freeman?" Holly asked.

"I'd prefer to walk in the garden," Peter answered.

A half-hour later Holly fetched a light wrap from her room and went out by a side door into the hotel gardens where, by a lanterned fish pool that sprinkled in the soft young summer night, Peter Freeman waited to see what chance had thrown his way and what might come of it this time around.

oooooooo
ooooo
ooo
o

2

The Night and the Music

Maurice Beckman was no saint. He had a large string of lady
friends and only a gentlemanly concern for probity that was
almost arcane saved him from becoming known as a rogue.
At first glance Maury did not appear to be cut from the cloth
out of which charmers are made. He was tall, broad-
shouldered, fresh-complexioned, with receding brown hair,
and looked his age – forty. It remained a mystery to envious
associates how a fellow who presented such an air of sergeant-
at-arms brusqueness could command the devotion of squads
of quality women. They deduced that Beckman's aura of
wealth was the principal source of attraction. They were
wrong. Maury's female companions might have disabused
curious males with a few home truths, but Maury's female
companions were not the types who kiss and tell.

Maury did not go out of his way to impress the opposite
sex. He was civil but not smarmy, attentive but not arch. He
treated women as equals, not as sweet little things to be
nibbled like Turkish Delight or snapped up at a bite like
marzipan fingers. Dining out with Maury Beckman, if you
were fortunate enough to be asked, did not commit you to
spending the night with him. He was more interested in lively
conversation than flirtatious chit-chat. No bubbling little
show girl, no matter how cute, had ever shared Maury's table
or his bed. On the other hand, many a married lady, wife of a
client or temporary partner, stopping over in town had

thoroughly enjoyed an evening *a deux* with Maury, secure in the knowledge that even if she felt inclined to round it out with a bit of extramarital hanky-panky, Maurice would ignore the bait like a fish without a mouth or, if she persisted, would rapidly escort her to a taxi cab and never ask her to be his dinner guest again.

Unmarried women, of course, were quite another matter. Maury credited them with having minds of their own – which most of them certainly had. If the talk was interesting and they both felt inclined, Maury saw no reason why they should not return to his flat in Heaton Court and continue their conversation there, in bed or out of it.

Maury would certainly not be returning to Heaton Court with that evening's dinner guest. Jane Tatton Swale, Oxford don, historian and author, was far too valued a friend to insult with the suggestion of casual intimacy. In spite of her strikingly regal bearing, famed in the groves of academe, Maury just didn't fancy her in that way, nor she him. They would eat, drink and talk politics far into the night tucked away at a corner table in the Vicar of Wakefield in Wine Office Court close by the City Women's Club where Jane 'camped' when she was in town.

Give or take an hour, while his sister Holly was walking with Peter Freeman in the gardens of the Hotel Britannique in Monte Carlo, Maury Beckman stood before his wardrobe mirror wrestling with his tie, wondering what Jane would have to say about de Valera's recent refusal to pay land annuities to Britain, or if she had changed her position on the value of the Geneva Disarmament Conference since last he'd talked with her.

Maury had settled the recalcitrant necktie to his satisfaction when the doorbell chimed.

Maury paused, frowning.

He expected no callers.

He was not a particularly unapproachable man and his telephone rang at all hours of the day and night, but it was unusual for somebody to arrive unasked to his flat door.

Maury slipped his dinner jacket from the wooden valet and put it on. Except that he still wore a comfortable pair of slippers instead of his leather shoes, he was dressed for the evening.

The doorbell chimed again.

Maury glanced at his watch. "Damn!"

He had no conscience about employing servants – in fact, he employed a domestic staff of three – but he valued his privacy too much to have them 'live in' and the trio departed on the stroke of six o'clock. If he was spending a quiet evening at home, which was often the case, Maury would cook his own supper from the well-stocked larder and the huge Frigidaire in the kitchen. Under such an arrangement Maury did not have to concern himself with house-keeping and yet retained a degree of self-sufficiency that was valuable to him.

The bell was insistent.

"All right, hold your horses."

Maury crossed out of the master bedroom into the square wood-panelled hall. He had lived in Heaton Court for less than five years. Before that he had dwelled 'in obscurity' in a villa in Peckham and had 'done for himself' entirely. Even a person as devoid of snobbishness as Holly, however, had finally remarked that it was ridiculous for one of London's most prosperous builders to reside in a 'clerk's shoebox' in the suburbs. Maury had concluded that his critics had a valid point. He had leased the villa – wouldn't sell in case hard times ever drove him to premature retirement – and had purchased an angular Victorian mansion in Wintle Street, off Marylebone Road. With an architect's assistance, Maury had designed plans for its modernisation. He had commandeered the entire top floor for his own use and selected tenants for the seven remaining apartments carefully. He had to admit that his new home was comfortable, easily managed and exceedingly convenient. For reasons that only Holly fully understood, however, Maury Beckman defended his property with a battery of alarms and burglar-proof devices, including special electric fitments on the window casements and a Varley voice amplifier and identification kit built into the oak door.

Maury flicked a switch. The amplifier crackled.

"Who is it?" Maury asked.

"Stan Nuttall."

"Who?"

"Stan. Stan Nuttall, from Bishop's Row, Lambeth. Don't say you've forgot me, Maury?"

The Varley kit made all voices sound the same but the name was so unexpected that Maury did not doubt the speaker but he was surprised, even a little dismayed, to hear from a man that he hadn't thought about in ten years. "Stan, with the eye-patch an' the . . ."

"I remember," said Maury. "Hold on."

He opened the door and stepped cautiously back, an ingrained habit dating from the period, mercifully brief, when he had become involved in Ritchie's sordid affairs. A dozen years ago Stan Nuttall had been one of Ritchie's cohorts.

"Oh, you're goin' out," said Stan. "Shan't keep you more than a couple of minutes, Maury."

"Come in, then."

Stan had lost the starved mongrel look. The ugly patch that he had worn over an empty eye socket, a relic of Mons, was gone, and the glass replacement, though detectable, improved the man's appearance. The left hand remained gloved, however. Presumably not even medical wizards could satisfactorily replace three missing fingers with something that would not offend. It wasn't only the extra flesh and the eye that made Stan seem different; he was geared in an expensive raglan overcoat, a snap brim, soft felt hat and shoes of brown willow calf; better dressed than most of Maury's contractors and, what was more, carried it off without flash.

"I really don't wanna hold you up, Maury."

Maury smiled sardonically and Stan, quick to pick up the gaffe, gave a curt bark of laughter. "Hell, I'm no mug artist these days, Maury."

"So what are you doing with yourself?" Maury led his visitor into the library. "You look prosperous enough."

"Can't grumble." Stan removed his hat and twirled it on his forefinger, inspecting the room with unabashed curiosity. "Gone into advertisin'. Pays a treat."

Maury folded down the front of a cocktail cabinet built

into the shelves. The cabinet's interior blazed with light reflected from crystal glasses and decanters. A tiny refrigerator coughed out ice cubes.

"What'll you have, Stan?"

"Whisky, on the rocks."

"Sit yourself down." Maury handed Stan a drink, saying, "Excuse me, I must make a phone call."

"Sure."

Stan did not apologise for the disruption his unexpected arrival had caused. The former tannery boy had come a long way but not, Maury suspected, in advertising; for sure Stan wasn't selling column inches for some local rag.

In the office that adjoined the library, Maury telephoned the City Women's Club and left a message for Miss Swale to inform her that he would be a half-hour late for their dinner engagement. Jane would understand. She also led a busy life in which the ends didn't always quite meet. On returning to the library Maury found Stan by the bookshelves, glass in hand. He still wore his overcoat but had laid his snap brim and one hogskin glove on the wine table. Maury's library was no 'purchased by the yard' array of calf and gilt. Most of the books had come from Foyles or Bumpus, bought by Maury because they interested him. He read widely. The books had the homely appearance of companions, informally exhibiting the kind of information that Maury fed on; architecture and decorative arts, biography, politics, history, economics, through to the latest novels by Dreiser, Wyndham Lewis, Priestley, Hemingway and Pearl S. Buck. In the revolving bookcase by his armchair, Laski, Leavis and Keynes rubbed shoulders with Dos Passos and Virginia Woolf.

Stan tapped a novel with a gloved knuckle. "Read this?"

"What is it?"

"*All Quiet on the Western Front.*"

"Yeah", said Maury. "I've read it."

"Takes you back, don't it? said Stan. "Stuff like that. Stuff like *Journey's End.*"

"Seems like another world, the trenches." Maury deliberately inserted the cliché.

Stan gave another bark of laughter, "Not to me, buddy,"

he said. "Not to you neither, I wouldn't be surprised."

Maury nodded. "You're right. But look, you didn't drop by to talk literature. What can I do for you?"

Stan could also be blunt when it suited his purpose. He leaned against the reading table, sipped whisky, then said, "I'm lookin' for a property."

Balanced on the arm of the deep-button leather chair by the unlit fire, Maury said, "I build them. I own them, but I don't actually do the selling, Stan. My agency handles that sort of thing."

"Bannister, Hepburn and Foss."

"Right."

"A special kinda property," said Stan.

Maury, who seldom drank before dinner, lit a cigarette and settled himself more comfortably on the arm of the chair. He could also be oblique when it came to it. "What's the name of your advertising firm?"

Stan went with him. "Apex."

"What's your position there?"

"General manager."

"So it's an office suite you're after?" said Maury. "For Apex?"

"Nope, a private residence."

"For yourself?"

"For a friend."

"A lady friend?"

"Could be!"

"Last I heard you were happily married, Stan."

"Wrong!"

"But what about, what was her name, the flower . . .?"

"Marigold! She left me nine years ago."

"Sorry to hear that."

Stan shrugged and put his empty glass on the library table. "I got charge of 'er kids. She signed them over, legal like, made me their guardian. Bloody Marigold! She brought in a real sharp brief. He carved it up. Cost me a bob'r two but it was worth it. Always liked 'er kids better'n I liked 'er."

It was obvious that Marigold's desertion still rankled. For a moment the tempo of Stan's speech quickened, his South

London accent no longer suppressed. Maury kept silent, hoping that Stan would reveal the true reason for his visit. But Mr. Nuttall was nobody's fool. He checked himself. "Never mind the story of my life. What about it, Maury? A domestic dwelling? For old times sake, give me a professional shove in the right direction?"

"What exactly *are* you after, Stan?"

"Bright, airy, sunny, modern, big – say ten rooms, like – in a location handy for the city."

"House or flat?" said Maury. "To buy or to rent?"

"House preferred," said Stan. "To buy."

"Leasehold or freehold?"

"Don't matter."

"Price range?"

"Don't matter neither."

"It would help," said Maury, "if I could match the occupant with the domicile."

"Stow the double-talk, Maury."

"Is the house intended to be a statement of well-being?"

"A monument t' gracious livin', yer," said Stan. "But's it's gotta be very habitable, an' very modern."

"That's not too tall an order."

"You got somethin' in mind?"

"Possibly," said Maury. "It won't be available until mid-summer, however."

"That's fine," said Stan. "It's not needed 'til August or September."

Maury said, "Leave the matter with me for a couple of days, Stan."

He did, in fact, have a house that would suit Stan's requirements to a tee, a four-year-old, brick-built, stucco-finished beauty with superb curved elements. He had seen the building through construction at the behest of Sherbrook Winter, pioneer of the modern movement in architecture. He had hacked through a jungle of by-laws and technical regulations that the local authorities threw up out of bloody-mindedness and sheer aesthetic prejudice. He had dealt under committee-room tables, trading specifications on a housing extension scheme in exchange for relaxation of demands on

No. 44 Vallois Street. He had even gone briefly into hock on three projects that the boors in the Borough Hall had shelved as part of their campaign against innovation. But he had finally triumphed and No. 44 went up exactly as Sherbrook Winter wanted it.

Winter had occupied the house since its completion in the autumn of 1928. Initially he had thrived on the controversy and ridicule that the House of the Future had brought on him. It had been called, variously, 'Winter's Folly' and 'Sherbrook's Sugar Cake' and had inspired a clutch of cartoons in *Punch* and one abysmal mock-epic poem in *Hearth and Home*. Lately, though, Winter had grown weary of English philistinism, or perhaps of the fact that his twenty-first century mansion was no longer considered that unusual. In the summer, so Maury had heard, Winter was packing up and leaving for San Francisco where he thought he would be more 'at home' than in London. Whether Winter intended to sell No. 44 or merely lease it, Maury did not know. A couple of telephone calls would answer that question.

"Let me ring you, say Friday, Stan."

"I'll call you."

"Please yourself."

"Appreciate the personal interest, Maury."

"For Old Lang Syne, Stan. Least I can do."

"How's Holly?"

Back in Lambeth when they had all been little more than children, Stan had doted on Holly. Perhaps if the war hadn't come along, if Holly hadn't become co-owner of a little antique shop, if there had been no . . . Maury cleared his throat and blinked several times. He could not think of the 'old days' with affection, only with anger. He did not wish to tip his suspicions to Stan in any manner at all.

"Holly's bloomin'," Maury said, another worn cliché from God knows when.

"Some business she's built up."

"She worked for it."

"Sure she did. Always was a grafter, your Holly." Stan lifted his hat and glove and put them on. Maury escorted him into the hallway. "But she's hit the jackpot now; the international art market. Hot stuff!"

"You've kept track of her!"

Stan shrugged once more. "Couldn't help hearin' the odd rumour. Apex handles the accounts of a couple of London art dealers. You get to hear the talk."

"Apex don't handle Kings' advertising, do they?"

"Hell, no! The Kings have everythin', and I mean everythin', buttoned down and sewn up; even advertisin'." Stan held out his ungloved right hand. "Good to see you again, Maury. Give my love to Holly when you run across her."

Maury shook the offered hand.

"You'll call, Stan; about the house?"

"Course I will. Why I came, 'n't it?"

"Friday or after," Maury said. "I'll have accurate information by then."

Stan passed out of the apartment main door into the corridor. It was carpeted and set with tables in pure white bakelite each bearing a flourishing potted plant. The elevator – no mere 'lift' in Maury's block – was to the right. Stan went that way.

Maury waited, then, abruptly, stuck his head from the doorway.

"Stan, I wouldn't *know* your client, by any chance?"

"Doubt it," Stan said, and added ambiguously. "Not now, you wouldn't know him now."

Maury closed the door, activated the alarms, switched off the Varley voice-box and returned to the bedroom. He put on his shoes, whisked a brush over his hair and switched out the light. He went into the hallway then through it to the library again. He poured himself a neat gin, and drank it slowly, feeling the clean-tasting alcohol cutting into the tension that Stan's visit had created. It wasn't a secret, of course, that could be kept for long. Maybe just long enough to link him to the house sale. He would avoid that, scrupulously avoid it. If Winter wanted a buyer, it could be arranged between solicitors and he, Maury, and his associated agents need have no part in it at all. He would forego profit for sake of caution – and conscience.

Tomorrow he would begin enquiries into Apex Advertising and its directors. Stan would not have been so free with his information if there had been anything obvious about the firm. Even so, Maury had a hunch, a shivering little hunch that behind Stan Nuttall, brother Ritchie stood waiting in the wings.

* * *

The fish pond by the low wall, under the soft rose lanterns, was the kind of setting that Mr. Lubitsch would have taken a day to light; Peter had consciously placed himself in an appropriate pose, left hand nonchalantly tucked into his jacket pocket, one foot on the crown of the wall; the featherweight hero with a touch of the cad. It came easy to him, not because he had been born to the gay planes of romance *vis-à-vis* the Hollywood dream, but from the blood, sweat and tears of thousands of hours of practice and rehearsal and the experiences of hundreds of matinées in snowbound hick towns and countless midnight finales in sweltering cities; he had learned how to be perfect and perfectly suggestive, the sum of all the basic parts he had ever played, the debonair fellow who got off with the girl in the end and proved himself to be no more than a skin-deep scoundrel. But Peter could not be sure, sure of himself or the validity of his role on stage and off. The girls, real girls, were never silk-clad and immaculate or merry-eyed and innocent; their surrender was as ersatz as his own. They too sweated and snapped, jabbered, sulked and screamed dirty words at dressers, drank buckets and played the cotton candy love game that led inexorably to morning revulsion. For all that Peter clung to the illusion that he had just enough romance in him to excuse opportunism and that the women, most of whom were predators, got no more, and no less, than they deserved.

Dancing was his defence against disenchantment. He was a strategist of the dance. He laboured with his body to keep it fit and hold poise against all life's crookedness. But the burden of reality was close to insupportable and he clung to the image he had created to seduce audiences – and anyone else who happened to come along out of the blue, like the good-looking English woman. Her entrance, he figured, was one of the purer moments; she shared the garden, the lanterns, the faint music of the hotel's orchestra, the evening's supple elegance. In the pool a fat carp flopped and the ripples lapped against the parapet. It was all a wanton falsehood, sure, but almost worth the bitterness of discovered truth.

She was no slender half-starved *ingénue* slaving to pretend she was stylish. God, she had style, real genuine twenty-two carat style, something uniquely her own. He wished that he could stroll with her through the lemon trees in silence, bonded only by the sounds of the night and the distant music, figures in the dream landscape he professed to despise.

"I hope Howard didn't offend you," he began.

"Not in the least."

"He's harmless."

"I've met one or two men like Mr. Crocker; their harmlessness is what makes them appealing," said Holly. "Have you known Marion and Ray for long?"

"Three, four years."

"Do you know them well?"

"They're chums of Howard. He coaxed Ray into backing a show."

"How does that work – backing a show?"

"The production is costed – salaries, costumes, sets – and put on top of the price of the book and the payments to the guys who write the music. The total cost is divided among two, three, five, ten people; the backers. If the show's a success they get back their original stake plus an agreed percentage of the profits."

"It's another form of gambling?"

"Sure, but rich folk clamour to back shows. They get to meet the stars and lots of pretty girls, to brag to their friends about the show as if it was their success. It isn't just the rich who buy in, come to think of it. Three years ago Howard bankrolled a tour of a musical play called, appropriately, *Rich Kid*. He scrambled the money up from the leprechauns."

"Leprechauns?"

47

"The little people; small time investors."

"Did they lose their money?"

"The hell they did. This was right after the market crash, so the main Broadway backers were broke. Howard had *Rich Kid* all ready to roll, but not enough in the cookie jar to get us to Hoboken. He had wrapped up his savings in it – and most of mine. But Howard's no quitter. He went out into the streets and drummed up close to two hundred small-time investors – leprechauns – the kind of two-bit gamblers more at home at the track. It was some piece of Barnum and Bailey, I can tell you. Know what he did? Took them all to Boston for the opening. Yeah, a train load of 'financial participants' rolling on up to Boston for the gala opening. The show hit, and the party lasted three days. God, I was one of the walking dead by the week's end. We packed 'em in, though, on the road through Denver, Detroit, Pittsburgh, Akron, all through the north states. Packed 'em in. Howard was offered a Broadway house but he figured if we struck out in New York it would spell disaster. He turned it down, extended the rustic tour for another twenty weeks and came out gleaming financially. The leprechauns got their money back and a bundle of clean bills on top, plus the kind of memories money can't buy. It was some finagle, believe me."

"Have you always been a dancer?"

"Since I was five years old."

"Five?"

"Aged five, I danced the *Little Mouse Minuet* on the stage of the Palmer Rose Vaudeville Theatre in New Jersey with my Uncle Ben, Aunt Irene and Cousin Lakey. They were the troupers in the family, my mother's sister and her husband. My pa was a stay-at-home. He was a CPA, a bookkeeper, with the gas and coke company in Baronsville. It was only after Pa died we had to scratch for a living. By then I was even more stage-struck than Ma. I had ten years of dancing lessons behind me and lots of experience doing 'guest spots' with Ben, Irene and Lakey when ever they swung close to Port Chester where we were living by then. After Pa died nothing seemed more right than I should go on the road in a double act with my cousin Lakey.'

"What happened to your family?"

"Ma lives with my married sister in the Borough of Queens, in New York. She comes to all my openings, sailing in like a galleon with Irene and Ben and all my relatives tailing along behind her."

"She must be proud of you?"

"Sure, she is."

"And Lakey?"

"Lakey died."

The strains of a waltz filtered through the lemon trees. Peter listened to the mellow sounds for a while, saying nothing. The woman on his arm did not press.

At length he said, "Lakey was nineteen. It was up in Seattle, in a lousy hotel room in Seattle. She was sick but not sick enough, she said, to duck the shows. She did three shows, then – well, then she just up and died. Pneumonia. I was with her. Me. Nobody else. Uncle Ben and Aunt Irene were home in New York. Ten o'clock, Lakey was out in the spot, singing, dancing, pretty as you like in her apple-blossom dress, all pale pink froth . . . Hell, it was a long time ago."

"It still hurts you to remember it, doesn't it?"

"Sure it does."

"My first husband," said Holly, "was killed in a fire. My grandfather, whom I loved very deeply, died in the same fire. My shop, my first shop, was razed to the ground. I've never quite got over it. Even now, when I'm feeling low, I shed the odd tear when I think of Christopher and Grandpa Tal. But, you know, I'm not sad about it. The hurt's almost comforting."

They had stopped walking and were standing by the balustrade that soared out over the tennis courts, over the curve of the avenue. The lights that wrote their signatures on the sea were remote.

Peter said, "Don't you want to hear about all the stars I've worked with?"

"I'd rather hear about you."

"There's no more to tell."

"I'm sure there is," said Holly.

Peter grunted and said, "You know more about me already than most of the women I've . . . Lakey; hardly anybody knows about Lakey."

"Why did you tell me, Peter?"

"Let's go inside now. I could do with a drink."

"Not yet, please," said Holly.

"Hasn't . . . Look, didn't Marion warn you off?"

"I don't understand."

"I've a 'reputation', a bad one. I'm supposed to be a . . . a womaniser."

"Are you?"

"Yeah, I am."

"Are you telling me this to impress me?"

"Let me take you in now, Holly."

Holly laughed. "For my own good?"

"I don't kid around."

The woman paused, then said, "Nor do I, Peter."

He clasped her arm tightly and led her towards the path that would take them back to the hotel. "That's what I'm afraid of, I guess."

"I'm flattered."

"Don't be," Peter Freeman said. "Be warned."

*   *   *

Kennedy put down his Dornford Yates novel and peered over the tops of his reading glasses at his wife. In plain Vyella pyjamas, hair rumpled, Kennedy contrived to look like an invalid. Even the gilded magnificence of a Hotel Britannique single divan did nothing for him. He seemed ill-at-ease in it as if he expected it to snap shut like a gigantic mousetrap. Holly studied her husband's reflection in the dressing-table mirror as she brushed her hair and removed her make-up. Already she had begun to behave with an uncharacteristic furtiveness that made her feel awful.

"Is that all Freeman told you?" said Kennedy. "I was sure you would wring his entire life history out of him."

"I did most of the talking."

"You were out there so long, Marion suggested you were waiting for sunrise."

"Such a beautiful night," said Holly. "You should have been with us, Kennedy, instead of incarcerated in the card room. How much did you win, by the way?"

"Only a tenner. With much effort. That Crocker chap's a dashed good player. I'm told he's even better at poker. Remind me not to try him out."

"Did Marion or Ray mention the Holbein?"

"Not a word," said Kennedy, "was spoke."

"It must have been difficult to avoid the subject."

"Mr. Crocker – what's it? –'carried the ball'. It seems I acquired more stage gossip than you did, m'dear. All very fascinating, I must admit."

"What sort of gossip?"

"Apparently it's Howard Crocker's avowed intent to transform Peter Freeman into a picture star. Can't see it myself. Can you?"

"Yes," said Holly. "I can."

"Seems too fragile to me. Not like Hoot Gibson."

"I doubt if he'll ever be cast in *Riders of the Purple Sage*," said Holly. "He's a dancer, Kennedy, not a cowboy."

"However, Crocker's very devious. With the Broadway theatre in a depressed state, Crocker hopes to 'springboard' young Freeman by transferring his American success to London, but West End managements won't play. It's all Jack Buchanan and Ralph Brooks these days. So, clever Mr. Crocker invests some money and commissions a special show with a London setting, *Step Out Along the Strand*; an American in England, you know the sort of thing. It has *two* leading roles, you see?"

Holly turned round. "One English and one American?"

"Very clever," said Kennedy, "Don't you think?"

"Peter's coming to London?"

"It seems to be in the balance," said Kennedy. "Crocker won't commit himself. Depends on whether he can secure the services of Buchanan or Brooks for the English part."

"Wouldn't that be wonderful," said Holly.

Kennedy removed his spectacles and wagged them at his wife. "That's only half the story; if the show is successful in the West End, Crocker plans to make a picture of it. Isn't that clever of him? Peter Freeman has already been – what's it? – 'tested'? Yes, tested by Hollywood. One studio actually offered him a seven-year contract but the terms weren't good enough. Howard Crocker is determined that your Mr. Freeman will become a Hollywood star."

"He's not my Mr. Freeman," said Holly.

"Don't you like him?"

"Yes, I do," said Holly. "I hope Mr. Crocker's schemes bear fruit."

"So that Freeman will come to London?"

Holly hesitated for the merest fraction of a second. "I'd like to see him dance."

"To your tune, Holly, eh?" Kennedy said. "To your tune?"

The display of pique was over almost before it had begun, so unlike her husband that Holly could not take it in and was left confused.

"I . . . Kennedy, I don't . . ."

Her husband puffed out his cheeks and touched his hand to his forehead. "I'm sorry. I'm sorry. I don't know why I'm so bad-tempered. I think it's the heat. I never feel comfortable in France."

"Why don't you go home, Kennedy?"

It was out before she could help it.

He looked at her steadily. No trace of anger remained in his eyes, only speculation.

"Do you want me to leave?" he asked quietly.

"Of course not."

"Then why suggest it?" A flash of temper for a second, final, time. "If you *want* me to leave, *say so*."

Holly put down the hairbrush and, smoothing her night-gown over her hips, crossed to Kennedy's bedside. "I *don't* want you to leave." She touched his brow. "Head-ache?"

"Shall I put a compress on it?"

"I'll be all right after a night's sleep."

"Kennedy, look at me."

"What?"

"I'll display the Holbein tomorrow night. We'll be out of Monte Carlo by Thursday."

"Oh, Ray Hillis might . . ."

"Thursday."

Kennedy sank back against the pillow. Holly noticed a sleek sheen of perspiration on his brow and under his jowls. He looked older than she could ever recall.

"Aren't you well, Kennedy?"

"The headache, that's all." He sought for her hand. "Really, that's all. Nothing to worry about. Be right as rain as soon as I'm home."

She hugged him.

Four or five years ago she would have slid in beside him, he would have stroked and petted her, taking the initiative after she had given him a sign that she wanted him. He would have been expert and gentle and tender and demanding and, most of all, loving. Her response would have been complete. But not now; not in a strange bed in a strange town in an alien country. Kennedy's response was not sexual, could not be sexual. He held her rather as young Chris used to hold her when he wakened from a fever dream, clingingly yet struggling to hide his need of her.

"Holly," Kennedy said. "I want you to be happy."

"I am happy," Holly said. "You've always made me happy, darling."

"If only Christopher hadn't died." Kennedy shook his head.

"Don't, Kennedy, please don't say it."

"I just want you to be happy, that's all."

He inclined his body away from her on the pretext of putting his spectacles on the night table. When he glanced back at her he wore a small pursed smile. "I think, m'dear, I'm getting old."

"Nonsense!" Holly tucked the coverlet around his chest. "Shall I open a window?"

"Please."

She went to the window and brushed aside a fold of the long drape. The sky over the bay was not black but blue, a strange electric blue, like evening not midnight. The window was already open. She stood by it, enjoying the cool air upon her limbs, looking out across the water, until a movement in the garden below caught her attention.

Peter was oblivious of her presence. She watched him without his being aware of it, looking down on an angle of the garden where flagged paving cornered on to the breakfast terrace.

Peter had removed his dinner jacket. His shirt was pure white in the faint light from the Avenue. He seemed to be etched by the light, like a silhouette. Completely absorbed, he stepped up, stepped down from the knee-high wall to the paving. Down and up, down and up, until the step became a little leap, the motions more elaborate, the footwork daintier, arms and hands extended; a boy's game, a dance routine, an exercise?

"Hm, what is it?" Kennedy asked.

"Nothing," said Holly. "Only the moonlight."

She let the curtain drop and crossed to bed.

She slid in and lay on her back.

"Right?"

"Yes."

Kennedy put out the lights.

On her back, breathing softly, Holly listened; imagination, only imagination, the whisper of his shoes on the stones outside.

A dance, an exercise, a game?

"Don't step on the cracks, Peter," she murmured under her breath. "If you step on a crack, the world will fall down."

"Hm?"

"Nothing, Kennedy. Go to sleep."

"Good-night, m'dear."

"Good-night, darling." Holly said.

*　　*　　*

Cushioned *chaise* on Larvetto Beach, lido mats smelling of rubber and salt, thick cotton towels, a Japanese parasol with a silken fringe, a gaudy awning on weathered poles, a knee-table to protect the sandwiches from ants, a bottle hamper, beach balls and books, oils, unguents and repellent sprays, a ukulele, a Smakbak Captive Golf set that no one had the nerve to use, cigarettes, cigars, a Leica camera –

"Smile, smile, for Heaven's sake, and watch the dickie bird."

"The *what*?"

"You heard."

– gingernuts, binoculars, champagne, tea flasks like mortar shells; an HMV portable gramophone that ground out Duke Ellington's *Black and Tan* –

"Duke who?"

"Ellington."

"English, I assume."

"Darling, he's a nigger."

"Oh, my mistake!"

– and later Johnnie Boles' striving vibrato number from *The King of Jazz*, over and over and over again –

"Gulls don't seem to like it."

"Can you blame them?"

"I like it."

"You're not a seagull, are you?"

"Not in my present incarnation."

"Darling, turn – it – off. *Please.*"

– and then just the waves and the gulls and an engine sighing in the glass-roofed station, children's laughter, traffic not far off above the boulevards, two silly slender girls shrieking on the rocks; the Ogden Hillises' encampment took a breather from small talk.

Captain Quayle had nosed the steam launch from the shadow of the harbour wall, not for any particular reason except that it was also part of Ray and Marion's empire and had to be seen to be believed. It sat like a paper cut-out on the blue, blue sea.

"We should have driven down to Pointe de la Veille."

"What's wrong with right here?"

"It's so narrow and crowded, so vulgar."

"Howard wants to be close to a telephone."

"Important call, important call expected. *Trés* important."

"From London?"

"Uh, yes, London."

Ray rolled over and, propped on an elbow, surveyed his wife.

"It's quite like old times. Remember that summer on Hampton Bay, at the Colonel's place? Picnicked every day for the whole month. Remember how hot it got, the sun? You looked like Pocohontas."

"I looked like a stick of pemmican."

"Not to me. To me you looked lovely."

"Then as now," said Howard.

"Thank you, Howard," said Marion.

Their limbs were anointed, nourished and smooth and yet they seemed less physical here than they did indoors at night, under electric candelabra. Sky and sea dissipated their identities.

Mine too , Holly thought: I'm not accustomed to this sort of idleness.

She watched Peter; he seemed relaxed, happy. His body looked less leggy in neat black swimming trunks, more compact, more desirable. She could believe in him this morning; he gained from the sun. Catching her eye he smiled at her. She smiled back, protected by the floppy brim of her hat. She wore wide-legged loungers and a plain halter top with broad enamel buckles on the straps. He admired her body covertly.

"*Desert Island Dreams.*"

"Pardon?" Peter said.

"Put it on. Haven't you got it? I though you had it. *Desert Island Dreams*; the Columbia album," Marion leaned forward, showing oval breasts. "Play it, Peter."

"I left it in my room, sorry."

"Oh, damn you!"

He shuffled the black hard discs, sitting cross-legged like a tailor. "*Ramona*?" he offered. "*Broadway Melody*?"

"Never mind."

"*Luff Yore Spell iz Effryvare*. How about that, Marion?"

"Gloria Swanson," said Howard. "Such a nice girl."

"Marion?" said Peter.

"Never *mind*. Thank you all the same."

Howard sat up from his recliner. "Come," he said. "Come, fill the Cup, and in the Fire of Spring, the Winter Garment of Repentance fling.) "

"Champagne, old man?" said Kennedy. "Is that what you're after?"

"Uh, no, tea I think," said Howard.

Kennedy reached down and extracted a flask from the sand. He poured tea into a tin cup and handed it to the American. "Fond of *Omar Khayyám*?"

"Never touch the stuff," said Howard.

"Goes right to his head," said Peter.

"I have been through all this before," said Howard, abstractedly sipping tea. "Produced a musical from a book by Schnee and a score by Riggs on the life of the, uh, poet feller."

"Guess the title," said Peter.

"Shock me," said Kennedy.

"*Come, fill the cup.*"

"That's not so awful," said Holly.

"Madam, you should have seen the show," said Howard.

"We opened in Boston on Tuesday, closed Boston on Saturday; and that was that," said Peter. "Only stout-hearted Bostonians could have endured even six performances. I had to dance with a camel."

"A *real* camel?" Ray asked.

"A real camel," said Peter. "Vicious brute, name of Achmed. It had the maddening habit of upstaging me."

"You mean, darling, the camel actually danced?"

"Loved dancing. Trained to it. Uh, born to it, really," said Howard. "Not the worst partner Peter's ever had, if you ask me."

"Achmed's jig-hops and pendulums were stunning." Peter rolled his eyes and rattled his head with his palm. "Really stunning."

"Surely you're pulling our legs," said Kennedy.

"Cut my throat if I tell a lie," said Peter.

"Well, I never!" Kennedy chuckled. "A dancing camel!"

"Sang too," Howard solemnly announced.

There was a moment's astonished silence then Peter burst

out laughing. "Now he is pulling your leg."

The morning wore on.

There was talk of the evening, what they would do then. Planning occupied much of the conversation, complicated arrangements stemming from Marion whose boredom had become palpable but, Holly suspected, was not wholly sincere. Beneath the affectations, Ray Ogden Hillis' wife would be trying to manipulate them to suit her own ends, whatever those ends might be.

"The new casino," Howard said to Kennedy. "What, uh, what d'you think, old boy? Team up? Break the bank?"

"Don't much care for roulette," said Kennedy.

"*Vingt-un*?"

"They still deal *Trente-et-Quarante* in this part of the world," Ray Hillis informed them. "It's fast, furious and fun."

"Perhaps," said Kennedy. "Perhaps we may do that after dinner."

Holly watched a sailboat tack against the currents at the harbour mouth, canvas bellying in the breeze that had sprung up soon after one o'clock.

She tried to phase them out, all of them; Kennedy and Peter in particular. If it hadn't been for Peter Freeman she would have found the inconsequential prattle a frustrating waste of time – yet she might have gone with it, accepted it as another manifestation of cat-and-mouse bargaining. It had become more than that, however. She would have been content to let it drift, to let herself drift through days, even weeks of this nothingness because Peter Freeman gave it meaning. It was that acknowledgement that caused her to swing her legs from the *chaise* and square herself to face Ray Hillis.

"After dinner, Ray," Holly said, "we'd better get down to business, hadn't we?"

"You mean the Holbein?"

"Of course."

"What's the rush?" said Marion. "Aren't you having fun, Holly?"

"Kennedy and I must leave the day after tomorrow." Holly spoke directly to Ray, ignoring the woman. "You must have an opportunity to study both the miniature and its history; that's only fair."

"Twenty-four hours seems a trifle inadequate," said Marion.

"Where is the picture, Holly?" Ray asked.

"In the hotel vault."

"Bring it to our suite," Ray said.

"When?"

"After we've eaten," Ray answered. "Later tonight."

"If you need more time . . ." Holly said.

"We'll discuss the price tonight," Marion said tersely.

I'm looking forward to seeing it, Holly," Ray Ogden Hillis said. "If it's as fine as your description . . ."

"Ray, darling," Marion interrupted. "I'm beginning to peel. Take me back to the hotel."

The beach party broke up within minutes.

*　　　*　　　*

It was a lacklustre period in the Hotel Britannique's busy day, the hour in which nobody could quite make up their minds what to wear or what to do until seven thirty when it was practically mandatory to waft into the cocktail lounge for small talk before dinner. But at five thirty the cocktail bar was still shuttered and the tea-lounge, having lost the sun, had lost most of its elderly clientele too. Through the door from the courtyard guests in informal attire, trailing golf clubs, tennis racquets or beach toys, headed straight for the lifts, grumbling and a little out of sorts after a long day in the sun. Staff were not much in evidence; a languid boy in uniform lolled against a pillar, and a couple of waiters, hot from service in the tea-lounge, carried away silver tassies and decimated cake trays.

Sprawled in a chair by the half-open window, unpicking the *Times* crossword as best he could, Kennedy was resting in the Kings' bedroom. Bathed and groomed, Holly was too restless to 'put her feet up for a while' as Kennedy suggested. She slipped on an afternoon outfit, a white linen dress and navy jacket with a tab fastening.

"Where are you off to, dear?" Kennedy enquired.

"I want another look at the painting."

"Why?" said Kennedy. "Are you frightened it has withered to dust?"

"I'm just a little nervous, that's all."

"Go on," he said. "I'll probably catch a bit of a nap."

Holly did not go in search of the manager to ask him to give her access to the basement vault. She could not be sure in her own mind whether she had told Kennedy a lie or had just thought better of it. Kennedy was not the sort of husband who would read mischief into inconsequential actions. He was almost too patient, too understanding. Perhaps, without knowing it, she had been spoiled by his indulgence.

She was nervous, that much was true. But her nervousness did not stem from the sale of the Holbein.

Music attracted her. The Britannique was not one of these establishments that went in for dancing at odd hours and piano players and string orchestras practised off the premises.

"Wait, wait, my boy." Howard Crocker's voice said. "Hold it. One two three *tap*, long slide, *hop*."

The room off the laundry corridor lay at the foot of a short flight of stairs in the hotel's cavernous basements. Windowless, it was lit by four fine crystal globes but denuded of furniture, except for two canvas camping chairs and a folding card table, on which sat the gramophone. The wood-block floor was even but unpolished, the odour of dust pervasive. The swing door creaked a little when Holly leaned on it and peered through the crack.

The men were too absorbed to notice her.

Howard was enthusiastic. "Looks great, great, but, uh, won't it anticipate the polka sequence just a touch?"

"No, Howard. A simple souped-up travelling step, is all. It fits okay with the polka. If it comes to it I can cut out the polka tap step and go through to an abbreviation."

Both men had changed into casual slacks and cotton shirts. Howard's pants were held up by a necktie in Princeton colours.

"Show me," Howard said.

"Give me the four bars."

"Never mind the music."

La-la-ing for timing, Peter rattled a series of single, double and triple taps for a wing then slid and hopped as he had done before.

"Go on, go on, you're getting, ah, there," Howard urged.

Peter did a swing and a shimmy, his body alive with sensual rhythm, his outspread fingers playing an invisible keyboard suspended in the air above him.

He stopped.

"How long?" Howard asked.

"About twelve seconds, I guess."

"Fine. How long would you hold the pose?"

"Not long. I'm on three thirty now and there's still some slack at the end, so we score for a fade and a drum roll hold."

To Holly it was a foreign tongue, the pidgin English of professionals. Her own trade talk would be equally unintelligible to Peter. She began to relax a little, to enjoy the privilege of watching Peter and Howard hard at work and, in a way, defenceless. Peter's sexuality was patently evident even in a repetitive practice session, not a blatant jazzy quality but a haunting suggestiveness, both ethereal and earthy. Holly saw how strongly the skill of the dancer came forth, stripped of costume and make-up, orchestra, chorus and spotlights.

Howard cranked the gramophone. "Ready?"

"I figure I could finish with the old Juba," Peter said.

"Nobody's used the Juba step in thirty years."

"Maybe it's time it came back into vogue."

"I'm, uh, not convinced."

"Let's give it a try, from the top."

Peter tapped his pump on the floor and Howard grooved the needle precisely. The dancer whirled smoothly into a sequence of controlled slides, wheels and taps, fusing music and movements into a graceful, narrative flow. Peter held the piano-playing mime then, with Howard growling a simulated drum roll, swung and leapt high to land in an outrageously theatrical pose on bent knees with arms outstretched.

"Agreed," said Howard. "The Juba works. Then what?"

"I cossack out of it."

"Good, uh, fine." Howard silenced the gramophone.

"Better than Buchanan?"

"Miles better, but I figure you'll be playing to Brooks."

"Have you heard – officially?"

"Not just yet."

Peter towelled his neck and face vigorously.

"I want it, Howard," he said. "Don't screw it up for me."

"Odd, I didn't think you were keen on London."

"Sure, I am."

"She isn't for you, Peter."

"*She* thinks she is."

"She's . . ."

"Married?"

"I was going to say, uh, different."

"Hell, Howard, they're all the same."

"Nonsense. Mrs. King . . . she . . ."

"Why do *you* do it, Howard? You're a skirt-chaser. *You* know where the fun is."

"Girls, just girls."

"It's time you graduated to women, believe me."

"Like Marion Hillis? Women, uh, like that?"

"She didn't mean a thing."

"God, how callous you can be, Peter."

"Forget it, Howard."

"I, uh, the King woman – please, don't make a fool of yourself."

"Want her for yourself?"

"I don't want her taking your mind . . ."

"My mind!" Peter shouted. "I haven't got a goddamned mind. Since when have I had a goddamned mind? I'm Pete the Human Robot. Wind me up, I dance."

"Peter, Peter, someone will, uh, hear."

"Let them hear. Tell them it's a new song. Look, what I do with Holly King's my business. Keep your nose out of it. You've got no right, Howard."

"It'll be Rose Lambert all over . . ."

"I wasn't to blame for what happened to Rose."

"Another few minutes and that poor woman would have been dead," Howard said.

"She was a neurotic. Anyhow, I didn't encourage her."

"You, uh, took her to, uh, bed, didn't you?"

"Only that one time."

"It seems, Peter, once was enough."

"*Forget it, Howard; you hear me?*"

"You intend to have her, don't you?"

"What if I do?"

"Oh, dear! Oh, dear, dear, dear!"

"*Cut it out, Howard.*" Peter cried angrily, then, "Just play the goddamned music will you?"

As the gramophone issued its tinny sounds once more Peter flung the towel furiously into a corner and braced himself. More like a boxer than a dancer he strutted into an angry, assertive crazy-walk, a thing too ugly to be comical, yet in perfect tempo and utterly controlled.

"Not that, Peter, not, uh, that."

"*Go screw, Howard.*"

Hardly daring to breathe, Holly slipped quietly away.

She had seen him now, the strange depths hidden by his charm, his angry passion and his despair. She wondered who Rose Lambert was and what the woman had done that had so punished Peter. Now, Holly believed, she had no illusions left and nothing to sustain her need of him.

And yet, still, she wanted him.

She was no blind child, as she had been when David Aspinall had taken her virginity. She was too mature to confuse sexual need with love. But she could do nothing to stay the swarming emotions in her, the wilfulness that she had long, long suppressed.

More than ever, she wanted him.

Tomorrow, come what may, she must steel herself to leave Monte Carlo and never see Peter again.

✳   ✳   ✳

Nobody drank much at dinner. The interval between the social and business halves of the evening was abbreviated as much as courtesy would allow. Even Marion was less gushing than usual and it was left to Howard and Peter to push the conversation along. No rule of etiquette said that the sale of an art object had to be preceded by solemnity or that preliminary discussions could not be made at the dinner table, but fashionable reticence and the faint fond hope of gaining an edge in bargaining kept the Kings and the Hillises off the subject of the Holbein in the pretence that it was not the sole reason for their 'friendly' congregation in Monte Carlo. It was almost eleven o'clock before the couples said good-night to Peter and Howard – who indicated that they would while away an hour or two at the casino before bed – and went upstairs.

The Ogden Hillis suite was magnificent. French doors lead to a balcony and the lounge was crowned by a superb chandelier that would have graced a ballroom without shame. Under the chandelier a round table had been draped with a plain baize cloth, as if for a card party. Servants had been dismissed for the night and Ray Ogden Hillis closed the window drapes while Holly and Kennedy, standing, waited.

Marion returned from the bedroom where she had divested herself of her wrap and had touched up her hair and make-up. "Kennedy, darling, pour me a cognac, a teeny-weeny one."

Kennedy served the woman from the suite's small bar.

"Holly?"

"No, not for me."

"Ray?"

"Thanks, I'll pass."

"Well," said Kennedy, handing Marion her brandy, "shall we have a look at the painting?"

"Why not?" Ray said, "That's what we're here for."

Holly opened her long leather purse and withdrew the case, unlatched it, extracted the miniature and placed it on the table's baize cloth.

Drink in hand, Marion peered down at it.

Against the green cloth it was as bright as a gem, its colours as vivid as if they had been applied only that morning and not four centuries ago. The plain ebony frame seemed more fitting than one of jewel-encrusted paste, rock crystal or ivory. Almost four inches in diameter, the portrait was slightly larger than most miniatures of the period.

Ray pulled out a chair, swung himself on to it. Hands thrust between his thighs, long body poked forward, he gazed in awe at the treasure. "Dear God!"

Marion remained silent.

"Dear God! It's a Holbein and no mistake. I've never seen one of this calibre. Must have been done towards the end of his life. The second English period?"

"Fifteen thirty-nine," said Holly.

"Yes, the Hornebolt influence is hardly apparent. I mean, sure, young Hans was a genius at reducing images without loss of clarity – but this –!" Ray shook his head in wonder. "Incredible!"

"Looks odd," Marion declared. "Beautiful, yes, but odd."

"Technically it reminds me of the Christina of Milan portrait." Ray inched the portrait closer, shifting the angle. "Its freshness makes it seem singular, that's all."

"I can detect no trace of retouching," said Holly.

"Watercolour?" said Ray.

"Yes, watercolour on parchment or shaved vellum."

"And the backing?"

"Card."

"One of his favourite French playing cards?" said Marion.

"That's certainly what it appears to be," said Holly.

"Have you had it examined scientifically, Holly?" Marion enquired.

"No."

"Why not?"

"It's one thing to allow experts to slice pieces off a huge Rubens or Titian but I wouldn't fancy them mucking about with something this small and delicate."

"Right!" Ray agreed. "That's the problem with authenticating miniatures by science; the risk of damage. For instance, the Henry Eighth miniature in the Morgan Collection is set so tight behind crystal and ivory it's *never* been removed."

"You're not J. P. Morgan," said Marion. "So don't go off the deep end."

"Is it really Anne of Cleves?" said Ray.

Holly knew how important the identity of the sitter was to

the Ogden Hillises. She opened her memorandum and produced from it a neatly typed provenance, fifteen pages stapled in a stiff cardboard binder.

"This particular miniature, by title, is unrecorded," she said. "There are, however, two – possibly three – Holbein limnings of Anne of Cleves. The physical resemblance is striking. But the miniature portrait of Anne in the Victoria and Albert Museum in London and the three-quarter length in the Louvre are what you might call 'standard Court commissions', flatter, more formal and less dense than our miniature. I have reproductions for you to look at." Holly put two page-sized reproductions on the table. "I think you'll agree there's a strong similarity."

"Yes," said Ray without hesitation. "For my money, all three depict Anne of Cleves."

"Don't jump to conclusions, Ray," Marion warned.

Ray spared her a glance. "Aren't you convinced?"

"I prefer to keep an open mind, darling."

Holly said, "A third Holbein portrait appropriate to our studies is housed in His Majesty the King's collection at Windsor."

"The Royal collection?" Even Marion was impressed.

Holly said, "The drawing from the Royal collection is catalogued merely as 'A Lady: Unknown' but art scholars argue about the identity of the sitter and some experts are adamant that it's a more intimate rendering of Anne, probably done as a preliminary study for the two formal portraits."

"Holbein could work at incredible speed when he had to," Ray put in. "You know, his preliminary study for the Christina portrait is reputed to have been done in three hours."

"I think," said Holly, "that Holbein worked through the Windsor drawing to our miniature, then formalised his work for the V. and A. miniature and the Louvre three-quarter portrait."

"Can you substantiate your theory?" said Marion.

From the folder Holly brought a third reproduction taken from the original chalk and ink drawing in the Royal collection.

She slid it in front of Ray.

He frowned down at it. "Now *that* may *not* be Anne."

Deftly Holly arranged the three reproductions and the framed original into a sequence across the table. "Now look at them."

"Gee, yes!" Ray said. "I see what you mean, Holly. The transition's obvious: the Windsor drawing – our miniature – the V. and A. example – the Louvre portrait."

"The flattening, formalising process is deliberate and apparent," said Holly. "Do you agree?"

"Young Hans doing his duty for Henry, earning his commission," said Ray. "I'm with you, Holly."

"Kennedy, what's your opinion?" Marion asked.

"I don't think you can ignore the similarities," said Kennedy, warily.

"The Louvre portrait is ascribed to a date in July, Fifteen thirty-nine," said Holly. "Safe to assume that our miniature was completed in the spring or early summer of that same year.

"How many of these facts did *you* dig up, darling," Marion asked, "and how many came via the seller?"

"My source bought the miniature as a Holbein but the seller did not know the identity of the woman portrayed. My source connected it with the Louvre portrait and made the initial comparisons."

"And convinced you?" said Marion.

"Convinced me enough to buy it," said Holly. "Naturally I extended the research and expanded the history. It's all in the provenance. Everything."

"Quite a find, Holly. God knows, I wanted a Holbein but I never thought I'd run across one as monumental as this," said Ray.

"Holly, do *you* believe it's authentic?" asked Marion.

"Yes," said Holly. "If I had any serious doubts I wouldn't have offered it to you."

"What convinced you?" Marion asked.

"The painting itself," Holly replied. "The fact that it isn't an exact copy of the recorded portraits. Clothing, headware, draping, though similar, aren't identical. The jewelry's quite different, the shoulders of the gown are more relaxed, the stitching on the collar too."

"Did you check the costume details?" said Marion.

"There are no anachronisms."

"I take it you also put the painting under a strong glass?"

"Of course."

"Find anything useful?" asked Ray.

"One or two things. Notice the muted highlight on the chain of the crucifix – ochre and powdered gold, I'm sure."

"Favourite mix of Holbein's," said Ray.

"Chemical analysis would confirm it," said Marion.

"Yes, if you want to risk it," said Holly.

"I'm not entirely happy," said Marion. "The painting's *so* luminous."

"Young Hans was a master craftsman," said Ray. "He probably worked some small wonder with his pigments or with the parchment dressing: the old cough linctus?"

"Balsam and a trace of honey," said Holly. "I thought so too."

"What about the brushwork?" Marion said.

"On this scale, even with an enlarger, it's very difficult to evaluate the brushwork of a watercolourist. But it seems right to me!"

"Everything about the painting cries 'Hans Holbein'," said Ray emphatically.

"Where did it come from, Holly?" said Marion.

"I'm not at liberty to divulge my source," said Holly.

"English dealer?"

Holly paused. "No."

Marion seated herself at the table and reached for the miniature. She handled it lovingly. Somehow the object brought out a gracefulness that was not usually apparent in the woman.

"You must name your source," Marion said, "or it's no sale."

"Come on, Marion," said Ray. "Holly has every right to protect the seller. All I've got to know, Holly, is – can we publicly display the painting?"

"Of course, Ray."

"Fine. Fine. Now show me the history."

Holly handed him the folder.

Ray scanned the typed text. With typical thoroughness Holly had built up and annotated the notes that de Rais had given her.

Ray read a passage aloud. "Reference from footnote in the Dallaway edition of Walpole's *Anecdotes* says – 'The likeness of the Queen is much treasured by my great-uncle Hathersage who hath it from Tuck of St. Martin's.'"

"No mention of Holbein or Anne," Marion pointed out.

"There's more." Ray read, "'In smallnesse there is much virtue and shew of Mr. Holbin's skills.'"

"All right, a Holbein miniature," Marion conceded. "Is it this one, or another?"

Kennedy cleared his throat. "The Tuck family of St. Martin's Court were picture dealers of some repute throughout the eighteenth century. They only went defunct a few years ago. There are records of many of their sales but not of this one; it's too early. On the other hand Tuck did sell the 'official' Anne of Cleves miniature, the one now in the Victoria and Albert Museum. It's accurately recorded that Anne handed that miniature to a lady-in-waiting, of the Barrett family of Kent, who kept it until eighteen twenty-six."

"What's your point, Kennedy?" said Marion.

"Perhaps Anne gave this miniature to another lady attendant."

"Tenuous," said Marion. "Just guesswork, really."

"Whatever!" said Ray. "Hathersage keeps it for sixty years then his grand-nephew sells it to a Dr. Wilbrew: there's a note of the sale in the Hathersage House Book, but no price. How did it get to France?"

"Wilbrew emigrated," said Holly.

"So he did now, so he did," said Ray, eagerly. "Here's a copy of a letter sent by Wilbrew and published in the *Gentleman's Magazine* concerning the public water supply in great cities, mainly Paris. How the hell did you discover that, Holly?"

"I didn't. It came with the original history, from my source."

"The mystery man," said Marion, with a trace of sarcasm. "How clever *he* must be."

Holly said, "In the original article quoted in the history, Wilbrew mentions a son. Presumably he had his family with him. So that puts Wilbrew, and the miniature, in Paris in eighteen thirty-one or two"

"How do we know it's the same painting?" asked Marion. "That's the rub."

"Well, we know the doctor owned a similar painting," said Ray, "and we know he lost it – because of this handbill." He held up the bill. "My French isn't up to reading it."

"There's a translation on file," said Holly.

Ray found it, read, "'Be it known that from his domicile at Number Eleven, Rue Flavine, Doctor G. R. Wilbrew had this day stolen from his possession a fine small painting showing the likeness of a lady dressed in costume of the English Tudor Court. If a painting of this image which, when stolen, was framed in gilt paste, is offered for sale be it recorded that it is the property of Dr. Wilbrew and the purchaser will be generously rewarded for the safe return thereof.'"

"To whom did Wilbrew send the handbills?" asked Marion.

"Curators of museums and galleries and the better-known French art dealers," Kennedy informed her. "Common enough practice. Notice that old Wilbrew doesn't mention the artist's name. Even in eighteen thirty the whisper of a Holbein on the loose would have been enough to make all the scallywags in France prick up their ears."

"The painting didn't surface, though?" said Ray, consulting the text. "It went missing for a century."

"It came to my source from a junk dealer who bought it with scrapings from the house of the Perrin d'Armans family at La Plaine-St.-Denis, near Paris," Holly said. "I've included all that my source could learn about the Perrin d'Armans pedigree. The Holbein is just the sort of thing that Yves Perrin d'Armans, head of the household in eighteen thirty-one, might have picked up from an unscrupulous trader. He was, a magpie, a hoarder and a miserly sort of chap all round.

There are records of sales made by the Perrin d'Armans during the eighteen nineties, a few quality pieces leaked on to the market. The family fortunes were failing by then. They continued to dwindle until the last surviving member of the house – a spinster in her eighties – died this year. There was a sale but it was poor quality stuff and the ragpickers had a field day."

"One hundred years is a long time for a Holbein to be out of sight," said Marion. "Surely somebody in the d'Armans family must have recognised its value?"

"Not if old great-great granddaddy Yves bought it secretly and, knowing it was stolen, hid it away," said Ray. "That sort of thing's legion in the collecting game."

"I won't deceive you, Ray," said Holly. "The provenance isn't as pat as it looks. There are several grey areas. My theory, however, is that Wilbrew's son *may* have stolen the miniature from his father's keeping and *may* have sold it to a dealer, perhaps directly to Yves Perrin d'Armans."

"Too far-fetched," said Marion. "There's nothing to indicate that young Wilbrew knew old d'Armans."

"Rue Flavine," said Holly, "is in the Paris suburb of La Plaine-St.-Denis. The old quarter was torn down long ago but the street's still there - a half-mile from the Perrin d'Armans' property."

"Really!" said Ray. "That's hardly the kind of coincidence you can ignore. Yes, I like your theory, Holly. Sonny robbing Daddy to pay for wine and women. Anyhow, if the Holbein was stashed away in cool, dry hiding-places for much of its life, that would account for its freshness and fine state of preservation."

"I see you *want* to believe it, Ray," said Marion.

"Hell, it's better documented than that goddamned Lancret you jumped at last year." Ray spoke with a certain acerbity. "It had no history to speak of. But you liked it, therefore you convinced yourself it was genuine. Right?"

"But the Lancret was a bargain, a give-away; cheap," said Marion. "You can bet your boots this Holbein won't be."

Ray lifted the miniature between forefingers and thumbs and looked straight into the painted eyes. He emanated desire

71

for possession, not mere greed but that brand of longing that marked the true collector from the dilettante. Holly understood it well. In addition, Ray would be thinking how he could enhance his reputation through the painting, how he would evolve a whole theory around its unusual qualities, climb right on board the Holbein bandwagon by having found – rescued – a miniature as fine and important as any in the Morgan collection. It was strange how American collectors measured themselves against Morgan. As if to confirm Holly's judgement of his character, Ray said, "Boy, this'll knock Teddy on his ear. He never *saw* a sixteenth century this good."

Marion said, "How much?"

The sudden question caught Holly off-guard. She had not quite decided on an exact sum; a leaf of her memorandum was covered with calculations of exchange rates and profit margins.

"Well, Holly, just how much do you intend to sting us?" said Marion again.

There was no accurate gauge as to what the Holbein might be worth on open market. Certainly sixteenth-century masters were 'high', but it had been many, many years since a miniature of such quality had landed in an auction room. It was one of those pieces of art that command their own price.

Holly took a deep breath. "Twelve million, five hundred thousand francs. That's fifty thousand dollars."

"Wow!" Ray exclaimed.

"Fifty thousand, and it isn't even jewel-framed," said Marion. "Robbery!"

"I'm sure the frame was changed by Yves Perrin d'Armans, or perhaps Wilbrew's son sold it separately," said Holly. "I'm offering the painting, Marion, not the frame."

"Holly, you've got to admit," said Ray, "it's a helluva price."

"It's a hell of a painting."

"That is true; that is very true."

"And it cost me a great deal of money. I didn't stumble across it in a fleamarket."

Kennedy said, "I assure you, Ray, Marion, that Holly and

I are not profiteering."

Kings', in fact, would reap only twenty-one percent profit on the transaction, a modest return by art market standards.

Ray said, "Holly, not even Duveen would have the neck to ask for that amount of money for a miniature. It's unrealistic, out of kilter with values."

Holly lifted the leather purse and her memorandum and got to her feet, not brusquely but with excessive politeness. She had made no case for the astronomical asking price, no case at all. Marion was surprised and a little dismayed by Holly's refusal to haggle.

Holly said, "Will the painting be safe here?"

"I'll watch it like a hawk," Ray promised.

"In that case," said Holly, "we'll leave it with you to let you examine it thoroughly."

"And the price?" said Marion.

"The price is fixed."

"Kennedy, can't you make your wife see reason?" Ray said.

Kennedy shrugged.

"Apparently not," Marion blurted out.

Ray said, "When do you want an answer, Holly?"

"Tomorrow afternoon or evening."

"Wait," said Marion. "Let me ask you something, darling; what kind of fix will you be in if we don't buy it?"

"No fix, Marion. I'll find another client," said Holly.

"But the capital outlay," the woman went on, "must have drained your resources quite a bit."

"You're being less than polite, darling," Ray remarked.

Holly paused. She held purse and book against her breast, standing close to Kennedy, in unity with him. "Not quite, Marion," she said. "If I don't sell to you I'll sell to Edward Lathrope."

"But you . . . you don't know Teddy Lathrope."

"I think a Holbein miniature would make a suitable calling-card, don't you?" Holly said.

Ray gave an amused snort. "You said the right thing, Holly King, exactly the right thing."

"Tomorrow," said Holly. "Until then please keep it safe."

"Count on it," said Ray Ogden Hillis.

*　　*　　*

"Kennedy, are you concerned?"

"Concerned, dear?"

"Worried."

"About what?"

"Anything?"

"Will the Ogden Hillises buy? Is that what you mean?"

"I suppose so."

"No, I'm not worried. As you shrewdly pointed out, if they don't buy somebody else will."

"But that's bound to mean delay. I'd have to approach a client stone-cold – Teddy Lathrope, perhaps – convince him I was honest and that the price wasn't extortionate."

"How long a delay?"

"I can't say – weeks, months."

"Cold feet?"

"A little. Marion's guess was spot on, wasn't it? If we don't clinch a sale then the business will be hampered in purchasing power until we do."

"That's the risk we took, dear."

"Most of our working capital, plus the little loan on the securities; Kennedy, what if . . .?"

"What on earth's wrong, Holly? I've never seen you so agitated before."

"The price is so high."

"Holly, please tell me what's wrong."

"It's . . . oh, I don't know!"

"Do you doubt the Holbein?"

"Heavens, no!"

"What, then?"

"I wish I knew," said Holly.

*　　*　　*

"Of course she won't sell it to Teddy. Teddy may want it, would want it, but Teddy's tight. Tight as a duck's tail.

Darling, can you *imagine* Teddy Lathrope signing a cheque for fifty thousand dollars for a *single* miniature from a dealer he's never *met* before?"

"Put like that . . ."

"What other way is there to put it? If she sticks it up at Sotheby's or Cortlandt Bishop's it's unlikely to fetch anything like that figure. Auctions are a lottery and she knows it. God, if anyone knows it, Holly King does."

"Might be a runaway, though."

"Possible, I admit. But what are the chances, darling? These days? Erratic prices. Unpredictible fashions. I mean, my God, who's got fifty to throw out on a miniature?"

"We have."

"I have, darling, I have."

"All right, Marion, *you* have."

"I've never seen you so eager before, Ray. You must want this Holbein very badly."

"Isn't it obvious?"

"Stall the King woman. She isn't going to walk away."

"She might."

"Oh, I agree, darling, she might walk away from fifty thousand dollars but she won't walk away from Monte one minute before she has to."

"What's that supposed to mean?"

"Don't be such a cluck, Ray. She's fallen for dear Peter."

"Holly isn't that kind."

"It seems they're *all* that kind; she's only an extra in a distinguished cast, darling, from Margaret Nicholls up to poor Rose Lambert."

"Does that cast include you, Marion?"

"Of course."

"You're a bitch sometimes."

"Don't go all sulky, Ray. You've never accused me of fidelity in the past, why start now? Besides, don't pretend you didn't know about Peter and I."

"Sure, I knew, but I thought it was over."

"It is, long over."

"Now he's just – what? A friend?"

"He tired of me too, Ray."

"How that must have hurt you."

"It did, but not enough to make me take an overdose like poor little neurotic Rose who, I do believe, had never been spurned before."

"No, usually she did the spurning."

"Rose, New York's praying mantis. It served her right."

"Did you . . . was it fun?"

"Great fun."

"Is he . . . you know what I mean?"

"It's all make-believe, Ray."

"Hah, I'll bet!"

"It's true, I swear. It's not what Peter does that's especially alluring; it's the fact that dear Peter can make you believe it's romantic. I suppose that's why women like Holly King, hard-headed practical types, find him irresistible."

"Is that why you find him irresistible, Marion?"

"I suppose it is, really."

"Well, I reckon Holly King's got more . . . she won't fall."

"She's fallen already."

"Already? You don't mean . . .?"

"God, no! Peter will play with her like a cat does a mouse. I honestly believe that's the part of it he enjoys; the – what – courtship ritual, the seduction. Afterwards, he soon loses interest. And, oh, how that rankles."

"I never did like him much."

"You've never liked any of my men, Ray."

"I guess I'm just an old-fashioned husband."

"I find that rather sweet."

"Fact is, Marion, I hate the sons of bitches. Freeman included."

"You hide it very well, darling."

"Because I . . ."

"Need me? Of course you do. Besides, you know I don't take them seriously."

"Not even Freeman?"

"Not even Peter. The only man I've ever taken seriously is you."

"But if he, if Freeman . . .?"

"He won't; not now. I admit I wouldn't refuse him. But,

no, darling; Peter has passed me by long ago. It's Holly King he's pursuing."

"If Kennedy's wise he'll close the deal and get her out of here fast."

"Kennedy King does not call the tune, which is the reason I suggest that we don't meet the asking price on the Holbein. They're stretched very thin, darling. And Holly doesn't have her mind wholly on business. We can take advantage of the situation."

"Wreck a marriage just to save a few bucks?"

"In my estimation the marriage is not so stable as it seems. However, what do you calculate she paid for the miniature?"

"Twenty-five, thirty; something like that."

"I think she paid more like forty."

"So what? The Kings have more than five times that in stock in their shop in the Chalfont Arcade."

"Stock, not working capital."

"I see what you mean, Marion. Even the Kings have to turn over their investment rapidly these days. It might be a blue chip trade they're into but the damned profit margins have shrunk so much since the crash that, like dealers in New York, they must run pretty close to the edge. A delay on a big sale could pinch them enough to hurt, I suppose."

"Pinch her then. Make her wait. We could take them out on the yacht, couldn't we? Better still we could persuade Kennedy to stay ashore with Howard, contrive to get Peter and Holly alone, shake them together . . ."

"No, Marion. Pay her the asking price."

"Scruples?"

"Some, yeah!"

"Since it isn't your money, darling, I don't see how you can afford to have scruples."

"Listen, I won't serve Freeman another lover on a silver plate, not for all the bloody Holbeins ever painted."

"You're amazing, darling. You're making more fuss about a woman you hardly know than you did about me."

"Why are you trying to hurt her, Marion?"

"She's such a stuck-up prig, that's why."

"Holly King? She's no prig. I reckon you're jealous of her,

Marion, because she came up the hard way, without the silver spoon, and made it to the top."

"Do you call Kings the top?"

"Or, maybe, it's because Freeman ditched you and has eyes for her instead."

"I can't even stand that husband of hers, that *old* man."

"He loves her."

"Meaning what?"

"Meaning . . . Geeze, Marion, all I want is the Holbein."

"Aaww, does widdle Way wanna nice new paintin'?"

"Yeah, I do."

"Okay, big boy. It's yours."

"What?"

"You can have it."

"No stalling?"

"No stalling."

"What's the price, Marion? What do I have to do?"

"Nothing at all. 'Cept give me a kiss and say thanks."

"Why did you suddenly change your mind?"

"Peter will have her in his own good time. He doesn't need my help. Buy the Holbein. Let her run away. It won't matter."

"Well . . . Fine."

"What about the kiss; a little sign of gratitude, darling."

"Can I close the deal in the morning?"

"Yes. Now. Kiss. Kiss."

"Just let me put the Holbein safe in its box."

"*Now*, Ray."

"All right."

"Thank me properly. Improperly."

"Marion . . ."

"Tell me how much you love me."

"I love you," Ray said. "I love you very much."

"That's more like it," Marion sighed.

* * *

"Who the hell do they think they are? Who do they think *we* are? I wouldn't offer a deal like that to a kid fresh out of dancing school." Howard thumped the receiver into its hooks and paced up and down the room a couple of times before going out through the French doors on to the breakfast terrace. "I've met some cheap chiselling, uh, sonsabitches in my day but Jopman takes the biscuit."

In the light of morning, Howard presented a less than urbane image to the world, grey hair dishevelled, Brooks Brothers dressing-gown carelessly pulled around him, belt trailing like a prehensile tail. At the breakfast table, Peter was cool-looking in tailored grey slacks, dark blue shirt with a cravat tucked in at the throat, freshly shaved, hair brushed neatly back. He spread marmalade on toast.

"You knew before we left home the kind of deal R.K.O. had in mind, Howard."

"I thought I'd scare them into upping the offer."

"Guys like Opman don't scare easy."

"*Dance* was a smash. A, uh, total, unequivocal smash. What am I doing here? We should be in Hollywood, uh, right now." He glanced at Peter. "For God's sake, will you leave that toast alone and listen to me."

"I'm listening." Peter bit into the toast.

"You're so calm, always so damned calm."

"Howard, the reason we're sitting in the sun in France is that you spiked the deal weeks ago. Do you suppose they'd call you transatlantic just to tell you they're offering the same money and the same terms if they weren't worried?"

Howard seated himself, reached for a glass of orange juice. "Uh, yes. Never thought of that."

"They've been stupid," said Peter. "Tipping their hand."

"Quite right, quite right!"

"Besides, if the London show comes off we couldn't take R.K.O. up on *any* kinda contract. And the London show will come up, won't it?"

"Oh, I can cobble something together."

"Cobble something . . . with Ralph Brooks – and me?"

"Uh, yes, an ill-chosen phrase. I thought you didn't want to go to London."

"I told you yesterday, I've changed my mind."

"Has she given you any encouragement?"

"She's a lady, Howard."

Peter finished his coffee and got to his feet. Though Howard and he had stayed at the casino until after one, Peter seemed as energetic as ever. Sourly, Howard watched him execute three or four limbering-up steps then, grinning, give his manager a crisp salute.

"Think I'll go for a stroll, Howard."

"Be back by September, will you?"

"I'll try."

There was no arrangement, no rendezvous. For all that, Peter Freeman was hopeful that Holly King might also 'feel like a stroll', might return to the gardens where they had walked together the night before last. For all he knew the Kings had conducted their business with the Ogden Hillises and had taken the early train out. Hubby might have gotten wise to what was happening and, rightly, have whisked his wife out of harm's way. There was no harm in it yet, of course. But there would be. Sure, there would be. He was still falling. He hadn't stopped, hadn't grounded. It wasn't just when he was with this stranger from England that excitement warmed him. It was all the goddamned time. Excitement? More than that. He had never experienced it before. It was a bit like pulling off a sequence of steps that hadn't been planned, the uncertainty of it all was exciting but made him anxious too. He had agreed to tag along on the Riviera trip in the hope that it would lift the depression that had stolen over him during the long winter in New York when the grind of the show – and the sick business with Rose Lambert – had culminated in Hollywood's refusal to snap him up. His pride had been wounded. Couldn't they see that he was the most talented performer of his generation, next to Astaire? His work rate was five times higher than anybody else's. He was a law unto himself. Rose should have realised it. How did he know she was close to blowing her cork? He was the one who was supposed to be sensitive, not the rich lacquered women who threw themselves at him. Women like Marion. It pleasured him to be there with her, aware that she still wanted him but could not have him now, not with Ray around, and that he would not permit her to back him into a corner. She had no claims on him. He had never pretended to be in love with her or led her to believe that their affair would be other than fleeting. When it came to it, he was more deceitful and more rapacious than any of the spoiled women whom he had bedded, more than a match for any of them. He would not be used. He would not put himself in a position to be hurt again, as Lakey had hurt him.

Peter emerged from the side door of the hotel and paused to take a deep breath of the morning air. Clipped hedges, massy evergreens, flowers, the Avenue – a perfect day, enlivened by a brisk breeze from the sea. Flags snapped on the hotel's painted poles and the town climbed up, clean and sharp in the sunlight.

"Peter?"

Holly King stood by the corner of the embrasure where the path sloped down to the gates. She wore an off-white jumper suit and the breeze plastered the folds against her limbs and ruffled her dark hair. She waved to him and called his name once more.

Peter waved back.

To hell with Marion Hillis. To hell with Rose Lambert.

It was this woman, this quiet Englishwoman, that he wanted right now. And he intended to have her, whatever the cost.

*   *   *

Holly was afraid. Never before had she been so drawn to a man. Her love for David Aspinall had been little more than a childish infatuation. Her love for Christopher had been, at first, expedient and had grown only slowly, so slowly that it had not had time to come to full flower. Her love for Kennedy was too solidly founded on respect to bear comparison with her feelings for the American. The rapidity with which she had stepped into a relationship with him was appalling, the kind of thing that she would have condemned if it had happened to another woman. She tried to pretend that she had lost volition, that her meeting with Peter was the fulfilment of a destiny. But she did not believe in destiny.

Christopher had been a fatalist; there was no romance in the philosophy, not one drop. It was impossible to bring her feelings into perspective on that bright brisk morning, knowing what Peter was and what her flirtation signified. He was not a man she could admire or with whom she could share her life. Perhaps that was part of his attraction – or all of it?

"Did you have a profitable night at the casino?" she began.

"You're kidding?"

"Lose much?"

"Twenty bucks or so. I never did go for mechanical gambling," said Peter. "I'm a sucker for horses, though. One reason I came on this trip was to attend the spring race meeting at Longchamp. I lost my shirt, but it was worth it. I hope to be back in Paris for the Grand Prix and the d'Auteuil in une."

"I thought you were planning to come to England."

"If Howard swings it, sure."

"You must dine with us. My son would love to meet you."

"How old's the boy?"

"Thirteen."

They walked side by side down the path towards the gates, wanting desperately to touch each other. The affinity was physical and arousing and it disturbed Holly deeply. She had been an introverted girl and a woman who prided herself on her self-control. It was ridiculous that, at this stage in her life, the blood would not be denied, the angry appetites that, she believed, had shaken her mother and caused her to ruin her life by marrying the strutting little bantam, Leo Beckman, a man so different from her, so far beneath her that the match was doomed from the outset. For a single instant she felt as if her mother was there in the garden with her, no ghost but an unseen observer nodding and smiling and egging her on. Was the Kirsanoff inheritance, in the long run, inescapable? The passion, the selfish desire, the webs of conflicting emotional and sexual need spun fine by the intellect? Wryly Holly supposed that her Russian ancestors would have approved of such madness and that the gardens of the Hotel Britannique on a blue spring day were no less suitable for wilful folly than the snowy streets of Moscow or the fog-brown slums of London.

She had no patience with the foibles of her imagination and had learned no lesson about herself from the fact that she had been loved in turn by a gambler, a poet and a fine art dealer. In the child-like core of her being, the region that remains untouched by maturity and experience, Holly could not separate what she had made of herself, what she had achieved, from the matrix of her character, the unalterable background that gave her identity. So lacking in fundamental confidence was she that she truly believed that any woman would have done as well for David, Christopher and Kennedy. Now Peter Freeman, a womaniser, appeared to confirm her belief; and for that, strangely, she was grateful to him.

"Holly, when I come to London, it's you I want to see, not your family."

"That's not how it's done, Peter; not in England."

"Jolly old England," he said. "Must do the decent thing, what?"

"Kennedy isn't like Ray Hillis."

"And you're no Marion, thank God."

"If you come to London, we could be friends."

"God!" Peter exclaimed. "Friends! It's too late for that."

"In that case . . ."

"Go ahead, dish out the ultimatum."

"Won't you even allow me to say no?"

"Yeah, you can say no – just don't count on my cooperation."

"What?"

"I may even take you at your word, Holly? Are you sure that's what you want?"

"Did Rose Lambert say no?"

"Who told you about that? Was it Marion?"

"How serious was it, Peter?"

"Not very. Rose . . . Christ, I don't want to talk about her to you."

"What did she do?"

"Drank poison, not poison, stuff to make her sick. She didn't intend to kill herself. I *know* that. She wanted to punish me – and she did. I didn't mean her any harm."

"But you did her harm."

"It would have happened any way. Her second marriage was on the goddamned rocks, and she was broke – though nobody knew that, not even me."

"What happened to her?"

"Nothing bad. I don't know. I haven't seen her since. I hear she's in Baltimore with a new husband; starting over. Is that what you wanted to learn."

"It's hard for me, Peter, don't you see?"

"I know."

"Do you?"

"All you seem to do is ask questions."

"It's safer than having to give answers, make promises," said Holly. "I don't know where I am."

"You're here, in Monte Carlo, with me; that's all that matters."

"But if I leave Monte Carlo, will I leave you too?"

"Questions?"

"Answer me."

"No, you won't leave me; I think you know that."

"It isn't imagination, then; too much sun, too much *vin blanc*?"

"It isn't for me."

"You've nothing to lose, though, have you, Peter? I came to France to sell a miniature painting. Now I couldn't care less about the blasted painting, or Ray Hillis's money or anything else. I feel as if I'd been torn away from a mooring."

"Maybe you have. Maybe I have."

"For ten years, Peter, I've kept occupied, buying and selling antiques, building a fine business, being a wife to Kennedy and mother to Chris; now . . ."

"Don't tell me you think it's all been meaningless?"

"Of course it hasn't. I'm not *bored*, Peter. It *isn't* boredom."

"What is it then? What is it between you and me?"

"If you took me upstairs, to a bedroom . . ."

"That wouldn't end it, Holly."

"Are you sure?"

"Sure I'm sure."

"It might end it for me."

"Do you want to try?"

"That's pretty cruel, Peter."

"No more cruel, no more cold-blooded than discussing what's between us as if it was a . . . . a deal you were doing."

"You're right. I'm sorry," Holly said. "Once I'm back in London, in my own house, with my son close by . . ."

"You're running away."

"Yes, I am."

"Before we've really gotten to know each other."

"Oh, I know you well enough, Peter."

"You've met 'my kind' before, uh?"

"Never, never anyone quite like you."

"Close enough?" said Peter. "My kind aren't safe to be around, is that it?"

"Don't you understand?" said Holly. "It's me I'm afraid of."

"When I saw you through the window . . ."

"Please, don't."

"It isn't supposed to be like this. I'm not a damned puppet. I'm not being jerked around by all the guys I've played. It just *isn't* supposed to happen."

"I'm surprised too," said Holly, "if it's any consolation. But I'm not . . . well, I'm *not*. Let's go back now. My husband will be up and about, probably wondering where I am. Take me back."

"All right."

"Talk about something else, anything else. I'm afraid I'm not used to such personal topics."

"Why are you going to Paris?"

"To look at paintings," said Holly.

"More paintings," said Peter. "I thought the sale of this Holbein picture would be enough for a while."

Relieved that the conversation had come down in pitch, and on safer ground, Holly explained, "I said I was selling the Holbein for a record price; that's true – but only for a miniature. It's a rising market but not in any one particular area. Up and down. Nobody truly understands it. Tastes change overnight. Fashion has too big a hand in it. Kennedy trusts my judgment."

"I would too. If I wanted to buy a nice miniature painting what would it set me back?"

"The Holbein is very special," said Holly. "It has a unique place in the artist's history. But a Cosway or Fragonard could be had for a couple of hundred guineas, about eight hundred dollars."

"What if I wanted something really old; a piece of olde England?"

"A Hilliard miniature from the time of Queen Elizabeth could be found for as little as a hundred pounds – if you knew the right dealer."

"You know a lot about paintings, don't you?"

"I'm no expert," said Holly. "I'm not being modest. I'm a dealer in fine art objects – from snuffboxes to tea-services, from silver plate to, oh, Dresden figurines. You had your vaudeville apprenticeship, Peter, I had my days tramping round the Friday outdoor market up Camden Road in the rain, picking over the pitches, or sitting for hours in draughty auction rooms. I didn't always do business in the Hotel Britannique in Monte Carlo."

"Would you go back to the Camden Road days, Holly?"

"Never," Holly said. "I couldn't, not now."

"What's next for you?"

"Can't say."

"Sell something to the King of England?"

"By appointment to His Majesty," said Holly. "Kennedy would like that."

"But not you?"

"Yes, it would look impressive on our headed notepaper."

"But it wouldn't . . . thrill you?"

Holly did not answer. They were standing together in full view of the hotel, unscreened by trees and ornamental shrubs, close to the spot where she had watched Peter go through his elegant little exercise the night before last. Holly did not have to struggle to recapture her emotions of that moment; they were with her still, undiminished by her decision to get out of Monte Carlo and away from Peter Freeman as soon as she could. As she had suspected, it was not a fleeting daydream, an unusual fancy. Even talking about it with Peter did not dispel her desire to be with him.

Holly said, "You asked about Paris; I have a friend there, a dealer. He's offered to introduce me to a Count and Countess who are considering selling some family heirlooms. My friend, Monsieur Lenormant of the Galerie Voltaire, appreciates that the Count and Countess do not wish the articles to appear on the French market, either in a dealer's catalogue or at auction. They have no objection to the stuff being sold in England, however."

"Proud French aristocrats?"

"I haven't met them yet."

"You'll take the stuff – paintings?"

"Probably."

"What does Lenormant get out of it?"

"Ten percent of the sale, split between buyer and seller."

"Most theatrical agents skin you for twenty percent."

"Also," said Holly, "if a similar situation arises in which I require a French dealer I put the business in Monsieur Lenormant's hands."

"Trust and friendship?"

"Yes, I've known Monsieur Lenormant for years."

"Young guy?"

"Ancient," Holly smiled. "He has snow-white hair and a dowager's hump."

"What's that?"

"A hump – like this."

Holly demonstrated, hunching her shoulders and thrusting her head forward.

Peter laughed. "You look a bit like a stork."

"That's exactly what Monsieur Lenormant does look like – a stork."

Above the couple, flags snapped crisply in a gusting breeze that brought a hum of sound up from the Avenue, the rhythm of surf scudding on rocks and the harbour walls. Holly's relaxed mood vanished. When Peter laughed, her attraction to him became unbearable; the thought of not seeing him again engulfed her. She wrapped her arms about her as if the warm breeze chilled her to the bone. "I'm going in now."

"Wait, please, let's talk a while longer."

"No, Peter."

"Holly?"

"Good-bye."

"Hey!"

The door shuttled behind her.

Peter watched it swing, slow and settle. He hoped she would change her mind. But Mrs. King, he guessed, was a woman of great self-control; once her mind was made up she would not go back on her decision, not for him, not for anyone.

Disconsolately Peter Freeman seated himself on the low brick wall.

He lit a cigarette.

He studied the toes of his shoes.

He was right; Holly King did not return.

By noon that day the English woman and her husband, with Ray Hillis's cheque for fifty thousand dollars in their luggage, had left Monte Carlo for Paris.

OOOOOOO
OOOOO
OOO
O

3

The House that Beckman Built

Another city, another hotel, another set of circumstances, new faces, real and painted, another financial transaction; Holly had thought that she would find Paris comforting, that her business with the gracious Monsieur Lenormant would salve the sense of loss that she experienced on quitting Monte Carlo, on leaving Peter Freeman. Even Kennedy had remarked that their winding-up of the sale of the Holbein at eleven o'clock in the morning and their subsequent departure *sans* lunch had been so abrupt as to seem hostile. Holly had snapped at him, sharply reminding him that *he* was the one who wanted to watch Surrey play cricket on Saturday, telling him, with wounding truth, that she would have been more than happy to stay on and enjoy the sunshine and the good company that the Ogden Hillises provided. Though patient to a fault, Kennedy had been so caught out by this unexpected display of temper in his wife that he had gone into a sulk and had said hardly a word to her during the long train journey to the capital.

Their relationship had never been marred by petty bickering, but the potential for friction had always been there, deep in each of them. Kennedy was afraid that it would surface now, forced up by his wife's sudden, incredible infatuation with the American. At home he would have treated Holly more indulgently, but he was too weary and physically out of sorts to humour her, particularly as she was in the wrong. He did the next best thing, he prudently retreated.

On Thursday afternoon he flew back to Croydon from Le Bourget 'to deposit our dollars and make sure that there's enough in the trading account to let you spend again'. Holly was glad to see him go. It removed the need to disguise her mood and allowed her to schedule her appointments less rigorously. To her surprise, with Kennedy gone, she almost began to enjoy herself. The bitter-sweet aftertaste of an affair that never was, with no harsh sediment of guilt to spoil it, seemed ideally served by that most open and romantic of all cities – Paris.

Though she stayed as usual at the Regina on the Rue de Rivoli, Holly did not make use of the hotel's facilities and did not long remain brooding in her room. After telephoning Monsieur Lenormant to check her appointments for the following day Holly gave in to restlessness and went out into the city's streets. Aimlessly she wandered along Rue St. Honoré looking at the expensive trinkets in the shop windows, for once without the parchment-covered notebook tucked under her arm. She drifted back by the corner of the Place de la Concorde to the gardens and with curiously tender envy observed the hosts of lovers that the warm spring twilight had lured on to the terraces and paths of the Tuileries. She tried to blank out the *petite bourgeoisie* who seemed so out of place at the little café tables under the chestnut trees, couples who sat in severe silence, separated by too many years of intimacy. Nor did Holly pay much attention to the men who lounged on the café chairs and assessed the girls and young women with the calculation of stock merchants, their quiet arrogance hinting that a sexual encounter with them would be an admirable substitute for romance. Among the *pavillons*, under the plane trees, in pastel shadows and the auras of the street lamp lights, a dozen times Holly imagined that she glimpsed Peter and, catching her breath, believed that she had willed him to follow her, to find her alone in Paris on that velvet April night.

There was no such nonsense, of course. Idle wishing was its own fulfilment and Holly could not sustain it for long before it became, to her, too juvenile and – because she found it so – rather sad.

She returned, tired, to the Regina.

She asked at the desk if there had been a message for her, a telephone call perhaps, a note, a visitor?

She knew what the answer would be.

She went up to her room, bathed and put on her evening gown and went down alone to the dining room and ate dinner.

By eleven thirty she was in bed asleep, the parchment-covered notebook and a pocket manual of sale prices laid close by her on the bedside table to ward off her jejune dreams.

*   *   *

"Gawd strewth!" Leo Beckman exclaimed. "If it ain't Lord Muck."

"Evening, Dad," said Maury amiably.

"What you want, this time'r night?"

"I was in the neighbourhood so I thought I'd drop in for a cuppa."

"In the neighbourhood? Puttin' in a offer for Lambeth Palace, was yer?"

"How'd you guess?" said Maury. "We're converting it into flats."

Leo looked startled, not twigging that the joke had been reversed and, dazzled and bewildered by his eldest's success, almost inclined to believe it.

"Going to keep me on the step all night?" said Maury.

Leo squared himself in the doorway of No. 5, end house in the cul-de-sac of Abraham's Terrace, the infamous 'Abraham's Box' where Maury, Holly and Ritchie had been born and raised. The Box had changed little in appearance in the past decade, except to grow seedier and less rowdy, but in the backwaters of boroughs like Lambeth, depression and unemployment had taken their toll and the cheery heart of the district seemed to have been stilled. Cavanaugh's Patent Medicine factory had been forced to close in 1928 and the building had remained empty ever since, brick walls crumbling, windows broken. The tall chimney of Dorking's Light Iron Works had been smokeless since 1930 and many of the small trades shops had locked their doors forever. Fine new white buildings across the Thames and the splendour of the new Lambeth Bridge seemed as remote as the Potalla in Tibet to the natives of Lambeth. Even the Admiral's Hat, the corner pub, had gone flatter than its own cheap beer, its gaudy stained glass replaced in part by plywood boards plastered with handbills and wrinkled posters. Even Leo – especially Leo – had given up all loyalty to his once-favoured haunt and rolled a quarter mile east to the Paradise where there was light, laughter and a better class of women in the lounge.

"What the hell's wrong with you, Pa?" said Maury. "Got somebody in there?"

Ignoring the question, Leo tightened the cord of his Superior Quality All Wool Camel dressing-gown and stepped from the door to squint at the staid Humber motor-car drawn up at the kerb.

"Still drivin' that old bus?" he growled, slyly cocking his head to survey the length of the terrace. "High time you 'ad a Rolls-Royce, son. It's what a bloke in your position should be drivin'."

"I'll order one next week," said Maury.

"Locked it up, 'ave yer?"

"Want me to wheel it inside?"

"Well, can't be too careful these days," said Leo. "Gawd, the things that 'appen round 'ere! Steal the sugar outta yer tea, kids would. Bleedin' young 'ooligans!"

"Pa, are you going to let me in?"

"What? Oh! Yer!"

Leo made room for his son to enter the tiny hallway. As Maury did so, Leo struck up with a loud speech of welcome that Maury guessed was not intended for his ears alone.

"Good t'see yer, *Maury*. Go into the livin' room, then. The *livin' room*. Not every night *my son* comes callin'."

In passing, Maury glanced up the narrow staircase at the faint glow of light under the bedroom door on the first floor landing. As he suspected, Leo was 'not alone'. Most likely the old reprobate had a tart up there. At sixty Leo Beckman seemed to have found second wind as far as women were concerned. He had little enough to occupy his mind, Maury supposed, except the indulgence of basic appetites. Maury was more amused than disgusted. "Got company?"

"What? Nah! Must've left the lamp on. Was in me bed. Just gone."

The years had been kind to Leo. In fact he looked better now than he had ever done; the selfish simian ferocity had diminished and he had put on weight. He took more care of his appearance. His iron-grey hair was cropped close to his skull and, Maury reluctantly had to admit, the old codger still gave off a vigorous, vulgar aura of self-confidence, like an ageing rooster. Maury had, of course, noted the brand new dressing-gown and wine-red mock-silk pyjamas. On entering the living room, he found other clues to confirm his suspicion that Pa was having himself a last long fling.

The room had also changed; it was tidy, clean and well-furnished, a Magilog electric fire in the hearth, a Mullard wireless set on a teak cabinet by Leo's leather armchair. The transformation of Leo's hollow had been gradually accomplished by Mrs. Ida Fest who rode up to Lambeth from Battersea every weekday morning to 'do' for Mr. Beckman. Ida had been Maury's choice of housekeeper. Though Leo referred to her grandly as 'my char', the master-servant relationship had become confused over the years so that Leo, without being aware of it, did more or less what Ida told him and not the other way round. Ida was paid by weekly postal order sent directly to her home address by one of Maury's clerks. It was Ida Fest who had cajoled Leo into keeping himself clean and reasonably smart, who not only swept and polished the furniture but made Leo's meals and even bought clothes for him – for all of which Maury paid. Ida left Leo free to stroll about Lambeth like the Duke of Ditchwater, toddling from the Paradise to the bookie's shop to the Rex picture house. Ida was a gem, and Leo knew it. But it certainly wasn't Ida Fest who, at that hour of a Thursday night, was hiding in the bedroom upstairs.

Maury knew better than to wait for his father to offer him refreshment. He took off his hat and overcoat, slung them on the sofa and went directly into the kitchen.

"Want tea?" he called.

"Yer, yer, since you're makin' it."

Maury put the kettle on the stove and lit the gas.

From the living room, Leo shouted, "Would yer rather 'ave a drop o' the 'ard stuff, son? Gotta nice bottler Scotch. Port, Sherry, or . . ."

"Tea'll do me," said Maury – and stepped suddenly back into the living room.

He had already spotted the box of Perfectos Finos cigarettes, Caprice chocolates and two stemmed glasses sitting stickily on the edge of the wireless cabinet. An evening with Don Juan, Maury thought. At first it crossed his mind that he had tracked Ritchie with unexpected ease. But there was no reason for Ritchie to spend a social evening in Abraham's Box. Besides, it would have been far too much of a coincidence after – what – twelve years. Expensive fags, chocs, port wine? Not Ritchie but a bit of fluff, a rather special bit of fluff to prompt Leo to go to all that trouble. Maury felt like blurting out, "How long has this been going on?" but the question, let alone the implied reprimand, would have been ridiculously out of place. Leo had always had the morals of a polecat; Maury was just thankful that he no longer smelled like one. Even so, the sight that met his eyes when he popped back into the living room astonished him.

There was Leo, sneakily trying to hide the evidence, caught on his way to the door.

"What the hell have you got there?" said Maury.

"Ah . . . ah . . . nothin'."

"Pa?" Maury advanced.

"Ain't nothin', ain't nothin'." Leo tried to stuff the objects into the breast of his dressing gown, cheeks scarlet with embarrassment. "Nothin' t'do with you."

"Give 'em here."

For all his veneer of civility, Maury had been reared in rough schools and was rock-hard underneath. He had not forgotten the value of direct attack. He grabbed his father's shoulder and spun him round.

The tambourine fell, jangling, to the carpet; a round, well-worn tambourine, an instrument, not a toy, and with it an unmistakable poke bonnet in stiff black-painted straw.

"God Almighty!" said Maury.

"Ssshhh! She'll 'ear you. Cissie don't like folks t' take the Lord's name in vain."

"You mean," said Maury, "you mean you've a Salvation Army girl up there in your bed?"

"Shh!"

"A Godless little ex-Jew like you! I can't believe it! How the hell did you talk her into it, Pa? I mean, God Almighty!"

"She ain't no girl, she's a captain."

The inappropriateness of the liaison struck Maury as hilarious. He bellowed laughter, while Leo pranced on bare feet and begged him to shut his mouth.

"What's she doing it for – Army funds?" said Maury.

"Ain't like that. Really it ain't."

"Port wine, ciggies, chocs; what ever happened to self-denial?" Maury laughed again. Lifting the tambourine, he shook it gently and declared, 'Saw the Light, Hallelooyah!"

"Maury, Maury! I'll bleedin' kill yer, if you don't stop makin' that racket," said Leo. "Told you, it ain't like it seems. She . . . Cissie *likes* me. She ain't serious about the Army no more. It was her Pa – her Papa, she calls 'im – he was a bleedin' looney about Salvation. Wouldn't let Cissie marry, not even an Army bloke. She's no chicken, Maury. I mean, she ain't a kid."

"I don't believe this, I just don't believe it."

"Ahh!" Blushing, Leo hung his head.

"What age *is* she?"

"About forty, like that."

"Introduce me."

"*What*?"

"I'd like to meet her."

"Not, not t'night, son. Wouldn't be right. It'd embarrass 'er. It's supposed t' be a secret 'til she gets shook o' the Army, resigns like. Old man's only been dead six months."

"I see," said Maury, nodding. "Are you going to marry her?"

"Well . . ."

"Salvation, Pa?"

"Well . . ."

In the kitchen the kettle sang and Maury, still chuckling, went through to make tea. He found a stale cream bun and two Eccles cakes in the bread tin and put them on a plate, the plate on a tray and carried supper through. His father was slumped at the table, a Perfectos hanging from his nether lip, bonnet and tambourine placed on the cloth before him like votive offerings or exhibits in a criminal trial.

"I ain't ashamed, Maury," said Leo belligerently. "Caught me on the 'op, that's all. I got no reason t' be ashamed o' Cissie."

"I won't say a word," Maury assured him.

Leo removed the cigarette, absently lifted the cream bun, demolished it in three mouthfuls, head still resting on his hand, elbow propped on the table. Maury stirred his tea for him and pushed cup and saucer close.

"Don't look so dejected, Pa."

"I wanted it t' be a surprise, like."

"It was, Pa, a real surprise."

"You 'ad t' come tonight, didn't yer?"

Maury seated himself, sipped tea and helped himself to a cigarette. It was years – uncountable years – since last he'd sat like this with Leo. In fact, he could hardly recall having shared such a degree of intimacy with his father before; no, not intimacy exactly. With gratification, Maury realised that they were not equals. Leo had been chastened by comfort, by the flight of his sons and daughter. Maury had no doubt that Leo considered it an excellent exchange, moan though he would about neglect. But he, Leo, would do it again, swap all three kids for a tidy monthly pension.

"Told Ritchie yet, Pa?" Maury asked. "About your intentions?"

"Not told nobody."

"Ritchie will be pleased. He always said you should marry again, find a good woman to look after you, in all respects."

"Did he?" Leo glanced at his elder son. "Did Ritchie say that?"

"Oh, sure. But you an' he were always thick. Know what Ritchie told me once – before he left – told me if I didn't look after you properly he'd come back and break my bleedin' neck."

"Gerroff?"

"He did, I swear," Maury lied.

"Well, I never guessed."

"Write him. Tell him the news. You know Ritchie, he was always generous; probably send you a wedding gift."

"Don't 'ave to write," said Leo.

"You mean Ritchie already knows about your . . . your ladyfriend?"

"I can tell 'im man-to-man."

Leo had walked straight into Maury's trap.

If Ritchie had known that his father would yield up 'secrets' so readily no doubt the man would not have heard one word from his son over the last decade. For all Ritchie's cynicism, however, there was attachment here, one slender strand of sentiment. Maury had banked on Leo's loose-tongued pride in his favourite's achievements which, embellished and coloured by Leo's vivid imagination, rose above the merely criminal to become like the conquests of an emperor.

"Can you now?" said Maury. "How's that?"

"Be 'ome soon, Ritchie will. Home for good."

"Really!" said Maury.

"Yer. He's made his pile. More'n you – well, maybe not more'n *you*, Maury, but more'n *her*." Leo, of course, meant Holly. "Rollin' in it, is our Ritchie."

"Always knew he'd make good."

"Good? He was big time. Hear that? Big time in America. Had dinner with Al Capone. Even worked for the Big Fellow. Knew them all – Bugs Moran, Machine Gun McGurn; all them fellers. All the big fellers."

"Really!" said Maury again.

He didn't believe a word of it. It was not that he doubted Ritchie's ability to impress himself on the gang-bosses of

North America, even to work for their violent organisations – that was Ritchie's element – what Maury doubted was that his brother would ever be stupid enough to breathe a word of his professional dealings to a lip like Leo. So – either Ritchie had never been involved with bootleggers and had invented the story to delight his father, or Leo had devised the whole legend from innocent remarks in the boy's letters.

"Got too 'ot for 'im in Ill'noise. Saw trouble comin', did Ritchie."

"He's not in Chicago now, then?"

"Nah! Been outta Chicago since, since . . . twenty-nine, I think."

"But he's coming home for good?"

"Yer."

"How do you know?"

"Told me, in a letter."

"May I see the letter, Pa?"

He had pushed too far. Suddenly Leo was suspicious, on his guard. "Wha' for?"

"I'm interested."

"Not you, Maury. You allers 'ated Ritchie. Never understood 'im. You an' *her* both, never liked 'im. Never gave 'im a chance."

"Listen." Maury's tone hardened. "Don't preach bloody Ritchie's virtues to me, Pa. I'm not asking where he is and when he's coming home so I can throw the little swine a welcome party."

"See, there yer go . . ."

"Look!" Maury stuck out his arms, jutting his wrists clear of the cuffs.

The flesh was still pinkish and cratered, raised up in badly-healed weals on which no hair grew.

"See those marks?" said Maury. "Remember how I got them? I still think Ritchie landed us in it, left me with these."

"Never proved. Never no proof at all."

"The fire that destroyed Holly's shop, killed Grandpa Tal and Christopher, was supposed to be revenge on Ritchie."

"In a pig's arse," Leo snapped. "It was an accident."

"I don't think so." Maury reined his anger. He slid his

cuffs over the burn scars and reached for the teapot to freshen his tea. "In any case, if Ritchie is coming home, Pa, I want to know about it."

"I told you. He's comin' home."

"When?"

"Dunno!"

"To do what?"

"Dunno!"

"From where?"

"Dunno!"

"Pa, do you want me to go upstairs and talk to your ladyfriend? I'm sure a nice Godfearing woman with a Sally Ann background, even if she is sewing a wild oat or two right now, would like to know what she's latching on to – what kind of a stepson she's liable to wind up with. I suppose you didn't sing dear Ritchie's praises to – what's her name – to Cissie?"

"Leave 'er out of it."

"No, Pa," Maury put down the cup, got to his feet, looked up at the ceiling then moved towards the door.

Leo grabbed his sleeve, snared his elbow and dragged him back to the table. "Don't want Cissie told. Less she knows about . . . about *any* of yer, the better. Strewth! None of yer – 'cept Ritchie – are much t' be proud of. Never comin' round 'ere. Never sparin' a thought for your poor old . . ."

"When's Ritchie coming home?"

"August, September."

"To do what?"

"Advertisin' business."

"Where is he now?"

Leo paused.

In a silky tone, Maury said, "Come on, Pa. What harm can it do, telling me?"

"Ritchie told me t' say nothin', not to nobody."

"That's 'cause he's still scared of Vince Shotten."

"Vince Shotten! Our Ritchie's scared o' nobody."

"Answer my last question, Pa, and I'll toddle off and let you get back to b . . . upstairs."

Leo hadn't changed. He might be smoother, more mellow,

more outwardly respectable but he still had an eye for the main chance. "'Ow much, Maury?"

"Good God!" said Maury, shaking his head. "I've been supporting you for ten years. Where do you think your monthly handout comes from, the bleedin' fairies?"

"Conscience money," said Leo. "I know what it is!"

"Want to see how quick I can square my conscience," said Maury, "by cutting off your allowance?"

"Ritchie'll see me right. Don't need you now."

"Are you certain enough to try it?"

Leo had the audacity to consider his reply.

"Yer. You're right, son. I'd best hold on a bit."

"So tell me then, where's my brother now?"

"In France," Leo Beckman said.

* * *

The decline of the House of Dubriel had begun one morning in September, 1914, at the Great Rout of the Marne. There, in the course of a single day, three of the five sons of the Comte and Comtesse met their deaths. Another son died in the forest of Vosges only weeks later. The Dubriels' sole heir survived as a prisoner in the German concentration camp at Cottbus. Weakened by stomach wounds, however, he succumbed to dystrophy in the spring of 1918. With him to the grave went the hopes and aspirations of a banking family that had endured and triumphed over a multitude of national disasters since the Reign of Terror. The handful of cousins and nephews who trailed home from the trenches had no more heart for the future than had the Comte and Comtesse who yielded without a struggle to the turmoils of post-war Europe. Company holdings were sold off, directorships lapsed, estates in Limoges were mortgaged. The bank itself almost went under and only the discreet removal of the 'old' Comte – he was forty-nine that year – saved it from final collapse. Throughout the ebbing of their fortunes the Comte and Comtesse sat in their house and did nothing.

The drawing room of the house of the Dubriels, in reality a labyrinthine apartment in a red brick block off the Boulevard de Sebastopol in the 4th arrondisement, contained all the treasures that had been withdrawn from the frontiers of their empire. The conglomeration of furniture and ornamental art was overwhelming. Only a room of such massive proportions could absorb the trophies and still preserve an atmosphere of monastic austerity, a dusty, webby, tomb-like air that denied the splendour of wreaths and eagles and Bourbon acanthus scrolls. Pelmets swooped over the windows. Secretaires, swan-breasted chairs, sabre-legged stools, bookcases, divans *Egyptienne* and several beautiful little teapoys – offhand Holly could not recall the exact term for French pillared tables – seemed welded to the Saint-Ange carpets, faded with use and listless neglect.

In the midst of it all perched the three stuffed birds; Holly could not put Peter's remark out of her mind, try as she would. She did not find it comical now, however, for the analogy was disturbingly accurate. If Monsieur Lenormant was a stork, the Comte and Comtesse were, respectively, a dewlapped pelican and a horned owl – he pale and boney and big-billed; she, in a drab gown of cinnamon satin, with a round head, large eyes and a liverish brown complexion. They spoke rusty English, politely disregarding Holly's fluent French.

In that quick dabbing way of his, Monsieur Lenormant had managed to convey to Holly a warning that the Dubriels would be less than friendly. After all, Holly was a woman, young and beautiful – an amalgam of elements that the Dubriels had pruned from their lives in the name of mourning. Holly had questioned the wisdom of a meeting but Monsieur Lenormant had assured her that, when it came to it, the Comte and Comtesse would not allow prejudice to stand in the road of profit. The Comte and Comtesse Dubriels were not the first 'coy' sellers that Holly had encountered in her career and they would not be the last. She was prepared to be patronised. In this case she felt that the august history of the family gave the couple some entitlement to pride – and to prejudice – and consequently she left the twentieth-century at the apartment door and with it any inclination to be impatient. It was just as well that Monsieur Lenormant had briefed her on what to expect. The Dubriels were quite the most irksome clients that Holly had ever had to deal with. She was used to being treated like some kind of bailiff, one step up from a thief, but the suspicion with which the Dubriels greeted her was close to slanderous. If it had not been for her promise to Monsieur Lenormant, Holly would have turned on her heel and walked out of the apartment regardless of what masterpieces the blasted family had in its vaults. The conversation was stilted, limping along in a mixture of formal English phrases and rapid French. At first it was conducted exclusively through Monsieur Lenormant, even in Holly's native language, as if the Dubriels resented having to address her directly. No refreshments were offered. Smoking, clearly, was not permitted – a great strain on Lenormant who toyed nervously with his little amber holder all the while.

It took an hour to reach the beginning of 'discussion' concerning the fact that the Dubriels had paintings to sell. In that time few pleasantries were exchanged. The talk was of the doleful state of the art market which was suffering the most serious slump in prices since 1888. An expansion into political topics might have seemed natural but to the Dubriels the world outside was a world apart. They obviously cared nothing for the hungry, jobless masses of Europe and America. They were, however, well-informed about sale prices and the movement of *objets d'art*, though they feigned ignorance of the 'slump' and stiffly protested to Monsieur Lenormant that it was not so, that he was exaggerating – lying – in an attempt to beat them down on his offer, to cheat them. Holly, it was implied, was his accomplice.

At first Holly did little to support her colleague who, it seemed, knew the Dubriels well enough not to take offence but to parley with them and parry every nasty thrust with a soft answer. Gradually it dawned on Holly that the Comte and Comtesse were probably desperately in need of the money but that it hurt them to have to sell their heirlooms, to strip away pieces of the family's illustrious past. The syndrome was common among English aristocrats and recognition of it gave Holly increased patience, even a modicum of sympathy for the French couple.

"A fine large Gauguin," Monsieur Lenormant was saying, "sold only last week. The price – less than fifteen thousand francs."

"It is more," said the Comtesse, "than that immoral man deserves. We have no Paul Gauguins here."

"El Greco," said Monsieur Lenormant; "*Our Lord at Emmaus*, a brilliant painting. How much did it fetch at Sotheby's, Madame King?"

"Only two hundred pounds, sterling; twenty-five thousand francs."

The Comte swallowed his accusations, silently gobbling them down into his throat while his jowls rippled as if he was choking on a dead fish. But the Comtesse gave a solemn nod, indicating, Holly thought, that she had studied the sale price catalogue of that particular shambles.

"We do not believe El Greco to be worth more," she declared.

Kennedy, thought Holly, would have been perfect with them. They would have respected his age, his drowsy patience, and would have found him in complete agreement with every opinion they offered. Holly could not bring herself to deny her taste, to condemn El Greco, Gauguin and, in turn, Bruegel, Cézanne, Fragonard and even Botticelli. She began to wonder just what artists were considered 'fit' to be given house-room by the Dubriels.

She tested the water.

She said, in English, "Not all artists are out of favour in our auction rooms."

Peering across the vast acres of the drawing-room in the dim light, the Dubriels stared at her. The Comte shook himself a little, lifting his wattled neck from his shoulders, while his wife clocked her head this way and that as if to seek the source of the voice.

Holly went on, "Sir Henry Raeburn . . . you have heard of him?"

The Comtesse leapt a little in the Empire chair as if her tail feathers had been singed. Holly, of course, was being mischievous as well as probing. She would have wagered Ray Hillis's cheque that none of the Scottish Academician's portraits had strayed into the Dubriel's collection. But she had told the truth; Raeburn was fetching high prices.

"We – have – heard – of – him." The Comte took thirty seconds to deliver his five word answer.

Holly smiled; she did not wish to antagonise them further – for Monsieur Lenormant's sake – but she sought to establish her expertise, to gain authority before she was taken into the gallery to see whatever it was the Dubriels wished to sell, if ever they got around to it.

"Even in a depressed market," Holly said, "it would be unreasonable to expect less than ten thousand *pounds* – over twelve million francs – for a good Raeburn portrait."

"*Oui*," said Monsieur Lenormant. "We have been negatif in our talk too long a time. Madame King is correct. We must be positif. No?"

"We have no Raeburn," said the Comtesse.

"Turners, too," said Holly, "are valuable."

"And works by Sir Edward Burne-Jones," put in Lenormant who had quickly picked up Holly's intention and her method of moving things along. "And Joshua Reynolds, am I not correct, Madame?"

"Quite correct," said Holly.

Husband and wife fluttered, exchanging singular signals, not with their eyes but with their hands.

"All – *English*?" said the Comte.

"In England, the English are wanted," said Holly. "Unfortunately, as I understand it, it is necessary for you to present your paintings in England."

This time the Dubriels did not consult each other by digital semaphore; they said nothing, remained motionless.

Holly said, "Dutch artists are also popular."

The response was slight but gratifying. The Comtesse blinked, a slow lowering and raising of the lids. The Comte finally swallowed his dead fish and his jowls relaxed into comfortable folds.

They had Dutch paintings.

Holly thought out her next sentences with great care. There was the possibility that she might have the pick of whatever works the Dubriels had. She could sense their interest now, like a tug on a baited line. Perhaps the reason they had not been specific to Monsieur Lenormant was that they had no attachment to particular paintings, that the act of selling *anything* was anathema to them. In that case, money, market value, would be the only criterion of choice. Cautiously, Holly advanced names, fashionable names, the names of artists currently in vogue and who, reasonably, might be represented in the Dubriels' collection. Though she had no notion of how many works the Comte and Comtesse might wish to dispose of, or of the quality, Holly experienced a quickening of interest that fired her imagination with visions of huge Rembrandts, Steens and uncatalogued Vermeers of impeccable provenance. One advantage to buying Dutch rather than French masters was that there would be less fuss in obtaining export licences, about which the authorities had become somewhat sticky of late.

"Van Dyck is held in esteem, of course," said Holly, "not only by English collectors but by American museums."

She made a few remarks about Sir Anthony and observed that the Dubriels did not pour scorn on lucky van Dyck.

Encouraged, she tried them with Pieter de Hooch.

Comtesse Dubriel praised de Hooch's Delft period, damned his Amsterdam period, and did not otherwise commit herself. Monsieur Lenormant took a hand and introduced the name of Albert Cuyp by praising the large glowing landscape that hung in the Louvre. The Comte said that he and his wife rarely visited the Louvre now but he offered a word or two of praise for Italianate Dutch painters in general. The Comtesse added that she had a particular fondness for *les interieurs*, meaning, Holly thought, the school of Vermeer. It was consistent with what she knew of their background that the Dubriels should favour the quiet Dutchmen. Given a shaft of sunlight and a little simplification, the décor and the drawing room would have made an ideal subject for any of the maestros – though she could not imagine the Comtesse with a jug on her shoulder or the Comte in leather thigh boots.

Warming, the Dubriels discharged more information than perhaps they had intended, displaying knowledge not only of periods and painters, but again of current market values – and, Holly noticed, of the prices they might expect for their own paintings. Eventually it would have to come to a 'showdown', or possibly a 'show up'. Holly did not now suppose that the Dubriels were merely boasting or making empty promises that they could not fulfil.

At the end of another hour, more interesting than the first, the Dubriels were ready to allow Holly and Lenormant entry into the holy-of-holies. Head spinning with names and prices, Holly was startled when the Comte rose and, without a word, walked the length of the drawing-room to a double door on the inner wall. He opened it, pushed the doors before him and disappeared.

Comtesse Dubriel rose too.

"Come," she said, and with an odd rolling arthritic gait, followed her husband into the apartment's inner chambers.

The dining room faced east across the angle of the Boulevard de Sebastopol and caught noonlight through tall windows of tinted glass. The room was over a hundred feet long. It contained nineteen paintings.

The majority were hung on line above oaken dressers but over the fireplace was a magnificent de Hooch – a courtyard scene with lacy snow upon red tiles, a melting ruff of icicles on a water barrel and a man and woman, domestics perhaps, stooped by a frozen pump. Holly dug into her memory. The last de Hooch to come to the London block, a less typical example of the artist's work, had been knocked down for £14,500; two seasons ago, to Lord Rossmore. She hesitated before the courtyard painting, awed by its quality, then turned to the main collection along the interior wall.

The Dubriels moved ahead of Holly and Lenormant – to whom the spectacle was also quite new – saying nothing, walking like royalty, making no sound on the Turkish runner. Neither husband nor wife passed comment when Holly paused before a particular work. They put no pressure upon her and left the English woman in a state of mounting suspense as to which of the masterpieces would be offered for sale. Holly knew that she could clear the room, that she and Monsieur Lenormant between them would have no difficulty in selling all or any of the nineteen canvases. There was no inferior work here, no forgotten apprentice pieces, no 'work-shop' landscapes. What was more, the paintings had been well cared for. Most had been lovingly cleaned. Ivory cards attached by cords to the base of the frames gave the date and details of cleaning work. Only one, an unusually large de Heem still-life of goblets, fruit and a dead game bird, remained opaque with age. There was a card on it too, a very yellow card, which said in French – *Jan Davidsz de Heem? Attribution suspect?* The still-life's doubtful origin explained perhaps why it had not been sent along to Robelates in its turn in the decade before the world war.

The earliest work that Holly could identify was a Massys' duel portrait, pale, clear and cool but a little over-florid in its detail. A plaque on the base of the frame gave the title *Tax Gatherer in his House*.

"*Ah, non!* That one is not for sale, Madame." The Comtesse's voice echoed slightly in the long, long room. "Not at any price." She hesitated then jerked her head away as if she had already revealed too much.

Gravely, the Comte explained, "A gift from our departed son Edouard."

Holly and Auguste Lenormant completed their preliminary inspection. No notes were taken; in the House of Dubriel that would have been totally *infra dig*. But to each canvas Holly mentally ascribed a price, except on works of less familiar artists where, she hoped, Monsieur Lenormant's expertise would bolster her own. In more usual circumstances she would have had plenty of opportunity to check and recheck, to delve into the volumes of *Art Auction Records* and *Sale Prices Current*, but the circumstances were far from usual. The formality with which the Dubriels presented their collection indicated that they would have been deeply insulted by the very suggestion that research was necessary, that their paintings were inferior or, worse, suspect. Records of purchase, dating back a century or so, would not be thrown open to the dealers. It was possible that some of the works had come into the Dubriels' hands in payment of debts incurred to the bank. Nobody would be more scrupulous than a banker when it came to establishing authenticity, few bankers more scrupulous than the Comte Dubriel, *père et fils.*

From the Collection Dubriel would be sufficient guarantee to any prospective buyer.

Side by side at the end of the dining room, the couple waited while Holly and Lenormant finished their tour. The Comte and Comtesse had become even stiffer in manner. They were both tense, radiating not so much superiority as anxious pique now that the moment for stating terms had finally been reached. Holly still had no idea what the couple intended to sell. It must be obvious to them, however, that the expert from England was no less impressed than the expert from Paris. The advantage was all on the side of the seller.

The Comte had his speech rehearsed. He said, "We will agree on a price. Madame King will be the purchasing agent. It is to the English firm that the Comtesse and I will make our sale, not to the Galerie Voltaire. It must not be known that we are . . . releasing. We do not wish it known in France. We will pay to Galerie Voltaire a fief, a . . ."

"Fee," said the Comtesse.

". . . fee of five percentage of purchase price. The arrangement between Madame King and Galerie Voltaire is not of our concern."

"On these conditions, your word, please," said the Comtesse.

Holly left it to Monsieur Lenormant to ask the obvious question. "How many works do you have for release?"

"The terms first, if you please," said the Comte.

Holly said, "In principle the terms are agreeable, Comte. I will sell the painting or paintings in England, privately or through auction. You have an objection to auction?"

"It would be preferable for private sale."

"I see," said Holly. "In that case, sir, I would like to identify the Dubriel collection as the source of the painting to my client – assuming that the client is not French."

"It is necessary, Madame?" asked the Comtesse.

"It is preferable," said Holly firmly.

Comte and Comtesse debated in hushed voices, speaking

rapidly, heads literally touching as they breathed words into each other's faces.

Holly thought of de Rais who at least had style to mask his conspiratorial attitudes: this pair wore their cunning with regal sleaziness. Her sympathy had evaporated. She disliked them intensely and, while they conversed, turned her back on them and looked down the length of the room picking up on a few scattered phrases of what appeared to be an argument. The Comte talked of *circonspection*; caution. The Dubriels were fiercely protective of their reputation. And yet they needed the francs that the sale would bring. For what purpose, Holly wondered; to support this fantastic mausoleum? Rising costs must have whittled away their income.

"It is agreed, Madame," said the Comtesse, at last, scowling down her doubtful husband. "In words, you may tell the personage, the buyer, that the work is from the Dubriels."

"Thank you, Comtesse," said Holly.

"*Maintenant*," said the Comtesse, taking the reins from her husband. "We will hear the offerings."

"On what painting?" said Holly.

"On each," said the Comtesse.

"You are selling all?" blurted out Monsieur Lenormant.

The Comtesse smiled thinly. "What we need to sell, only."

Holly understood; the Dubriels had a specific requirement, a precise sum. They would evaluate her offers and sell her either a single large canvas or three or four lesser works to make up what they needed. She had done business this way before, though not often. Monsieur Lenormant, however, was bewildered. It was left to Holly to explain to him what was what. She did this openly and without embarrassment while the Dubriels listened. Glumly, Monsieur Lenormant nodded. For a wild, improbable instant he had thought he was in line for ten percent of the entire collection.

At a snail's pace, the four returned down the length of the dining room. Holly and Lenormant took a great deal of time; being professionals they were not to be rushed.

The paintings were handsomely framed in a style that was almost uniform, varying only in weight of gilt. Not all were glazed so that the dealers were able to examine surfaces closely, brushwork and varnishing in particular. The information on the little cards, though terse, was useful. At the end of the inspection, Monsieur Lenormant requested a minute or two of private conversation with his English colleague, and the Comte and Comtesse wandered off up the room. Lenormant produced a notebook from his vest pocket. Holly and he conferred, agreed prices which Monsieur Lenormant duly jotted down in his book. It might have been a junk auction, so casual did it seem now, yet the mounting column of figures, in francs and sterling, was staggering. One, almost any one, of the Dubriels' masterpieces would have kept a miner's family, or a docker's, in clover for several years. But Holly did not think of such things now; she had been too long in the trade to make such invidious comparisons.

Monsieur Lenormant indicated to the Dubriels that the final phase of the transaction was imminent. Rather briskly the four began the long walk for the last time. The Comte took no notes, made no comments, merely nodded as Monsieur Lenormant placed a monetary value on each of the paintings in turn.

"Jan Steen – one hundred and thirty-five thousand francs."

"Fifteen hundred pounds, English," Holly added.

"Van Goyen – a landscape in summer – thirteen thousand francs."

"One hundred and fifty pounds."

The Comtesse gave a little grunt, perhaps of disappointment.

The Comte nodded.

"De Hooch – a courtyard in winter – the Antwerp period."

"The Delft period," the Comtesse corrected him.

The Parisian dealer bowed, said, "One million francs."

Holly said, "Twelve thousand pounds."

The Comte nodded.

"Albert Cuyp – a gentleman on horseback – one hundred thousand francs."

"Twelve hundred pounds.

Nod.

The valuation continued.

Finally the last painting was reached.

"Meindert Hobbema – a wooded landscape – nine hundred thousand francs."

"Ten thousand pounds," said Holly.

She hoped the Dubriels would part with that particular work which she knew she could dispose of at a tidy profit almost immediately. Hobbema was still much prized by English collectors and a certain Mr. Russell of Kensington would snap it up. Hobbema was his passion, one which he could well afford to indulge. The Dubriels were human enough to express restrained surprise at the high value placed on a painter who, it seemed, they considered slightly inferior. It was their turn to confer in private.

Holly and Lenormant retired out of earshot.

Holly said, "Have you bought from them before – Dutch works, I mean?"

"No. Furniture only. Very valuable."

"But I was under the impression that you dealt with them frequently."

"That is true, but only with *objets d'art*. In the most, furniture, but a Ming wine jar, gold spoons. In pieces."

"Piecemeal?" Holly murmured.

"Yes, a little at a time over ten years."

"But you've never seen the collection before, the paintings?"

"No, I have not. Why do you ask, Madame?"

"I thought there would be more."

"Is what you see not good enough?"

"Marvellous!" Holly agreed. "But yet, I thought there would be more. There are sales records; the Comte's father was a keen collector – of Italian art."

Monsieur Lenormant shrugged. "They keep."

"Obviously," said Holly. "But if this is an example of their Dutch stuff, their Italian works must be priceless."

"What do you hope it is they will sell to you?"

"The de Hooch and the Hobbema," said Holly without hesitation.

"I think they know that too," said Monsieur Lenormant.

Side by side the Dubriels waited, she with hands neatly bridged, like little brown claws, at the level of her waist; he with the tips of his fingers cradled in the vee of his vest, a touch of the Napoleon Bonaparte.

"We will sell to you, Madame King, the landscape of Hobbema, at nine hundred thousand francs."

"The de Hooch . . .?" Holly could not hold back.

"The Hobbema," said the Comte. "Only the Hobbema – at this time."

"Nine hundred thousand francs," said the Comtesse, as if she expected Holly to retract.

"I am grateful," said Holly, "to have had the opportunity of viewing your collection and of purchasing such a beautiful painting."

The Comte did not acknowledge the polite compliment nor did he offer his hand to seal the bargain, not even to Monsieur Lenormant.

"The offer will be consigned in script, Madame?" he asked.

"Yes, by letter of agreement of terms."

"I will, with permission, arrange collection and shipment to London," said Monsieur Lenormant.

"When?" asked the Comte.

"As soon as possible."

"When will you, Madame, meet your obligation?"

"Within a week," said Holly.

She thanked God that the deal on the Holbein miniature had not been delayed. The spiral of demand on the purchasing account was becoming formidable. But Holly had no real worry on that score. She was quite sure that the Hobbema would hardly touch down in the Chalfont Arcade before it would be sold. All it would require would be care in making the arrangements, and a day or two's delay in paying the Dubriels; nothing drastic.

The Comte nodded.

The Comtesse nodded.

And, much to Holly's surprise, the couple walked out of the dining room without a word of farewell. Now they had what they needed there was no more to be said.

An elderly man-servant showed Monsieur Lenormant and

Madame King from the house.

"Well," said Holly, as she stood with Monsieur Lenormant on the corner of the Boulevard de Sebastopol, "I'm glad my English clients aren't that abrupt."

Hastily lighting a cigarette, inhaling with a sigh of relief, Monsieur Lenormant said, "Ah, but you are pleased with the transaction."

"Without doubt," said Holly, in French, "I will be able to sell the Hobbema at a profit. And you, Monsieur Lenormant, are you satisfied?"

"It is good that we have established relations with the Comte and Comtesse," said Lenormant. "They are satisfied, and that is what is important."

"Do you think we will hear more from them?"

"But yes – I am sure of it."

"Monsieur Lenormant – alas – was quite right.

*　　*　　*

The grand tour of No. 44 Vallois Street took less than an hour. Even at that, Maury was more thorough than Stan would have wished. But he did not hurry the big fellow, letting him do his job according to established routine. Stan – wrongly – assumed that showing clients round houses was part of Maury's business.

Maury had prudently shuffled off the Sherbrook Winters for the afternoon, husband, wife and three small daughters, and the house was occupied only by the resident house-keeper, a thin young woman in a starched white overall that made her look like a dairymaid. She did not tag along on the tour of inspection but confined herself to the basement, to the huge brushed-steel kitchen which, Stan thought, was more like the engine-room of a Cunard liner than a place where supper was cooked.

Though faintly bored by the procedure, Stan made careful mental note that there were two bathrooms and four water closets, and a separate servants' apartment tucked away in the wing, that the garage had electrically-operated doors and an inside lobby entrance that led to stairs to the lounge. He was very particular about entrances and exits – not out of any intrinsic interest of his own but because he had been thus briefed by his boss who, not unnaturally, was much obsessed with security.

Even Stan, whose taste ran more to cosy 'holes' and big black kitchen ranges, open fireplaces and standard lamps, had to admit that the bedrooms and lounges were magnificent. He began to understand why Maury rated the joint so highly and why the Winter bloke was considered – by a knowledgeable handful – to be hot stuff as an architect. Even on a dull Saturday afternoon, with cloud like used blotting-paper pasted down over the park, the house seemed light and airy, like villas Stan had read about on the Italian Riviera or, now that he thought of it, like the places rich folk lived in in Hollywood. He could just imagine Norma Shearer in a slinky gown coming on down the spiral staircase that split the lounge from the cocktail mezzanine, or see dark-eyed fragile Sylvia Sidney kicking off her tiny shoes to flop on the marshmallow bed. Stan had an average sort of dream-life, really, but there was something about No. 44 Vallois Street that brought it out, projected it. He wondered if it would have the same effect on his boss, if Ritchie would strut about like Cagney in *Smart Money*.

Probably not.

Unaware of Stan Nuttall's fancies, Maury droned on about plumbing and ventilation, pointing out the ultra-modern devices that Winter had designed and that Maury Beckman's builders had skilfully executed. It was, Stan remarked, some domicile.

Having reached the summit of Winter's 'bridescake', Maury led Stan across an upper lounge, through electrically-controlled sliding glass doors on to a flying wing balcony; a marvellous piece of architectural ingenuity, Maury enthused, that defied the narrowness of the original site. Stan could not but agree. The balcony – an airy patio – soared over the garden's retaining stucco wall and hung poised over Regent's Canal. It was protected, though, from traffic on the Prince Albert Road by chestnuts and willows in dripping bud.

Maury closed the huge glass doors and joined Stan at the rail.

"Where exactly are we?" said Stan.

"Officially – Primrose Hill," said Maury. "But you can throw buns to the bears in Regents Park Zoo; and that's Camden High Street just over there. On a clear day, through the gap in the trees, you can see the Crystal Palace."

"Nice," said Stan.

"Think Ritchie'll like it?" Maury asked.

"Ritchie?"

"Come off it, Stan! I wasn't born yesterday. Anyhow, you didn't make much effort to keep it secret, did you?"

Stan smiled, shrugged. "Maybe not."

"Why's he coming back?" said Maury. "What's he up to in London?"

"He's gone legitimate," said Stan. "Apex Advertising is his pride'n'joy. He owns it."

"Not according to the Register of Companies."

"Been busy, ain't you, Maury?"

"You fed me enough to make it easy."

"Well, Ritchie's gotta be careful because of that record of his – you know; the year he did in clink when he was a kid."

"He was no kid," said Maury. "And I always thought he got off light."

"Wouldn't know, would I?" said Stan innocently.

"How the hell did he persuade you to work for him?"

"Wasn't hard. I needed the loot," said Stan. "Listen, you're not gonna tell Ritch I told you, like?"

"If Ritchie'd wanted it kept as a *real* dark secret, he wouldn't have sent *you* to ferret around. But all right; if ever my dear brother and I do meet, I'll keep mum about it."

"Listen," said Stan, "you're not gonna refuse to sell 'im this 'ouse, are yer?"

"It's not up to me," said Maury. "I'm not the owner. What I'm *not* going to do is get involved. In no way, shape or form do I want to be tied in with Ritchie. But if he tenders an offer to Sherbrook Winter I won't put a spoke in his wheel."

"I'll be makin' the offer."

"Do it through a reputable lawyer."

"Right," said Stan. "I'll keep you out of it."

"If Winter asks my opinion," said Maury, "I'll just say I don't know the buyer."

"Fine," said Stan. "Will money talk?"

"Uh?"

"If the offer's big enough will Winter bite?"

Maury said, "Oh, yes! Winter's as greedy as the next guy. What kind of money's Ritchie using these days – blood money or just dirty money?"

Stan grinned. "Smart money, Maury. Smart money."

Maury was not enough of a film fan to pick up the allusion. He said, "I'm still surprised, Stan. I really thought you'd more sense than to get tangled up with my brother again."

"Better'n starvin', old son," said Stan. "I was at rock bottom when he got in touch with me. He sent me a letter askin' if I'd work for him in London."

"Doing the odd bank robbery?"

"Nothin' like that, Maury. It's shady but not criminal. I'm the front man. Know what that is?"

"Of course."

"Anyhow, I'd two kids to raise an' no regular job, no prospects – and no conscience. Between the bloody Depression an' Marigold, I was trapped. Didn't want my girls growin' up in a stinkin' back room in Lambeth like I'd done."

"Did Ritchie come to London to see you?"

"Yer. He's been over ten, a dozen times since 'twenty-seven."

"Over from where – France?"

"Stan frowned. "You 'ave been sharp, Maury."

"How long's he been based in Europe?"

"Dunno – an' if I did I wouldn't let on," said Stan. "I may not be twenty-two carat, Maury, but Ritchie pays me enough to be entitled to a certain amount of loyalty."

"Why are you talking to me about him at all, then?"

"You're family."

"Far as I'm concerned," Maury said, "blood ain't thicker than water. Not after what Ritchie put us through."

Stan said, "Well, I dunno about that. I just don't think he was responsible for what happened. Not entirely. Vince

Shotten's chimpanzees got outta hand, way I heard it. Vince didn't like it; took his own revenge."

"Is that who Ritchie's after? Vince Shotten?" said Maury.

Stan laughed. "Hell, no! Vince Shotten's lost his bottle. Anyhow, Ritchie ain't comin' home to start up old wars. Vince won't interfere with him, an' he won't interfere with Vince."

"So it's bigger fish Ritchie's frying?"

"Legitimate business," said Stan.

"Through and through."

"Well, maybe not all the way through, like, but close enough."

"What's he into, Stan?"

Stan made his eyes round, so round that the glass one looked obscene in its socket. Maury glanced away.

"Advertisin', that's all," Stan said. "Honest injun!"

"All right," said Maury. "Have you seen enough here?"

"I don't need to see no more. It's ideal," said Stan.

Maury touched the steel plate that flushed the patio doors open. The men walked across a barley-coloured carpet that covered the forty-foot long lounge from wall to wall. They descended the open staircase, Stan leading.

Maury said, "Is there a family?"

"You mean, does Ritchie 'ave kids? Nope, no kids."

"Is he still with the Erbach girl?"

"You're kiddin', " said Stan. "He dotes on 'er."

"I'm surprised." They went on down an interior staircase to the ground floor. "I thought he'd have shucked her off years ago."

"Seems not," said Stan. "I've never met 'er, you know."

"I wonder if her folks know she's coming home?"

They reached the entrance foyer where the housekeeper waited. Maury thanked her. She let them out into the front courtyard where Maury's Humber was parked.

"What do they do?" said Stan.

"Hm?"

"Ritchie's wife's folks; what line of work they in?"

"Furniture repair," said Maury. "Do you want a lift back to town?"

Stan put his hands in his overcoat pockets and glanced up at the sky. "Since it's dried up, I think I'll walk, thanks."

Maury opened the car door. "Suit yourself."

Looking up at the steep elegant white curves of No. 44, Maury hesitated. He had been – and still was – proud of his involvement in the building of this house. It gave him a weird pang of remorse to hand it over by proxy to his brother. He felt as if he was betraying the place, selling it up the river. There were those, of course, who would claim that it was the perfect residence for a vulgar advertising executive with a gaudy past; Maury would not agree. He could not be sure why he had done it; not out of fraternal sentiment; not out of ignorance. There wouldn't even be a few quid in it for him.

Why?

As if guessing what was going through Maury's mind, Stan said, "At least you'll know where he is, Maury. Right here." That was it, a subtle answer.

Ritchie was so incredibly unpredictable that, deep inside, Maury had always been just a little bit afraid of him. That gnawing fear had not diminished with the passing years; if anything, it had increased.

Dear God, Maury thought; I'm trying to appease Ritchie, to make up to a man I hardly know any more.

It's propitiation.

Pure and simple propitiation.

The imminent return of the native had him spooked.

"Ritchie'll be grateful, I'm sure," said Stan. "Maybe he'll even ask you round to din-din."

"Listen," said Maury, "I must rush. Three o'clock appointment."

"Never let up, do yer, Maury?" said Stan. "See you. And thanks."

Maury reversed the Humber and aimed the prow at the open black iron gates, then, engine revving, rolled down the window and called out; "Remember, Stan. I don't want to be involved any more."

"I'll remember."

Stan grinned and waved his dead left hand as Maury

powered the car out into Vallois Street and swung left towards Rolleston Crescent.

Stan walked out of the gates, found the lever that closed them behind him.

It was too late; Maury *was* involved, like it or not.

Poor old Maury could not escape, no matter how fast he roared away from Vallois Street.

Pausing, Stan looked back over great dense combers of laburnum to the soaring white wings of the house that Beckman had built and within which Beckman would be destroyed.

"Some joint!" he said aloud, then, shrugging, headed east to find his way out to the park.

OOOOOOO
OOOOO
OOO
O

Part Two

LONDON INTERIORS

1

Happy-Go-Lucky Holly!

September was warm; not a sprinkle of golden days left over from high summer but a snuff-coloured heat that stuffed the nostrils and made the head ache. The cavernous interior of Kings' Antique Gallery in the Chalfont Arcade was, for once, no cooler than the street. The air within hung stale and heavy, the rumble of traffic muffled and menacing, like growling thunder. Caldwell, an elderly shop servant, trolled listlessly about his chores, flicking dust from statuettes and china ornaments with a feather tickler, complaining all the while in a nasal monotone about the heat. Stone deaf Mrs. Mazollo diligently applied herself to polishing the parquet, her cheeks as red as Cardinal wax. In the basement Wilf had stopped whistling; Holly suspected that he had also stopped work on packing and crating a three-winged Morris screen that had been sold the previous afternoon to a dealer from Wales. She would be obliged to go downstairs and bark at Wilf for idleness; the thirty-year-old 'boy' would take heed of nobody but the Missus.

Holly set down the folio of drawings and, using both hands, fanned her hair from the nape of her neck. "London's insufferable in this sort of weather," she said.

Emma Chubb said, "Wish I'd gone to the Lakes this month instead of last."

"Well," said Holly, "at least Kennedy and Chris are having it fine. I hope the weather holds until the weekend. I could do with a breather by the sea and a bit of real sunshine."

"Hm, you do look a bit washed out, Holly," said Emma. "Small wonder, all that racketin' around you do."

"True. My hand feels empty unless its got the handle of a suitcase in it."

"Still, you've plenty to show for your travels, haven't you?" said Emma, adding in her throw-away style, "one way or another."

"What's that supposed to mean?"

"Experience, if nothin' else," Emma said. "Meetin' all those glamour boys."

Holly made no answer. Instead she quickly flipped open the pasteboard folder.

She lifted a drawing and cradled it gently in her fingers, studying the seated nude critically.

"Sturdy piece, ain't she?" said Emma. "Nearly as fat as yours truly. What do you think of it?"

"Not much," said Holly. "Boucher's drawings are notoriously inferior to his paintings."

"I'd hardly call 'em rubbish."

"They're insensitive," said Holly. "It's a recognised flaw. Boucher needs the texture of paint to bring out the line. No strength, you see."

Emma sighed. As an old friend, she was aware that a preachy tone was Holly's shield. Nobody, not even Emma, was allowed to come too close.

"Pardon me!" Emma said. "Takin' up your time with rubbishy Bouchers. I'll bring Daumiers in future."

"Emma, I'm sorry." Holly laid the drawing down, found her friend's hand and gave it a squeeze. "I didn't mean to sound ungracious. I appreciate the offer. Boucher *is* collected. I can sell them easily enough. Where did you pick them up?"

"Durham."

"Do you want me to make an offer, or would you prefer to give me a commission on the sale?"

"Got a client in mind?"

"No. I'll catalogue them."

"In that case, I'll sell 'em to you."

"Fine," said Holly. "I'll let you have a valuation in writing by the end of the week."

"No mad rush," said Emma. "And a verbal offer will do."

Holly tidied the six Boucher drawings, laid a tissue on the top, closed and tied the folder and put it carefully away in a drawer in a map cabinet.

"I know it's early," she said, turning, "but are you ready for a spot of lunch?"

"Don't know where I'll put it," said Emma, "but if you're standin' treat I'll force myself to toy daintily with a veal cutlet."

"The sale starts at one thirty, doesn't it?"

"Yer," said Emma. "I suppose we'd better be there on time. Not that I ever pick up much at Partington's these days."

"Everybody fancies themselves as an expert," said Holly. "You know, more folk are robbed in salerooms than . . ."

The front door clashed open, almost dislodging a Parian ware bust from its alabaster pedestal, prompting Caldwell to drop his tickler and rush forward, arms akimbo like a short-sighted outfielder. Startled, the women looked round as a lanky delivery boy in a moss green uniform charged into the gallery.

"Kink", the boy yelled. "Gotter Kink 'ere?" He did not wait for an answer but, bold as brass and clumsy as a bear, pranced down the carpeted aisle towards the alcove, bawling, "Lookin' for Kink. Olly. Olly Kink."

"Stop where you are," Holly shouted.

Surprised at having his mercurial briskness challenged, the boy froze in his tracks and glowered at Holly. "You Kink?"

"Yes, I'm Holly King."

"Rightio. Got blooms for yer. Sign 'ere." He thrust out a receipt book with one hand and a huge bouquet of long-stemmed yellow roses wrapped in clear cellophane with the other. "Roses'n'all," said the boy. "Somebody sure likes yer, missus."

Holly signed the receipt, gave the boy threepence and told him to go out a good deal more cautiously than he came in. She carried the flowers to the desk, unpicked the wrapper with her fingernail and sniffed the sweet perfume appreciatively, a fragrance like a breath of clean open country.

"Ain't there a card?" Emma fingered the dressing of ferns curiously. "Wonder who sent 'em."

"Kennedy, I expect," said Holly. "Who else would send me roses?"

"I would," said Peter Freeman.

He had entered the shop as the delivery boy had left and had been watching from a distance, unnoticed. Tanned and lean, he wore a blazer and pearl-grey flannels and carried a panama hat in his hand. In his buttonhole was a fresh yellow rosebud.

Holly was too confused to be flippant.

"Didn't you know I was in London, Holly?" Peter asked.

"Yes, I . . ."

"She read it in the papers, Mr. Freeman," said Emma, extending her hand in *grande dame* manner to demonstrate that she was not overwhelmed by Broadway stars. "It's a great pleasure t'meet you at last. Holly's told me so much about you."

"Peter, Emma Chubb, a colleague."

"An old chum," said Emma, "is what she means."

"So," said Peter, who did not quite know how to take Emma, "this is the hub of the Holly King empire." He looked round. "It's quite something."

"Interested in collectin', Mr. Freeman?"

"I'm afraid not."

"Perhaps Holly'll fire your enthusiasm," said Emma.

Still holding the roses, Holly had recovered from her surprise. She intervened before Emma's mischievousness slid into maliciousness.

She said, "Have rehearsals started?"

"Not just yet," said Peter. "I've been given a few days to settle down. I hoped you might be free for lunch, Holly."

"No," Holly said, sharply. "Emma and I . . ."

"She's talkin' rot, Mr. Freeman. We were just nippin' out for a spot of nosh when your bouquet arrived."

"Then the three of us . . ." said Peter.

"Wouldn't dream of it," said Emma. "Two's company."

"The sale" said Holly. "I have to be at a sale."

"I'll start for you," Emma offered.

It was typical of Emma Chubb to matchmake; she could not resist meddling. At one stage she had been Holly's confidante; at another Kennedy's 'go-between' in his court-ship of Holly. Though she had been the mistress of another antique dealer, Simon Black, for half her life, and utterly loyal to him, Emma still considered herself unbound by conventional morality.

"But, Emma, you don't know what I want," Holly protested.

"After fifteen years, I don't know what Kings' are interested in?" said Emma. "Give me your buyin' card and marked catalogue an' I'll do the rest while you pop off with Mr. Freeman an' celebrate your reunion."

"I . . ."

"Fetch your coat," Emma commanded, then, taking Peter by the arm, walked him away from Holly saying, "Have you met Ralphie Brooks yet? What a scrumptious chap he is. I've seen all his shows."

Short of blunt refusal, Holly had no alternative but to go along with Emma's plan. When she stepped into the cloak-room to find her hat and gloves her heart was hammering like mad and she knew there was no possibility of escape.

* * *

Even before *Step Out Along the Strand* opened and the publicity juggernaut rolled in pursuit of Peter Freeman, his face was familiar to several of the diners in the carvery of the Berkeley Hotel. The kind of Englishman who ate in the Berkeley, of course, would not deign to goggle or intrude upon an actor's privacy, or admit to being a 'fan' of the exuberant American dancer. Even so, Holly was conscious of covert scrutiny and felt, probably with justification, that some of the diners were discussing Peter and, by association, his companion.

She found it difficult to relax and be herself. She did not meet Peter's eye but looked down upon the traffic that clattered along Piccadilly, at sluggish rivers of pedestrians on the pavements under the shops' canvas awnings. She kept her hands in her lap, not daring to rest them on the table in case Peter touched her. It was not imagination; he too was tense. His eagerness, no longer easy and outgoing, had an awesome concentration of will behind it.

"I hope I didn't embarrass your friend by calling at the gallery?" said Peter.

"Emma's an incurable romantic and romantics are not easily embarrassed," said Holly. "They're too self-centred."

"That's pretty cynical, Holly!"

"Is it?" said Holly. "I don't believe a romantic person can be anything but single-minded – unless it's plain stupid; and Emma isn't that."

"She claimed she was an old chum; is that true?"

"I suppose it is," said Holly. "We go back fifteen or sixteen years."

"Was she a friend of your first husband's too?"

"No," Holly said. "She was – and is – a friend of my present husband."

"How is Kennedy?"

"He's on holiday in Devon."

"Ah!"

"What do you mean – ah?"

"I can't say I'm sorry Kennedy isn't going to walk in that door," said Peter.

"There's no danger," said Holly. "Even if he was in London, even if he knew that I was here with you Kennedy wouldn't intrude. He's far too much of a gentleman."

"If he knew how I'd missed you, Holly, he might be less of a gentleman," Peter said.

"A four-day acquaintance," said Holly, "almost six months ago, is hardly the basis for an undying . . ."

"Really? Why isn't it?" said Peter. "The first man you loved, whoever he was, didn't that begin with a meeting, an attraction, an hour or two of talk?"

Peter's perception was disturbing. How could he know how she had felt about Christopher, how her love for him had grown out of a strange mating of pity and need; or of

David Aspinall's calculated charm, his careless, ruthless, selfish, dangerous appeal? No one knew about David. She had been younger then, much younger, unschooled in life. Now it was very different. She assumed that Peter had made his point. But she was wrong; he wanted an answer.

"Didn't it?" he persisted.

"I think," Holly waved the menu at the waiter with an uncharacteristic lack of panache, "I'll begin with melon."

"You can't brush me off, Holly," Peter said quietly, as the waiter came to the table to take the order.

"At least," said Holly, "you might have the decency to let me try."

"You won't succeed." said Peter.

"Cold meats, green salad," Holly told the waiter and put the menu aside.

Peter attended to the selection of a light wine, then, taking his cue from Holly, turned to less personal topics. "Howard sends his best wishes."

"Isn't he in London too?"

"He comes and goes," said Peter. "He's a good guy to have around during preliminary rehearsals. He fights for my rights in a manner I wouldn't dare copy."

"He protects you from behaving like a conceited pig, is that it?"

"That's it," said Peter.

"Tell me about the show."

"We start rehearsals tomorrow. I've a principal cast meeting in the morning. We begin in earnest Wednesday, and – God willing – open in the Mayhew Theatre in Shaftesbury Avenue on November fourteenth."

"How long will you be in London?"

"For ever, I hope," said Peter.

"Be serious," said Holly.

"Ten months, maybe a year. If the Hollywood deal goes up in smoke it could be longer. Howard thinks *Step Out* has staying power. Hew Saracen, the English producer, agrees with him." Peter explained. "The Mayhew's Saracen's theatre."

"With you in it, Peter, I'm sure the show will run a

thousand performances," said Holly.

"Brooks is the banker's card, not me," Peter said. "Funny though, I do seem to have gathered a devoted following in England."

Throughout the meal they talked of the musical and of paintings. Peter admitted that he had spent some time in Europe's galleries that summer as well as leaning on the rails of its racetracks.

At one thirty Holly asked Peter if he would excuse her. She told him that she did not quite trust Emma to conduct Kings' business at the sale. In fact, it was to escape the strain of small talk that Holly stressed the importance of her afternoon engagement. Not that she found conversation with Peter difficult; the tricky part was avoiding intimacy. Having pushed him away, she was tempted to try to draw him back to her, to flirt with him. Until that moment her power over him had not been a factor in the relationship.

Peter paid the bill and escorted her down into Piccadilly.

"A cab?" he asked.

"No, I'll walk," said Holly. "It isn't far to Partington's from here."

"Can't I come with you? I've never been to an auction. I'd like to watch you at work."

"I'd rather you didn't, Peter, not today."

"Because your friend's there?"

"It won't be much of a sale," said Holly.

"Another time?"

"Perhaps."

"I'll call you tomorrow," Peter said. "Maybe even tonight."

"Don't."

"You can't just walk away again."

"Indeed I can."

"I'll call you. All right?"

She did not answer him, heading towards Sackville Street. Peter did not follow.

But from that moment on he never left her side.

*   *   *

Holly found Emma seated close to the auctioneer's dais in the large many-windowed room on the ground floor of Partington's. Emma had reserved a chair for Mrs. King though the room was packed with dealers and amateur collectors. There had been delay in starting and Holly pushed her way to the vacant chair by Emma's side just as the auctioneer announced the first lot, a handsome Dublin mahogany diner. It was gone before Holly could find the price in her catalogue. She was dismayed to see that she had estimated the worth of the diner at twenty pounds more than its fetched price.

"I thought . . ." Emma whispered.

"I missed it."

"Buck up. I'm in for this commode."

During the sale of the next five lots Miss Chubb demonstrated the qualities that had earned her a formidable reputation as a valuator of middle-range furniture. She rapped out her bids with a confidence that in no way reflected her personal financial status.

The gavel clacked.

"Ana lotsa eight ana ninea to Miss Chubb, sold as one. Account."

Emma preened herself as an omnium whatnot and a pretty little woolwork fire-screen were ticketed with her name.

"Lot ten; chairs, eight. William'n'Mary, ladez'n'gentlemen. Eight chairs, needlework seats. Handsome. Who'll start me at five hundred? Read yore catalogues, gentlemen. Quality here. Five hundred, do I hear? Four?"

Holly was lost in thought, staring at the wrong page of the catalogue in her lap.

"Three, I'm bid. Three hundred – right, guineas."

"*Holly*," Emma hissed.

"What?" said Holly.

"Three-five, on three-five guineas."

"Four."

"Four, I havea four."

Had she been a fool to snub him? What if he took her at her word and did not call on her again?

"*Holly*!"

"Oh, yes, five."

"Five bid. With Mizz King. Five hundred guineas."

Emma's charged whisper intruded into Holly's thoughts. "What's *wrong* with you, gal. Havin' a zizz or somethin'?"

"No, I . . ."

"Five hundred ana fifty, bid."

A smartly dressed out-of-town dealer with a flamboyant necktie and florid complexion smirked across at Holly, trying, perhaps, to bluff her out of the bidding.

"Against you, Mizz King," said the auctioneer.

"Holly, what's your marked price?" Emma hissed.

She had four nights to pass alone in her house in Chelsea. Kennedy was far away, Chris with him; Peter here in London. Four nights with nobody to answer to – except herself.

"Goin' once. Goin' twice . . ."

"Holly, give me your . . ."

"Sold to Mister . . .?"

"Ormsbee. Trade card and cheque."

"I thought . . . I thought we had the bid," said Holly.

"Are you sickenin' for somethin'?" said Emma. "Look at your price – seven hundred. You had a customer for them, didn't you?"

"Yes," Holly whispered. "One of Kennedy's clients."

"Now you are in the soup," said Emma. "Concentrate."

But Holly's concentration was totally gone.

Flustered, she missed the next lot too. Cheeks pale and tears in her eyes, she stared down at her catalogue, not daring to look towards the windowed wall and see there the ordinary man, the shabby dealer, that her imagination had transformed into Peter.

"Oh, yer, now I've got the picture," Emma whispered. "Did you ask him along?"

"Who?"

"Your American friend."

"Peter – where?" Then she saw that it *was* Peter.

He appeared to be quite at ease, leaning against the panelled wall, one hand in his trouser pocket, blissfully unaware – it seemed – of Holly's presence.

"My God, look at him!" said Emma. "No wonder you lost the place. What a handsome devil he is."

"La-deeez, please," said Coulter the auctioneer firmly.

"Here." Emma plucked the Kings' catalogue from Holly's fingers. "Don't go all to pieces, love. He's only a man, even if he does look like the answer to a maiden's prayer. I'll take over 'til you get sewn together again."

Although Emma could be sharp-tongued and malicious on occasions, she was not uncaring of her younger friend. She took over Kings' bidding as well as her own and gave way to Kings' higher prices where marked against competitive lots.

The pace of bidding quickened, spurred by Coulter's anxiety to be cleared up and off before dusk so that he might put in a half-hour in his garden with the watering can. He was not, at the best of times, a leisurely auctioneer and, though he'd noticed Mrs. King's rare lapse in concentration he made no adjustment for it and certainly did not recognise the suave stranger as being the cause. For Kings' Emma acquired an eighteenth-century lady's dressing-table, classified as a *bonheur de jour*; several such pieces had sprung on to the London market in the past months and the price was practically knock-down.

Embarrassed, vulnerable and ashamed, Holly dabbed her brow – and her eyes – with a handkerchief, trying to compose herself, to take stock of the fact that, for the first time in her life, she had muffed a bid at a public auction.

"Lota nineteen; parquetry cabinet; French; Louis Sixteen. Asa described," Coulter sang.

There was a flutter of bids from several quarters of the room but when the price rose beyond one hundred and fifty pounds only Emma and a balding, rather seedy little man stayed with the bidding.

"One seventy-five," said Coulter. "With Mizz Chubb."

"Hun'red an' eighty," snapped the balding man.

"Come, come!" said Coulter, peevishly. "Don't waste our time."

"Ninety, then," said the man.

"Against you, Mizz Chubb."

Emma smiled and gave a shrug so that the balding man relaxed, thinking she was abandoning pursuit of the cabinet.

Coulter clacked his hammer. "At one hundred ana ninety pounds . . ."

"Oh, two twenty-five, then," Emma called out, as if she was really a very silly girl for yielding to temptation.

The man's face fell.

"Two hun'red an' *fifty*," he announced savagely.

"Blow the little weasel," said Emma under her breath.

The cabinet was not worth more.

"Three hundred."

"God Almighty!" Emma exclaimed.

"Was that . . .?" said Holly.

"I'll say it was."

"Well – three hundred," said Coulter. "All finished at three. Sir? Right, gone to Mister . . ."

"Cash."

"Mr. Cash, it is," Coulter told his clerk. "Now, lota number twenty."

"What did he do that for?" asked Emma. "Is he furnishin' a house here in London?"

"I don't know," Holly replied.

"I think," said Emma, "He bought it for you."

"Emma, don't be ridic . . ."

"Was that a bid, Mizz King?" asked Coulter.

"Bid? On what?" said Holly, then, in total rout, thrust her catalogue back at Emma, said, "Finish for me," and left Partington's in an undignified hurry.

Peter caught up with her at the bottom of the stairs that led on to the street.

"Holly?" He reached for her arm.

"You shouldn't have come, Peter."

"The table; are you annoyed about the table? It's for you, if you want it."

"Three hundred pounds is more than it's worth."

"Not if it pleases you, Holly."

Again they were parting in the street.

"*Go away, Peter. Please, leave me alone.*"

"I can't" he said, simply. "I won't, no matter what you say."

"*Please, let me go.*"

"Is that what you really want, Holly? Never to see me again?"

"I'll reimburse you for the table."

"Is *that* all you can say? All you can think about – the table." Finally her attitude had riled him. He took her hand and gripped it hard, refusing to release her. "Forget the damned table. Look, I *will* leave you alone. I *will* let you go. But only if you tell me that's what you really want?"

She could not lie again.

This time he did not press her.

"I'm staying at the Savoy," he said. "Goodbye, Holly."

"Peter, the table?"

"Keep it. Sell it," he said. "I don't care about the god-damned table."

He stepped away from her and made his graceful way across the narrow street.

Holly went home alone by cab, ruined, like the day.

*   *   *

The Kings' house in Tite Street, Chelsea, rubbed shoulders with a dwelling once occupied by Oscar Wilde. For that reason, perhaps, a former owner had sealed the mansion's garden behind a high brick wall pierced only by a wrought-iron front gate and a rear door for tradesmen. The upper rooms afforded magnificent views of the Thames but the house was set at such a confidential angle that it did not receive much sunlight and the ground floor apartments were gloomy. 'Stygian darkness, it seems, is the price of privacy,' Kennedy declared, and frequently threatened to do away with the blasted wall if he could just think of something to put in its place. The gloom remained in spite of all that Holly could do to relieve it with pastel wallpaper, peach carpeting and more lights than Leicester Square.

The sitting room was Holly's domain. She preferred it to the formal drawing room. Furnishings were soft and comfortable in contrast to the dark warm woods of the little antiques and brilliant blues and yellows of the Crown Derby china that was displayed in a cabinet by the side of the fireplace. On arriving home that disastrous afternoon, Holly hid herself in the sitting room while the sun slid away and the evening sky filled with fluid blue dusk and russet clouds. Holly did not notice the spectacular sunset. She sat on the sofa, sipped dry gin and wished that Kennedy and Chris were not in Torquay. If her husband and son had been at home she might have invited Peter for dinner and put the whole ménage in proper perspective. Hopefully she might thus reduce her infatuation with the American to scale – Chris first, Kennedy second, Kings' third with Peter Freeman cantering back down the field.

She was considering pouring herself another gin, one more than she knew to be good for her, when Mrs. Andrews, the cook, popped in just to see that she was all right and to ask what she would like for dinner. The Kings' domestics did not live on the premises. Cook and parlour maids turned up each weekday morning and one or other would stay on until eight, at which hour, when Kennedy was at home, dinner was served. At weekends Holly descended into the kitchen and pretended she enjoyed messing about at the stove.

"Dinner?" Holly had no appetite.

"Aye, Mum. What would ye like?"

"Anything at all, Mrs. Andrews. May I have it in here, on a tray, please."

"A casserole, would that do ye?"

"Perfect," said Holly.

So, at eight o'clock, she ate dinner alone in the sitting room. She could not recall how she had passed the preceding hour. Peter was locked in her thoughts, like a portrait in one of those little Elizabethan love boxes. Why was she so attracted to him? Why had she chanced to meet him that particular year when she was restless and bored? Why not next year, last year – never?

She turned on the wireless, hoping that dance music would drown out the clamour of her thoughts, but like everything else, it reminded her of Peter.

It was a vast relief when the front doorbell clanged. Now alone in the house, Holly went to answer it, sure in her heart that it would be Peter and prepared to let him enter, eager for what would follow.

"Who is it?"

"Me!"

"Maury?"

"Of course; Maury."

She let her brother in.

Broad, strong, smiling Maury; she experienced a rush of affection for him as if he had deliberately saved her from a foolish mistake.

She took Maury's hat and overcoat and hung them on the what-not then, unusually, hugged him.

"What's up with you?" Maury enquired.

"I'm just glad to see you, that's all."

"Missing your old man, are you?"

"Yes, I am rather."

"Well," said Maury, going into the sitting room, "perhaps you'll be less glad to see me when you hear what sort of news I've got for you."

"What's wrong? Is it Chris? Has something happened in Devon, an accident?"

"No, no, nothing like that. Here, you *are* a bundle of nerves tonight, and no mistake."

"It's been a trying day; the heat, you know".

"Don't I?" said Maury. "I ventured out on to a building site, sat on a plank and drank tea. Enjoyed it, really, though I didn't cut much ice with the brickies when I told them their brew was almost as bad as their foundations. Offer me a nice whisky and soda, love. I've been saving myself all evening for a snifter of Glen Morangie."

"Have you eaten?"

"At the club. Where's the booze?"

"In the library. Help yourself." Holly followed Maury through the hallway into the library at the front of the house and watched him fashion himself a stiffish whisky at the drinks table. "What's your bad news, Maury?"

Maury added a whisper of soda to his whisky, switched out the lamp and, taking Holly's arm, escorted her through the hallway into the sitting room again.

"Is it father?"

"Oh, God, no! The old buzzard's as happy as a sandboy. Has himself a ladyfriend. I've dropped in several times in the hope of meeting the model woman – any female that can put up with old Leo must be a model woman – but he won't wear it. Hustles her upstairs out of sight before he opens the dashed door to me."

"Perhaps she's *déclassée*," said Holly; "or Leo thinks she is, which would be typical of him, wouldn't it?"

"Anyhow," Maury seated himself in an armchair and crossed his knees. "Anyhow, Leo isn't the problem. It's our long lost but, alas, not forgotten brother."

"Ritchie?" said Holly coldly.

"He's back in London."

"For a visit?"

"For keeps."

"Maury, are you sure?"

"Positive. He's bought a property. The Sherbrook Winter house in Vallois Street."

"You can't be serious?"

"I'm afraid I am," said Maury. "Ritchie's agents handled the transaction. Made Winter a fantastic cash offer."

"How do you know all this, Maury? Have you been in touch with Ritchie?"

Maury explained how he had been approached by Stan Nuttall and described for Holly's benefit his sideways manoeuvres to steer clear of involvement. He concluded, "I want no truck with brother Ritchie, or any of his kind."

"Why didn't you send Stan packing?"

"I should have, right enough," said Maury. "But I reckon if Ritchie *is* back in London it's best we know what he's up to."

"The grapevine?"

"Works wonders," said Maury.

"How on earth did Ritchie earn enough money to buy the Winters' place?"

"God knows!" said Maury. "You can bet it wasn't done legal and above board."

"Are you worried, Maury?"

"Candidly, yes."

"Why?"

"You know Ritchie. He'll use us, Holly. He may not have any particular scheme in mind that requires a reunion with you an' me but he'll be on standby, you can be sure. Look, Ritchie knows that neither of us is exactly broke. If he needs to further his ends and thinks that we can supply anything, from modest influence to capital, he'll use us any way he can."

"How can he use me?" said Holly, frowning. "Surely he can't hope to trick Kings' into resetting stolen goods for him. He tried it years ago and it didn't work; I'm a lot more cautious now than I was then."

"Depends on the goods, Holly," said Maury. "This much I have discovered – he's gone into advertising. The Apex Advertising Company; Ritchie's its principal shareholder. Apex seems to be *bona fide*, but my guess is that it's a façade, a front for some kind of illegal activity."

"Who are his clients?" asked Holly. "Do you know?"

"Amongst others – Tate Picard, John Groucher, and Braintree, Parker and Wolff."

"Ritchie is associated with *art* dealers?"

"See what I mean?" said Maury. "I don't suppose Ritchie has much to do with design and typography, but the Apex is certainly favoured by upper-bracket art firms. Mark you, Apex also handle money-mill accounts like Mariners' Toys and Bagshaw's Medicinals."

"If Apex have such large commercial clients why does it bother with specialist sidelines? Advertising isn't really a feature of the art trade?"

"Search me," said Maury.

There was a flash of fear in Holly's eyes; not apprehension – genuine fear. However much he might profess innocence and loyalty to the Beckman clan her brother was dangerous.

"I want nothing to do with him," Holly declared. "Nothing, Maury. I don't want to *see* him, *hear* from him, have *any* contact with him."

"Right," said Maury. "But will you . . . well, keep an eye open and an ear to the ground – just in case?"

"Is . . . is he married still? Is the girl with him; Ruth Erbach?"

139

"Yes, still married. But Ruth Erbach's hardly a girl now, Holly. Remember, love, it's twelve years since they eloped."

"She'll be twenty-nine."

"Is that all?" said Maury. "Never having met her I always think that she was a mature woman when she scooted with Ritchie. What was she? Seventeen?"

"About that."

"Do you ever hear from her mother and father?"

"Never," said Holly. "They still blame the Beckmans for what happened."

Maury finished his whisky.

Holly said, "Like another?"

He shook his head, turned back his cuff and consulted his wristwatch. "Sorry, love, I'll have to push off."

"Who's the lucky lady tonight?"

"Daughter of an American hotelier. I promised I'd pick her up at the air terminal and make sure that nobody ran off with her between there and Claridge's."

"Tuck her in and kiss her goodnight?"

"And sing her a lullaby," said Maury. "She's only thirteen years old. On her way to boarding school; poor kid."

"Doesn't she have an entourage?"

"I expect so," said Maury, "but I owe her father a favour. Besides, he's talking about building a splended hostelry in our fair city and I wouldn't mind having a finger in that pie if it ever comes to pass."

"Do you like Americans, Maury?"

"Salt of the earth – most of them," Maury said, "I've always found them tough but fair."

"Tough but fair," Holly repeated.

"Why do you ask?"

"No particular reason."

Maury put down his empty glass and got to his feet. Holly did not try to detain him though she longed for him to stay, to provide her with an opportunity to talk of her dilemma. It was possible that Maury might manage to cajole her into seeing her relationship with Peter for what it really was – an indulgence, a silly selfish indulgence.

She fetched Maury's hat and coat.

In the hallway, door already open, she said, "Thank you for telling me about Ritchie."

"I thought it best you should know." He kissed her on the brow. "Don't work yourself up about it. Don't brood. The situation doesn't warrant concern just yet."

"Oh, yes, it does, Maury."

Their eyes met, the calm Beckman eyes.

Unexpectedly Maury winked. "I'm no mug now, Holly. I can cope with Ritchie. If he tries anything nasty with either one of us, I'll trample all over him. Stamp him flat, like a cockroach."

"I believe you would, too."

"You bet I would."

He kissed her once more and went out into the darkness. A minute later Holly heard the roar of the Humber's engine as the motor drew away from the pavement behind the high brick wall.

She lingered on the doorstep, listening to the sounds of the river and the city, enjoying the salt breath of the distant sea that the flood tide brought with it up to the Reach and beyond.

Then, lonelier than ever, she went indoors again.

*　　*　　*

At eleven fifteen Holly gave in. She placed a call to the Savoy.

The suave reassuring voice of a receptionist asked with whom she wished to be connected.

"With Mr. Freeman," Holly said softly. "Mr. Peter Freeman."

*　　*　　*

Below the gilded cherubim and Arcadian pillars of the Mayhew Theatre lay a nether world of sweating steam pipes, fuse boxes, prop and costume mausoleums, timber stores, paint shops and two bleak rehearsal rooms where stars and choruses laboured to produce the magical spontaneity that entranced audiences season after season. There was precious little magic below decks, however, only the effluvia of Sloan's Liniment, Zubes, Germolene and Chlorodyne, and sad tangles of woollen binders, knee bandages and elastic ankle straps. "This," Ralph Brooks would remark, for the benefit of novices at his court, "is no rehearsal room; it's a damned field hospital."

There was more than a grain of truth in Ralph's observation. Tanned, elegant, graceful, lithe, limber and gloriously perfect specimens brought out of the spotlights, cleansed of greasepaint and powder, theatrical idols seemed even more mortal than ordinary folk. They were victims of contrast and the nervous strain of keeping up appearances. Ralph sustained himself on milk and Seidlitz powders, an addiction that led to Rosemary Case's famous jibe, "The purr in Brooksie's throat ain't sentiment; it's sediment." The lovely Rosemary was not free of erosion, though. Much of her conversation concerned 'nodes' on the vocal cords and 'hamstrings'. She would buttonhole poor chorines not nimble enough to get out of the way and regale them with hair-raising tales of 'nodes' and 'hamstrings', afflictions that became known as Case's disease and featured, in the 1937 smash *What's Sauce for the Goose*, as a firm of solicitors, Nodes & Hamstrings, a piece of show-biz whimsy that amused Rosemary not at all.

Director Giles Benedict and principal dancer Peter Freeman were not immune to the tensions of the first act run through that took place on Wednesday morning, though neither Benedict nor Freeman had allowed his talents to become blunted by weeks of neglect, by too many late nights, cigarettes, Gibsons and *plat du jour* dinners. Benedict, even slimmer than Peter, kept himself honed for his annual directorial stint by playing polo and tennis. He had sleek black hair and a pencil moustache and had been a lead dancer until a skiing accident had damaged his hip. Though only forty, Benedict had already directed a dozen lavish musicals for the Saracen management. Of the principals, Peter Freeman was the only one that Benedict had not worked with before. Being a cautious man, he did not push Peter too hard during the course of the morning though he had marked Peter as a compulsive worker, a professional to whom perfection was not an ideal but an objective. Benedict was too much of a realist to seek an absolute.

"Right, Jimmie," said Benedict to the piano player. "Sprightly – *da-ta-da-ta-deedle da-ta-te-tum*: there – while Peter crosses to centre. A two bar strict-tempo phrase before the pause when he and Ralph confront each other, then into the solo piece. Got it?"

"Got it." Jimmie laconically dipped the cigarette that loitered on his under lip.

The piano, a venerable upright in better tune than its scarred condition suggested, a dozen chairs and four buckled screens on squeaky wooden wheels gave all the dressing needed at this early stage. Ralph had commandeered three of the chairs to make a wobbly day-bed in a corner, a defensive position to which he retreated when not in motion.

Benedict clapped his hands. "We'll run through it from the beginning, I think. Don't worry if it doesn't flow. Early days, very early days. Ease into it but *do* try to sense the timing. It's a moment built for in the score. Rosemary, a half turn back, would give Peter a tiny inch more for the business; a startled thing, and the round eyes – *Ooo, I say!* that sort of expression. You find this handsome young American rather attractive."

"It's the truth!" Pertly Rosemary flashed her *Ooo, I say!* look at Peter.

"Ralph," said Benedict.

Tall, and canny in his movements, Ralph Brooks got up from his resting place and sauntered to the chalk mark on the floor.

"Am I still, or do I pick him up with my eyes?" he asked.

"I think you watch him on."

"Yes, I oughta, oughtn't I?"

"Ready?" said Benedict. "Jimmie: one, two."

The piano music, strong on every beat and without shading, rolled out and Rosemary Case performed her sprightly mime, the lady in the city street, the window shopper, while Ralph sang uncertainly, a charming song about the Man Who Waits – and Waits – and Waits – for a Pretty Little Thing Like

You. Peter on a chair behind what would eventually be the window of a barber shop, caught sight of the girl as she passed and jumped up, swirled away the cape and hurried out of the shop after her, pausing on the barber's whistle to catch his straw boater as it spun out of the door after him. Rosemary went into the wings; Peter followed. Rosemary emerged. Ralph concluded his song. The Man Who Waits met the Girl, who contritely made up to him.

Jimmie thumped the sprightly melody and Peter, dancing intricate steps, pursued the Girl from the wings and, undaunted by her beau, executed a courtship tap-dance that, in the final scene, would lead into a male duet and two distinct man-girl sequences of considerable complexity.

"Good, yes, promising! Well done!" said Benedict.

"Who choreographed Peter's sequence?" Rosemary Case asked.

Benedict glanced at her to see whether she was showing her pretty little fangs or not. He decided to be honest, and answered, "Peter did it himself."

"Is it wrong?" Peter asked.

"I love the retard, the walking step," said Rosemary.

"You want me to go through . . .?" Peter began.

"No, it's good," said Benedict.

"Pity I just have to stand there," said Ralph Brooks, with a counterfeit air of injury, "and watch."

"Catch your breath, darling," said Rosemary. "Let them ogle your marvellous profile."

"You could . . ." Peter began, anxiously.

"No, he couldn't," said Benedict. "Ralph must stay centre."

"Ignore old Brooksie, Peter," said Rosemary. "He's just looking for an excuse to sway languorously."

"Who called?" said Ralph, lifting his chin regally, "I am but a reed in the wind of mediocrity."

"So, Peter, beware," said Rosemary Case.

"Dear reed," said Benedict, "you have the stage alone for first scene change; you sing *and* dance at that point. Don't be greedy."

"I was never much good at doing two things at once," said Ralph.

"Or even one thing at once," said Rosemary.

"Oh, shut up! Peter," said Ralph, "let's burrow into my corner and discuss how we can thoroughly upstage our leading lady."

"And which of you intends to buy me dinner?" said Rosemary.

"The appetite of the lady," said Ralph, "knows no reserve. Perhaps we should both buy you dinner. Peter? Suitable?"

"Hey, I'm sorry. Not tonight."

"Tomorrow, perhaps?" said Ralph.

"I've no rehearsal call now until Monday," said Peter. "I thought I might see some of the countryside."

"Another time then." Ralph Brooks retired alone to his corner.

Peter drifted back across the room, idly tapping the toe-plates of his pumps, listening to the timbre of sound the flooring made. Benedict was talking in a quiet voice to Gwen Flowers, an ageing music hall actress who had found a new lease of life in minor roles in musicals. Gwen's face and figure were almost as scarred as Jimmie's rehearsal piano but she was equally in tune with the spirit of the production and, Peter guessed, would wring an excellent comedy performance out of supportive lines.

Rosemary touched Peter's arm.

"Don't be put out by Ralph. He's practically paranoid. Any least little thing he interprets as rejection. He'll snap out of it."

"Think he resents me – an American?" said Peter.

"It isn't that at all. I certainly don't resent you. On the contrary, Peter. In a couple of years, I've the feeling I'm going to look back on *Strand* and say with pride that I played the Mayhew with Peter Freeman, *the* Peter Freeman."

"Hey, that's nice!"

"Are you really going off to the country tomorrow?"

"As a matter of fact, I am."

"It's a girl, isn't it?"

"It . . . yeah."

"Anyone we know?"

"No, I don't think so."

If Rosemary was disappointed she hid it well. She shook her blonde curls, twinkled and sang in a tiny eggshell voice, "If'n you cain't be good, be caireful, my Poppa said tuh me-ah," a New York import that had proved too shocking for English theatre audiences three years ago but that Rosemary still occasionally performed at private parties where no holds were barred.

Peter found a smile. "I'll try," he promised.

*   *   *

September rain billowed softly out of the darkness and beaded the mullioned windows of the coaching inn. Below the bedroom sill a painted signboard creaked in the wind that wandered over the shorn fields from the hamlet of Minton and the village of Brattlesham and, Holly supposed, from Cambridge only ten or a dozen miles due east. With it the night breeze carried fallen leaves, pasting them flat against the speckled pane so that Holly saw them veined and vivid like fragments of rotted tapestry on a lighted screen. An oak leaf's startling hand plastered the glass before the weight of its thick dead stem tugged it away to join the scurrying flocks of autumn on the ground.

Window, oil lamp and bed were reflected in the dressing table's triptych mirror and appeared again, mysteriously detached, in an oval looking-glass affixed to the wardrobe door; a separate scene so reversed that Holly could not be sure that it did not represent true reality and that she, in the bed, had not become a mere observer of herself.

The Bell Cap Inn, far off the beaten track, was quiet that Thursday night. Holly had stayed in the inn several years ago and had been so taken with its atmosphere that she had unhesitatingly brought Peter here. Now, with dinner over and the local farmhands turned out of the public, Peter was still in the bar parlour chatting affably to the landlord with that casual guilt-free air that Holly found difficult to emulate. She wondered what the pair could find to talk about, what common ground. Perhaps Peter was telling his host about Iowa and Kansas where the wheatfields stretched for a thousand miles; a fitting subject for a country inn in damp autumn weather with a pint of best bitter on the counter. The subject of the conversation hardly mattered; Peter was showing remarkable patience, an apparent indifference to the woman upstairs that was all part of the subterfuge and supported the little white lie in the register that they were man and wife. Perhaps, too, there was an element of dominance in his delay; was he deliberately making her wait for him?

By the brass lamp's flame Holly glimpsed herself again in the mirror, shoulders bare, breasts heavy under the bodice of the lawn nightdress, yet with a calmness in her bearing and expression that hid her longing. She touched the palms of her hands to her breasts, lightly, and found that she was already aroused. Whatever doubts assailed her, desire for Peter made her bold, wanton and, perhaps, more beautiful than she had ever been. Dark hair loosed about her shoulders, her eyes were slumbrous, almost sullen, each passing minute increased her need.

The deception had been cleverly arranged. She had covered the trip to Cambridgeshire with a call on Ronald Hadley, a crippled war veteran who dealt in drawings and watercolours, operating from his cottage home in Brattlesham. That afternoon, alone, she had called on Ronald and purchased a Samuel Cooper miniature, a brittle little Hoskins and a small unframed Murillo that Ronald had 'let go' at a hundred and twenty pounds. Peter had remained in the village. She had picked him up again at half past four and they had driven along scenic lanes in the waning light to the Bell Cap Inn. Calculation increased her sexual anticipation; in conducting the affair so efficiently Holly had cancelled out the possibility of pretending that she had succumbed to impulse, that Peter had swept her off her feet and that the overnight affair was just a happy-go-lucky episode. To her it was an important testing; to Peter, she suspected, it was only an exciting diversion and she was, really, of no more importance to him than any of the women he had slept with. In the course of the afternoon and evening he had grown more confident, paying her compliment after compliment, touching her hands and body affectionately, gentling her along with a romantic foolishness that was, at one and the same time, flattering and insulting. How could he possibly know that she was free of anxiety if not of guilt? Having made up her mind to sleep with him, she looked no further than the act of love itself, the fulfilment and expression of an opportunism that had long been suppressed within her and that she was not prepared, in any way, to equate with the other forms of love that she had experienced in the course of her life. She had surrendered not so much to Peter Freeman as to restless sexuality, a selfish and illogical thing that she had not wished upon herself and had sought to evade.

Peter might think what he liked of her. In her heart, Holly knew that she was not so much giving in to him as to herself.

He knocked softly upon the door.

"Holly?"

"Come in, Peter," she said. "I'm ready."

*   *   *

In the moments before he opened the door and went into the bedroom Peter reminded himself that there must be no talk of love. It was not his style to trade on empty promises. Strange, though, how cynical he felt about his latest 'conquest', how disappointed that Holly had fallen for the same medley of compliments and attention that had wooed so many other women to his bed. No matter how Holly packaged it in picturebook villages, roast beef and English ale, in oil lamp light and the loamy scent of fall rain, it was the same soft surrender that he had received so many times before. He had expected more – did he mean less? – from Holly King. He had hoped that she would resist the cheap escape he offered, realise that stolen sex was only an abbreviation for needs that he could never satisfy, not without sacrificing himself – and that was something he would never do again.

Lakey had taught him that only a fool gave up everything for love. Love-making changed nothing. It was intensely pleasurable, and a great little substitute for many of the things that his dedication to a career, and his disorderly way of life, robbed from him. But it did not answer any of the big questions; it dispersed them nicely for a while. Only his body had any real wisdom. Inside he was a faker, like ninety percent of Broadway show folk.

Maybe he was all wrong about Holly. Maybe she wasn't seeking to salvage her capacity for love through him, the quality that time destroyed in men and women alike, and that like the blue, blue evenings of childhood could not be recalled. He had never made love to an innocent girl – except Lakey. He had had no reason to hide from Lakey; they had both been so very young.

In the bed Holly waited. She had not hidden coyly from him, nor did she pose. Her cheeks were flushed but her expression was calm, disconcertingly so. He went over to her at once, stooped and kissed her on the mouth, letting his lips linger. He wanted her now. The strength of his hunger surprised him. He drew her against him, felt her arms go around him, the weight of her body press against his chest. He kissed her again and fondled her breasts.

Stepping back, he undressed without ceremony. Holly watched him, saying nothing. Naked he was unspectacular. He wished that he had that streak of outrageous, unjustified vanity that would allow him to show off, carry mastery into domination, but he did not demand to be worshipped or even admired. He wanted only to give and be given an intimate, all-consuming pleasure; the bed was no stage, the woman no audience.

He pulled back the quilt, glimpsing Holly's legs and thighs, the nightgown mussed up over her belly so that he saw too the dark triangle of hair, her readiness. He slid in to the bed and turned against her, cowling the quilt over his shoulders. She caught him in her arms and hugged him to her. He felt her respond at once, opening her knees. He was against her, probing, angry at his impatience, the fact that she seemed to need no preliminary tenderness. Desire and anger twined in him; he dispensed with the luxuries of foreplay, the climax of wooing, the final secret acts of seduction. There was nothing quixotic in her willing and opulent cooperation. Peter was jealous of her freedom from guilt. Her mouth sought him as he slid his hand down to her thighs. They kissed breathlessly. He pulled his head away and buried his face in her hair. Touching her with his fingers, he found that her heat had mounted – yet there was still reserve in her, not a withholding of her body but a slight palpable detachment that stirred him to roughness. He grabbed her nightgown, furled it into a stiff roll and squeezed it over her breasts. Cocking it with one hand he bound her, braced, below him.

"Yes," she told him. "Yes, Peter, yes."

He entered her, not tentatively but completely, gasping as her flesh encompassed him. Holly cried out softly. Before he could begin to find a rhythm she cried out again and exploded wetly against him, the soft pulses of her vagina tricking him into a sudden thrust that bonded them in climax.

Minutes later, he took her a second time.

Hours later, with the brass lamp extinguished and the wind loud on the inn's mullioned panes, they indulged themselves in all the stimulations that they had previously neglected. Here his sophistication mastered her; his mastery made his own search for gratification all the more intense. The intercourse was lingering and explorative and their climaxes, when they came, complete, until along the petalled edges of orgasm, Peter slipped unguarded into a dreamless sleep.

*　　*　　*

Mist marred the vistas of village and coppice and shrouded the far flat horizons of harvested fields. The night wind had dwindled and the morning was still. Unravelled leaves lay thick by the roadside as Holly drove at no great pace along the narrow Cambridgeshire lanes, heading for Royston and the A.10 to London. The Sunbeam's heater purred. Holly wore a light tweed coat for it would be several hours before the sun broke through. She had eaten a substantial breakfast at the Bell Cap and felt more relaxed than she had done in many months – not carefree, though. The thought of a confrontation with Kennedy and Chris niggled at the back of her mind however much she tried to push it away. Beside her Peter smoked a cigarette, hunched in the passenger seat, his knees against the glove box in a peculiarly comfortable position. They had said little to each other in the bedroom or over breakfast; conversation would have been an unnecessary ancillary to their contentment. With just the faintest touch of irony perhaps, the landlord had said that he hoped they had enjoyed their stay and that he might see them again soon. Peter had said that he hoped so too, and had paid the bill in cash to avoid the embarrassment of a cheque. As soon as the car was out of sight of the inn, wrapped in a cocoon of mist, Peter had leaned over and kissed her on the mouth. The Sunbeam had slithered a little and Holly had braked down and stopped and they had kissed for a moment or two before she drove on again. Soon they would reach a town, the width of the road would increase and there would be traffic and people, London lying ahead – and an inevitable parting. Holly would be drawn at once into business matters for an hour or two before going to Paddington to catch the Great Western 'Torbay Express' that would carry her down into Devon for a long weekend with her family.

"Maybe I'll go to the theatre after all," Peter said.

He did not try to dissuade Holly from going to Devon, did not suggest that she telephone Kennedy and invent an excuse for staying in London. He seemed concerned that she should not short change her husband. But there was no longer certainty in anything and as the car gathered speed on the stretch between Buntingford and Ware, Peter said suddenly, "Is it Kennedy or the boy that'll keep us apart?"

"Neither." Holly's gloved hands tightened on the steering wheel. "What will keep us apart, Peter, is you – and me."

"How far will you go, Holly?"

"I don't understand."

"Will we see each other again?"

"Yes, if you want to."

"Sleep together again?"

"Yes, but I won't promise you more, Peter."

"I figure it's the boy, your son."

"Meaning it can't possibly be Kennedy?"

"No, but . . . Kennedy's not young, Holly."

"What's that got to do with it?"

"You enjoyed being with me last night. I know you did."

"Of course I did."

"You'll worry about the boy finding out?"

"It sounds to me as if you've had experience of this sort of relationship before?"

Peter shrugged. "I've seen a lot of movies, that's all."

"Chris is not a child now, Peter."

"But he's yours. I mean, there must be something special between you. You loved his father, didn't you? Deems?"

"Christopher Deems wasn't his father," Holly said. "There was another man, son of the owner of the antique shop where I started my career. His name's not important."

"Aspinall," said Peter. "You mean Chris is Aspinall's son?"

She could not recall when she had told Peter the details of her early life, of the stroke of good fortune that had broken the ties with Lambeth and had given her a Godsent opportunity to make something of herself. Whether it was she or another who had told the American of Aspinall's Antiques hardly mattered.

"Yes, David; David Aspinall."

"Is he dead too?"

"As far as I know," Holly said, "David's in the Far East. The last I heard – this was years ago – he was with a shipping firm, in their office in Hong Kong."

"Did he run for it?"

Holly smiled. "Rather than marry me, d'you mean?"

"I'm sorry." Peter was confused by the woman's revelations. "What I mean is, *why* didn't he marry you?"

"I didn't want him to," said Holly.

"Did Deems marry you knowing you were pregnant?"

"I suppose it's difficult for you to understand – Christopher was a strange man – but he married me, I think, *because* I was pregnant. I had no idea that Christopher would would die. To all intents and purposes, my son is Christopher's son."

"Why are you telling me this, Holly?"

"To help you understand."

"Meaning?"

"Meaning, I think, watch out."

"Are you trying to scare me off?"

"I don't know what you see in me, Peter, but don't take me at face value."

"Does Kennedy know about Chris?"

"Only my brother Maury knows the truth."

"Why in God's name did you tell me?"

"I'm not sure. Perhaps to prove to you that I can be ruthless too."

"You can trust me, Holly," Peter said. "The past has nothing to do with it, with us; it's over, gone, forgotten."

"Not forgotten, Peter. We live with it every day," Holly said. "So it isn't here and now; you and I – isolated. It never can be, really."

"Are you letting me off? Telling me it's over already?"

"No."

"Holly, I want you!"

"Even now you've had me?" she said. "Do you still want me as much as you did?"

"More."

"For how long?"

"I don't know. I don't think that way."

"You see, Peter; see how different we are."

"The way I live may look superficial but it isn't," said Peter. "I'm not like the fan articles make out."

Holly glanced at him once more. "In a month, two months, Peter, we'll be at the negotiating stage, won't we?"

The fact that he took her meaning at once told Holly that she had not oversimplified this complex man, and that his talk of affinity had been correct.

Peter said, "Who gives up what?"

"Exactly."

"I've nothing to give up," Peter said.

"Only your career?"

"My career? My dancing?"

"No, not your dancing; your stardom."

"That's a long way off – if you mean Hollywood."

"Don't lie to me, Peter, not even a little bit."

"All right," he said. "I want – yeah – stardom. I want it for

Howard, too; and that's the truth."

"And you can have it, can't you?"

"Given the breaks."

"Would you be willing to compromise?"

"By staying in England?"

"Possibly."

"No, I wouldn't," Peter said.

"I see," said Holly.

"Will that be your excuse for shucking me off, Holly?"

"I'm not looking for excuses," Holly said.

"What are you looking for?"

"A balance sheet," Holly said.

"How can you be so goddamned analytical, after last night?"

"A thriving business, a loving husband, a secure place in society – and a son whom I love very dearly," Holly said, "that's what I'm risking."

"Isn't it worth it?"

Holly did not answer him.

The Sunbeam slowed. Cottages had yielded to trim little bungalows, the kind that Maury had once built, then to a town street with church and shops and long-fronted plate-glass chain stores and brick houses. Provision vans and private motor cars and women with young children, perambulators, dogs on leads, shopping baskets seemed suddenly to swarm around the car. Holly was preoccupied with the gearstick, gloved hands decisive as she negotiated the high street's congestion, crossed a busy junction and settled the Sunbeam out through the town's narrow ring of suburban dwellings on to the open road once more.

Patiently Peter waited, busying himself with a cigarette.

Inhaling, he let the smoke out steadily.

"You didn't answer my question, Holly. Isn't it worth the risk?"

"Yes, Peter," Holly replied. "I think it might be."

*   *   *

With its palm trees and promenades and gigantic stucco

hotels, of all the towns in England Torquay was the one guaranteed to remind Holly of the Côte d'Azur. It was summer still in Devon, the sky hazy with the warmth of the day, the sea with a muted evening glitter. No tweed overcoats were in evidence, only shorts and smart cream flannels, open-collared shirts and sandals worn over socks of bright red or yellow, a concession that even the most solid citizens of Britain's conservative isles willingly made to the holiday mood. Chocolate machines, ice-cream kiosks and awninged booths hung with spades, pails and flags were still open for trade in the teatime town as Kennedy, carrying Holly's case, led the way from the station. Chris, who seemed to have reverted to being a ten year old instead of a staid young man of thirteen, pranced about his mother like an unbridled colt, clearly delighted to welcome her to his boy's paradise.

Holly studied her son, as she always did when she hadn't seen him for a while, searching his features for a likeness of his father but finding there instead, by some feat of the imagination, more resemblance to Christopher Deems than to David Aspinall, especially now that his dark hair was bleached a little by the sun. For all that, he showed evidence of David's ebullience rather than Christopher's reserve and, when he wished, could woo his mother with an easy charm.

"Swimming, every day" Chris chattered. "I've been out on a yacht too, a real yacht."

"Oh, how did you manage that?"

"A friend of Father's was passing through, sailing round the Lizard. He offered to take me with him but you were coming."

"Bennett," Kennedy called back. "You remember Bennett, my dear, the carpet dealer. Retired from business last year. Looks the better for it too. He has a house near here, Dartmouth way. Yachts."

"Father says he might retire from the gallery," said Chris. "Take up yachting. Imagine living in Torquay!"

"Your father's too young to retire," said Holly. "Besides, we haven't enough money in the bank."

"Oh, I don't know," said Kennedy. "You could open a shop here, Holly; give you something to do."

"Are you serious?"

"Only slightly," said Kennedy.

"You'd miss London."

"I wouldn't," said Chris. "I'd love it here."

Holly smiled and rumpled her son's hair. It felt coarse under her fingers, salt-licked. He looked gawky in the canvas shorts that had fitted him so well at the beginning of the summer. His legs were long and smooth and browned by the sun. Why had she never taken him abroad with her? Not because he would have been difficult to manage. Selfishness, she supposed; not wishing to have her mind distracted from the purpose of her trips. If Kennedy had been keener they might have taken a villa, a long, long holiday. But not now, not with Chris at the peak of adolescence, all jumbled up, switching back and forth from child to young man from minute to minute.

Boastfully, Chris said, "I've learned to shoot a fair game of billiards, Mother. There are three tables in the hotel, you see, and Father's been a sport. I can beat him now, now that he's shown me the ropes."

"If I wasn't so blessed short-sighted," said Kennedy to the boy, "I'd give you a frame per set and you wouldn't even chalk your cue more than twice."

"Rot!" said Chris then, pointing, "Look, Mother, that's the Princess Pier."

"Yes, love," said Holly. "I know."

"Don't mind the stroll, do you, dear?" asked Kennedy.

"No, I'm glad of it – after London."

"I'll carry Mother's bag, if you like," Chris offered.

"Why not?" said Kennedy. "But trot on ahead, please. I don't want to be bumped every ten steps, thank you very much."

"Oh, really!" Chris took the suitcase and hoisting it under his arm, stepped on ten or twelve paces in front of his parents, his interest in them suddenly diminished as some aspect of the view absorbed his attention.

Holly wondered what thoughts occupied her son's head. She marvelled at the concentration of his gaze, as if he intended to imprint forever upon his memory the evening sky, the sea and the crescent of hotels. There could not be much in Chris's storehouse yet; Latin verbs, a smattering of history, Malvolio's speech, wedges of information about cricket and aeroplanes, facts that drew him away from her and closer to Kennedy. But in five years – Holly felt with sudden deep panic – Chris would have so much that was inimically his own, that they did not and could not share, that they would be strangers, just as she had become a stranger to her father. There in the late-season resort, her husband's arm in hers, she thought of herself at Chris's age; a bit of a misfit in the slum house in Abraham's Box, a woman already shaping to life's essentials, unprotected against the harshness of the world. How fortunate Chris had been. How completely he accepted the blessings her hard work and self-sacrifice had brought him. But how could she blame him for his ingratitude? He had never known anything else. She had devoted herself to providing Chris with a secure and comfortable home, a sound education and a father – Kennedy. She could not look to that quarter for relief; guilt was with her now and would remain with her.

"And what've you been up to, Holly?"

"What?"

"This week, in London?" said Kennedy.

"I . . . I went out of town," said Holly. "An excuse to get away from the dust. I visited Ronald Hadley. He had one or two things. Quite good paintings. I stayed over at Brattlesham."

"Alone?"

"What?"

"I thought you might have taken Emma along," Kennedy said.

"No. I didn't take Emma," Holly said. "Oh, by the way, the William and Mary chairs at the Partington's sale – I didn't buy them."

"I'm surprised! What did they fetch?"

"Only five fifty," said Holly; the lie was ready. "I know you'd have paid one-five more, Kennedy, but I had a close look at them and they seemed suspect to me. I think they'd been doctored."

"Doctored? The needlework seemed so fine."

"It wasn't right," said Holly.

"Who bought them?"

"Ormsbee."

"Ormsbee – oh, yes, from Birmingham," said Kennedy. "Hm, perhaps you're right, Holly."

"I'm sure I am."

"Of course, of course." Kennedy squeezed her hand. "I'm glad you decided to come down. You're rather . . . I don't know, tense. Now you must relax, enjoy yourself."

"Yes," said Holly. "Yes, I will."

It was the beginning of a new relationship, not the end of an old one. She was acutely aware of each sullen little lie, how it stuck in her throat like a fishbone. More, she was struck even then by the fragility of her falsehoods, the realisation that the fraying of one thread would bring all the rest away, like a broken bead choker. If that happened then she would never be trusted again, not by Kennedy, not by Chris, not by anyone.

That was the price she would have to pay for loving Peter in secret.

"Ah, here we are," said Kennedy. "Splendid building, the Royal Devon, isn't it? The service matches its appearance. This is one place you've never been to before, Holly, aren't I right?"

"Quite right," said Holly.

On Kennedy's arm, Chris leaping ahead, suitcase tucked manfully under his slender brown elbow, Holly walked up the shallow steps into the hotel's gilded foyer, a prisoner of her conscience for the rest of that long weekend.

oooooooo
ooooo
ooo
o

2

Return of the Native

Sherbrook Winter's wedding cake house at No. 44 Vallois Street suited Ritchie Beckman's requirements to a tee.

Travel had rubbed the corners off the violent youth who had fled Lambeth with his teenage bride over a decade ago. Ritchie had quickly learned that more was to be gained by cunning than by strongarm tactics. The lesson had been rammed home in the early twenties when he hauled illicit alcohol from Canada on contract to a Chicago syndicate. Until he encountered the real thing Ritchie had arrogantly assumed that he was ruthless enough to wrestle anyone to the floor – he revelled in the memory of how he had humiliated Vince Shotten, the South London gang boss – but the Irish Americans, Italians, even the Greeks and Jews with whom he did business in the Windy City made dear old Vince seem like Casper Milquetoast.

Ritchie was no casual wheelman. He had invested a portion of the money he had stolen from Vince Shotten in shares in a Canadian liquor company and, with Prohibition roaring across the 49th Parallel, had cashed in on boom times. Even that hadn't been sufficient to satisfy his cravings for profit and excitement, however. In addition to whisky he ferried paintings and antiques – items mostly stolen or strayed – across the border to sell to Dean Alexander, a dealer, in Evanston, Illinois.

Perhaps it was lingering envy of his sister Holly's success

that prompted Ritchie to trade in collectors' goods. More probably it was the realisation that for sheer viciousness he was no match for the hoodlums from Five Points or the smart guys of the Gold Coast. Ritchie was lucky to survive let alone prosper during his years in Illinois. His 'Englishness' helped. It softened the bantering unctuousness with which he wheedled his way round the gang lords, killers and bent attorneys who were to become his clients. It also disguised the fact that, at bottom, he was as rapacious as any of them.

The crossroads in Ritchie's career came one bitter night in November 1923 in the course of a routine delivery of hooch to a warehouse on Chicago's infamous Taylor Street. Instead of minions waiting to unload the cargo Ritchie was confronted by Sicilian Mike Genna, a member of the clan that ran the notorious 19th Ward. Somehow Genna, had picked up the impression that the Beckman kid was 'misabusing' the family store by using the Genna contract to conduct personal business.

With Ritchie plastered helplessly against the truck's hood, Mike Genna supervised the unloading.

In addition to whisky, the truck contained a large framed painting by Caravaggio and a small Italian Renaissance sculpture of the Virgin Mary. Mike Genna was madder than hell at this obscene mingling of sacred and secular. He was on the verge of wafting Ritchie to the here-and-gone with a shotgun and would have done so too if Ritchie had not remained cool. The Limey did not plead for his neck, did not even protest that the goddamned truck was his property and that he could carry what he goddamned liked in it. Instead of displaying fear or anger, Ritchie acted hurt. This surprising reaction to imminent demise gave Genna pause, a pause just long enough for Ritchie's nimble tongue to come to his rescue. "Hey, Mr. Genna, what is this with the gun? I ferry these nice things down here as a present for your brother, Antonio, because I figure he'll appreciate them – and you're gonna kill me for *that*." Antonio, the Gentleman, was the brains of the Genna mob. Antonio was an artist who designed buildings as a hobby and knew more about opera than anyone north of New York. Even his crazy brothers feared and respected

Antonio. The very mention of his name was sufficient to cause Mike to lower the shotgun and – for the time being – spare the Limey's life.

From such inauspicious beginnings a whole new career flourished for 'English' Ritchie Beckman.

Antonio Genna was delighted with the gifts. He failed to detect that the Caravaggio was phoney, that the Renaissance Madonna had a pedigree that stretched no further south than a studio in Montreal; consequently he was flattered and grateful and, in due course, agreed to meet the Limey face to face. They got along just swell, talking big shot art, expert to expert.

Soon after, Antonio introduced Ritchie to Mr. ohn Torrio, a very powerful person, a guy sophisticated enough to know a shark from a bananafish, a guy who could make Ritchie vanish from the face of the earth just by snapping his delicate fingers. Naturally the Canaletto that Ritchie brought down from Montreal was more or less authentic, and clean as a whistle. Mr. Torrio hung the landscape right above the fireplace in his very own home – and passed Ritchie on to Tomasso Estrada, another leading light in the alky-cooking guild.

Under Ritchie's influence Estrada caught the collecting bug real bad. The infection soon spread throughout the Italian Republican Club to other mobsters with more money than taste, and to judges, attorneys, court clerks and politicans who wanted to show that they too were men of discernment. They swallowed all that Ritchie told them and bought everything he advised them to, regardless of price. In fact the more they paid for an article the happier they were with it. Ritchie reckoned he did more for the spread of culture in Chicago in six and a half years than half a dozen mayors had done in their collective terms of office. The only fly in the ointment was that Estrada insisted that 'his good pal Ritchie' move down to Chi from the backwoods and set up a nice legitimate business in partnership with several respected members of the Unione Siciliana, an invitation, Estrada let it be known, that was a big honour for a Limey and one that should not be turned down.

Ritchie may have been reluctant to leave the shelter of Toronto but, running true to form, eventually he let greed overcome caution. He sold his shares in the Canadian distillery, purchased a quantity of 'art stock', some of it genuine, with the proceeds and transported the collection, his wife and himself from a hotel suite in Toronto to a hotel suite in Evanston, which was as close to Chicago as Ritchie cared to be. He persuaded his old chum Dean Alexander to sell him a partnership though, to Alexander's disgust, Ritchie did not come in alone but was accompanied by four members of the Estrada clan, gentlemen more interested in high profits than high art.

By and large Ritchie dealt in forgeries, fakes and reproductions. The lines of demarcation between one spurious work and another were fine. An outright forgery was a drawing or canvas signed by and sold as the work of a particular artist but that had been done, complete with duplicated signature, by a living painter. A fake was, usually, an unsigned work done 'in the manner of' a famous artist, an item that could be peddled with reasonable safety provided you were careful never to state that it *was* the work of a Rembrandt or a Botticelli but merely to imply it. A reproduction was a copy, sold as a copy – unless, of course, it happened to be a very fine reproduction in which case the addition of a mark or signature might hype it up into one of the other, more valuable, categories. The operation of a *sub rosa* dealership and a 'fake factory' required a great amount of care. With so many scientists in on the act, primary materials had to be as close to authentic as possible. Ritchie was always on the scout for 'old canvases' and worn or worthless *objets d'art* that could be ascribed to a specific period. Skilfully cleaned or painted over, they provided a genuine basis upon which the restorer could exercise his art.

Ritchie's restorer, to use a favourite euphemism for a forger, remained in Montreal where he continued to work miracles with the aged canvases and weathered marbles that Ritchie found for him. The grizzled old French maestro was Ritchie's ace in the hole. The only forger as good as André was André's brother, who lived in Paris.

When business in the Evanston salon expanded to the point

where André could not match supply with demand, Ritchie hopped over to gay Paree and made André's brother a very fine offer to go on contract to Alexander & Beckman. Prompted by his daughter, André's brother agreed. When business in Evanston boomed some more and it became necessary to sweeten the pot with genuine works of art, André's brother suggested that Ritchie get in touch with Europe's leading hustler and wholesaler of collectable wares, Monsieur Hugues de Rais, which Ritchie did. After that, feeding the maws of the philistines in North East America was a breeze.

But nothing stays good for ever.

Some of Ritchie's clients were not exactly dumb. Disquieting little rumours about some of the items that Alexander & Beckman had sold to the city snobocrats began to get around. The rumours were given weight when one hoodlum collector tried to buy his way out of a tax evasion bind by offloading a gigantic fleshy Rubens to the Metropolitan Museum in New York only to discover from the museum's experts that the painting was 'some kinda pasta-itch' with, generously, four licks of Rubens' brush on it and the rest of the acres swabbed on later by another hand. The noose tightened gradually round Ritchie's throat as his deceptions came home to roost. In addition, about this period, the Beckmans were embroiled in a bit of connubial nastiness that, though not the first in their ten years of marriage, was certainly the most serious. Ritchie's petite Jewish wife had become involved with an Italian hitman named Cole Cuneo, a gentleman who wouldn't take – and wasn't receiving – *No* for an answer. The effort of checking his violent rage at Ruth's infidelity almost broke Ritchie. His nerves were already in tatters, to the extent that he could no longer sit tight for a haircut or enjoy dinner in a restaurant that had windows on to the street. To add to his miseries the bulletproof vest that he bought and wore gave him a livid underarm rash. Really, the Ruth-Cole romance was a blessing in disguise. Ritchie had already seen doom looming over the horizon like an armoured Packard and his wife's affair provided a face-saving excuse for quitting Chicago.

Ritchie had already set up two sweet-running little businesses in Paris and London to keep his ménage fed and to occupy his days. He planned to 'semi-retire'. He did not imagine that the lunkheads he would be dealing with in Europe would give him many sleepless nights compared with the fraternity he'd conned blind in America. Settling scores really did not come into it. Maury's guess was correct; Ritchie involved his family in his ventures merely because they were handy and in case he might need them some day.

On a humid overcast afternoon in August 1931 Ritchie finally folded his tents, escorted Ruth from their hotel suite to a waiting cab and, without a word about his intentions, drove to the airport and caught an evening flight to New York City. The following morning, Mr. and Mrs. Rascombe, as their forged passports identified them, sailed on a transatlantic liner bound for France and put America behind them for ever.

Eight days later, at one in the afternoon, Dean Alexander was gunned down on the corner of Madison and Dearborn. By coincidence, exactly one week later, Cole Cuneo was slain by Prohibition agents after a running gun battle across half of Cork County. Before the snows billowed down from Labrador that year Tomasso Estrada and three of his kinfolk were dead and buried too and events were moving so fast that the Limey kid's duplicity was virtually forgotten.

Safe and sound in Paris, France, with his adorable wife and a hundred thousand American dollars stashed in various depositories, Ritchie Beckman's frayed nerves soon mended. In his heart he acknowledged that his time in Money City had simply expired but, being Ritchie, he chose to blame his wife for his expulsion from Eden, and added that burden too to all that poor Ruth Erbach Beckman had to endure locked in her beautiful wedding cake house in London's Vallois Street.

*   *   *

Breakfast *chez* Beckman. Ritchie was dressed for the day in a tailored blue suit, soft-collar shirt and knit tie. His dark hair, thinning slightly, was sleeked across the crown. Plumper, smoother, he still had an edgy air of presumption as if anything he wanted was his for the asking. His hands were fast in the routine tasks, wielding a fork, lifting a coffee cup, buttering toast, slitting open the morning's mail. A wafer-thin Chaumet wristwatch glinted in the sunlight that streamed through the French doors of the breakfast room. By contrast Ruth, in fine lingerie and a lemon silk peignoir from Joly's of Paris, was ungroomed and uncosmeticised, a little rumpled, like something left over from a wild party of the night before, but still beautiful. She lolled over a bowl of Quaker oatmeal, toying with the stuff with a silver spoon large enough to anchor a liner. She squinted at her spouse as he extracted bills from their envelopes, glanced at them and battened them down under the salt dish, saying nary a word.

Ruth's dark eyes watched him sadly. She licked oatmeal from the tip of the spoon.

She would never learn. Extravagance did not rile him. Sable, mink, silver fox furs stuffed her wardrobes, a ransom in jewelry lined the wall safes, a chorus line of shoes danced on eight stepped racks. She had suits, dresses, gowns enough to change three times in the day, every day in the year, and no reason to accumulate more, nobody to model them for, nobody to impress – nobody except her husband. She had become a desirable reflection of Ritchie's prosperity.

One hundred and twenty pounds frittered away on a pair of silver-backed hair brushes that she would never use and had no room for on the top of the dressing table. She longed for Ritchie to toss the bill down, rage at her extravagance, cuff her across the cheek. But that was not Ritchie's way. He had never, ever struck her and his voice was always gentle when he addressed her. He reserved a special honeyed tone just for her, and a patronising child-simple vocabulary as if she was still the schoolgirl with whom he had first fallen in love, the starry-eyed child with whom he had eloped years – centuries – ago.

It was not Ritchie's inflexions that chilled Ruth but the inflexibility of his authority over her. Ritchie might worship her, but he did not love her as a husband ought to love a wife. Their marriage had been corrupted by the very power of

Ritchie's love for her, a jealous, dedicatedly selfish kind of love that demanded total obedience and gave no honour and no trust in return – only *things*, alligator shoes, peardrop earrings and the damned pretty silver brushes that her shopping expedition, her one and only jaunt in the week, under the stern eyes of Mrs. McKim the housekeeper and Fletcher her lady's maid, had yielded instead of pleasure.

"Know what they cost, those brushes?" Ruth said.

"Sure," said Ritchie.

"A waste!"

"You want them, you have them, sweetheart."

"Sheer waste!"

"You don't like them? Send them back."

"Oh, I like them. Don't you like them?"

"If you like them, I like them," said Ritchie.

"I don't know why I bought them. I don't need them."

"They'll keep." Ritchie scanned an airmail letter that had arrived from Paris. "In ten years they'll be worth twice what I'm paying for them."

Ruth pushed the oatmeal to one side and lit a cigarette. "Who's the letter from?"

"It's business, sweetheart, just business," Ritchie said.

"Who's it from?"

"Nobody you know."

"What are doing today, Ritchie?"

"Going to the office."

"All day."

"Yer."

"Can I go out?"

"Sure. Take a walk in the park – with Mrs. McKim."

"I'd like to go out on my own, without McKim holding my lead?"

"It isn't safe," said Ritchie, still reading the long hand-written letter on its blue airmail stationery, "a woman on the streets alone."

"Ritchie, we're in London now. London. I was born here".

Ritchie glanced up at her. "Fletcher'll go with you".

"On my bloody own. I want to go out on my own."

Stuffing the letter into his jacket pocket, Ritchie came around the table and put his arm across her shoulders, stroking the bare flesh under the peignoir.

"You look a little peaky, darling," he said. "Maybe you should go back to bed, catch up on your beauty sleep. After lunch, Fletcher . . ."

"Ritchie, *please* let me go out without either of *them* tagging along."

"You need looking after."

"Not in London."

"You said that in Evanston – and look where it landed us."

"That was ages ago. Anyhow, it was never what you thought with . . ."

"I don't blame you, Ruth," said Ritchie. "You're just too attractive for your own good."

"This isn't Chicago. What can happen to me out there? Look, just in the park; I'll stay in the park – but, please, on my own, please, *by myself*."

"Parks are the worst places for women on their own."

Ritchie continued to stroke her shoulder, his fingers moving down to massage the upper swell of her breast. It was not a sexual gesture, though, nor sadistic; he performed it almost absent-mindedly, in the belief that, even at that hour, his hot-blooded 'little wifie' was suffering from 'restlessness'. Into her ear, stooping, he whispered, "I'll be home early. We'll have dinner . . ."

"Let's eat out?"

"No, no," said Ritchie. "Just you and me, Ruth. Here, at home. The food's better here than in any bleedin' restaurant. Anyhow, I don't want to share your company with a roomful of gawping idiots. Just you and me. Make yourself pretty, will you? Give you something to do this afternoon. Fletcher will do your hair."

"Frig you!"

"Hey, now! I don't like that kinda language, Ruth. You know I don't."

She thrust the lighted cigarette into the oatmeal mush and pushed herself from the table. His touch seemed to have made her more dishevelled. The peignoir swirled about her, giving her husband a glimpse of her lingerie, the lacy-edged cami-knickers, the silken legs, and her breasts, free and unbound under the silk.

"*Are you trying to drive me nuts, Ritchie?*" she shouted.

Ritchie looked pained. "Ruthie, I'm your husband. It's my job to look out for your welfare."

She swung on him before he had an opportunity to step away. She pressed her body against him, rubbing against him like a cat. There was not one iota of subtlety in the seduction. It was an outlandish manoeuvre, one that never worked. But she had lost whatever imagination she had ever had, could think of no other means of imposing her will upon him, though Ritchie's will was like stainless steel, hers only straw.

"Lemme go see my mamma."

"Aw, Ruthie. We've been through all that."

"I wanna see my mamma."

"Ruthie, Ruthie, Ruthie." He detached himself, holding her at arm's length, his eyes full of cold sympathy. "We tried, didn't we, honey? I mean, it's no good. I went round there and she wouldn't even let me cross the doorstep."

"But if I went . . ."

"Now," said Ritchie. "Now, sweetheart; what happened when you telephoned?"

Defeat crept upon Ruth suddenly; the humiliation of the one monitored phone call that he had allowed her to make. It was part of his hold over her; the fact that he was always right, always, always right. If she *had* listened to him in the first place, had 'left it to him', she would not have been wounded by her mamma's response.

Thoughts of a reunion with her mamma and papa had sustained her during long airless months in a Paris hotel suite, had eased the pain of her parting from Cole. She hadn't liked Cole, not really, but he was the only man she had ever had a chance to meet who had the brass to stand up to her husband, who had the cocksure arrogance to take her right under Ritchie's nose. Cole's will had been stronger than Ritchie's. Cole would have killed to have her, if she hadn't prevented him by giving in. But it was the thought of misty, homely old London, of Mamma and Papa, of the old house in the old street, of all the things she had once despised, that had kept her sane during the last months in Evanston when Ritchie had had her guarded night and day, not just by McKim and Fletcher but by two dog-featured toughs with guns bulging under their coats; guarded, imprisoned, night and day, day and night, until she screamed and screamed inside her head for release, not just release from the four rooms, but from Ritchie and Ritchie's sticky web of emotionalism. But there, in Illinois, she was a victim and in some danger, and commonsense held her together – just. But in Paris, in Paris it had been punishment, and only the thought of London . . .

"What happened?" Ritchie insisted. "You know what happened?"

"She . . . she . . ."

"Your mamma hung up, didn't she?"

Dumbly Ruth nodded. There were no tears. She was dry, every duct in her body wrung right out. Some days she felt that if ever she learned to weep again she would find the strength to walk out on him. But if she did – where would she go where he couldn't find her?

"And what did your Mamma say?" Ritchie wheedled.

"Nothing."

"Aw, now, Ruthie; you know what she said. Tell me what she said when she heard it was you?"

Ruth tried to pull away from him but he held her; the velvet vice. She closed her eyes to blank him out. He touched a finger against her lashes, brushing them so that she blinked. His face was close to hers. For an instant it almost seemed as if the sympathy in his eyes was genuine.

"When you said 'It's me, your daughter, Mamma', what did she answer?" Ritchie persisted.

"She . . . she said . . ."

"She said?"

"She said, 'I've got no daughter. My daughter's dead.'"

Ritchie pulled her to him, hugged her tensely.

"You poor kid," he told her. "God, I could strangle the old cow. What a thing to say! After twelve years, you'd think she'd forgive us."

"Lemme go see . . ."

"And get hurt even more? Hey, now, Ruthie, sweetheart."

"I'll . . . I'll just, just look at the house."

"Next weekend, maybe next weekend, I'll take you round there in the car. You an' me, honey, just the pair of us. We'll drive to all the old haunts, all the places we used to leave letters, where we used to meet. You'd like that?"

"Yes." She could not even be sure that she would like it but it was something, wasn't it? She was hardly ever alone with him outside the rooms they inhabited together. She had lost all perspective of her husband because of it. Even to be alone with him in the Bentley, without McKim and Fletcher breathing on her, even that would seem like heaven. "Yes, I'd like that."

"All right, it's a date. Maybe this weekend. Maybe Sunday."

"Thank you, Ritchie, thank you."

He smiled, let her go and straightened the broad soft knot of his necktie, his hands moving again with nervy brusqueness.

"Today, you go for a walk in the park with Fletcher, right? Be home nice and early. We'll eat dinner together, just you and me."

He patted his pockets to make sure he had all that he would need on his person, all the notebooks and wallets and cards that were part of his essential equipment now and that lay close to his body in the tailored contours of his suits.

He kissed her.

"Okay?"

"Okay."

"See you tonight then. Oh, and go easy on the Martinis."

"Ritchie?"

"Yer?"

"Is it . . . is it definite – about Sunday?"

"A date," Ritchie said and went out of the breakfast lounge, closing the door behind him.

Mrs. Eunice McKim, who had been with the Beckmans since Vancouver and understood everything there was to know about the husband, the wife and the relationship, was waiting by the top of the stairs that led down to the garage.

She had Mr. Beckman's topcoat and soft blue hat, and the locked black leather document case that contained everything he could not snugly carry on his person. She fed Mr. Beckman into the coat, handed him the hat and briefcase.

"How is Mrs. Beckman?" Eunice McKim enquired.

"I quietened her down," Ritchie said.

"Will we be goin' out, Sir?"

"To the park, Eunice, just to the park."

"The usual hour?"

"That'll be long enough. An' keep her away from telephones."

"Yes, Sir."

"Goodbye, Eunice."

"'Bye, Mr. Beckman."

Ritchie went swiftly down the spiral stairs, paused and called back. "Oh, Eunice, one more thing."

"What's that?"

"Pack me a bag, will you? I'm flying to Paris first thing tomorrow."

"How long will you be gone, Sir?"

"Over the weekend," Ritchie said.

* * *

The Apex Advertising Agency operated from offices in Court Lane, on the shifty side of Goodge Street. The building was a warren of one-man businesses tucked behind unpainted doors and unwashed windows. The lift was attended by a club-footed Boer War veteran named Murgatroyd whose official cards of employment listed him as a building supervisor and who dwelled in a narrow cold-water flat in the basement. Murgatroyd had taken care of the Court Lane property since 1907 and had gone down with it as a captain might go down with a sinking ship. He knew everything about everybody and received regular 'backhanders' from all the tenants, though by tradition his weekly wage was paid, not by the owners, but by the leaseholders of the salubrious top floor.

The top floor had not been split into cubicles but remained a crowning glory, two thousand, one hundred and twelve

171

square feet of studio accommodation spread under skylights, impossible to heat and draughty as Salisbury Plain but spacious enough to house the nine young men and four young women that Mr. Titus Mitchell employed and still leave room for three trim offices. In its time the top floor had been a Servants' Hiring agency, a photographic studio, a printing house for 'saucy' postcards and religious tracts and, for the last seven years, home of the Apex. Murgatroyd had no illusions about the owner – now general manager – of the Apex. Red-cheeked, breezy, backslapping Titus Mitchell was just as much a chancer as anyone and got short shrift when it came to deference and respect, particularly after word drifted down the lift shaft that Mitchell was on the verge of going bust. One thing Murgatroyd had never been able to discover was which of the 'gentlemen' who now occupied the best offices up there was the actual moneybags and brains behind the rescue operation. Was it Mr. Nuttall or was it Mr. Beckman? For no other reason than that Mr. Nuttall was a war veteran, Murgatroyd plumped for him and did his grovelling act at Stan's hand-lasted shoes. Mr. Beckman he continued to treat warily. There was something disconcerting about Beckman, some quality that Murgatroyd, for all his worldliness, could not quite define.

Whenever Mr. Beckman and Mr. Nuttall happened to travel in the lift together conversation between them was suspended, inhibited by his presence, Murgatroyd felt sure. Same thing with Nuttall and Mitchell, Mitchell and Beckman. The veil of silence increased Murgatroyd's suspicion that all was not as it seemed to be up top. From the shiny new staff of artists, copywriters, typists and salesmen the caretaker divined what he could about the doings in Apex. But the staff were all young and stupid and he wrung little change out of them. What galled the caretaker most of all was that he could not gain midnight access to the agency's top offices. His pass-key failed to tumble the special Chubbs that had been fitted to the doors and he did not dare use force. Among drawing boards and desks there were no clues. Even the files in Mitchell's office did not answer such bewildering questions as how Apex had come up off the floor so quickly and why toffs like Nuttall and Beckman spent so much time there. Nuttall or Beckman or, for that matter, the despised Titus Mitchell could have furnished Murgatroyd with an answer in three simple words – capital, influence and profit.

Under Mitchell, Apex had been perpetually under capitalised. The cheery little backslapper had jumped into running his own agency far too soon and his flair and professionalism had been stunted by lack of cash. From this state, almost on the eve of closure, Mitchell had been rescued by Stan Nuttall, ex-husband – more or less – of his cousin's gone-to-the dogs daughter, Marigold; all of them good, honest Lambeth types. Mitchell had not been given the old heave-ho, as he expected; on the contrary he had been retained at a very generous salary to run the streamlined business, to concentrate on that which he did best, only this time with plenty of the wherewithal behind him and no cheese-paring in the quality of demos and presentations and with a staff young and varied enough to supply creative sap.

So much for the money side of it.

The application of 'influence' was a more complex and peculiar matter. Small accounts flocked in like pigeons and large accounts came thick and fast, all of them drummed up by Mr. Beckman who, in Mitchell's opinion, was the greatest salesman ever born, a real huckster who stole accounts from other agencies over cocktails or bribed with paintings and fine *objets d'art* influential directors of manufacturing industries and chain store bosses. Just how Ritchie actually did it was not Titus Mitchell's concern. He was there to make sure that nobody got short-changed, that Apex delivered the very best, from one-shot single-column block ads up to nationwide campaigns – and he did his job well.

Money bred money and influence bred influence, and the litter would soon give birth to that beautiful hybrid – success. Most of Titus Mitchell's dealings were with Stan Nuttall. He saw little of Mr. Beckman. He was given his instructions as to clients' requirements, post dates and the like mainly by memoranda or verbally by Mr. Nuttall. In a sense Mitchell was no better informed than Murgatroyd about 'the other side of it', the shadowy deals that Ritchie Beckman did in antiques, paintings and drawings, all of them, as far as he could gather, imported from the Continent for the express purpose of sweetening potential clients. Even so, Mitchell, unlike Murgatroyd, had far too much sense to poke and pry into his employers' concerns and did exactly what he was told to do and no more. The fact that there were three different sets of account books did not cause Titus Mitchell to go short on slumber. Everybody was a fiddler. Only dummies got caught at it.

Mr. Mitchell was out of the office that Thursday morning; hence it was Murgatroyd who uncovered some interesting facts about Beckman and the set-up in the Apex. Those facts, rubbed together with astute observation of the source, put the caretaker's mind at rest on some scores, and troubled it even more sorely on others.

The man who swaggered through the swing-doors from the street and advanced to the open door of the lift was the kind of man that Murgatroyd might have become if luck had been on his side. The expensive off-the-peg winter overcoat, the tweed hat and black ankle boots did not fool the caretaker for a single instant. He recognised a working class boozer done up for the day when he saw one and marked the man as a customer for the turf accountant on the second floor.

"Yer," said Murgatroyd, hardly glancing up from his copy of the *Daily Mail*.

"Lookin' for Beckman's office."

"Beckman?"

"'Vertisin'."

"What's yer business wiff *Mister* Beckman?" Murgatroyd folded the newspaper and hitched himself to his feet from the cushioned stool in the lift's far corner. "Ye're no client."

"He's me son'n'heir." the little man declared loftily. "So look bleedin' lively, right."

Murgatroyd feigned deference. But he moved slowly, like a turtle in a watertank, to close the gates and crank the machinery into motion. He said, "Sorry, sir. Can't be too careful, like. Hundesirables is everywhere these days."

"Yer, right you are," said Beckman senior.

The caretaker clashed the gates. He drew the handle and

the lift rose jerkily.

"Mr. Beckman, your son ain't in yet. No doubt he'll be along shortly. He expectin' you?"

"It's a surprise."

I'll bloody bet it is, thought Murgatroyd.

He said, "A grand chap yer boy is. Done real well for 'imself. Must be proud of 'im, ain't yer?"

"Takes after 'is dad," said Leo, without a blush. "Yer, done *real* well."

"This 'is only business?"

"Got dozens, all over the globe. Just come 'ome from Chicago. Yer should've seen the friends he 'ad there. All the nobs, all the big timers."

"Capone?" said Murgatroyd.

Behold, Leo Beckman took the jibe seriously.

"Yer, Capone; an' Torrio an' all them fellers. Knew them all, our Ritchie did. I mean, this ain't nothin' but a sideline for 'im. Keeps 'is 'and in, like, since he come back ter London."

The caretaker had the lift crawling. Beckman, puffed up with conceit like a bullfrog, did not notice.

"Surprised 'e come back at all, like," said Murgatroyd.

"Come back ter look after me, 'is old man, now I'm gettin' on in years."

And the Band Played Believe It If You Like, thought Murgatroyd.

He said, "Not just in advertisin', though, is 'e?"

In the space of two minutes Leo Beckman had unloaded every last scrap of information that he had acquired on Ritchie's past and present, about the fancy house and the pretty wife and the flights to Paris in France, about his brother who was a big business tycoon, and his sister who was London's top antique dealer, mingled with a lot of blather about how much all three of his kids depended on him, and how much they loved him.

Like a cat loves the bleedin' water, thought Murgatroyd.

But the caretaker was shrewd enough to sift the chaff from the wheat and, later, did some discreet checking. He ascertained that Maurice Beckman was, indeed, a big city tycoon and that there was a sister married to a Bond Street antique dealer and a great many other things besides, not the least of which was that Mr. Ritchie Beckman had once served a year at His Majesty's pleasure for burglary. All of this Mr. Murgatroyd salted in his memory. Soon he might have something worth a quid or two to his occasional drinking pal, Detective Sergeant Penworth of New Scotland Yard.

But on that Thursday morning, when Mr. Ritchie Beckman arrived, only minutes after his pater had wandered into the Apex office on the top floor, Murgatroyd said nothing, nothing at all. He did not want to spoil the surprise.

* * *

"Married!" Ritchie exclaimed. "You, at your age! I don't believe it."

"I ain't so old."

"Well, I admit you don't look ready for the glue factory but – Geeze, married! Hah, I'll have a new mamma, after all these years."

"I thought you should be the first ter know."

Leo was seated uncomfortably on a bakelite chair before a tiny desk in a disappointingly unprepossessing office that seemed to be all window; the view of a flat macadamised roof, sooty brick walls and an air vent was not what he had expected. Only Ritchie's leather chair and a battery of telephones and other queer machines hinted that his son had made it to the top metaphorically as well as locationally. Leo began to wonder if he had misjudged Ritchie, if the boy had just been bragging about his success and, more relative, his wealth. Maybe that was the reason why Ritchie had avoided him since his return to London; they had met only twice, not even in a house but in pubs. The first time had been a bibulous, sentimental reunion, the second, though, flat as stale beer. Leo was glad that he hadn't taken Cissie along or mentioned her to Ritchie on either occasion.

"What's her name?" Ritchie asked.

"Cissie."

"Widow?"

"'Course not, a vi . . . ain't never been married."

"How old?"

"Younger'n me."

Ritchie scowled. "I hope she ain't one of those cheap chisellers, Pa."

"She couldn't be more respectable."

"A Jewish lady?"

"Not egzactly."

"Not exactly Jewish, or not exactly a lady?"

"She's a Gentile. But I don't 'old 'er religion against her."

"You're all heart, Pa," said Ritchie. "Come on, then, out with it."

"Out with what?"

"The gory details. For instance, when's the happy day?"

"Yer, well, that's the problem, son."

"Hey, you mean you haven't asked her yet?"

"Yer, yer; I've asked 'er a dozen times. Gone down on me benders to 'er. She's, ahm, keen on me, son, but she's nat'rally, ahm, perturbed by the diff'rence in our ages."

"It's hardly spring and winter," said Ritchie. "What's the arithmetic matter; twenty years is nothing if you like each other."

"Nat'rally she's, ahm, perturbed about 'er future after, after I'm gone."

Ritchie sank back in the hide chair, grinning and shaking his head. "She wants a dowry, right?"

Above the ring of his hard starched collar, Leo's jowls were scarlet with embarrassment. He hung his head and stared at his pudgy fists, tapping his thumbs together. It had come out all wrong. Ritchie had been too quick for him. He would have got around to it in his own fashion, after a while. Now it sounded as if Cissie was a gold-digger or, worse, as if he, Leo Beckman, had grown so limp and lacking in bottle that the only way he could get himself a wife was to purchase one.

Ritchie let him sweat it out.

Leo swallowed. "I got no insurances, son. No 'ouse. Nothin' ter leave Cissie in the, ahm, tragic event of me death."

Ritchie said, "What does she do, this lady?"

"Do?"

"For her daily bread; her job; her work?"

"S . . . S . . . Salvation Army."

"*What!*"

"Been an Army lassie all 'er life. A professional, like. Her old pa, he was a Colonel, somethin' like that. Had insurance, 'er pa, but the money it brings Ciss got ate up by the costa livin'. She marries me, she'll 'ave ter give up the Army."

"Is she holding out on you, Pa?"

"Uh?"

"Bedwise?"

"Bedwise?"

"Won't she come across 'til she has a marriage certificate? Is that it?"

Dimly Leo perceived what his son was driving at. It hadn't occurred to him before that Ritchie took him for that much of a fool. What was the point of courting a woman you didn't go to bed with? It was the 'bedwise' bit that clinched it, with a few other plusses now that he was getting on in years.

"Nah, that *ain't* it."

"Aren't you comfortable in Lambeth any more?" said Ritchie. "I thought Maury'd fixed you up with a woman?"

"A *char*," said Leo. "Yer, I'm comfortable."

"So why change?"

"Cissie . . . since I knowed 'er . . . things ain't the same."

"Does Maury know about this?"

"He . . . Yer. But not that I wanna get married."

"And Holly?"

"That *cow!*"

"I see," said Ritchie. "All right, Pa; what sort of dowry – I mean 'arrangement' – does your lady have in mind?"

"An 'ouse."

"Property's more Maury's angle than mine."

"Don't wanna ask him for no more'n I 'ave to."

"Cissie wants to own a house?" said Ritchie. "She wants a document, I suppose, that'll give her full claim on the property after you snuff it – though, God knows, by the look of you, you could totter along for another twenty-five years. Okay, a house: where?"

"By the sea."

"Nice," said Ritchie. "Retirement by the sea. Any particular place?"

"Brighton, Eastbourne, like that."

"And when you become a house owner – by the sea – then Cissie'll present herself before a registrar and wed you legal and you'll both go live out of London?"

"Yer."

"Is that what you want?"

"Yer," Cissie had dunned the hesitation out of Leo.

"Won't you miss Lambeth?"

"Lambeth ain't what it was."

Ritchie said nothing for a moment or two and Leo did not leap in with more arguments in favour of the arrangement. He had just enough savvy to let his son mull it over in peace.

"You gonna, ahm, help me, son?"

Ritchie said, "It's a big undertaking, Pa."

"Not for a feller like you."

Ritchie got to his feet and came to his father's side, clearly an indication that the meeting was over. He patted Leo's shoulder reassuringly and Leo, to his own surprise, felt his eyes become moist with love and gratitude. He blinked and got obediently to his feet, blinked again.

"Sure, I'm gonna help," said Ritchie. "Leave it to me, Pa. Leave it all to me, okay?"

Though Leo did not know it, he had provided Ritchie with just the sort of excuse he had been waiting for, a valid reason for drawing the dismembered Beckman family together again. But he would wait until next week, after he got back from Paris, relaxed and refreshed and with two more of Claude Cazotte's brilliant forgeries to offload on the London art market.

"Leave it with me, Pa," he said. "I'll see what can be done."

"Ye're a good boy, Ritchie. I knew you wouldn't let me down."

*　　*　　*

"Gone? Gone where?" said Ruth.

Stan's face remained expressionless. He hated this sort of dirty work, even although there was no lie involved. It was typical of Ritchie not even to have the guts to tell his wife that he was shooting off across the Channel for the bloody weekend. Presumably he had had breakfast with her that morning, had slept in the same bed with her last night, yet he had avoided the scene that the news would give rise to, the shocked reaction, the near hysteria, that his departures inevitably incurred. Stan was not familiar enough with the state of the Beckmans' marriage to gauge the reasons for Ruth's exaggerated response to what was after all a fairly regular occurrence. Stan assumed that Ritchie had 'another woman' over there, some slinky French bit, that Ruth knew of it and was torn apart by jealousy.

"France," Stan said. "Paris. Urgent business. He had a cablegram this morning. Couldn't get out of it. He sent me round with his apologies. He'll see you Monday or Tuesday."

"Telephones; there are no telephones in his office?"

"He just didn't have time, Ruth."

"He knew he was going, didn't he? Knew yesterday, last week."

"Something came up sudden-like."

The woman had lost weight. Thin and pale she looked like a starved waif, sunk in the rigid geometry of the couch – a davenport, Ritchie called it – in the living room. For all that, she was still beautiful and pretty sexy, Stan thought.

"Did he say what I'm supposed to do?" Ruth demanded.

Stan shook his head.

"We can go shopping, Ma'am," said the lady's maid, Fletcher, who stood like a wardress at the door, away across the planed-out spaces of the room.

"I can go shopping on my own, Fletcher."

"Mr. Beckman prefers . . ."

"But Mr. Beckman isn't here. Mr. Beckman's in Paris."

"Yes, Ma'am. But we all know how Mr. Beckman regards you going out . . ."

Ruth interrupted. "Lay out my navy suit, Fletcher. I'm

going out for luncheon – on my own."

Fletcher hesitated. She put up no argument but she did not leave her station by the door.

Stan realised that it was only his presence that prevented a tussle of wills between the so-called 'maid' and her mistress. There was no doubt who would emerge victorious. Ruth would not be permitted to cross the threshhold of No. 44 unaccompanied. Stan supposed that the women were only doing their jobs, obeying Ritchie to the letter for fear that they would lose a secure and highly-paid billet. He wondered why Ruth did not display more imagination and cunning; it would not be too difficult to evade the watchers once she was out in the streets of London. Perhaps she was afraid of them – or of Ritchie. If he'd had to live with Fletcher and McKim breathing down his neck for umpteen years maybe he'd have been drained of self-volition too. He could not decide which of the pair was the more loathsome. Fletcher was the younger. She had frizzled ginger hair and rimless spectacles which made her colourless eyes appear nickel-plated. She wore a green two-piece and a shin-length green linen skirt. A string of hard wooden beads lay on her fleshless chest. She spoke a perfect, grammatical form of English that covered all traces of her Irish parentage and Canadian upbringing. McKim was a large, masculine type of woman who dressed in brown and beige woollens and brogue shoes. Stan would swear that she dyed her hair, for the chopped skullcap was as brown as pony skin in spite of the fact that McKim must be pushing sixty.

"On my own," Ruth repeated defiantly.

"We'll give the matter consideration," said Fletcher.

Ruth had not moved from the davenport, had not even turned to make eye contact with Fletcher. The angles of the room carried their voices. Ruth stared up at Stan, who, still in his raglan overcoat, had remained standing in the square made by the seats, the coffee table and the huge quiet rug.

"Unaccompanied," said Ruth.

"Mr. Beckman left explicit instructions, Ma'am, that you were not to risk shopping on your own." Fletcher had been forced to it.

"Then Mr. Nuttall will take me to lunch."

The unexpected statement caught Fletcher off guard.

"Won't you, Stan?" Ruth simpered.

"Mr. Nuttall?" Fletcher came forward to the edge of the shallow steps that led down to the level of the living area. The beads clacked against her breast and she held her palm over them to keep them quiet.

"Mr. Nuttall's my husband's business associate, Fletcher, in case you didn't know," said Ruth, still not turning. She stared at Stan with a satisfied smile on her lips. "After all, Mr. Beckman *sent* Stan here in his place, didn't he?"

"Mr. Nuttall?" said Fletcher again.

He was caught, had to choose, had to allow his inclination to aid the poor smothered little waif, to defy Fletcher and McKim, to be weighed against Ritchie's ire. He would be defying Ritchie – and, Gawd help us all, it was Ritchie who paid the bills.

"Take me out to lunch, Stan?"

"I can't"

"You mean you won't?"

"I've an appointment."

"Please, Stan."

She was desperate; he felt rotten.

"No," he said. "I really can't."

A glance showed him that Fletcher had relaxed. She smiled conspiratorially at him; he had been incorporated into partnership with the two bullying bitches.

"I've gotta go, Ruth."

There was no grace to it. She was only Ritchie's missus and anything she was liable to tell Ritchie would not be believed. She could do him no harm, no real harm. Ruth's happiness, her welfare, lay outside Stan's province; not one of the things he was paid to attend to. She screwed herself round on the davenport, clutching at the boxed arm, fingers digging into the fabric as if into his flesh.

"You bastard, you dirty bastard. What's wrong with me? I haven't got the bloody pox, Stan."

"Goodbye, Ruth."

"You bloody bastard."

"We'll take care of her, sir," said Fletcher, opening the door for him. "She just needs a little drink, that's all."

"You're all bastards," Ruth shouted.

"She's right," Stan murmured as he went out into the upper hall.

But Fletcher did not understand what he meant and closed the door behind him without response.

* * *

Escargots, bearded oysters and the like were too slippery to appeal to Ritchie who preferred something he could get his teeth into. But he had lived in France long enough not to be surprised when his companion for luncheon walloped through two first courses washed down with *vintage cuvée*. Hugues de Rais made no ritual of eating and the service in the tiny wooden-walled restaurant at the top of the Rue de l'Abreuvoir in the old quarter of Montmartre was sufficiently brisk not to strain Ritchie's patience. He contented himself with a simple dish of Brill Durand and a carafe of the house wine, followed by a Soufflé Monte Cristo to satisfy his sweet tooth. Hugues de Rais reached the coffee and brandy stage at last but the delay hardly mattered as Ritchie was not a drinking man and never mixed business and spirits.

Montmartre was a safe spot for a rendezvous. Here there were only artists, no dealers of the class that would be liable to identify *le Fantôme* and stir rumours in the galleries down town. The couple had met here frequently, especially when their partnership was in the embryonic stage and they were feeling each other out.

Hugues de Rais lit a cigarette, dabbed his lips, and, like a hockey player swishing the puck into play after a time out, said, "Madame King, I have heard how she sells our Holbein to Ogden Hillis for much more than it would seem to be worth.

"What did she get for it?"

"It is reputed to be in the region of twelve and a half million francs, but my information may not be accurate, precisely."

"That's – eh – one hundred and fifty thousand bucks.

Geeze!" said Ritchie. "Twice what we figured."

"*Non*, Riccardo" This was de Rais' pet name for Ritchie. "It is twice what *you* figured."

"You puffed up your profit?"

"Naturally."

Ritchie and de Rais grinned at each other, quite fondly really. No transaction was complete without a bit of double-dealing; it was, for this pair, a peculiar signal of trust between them.

"Your sister is more astute than you believed her to be."

"Even so, she didn't twig about the Holbein."

"She had no reason; like her customers, she wanted to believe that it was authentic. And, too, it was such a beautiful job; all the pieces of it, including the pedigree."

"Yeah," Ritchie agreed. "Almost too pat."

"Pat?"

"Too neat. I worried in case I'd made the detective work too easy for her."

"I have never seen a more convincing history," said de Rais. "To think it was all fictional."

"Well," said Ritchie, "that's what it's all about, when you come down to it; being convincing. Who ever questions a reputable dealer or a classy private collector?"

"Planting dubious works of art has become something of a speciality with you, Riccardo. Did your sister buy the Hobbema canvas from the charming Dubriels?"

"How did you hear about that?"

"I have big ears," said de Rais with another grin. "May I enquire what it is that you have against the Kings?"

"Nothing." said Ritchie curtly.

"I have always found them very attractive, very honest."

"It's Holly's honesty that's so valuable," said Ritchie.

"Do you dislike your sister so much that you set snares for her?"

"I told you, I reckon I can use the Kings," said Ritchie. "No, I don't dislike my sister. She's a snob an' a prig but I've got nothing against her. Haven't clapped eyes on her for years, in fact."

"Why do you do this?"

"Do what? If you mean, about my sister – drop it."

"No, no. You are a rich man now, Riccardo, but still you go on with the game. Why is it that you do, when the need is gone?"

"I can see you're gonna tell me, whether I like it or not," said Ritchie. "I sometimes think that's why it went sour for you, Hugues, because you thought too much about motive and purpose."

"An old man's foible, a failing of age. Riccardo, I tell you, we do it because it is fun. It is like gambling on cards or horses, is it not?"

"Betting isn't my kick."

"It does not have to be; you have a love of fear."

"Fear? Geeze, Hugues that's . . ."

"It defines life for us, Riccardo; *conflit*. Conflict. Courage, cleverness, power against power. Domination. Humiliation."

"For you, maybe; for me it's just money."

"Do you not miss Chicago?"

Ritchie was a little taken aback by the perceptiveness of the question. The truth was that he did not miss Chicago, not the physical lineaments of the city, not the cold lake shore or crowding brownstones but the tension, the feeling of being on edge all the time, on *the* edge. Maybe there was something in what de Rais was telling him. Dealing defined life. The more complex and devious the dealing, the sharper the definition seemed to be. He was pushing forty now. The electric excitements of his young manhood were mere memories; he knew that he could not recapture that degree of intensity. The *need*, the sheer grasping need had diminished but he had found other ways of giving himself purpose. Power, like the Frog said. Danger and uncertainty. But he had become civilised mainly to protect himself from the cruelty he had glimpsed within himself. As de Rais and many another dealer had discovered, the world of collecting was a world of intrigue, not a pastime but a passion. In the last ten years Ritchie had discovered what it was that had motivated his sister, what it was that made her seem superior, *better*, goddamn it, than he was. Not her smartness, her flair, her looks or her intellect. Not even her determination. It was the passion in her that he coveted. Okay, what if her aims were petty? Holly's sort of passion was not reduced by gratification, like sexual desire or clawing ambition. Ritchie did not 'collect' things. He fed – and fed on – other folks' possessive urges. In a strange way, Ritchie dimly perceived that he was paying the world back for the fact that he possessed nothing except money. Only Ruth. Ruth was the fulfilment of all his emotional needs and desires. Everything else was strictly business.

Warned by Ritchie's silence that he had come close to offending his colleague, Hugues de Rais stepped away from the precipitous edge of psychology and embraced a safer subject – fraud.

"For you, Riccardo, I have something very special today."

"Like what?"

"Three old Dutch canvases," said de Rais.

"In good nick?"

"Condition, *parfait.*"

"I take it the painters are not well known."

"*Sans nom. Sans honneur.*"

"Good," said Ritchie. "What period?"

"Late seventeenth century."

"How large?"

"Two, like so." De Rais demonstrated with his hands. "The other is a figures landscape, very large. They will be excellent foundations for the work of your friend. What is his name? Monsieur . . . ?"

"Forget it, Hugues." Ritchie laughed. "I'm not gonna tell you his name. Hell, you'd steal him from me if I did."

"I would try, certainly."

"So I'm not gonna risk losing my contract with the world's best restorer," said Ritchie. "You've seen his work. You know just how good he is. Fifty percent artist; fifty percent chemist."

"It is true. His preparation and his mixing of the pigments is of the finest. Such attention. Such knowledge. It would be a wonderful experience to watch him work."

"Not a chance, Hugues."

All the praises that de Rais heaped upon Cazotte's head

were justified, yet Ritchie could not find it in himself to give unstinting admiration to the passive little Frenchman. He could see with his own eyes the results of Cazotte's genius – that wasn't too strong a word for the man's talents – but he could not equate them with Madelaine's father. Self-effacement had robbed Cazotte of the status he deserved. He was no more than the sum total of all his fakes and forgeries. If Cazotte had been born with a silver tongue he would have shamed the art experts with the breadth and depth of his knowledge of painters and painting. But he was, by nature, inarticulate; he expressed himself in duplication and imitation. Every quirk of line, every peculiarity of shading, the seemingly inimical 'spirit' of creative artists, had been lovingly studied by the old man and flowed from his educated finger tips as naturally as his own signature. There was no formality in his rendering of other men's styles; they seemed to become part of Cazotte' own talent. In addition, Cazotte had astonishing patience. He would never hurry or permit himself to be rushed when it came to the preparation of a canvas or board or the selection and mixing of a specific palette. He had gathered a vast collection of charcoals, varnishes, thinning agents, cleansers, surface tinters and, of course, the raw pigments from which he mixed his colours. The walls of the studio were littered with shelves of china mortars and wooden pestles, grinding trays and bowls, testing fragments of papers and canvas, and with more pots of chemicals than you could find in a laboratory. Cazotte's quest for strange pigment bases was unending. His historical knowledge of materials was always correctly applied. He would go mad with delight over a jar of dried lampblack picked up by chance in a flea market or the stub of a pencil that contained no trace of graphite.

Ritchie sensed that Cazotte, rather like his sister, was in the grip of an obsession, but in the forger's case the grip amounted to a stranglehold that had choked all other interests and emotions and made him, as a man, as dull as an army blanket. What the hell did that matter when he could produce such immaculate works of art, 'perfect' Vermeers and de Hoochs, dozens of others too – including Holbein miniatures?

"Your man, he is very good with Dutch masters, is he not?" De Rais asked.

"He can turn his hand to almost anything," said Ritchie. "But, yes, he enjoys working with the Flemish painters. He says they're very 'pure', whatever the hell that means."

"For you, Riccardo, the Flemish masters mean good prices."

"The best, even these days."

"I would like your man to work on my three old canvases, to hire his services."

"To do what – complete restoration?"

"Exactly – complete restoration."

"You've got a buyer?"

"*Oui* – so I require a good history for each restoration also."

"Where does your buyer live?"

De Rais wagged his finger at this mischief.

Ritchie said, "Is he – or she – an expert?"

"No licences are involved," said de Rais. "Inspection will be very expert, however."

"So long as it's a private collection," said Ritchie. "I've heard tell that the museums and galleries are using X-ray detectors that pick out the brushwork – and you can't take 'restoration' that far."

"It is a private collector," de Rais assured him.

"I want fifty percent. You provide the raw canvases and the market. I provide the restorations and authentications."

"From the House of Dubriel?"

"Maybe," said Ritchie warily. "Maybe not."

"Half?"

"Half."

"How is it you will know what I fetch for them, finally?"

"My man'll put a reserve price – know what I mean – on them. I get at least half that sum. Anything more, I'm relying on your integrity, Hugues."

"*Ah, oui* – my integrity."

"Know what that means?"

"It means you will enlarge your asking price, no?"

"Right," said Ritchie. "Where are the canvases?"

"In the trunk of my limousine, close to here."

"Wrapped for travel?"

"Of course."

"Okay, I'll take them off your hands right now."

"I drive you."

"Like hell you will," said Ritchie. "I'll take a cab." They shook hands and rose.

"How long will it be necessary to wait for them?" asked de Rais.

"As long as it takes," said Ritchie. "One thing I learned early; never rush a genius."

"Who is this genius?" de Rais asked innocently as Ritchie helped him on with his overcoat.

"His name's Vermeer," said Ritchie.

Both men laughed at Riccardo's little joke.

*　　*　　*

Soft rain laid a sheen on the paving of the patio and on the leaves of the big dismal rubber plants in their troughs. It was not an invigorating rain but seeping moistness, like mist, that hazed the lights and enclosed the huge white house in Vallois Street. Friday night, Saturday morning – it made no matter to the mist. Two o'clock, or four – the mist was impervious to the hour. It had things its own way, the park empty, the streets empty, the canal like coal-oil deep down below. For once even the zoo animals were silent as if the mist had tranquillised their bored unrest.

Ruth was half-seas-over still, though she had slept a little, curled up like a foetus under silken sheets, just squiffy enough to take pleasure in guile which, at first, seemed no more than mischievous defiance, a game against Fletcher and Eunice McKim, a tingling childish prank, creeping through the quiet warm house, barefoot and in her nightgown, shivering slightly, waiting to be caught. But then the mischievousness went out of it, and the pleasure. The mist beyond the huge glass walls was too bleak, too real. It sobered her and brought the dull ache out of her head into her belly, nagging loneliness on the border of despair. She lay in the half-dark on the carpet, protected by the davenport, and slid the telephone down off the table. The mist served her, seemed to focus the salty pre-dawn light through the undraped windows so that, with her nose almost against the plate, she managed to dial the number she had memorised, the one telephone number that she knew, the only number that she dared call at – what? – four, four thirty in the morning.

She lay on her stomach on the carpet and pressed the receiver against her ear, hearing the dialling tone, the ringing. It stopped.

She heard. "Who is that, this hour?"

"Oh, Mamma, it's me."

And nothing: yes, something: a presence, the silent sound of her mamma just, just *standing there*.

"Mamma, it's Ruth. Please talk to me."

"Ruth who?"

"Your, your daughter, Mamma."

"This is a wrong number."

"*Mamma.*"

"I got no daughter. No daughter in this house."

"Yes, Mamma. Yes, you have. It's me."

With the tears, her nose began to run and she scrambled to her knees, holding the phone as if it was the handle of a raft and all that stood between her and drowning in that infinite sea of mist.

"*Please, Mamma, please, please.*"

But her mamma had hung up on her.

Kneeling, she frantically dialled the number again, with just enough control to make sure she got it right; no possibility of a wrong number, no other gruff Jewish matron dragged out of sleep by a ghost from the past; really her mamma, her own mamma.

The telephone rang and rang and rang.

And nobody answered.

She battered the receiver against the leg of the davenport, then lifted the body of the telephone and drummed it down on the carpet, clutching it in both hands like a rock.

"Answer me, Mamma. Mamma. Mamma. Mamma. Ans-

wer me. Answer me. Answer Mamma, Mamma, Ma . . . Ma
. . . Mmmmmm."

McKim and Fletcher were advancing down the avenue of
light from the open door; Fletcher and McKim, shoulder to
shoulder, one in cotton pyjamas like a baseball player's suit,
the other in a bell-tent gown, hair in a net, marching down on
her.

She jerked the cord, plucked at the receiver.

"Mamma, I want . . ."

Thinking, *No, don't crawl. Forget it. Ritchie's right. Ritchie's always right. She is dead. Mamma's right. You're dead.*

Thinking at the same time, *Who else can I call? Who else
would be pleased to hear my voice, to know that I exist, that I
thought of them at four o'clock in the morning. Who did I
know who doesn't love Ritchie, love what he pays them?"*

Eunice McKim caught her under the armpits and half-
dragged, half-lifted her away from the flailing instrument.

Ruth shouted, "NOBODY."

Grunting Eunice McKim pinned her arms and swung her
up and carried her across the room towards the stairs that led
to the level of the master bedroom.

Ruth shouted, again, "NOBODY, NOBODY."

"That's right, honey," crooned Eunice McKim. "There's
nobody here but us."

＊　　＊　　＊

Under a beaverskin quilt in the double bed in the long attic of
the house in the Rue Flavine, la Plaine-St.-Denis, nineteen-
year-old Madelaine Cazotte and Ritchie Beckman made the
beast-with-two-backs for the second time that night. The
girl's appetite was insatiable, her agility and inventiveness as a
lover so remarkable that Ritchie begrudged her nothing, not
the money she cost him, nor the time, nor the energy that he
expended on satisfying her, though it would take him half a
week, back home, to recover from the wild Parisian weekend
– one reason why he completed his business in the capital
straight away, putting it, necessarily, before pleasure.

The beauty was that the lithe, ash-blonde girl was not 'in

love' with him, no more than he was – at that period – with her. It did not occur to him to be conceited about his possession of the lovely Frenchie; the relationship was not built on shifting sands of vanity. What she did with herself when he wasn't there didn't matter much to Ritchie. All that mattered was that she should be around when he was in Paris – and she always was. Outside the attic bedroom, he called the shots. She was the same as any other employee, had to come up to the mark. No sweat, no problems. Madelaine was as intelligent as she was good looking. She understood precisely what was required of her and applied herself to the job wholeheartedly and with a disciplined cunning that Ritchie admired more than anything else about her. So precocious was she in running the Paris end of Ritchie's fraudulent empire that it always came as quite a surprise when he saw the youthful unblemished body and was reminded that she had not yet reached the age of twenty.

The truly incredible thing about her was her grasp of the business. He never had to explain *anything* to Madelaine more than once. Her patience and thoroughness as a researcher – an inventor of histories – surpassed anything that Ritchie had hoped for when he first took her on, at her father's request, thirty months ago. In maturity, she would be more formidable than any of them. With three or four years' experience behind her there was no saying what she could not achieve. That she would eventually desert him, Ritchie did not doubt. She would not leave him for 'another man', however; she would leave him only because she required the challenge of going it alone, of making her mark in the art world, of becoming a legend in the canon of collectors and dealers as de Rais, in his prime, had been. Ritchie would give her his blessing, try to retain a little piece, a percentage, of the action she would generate, for as long as possible. Madelaine would never really belong to him. Knowledge of her independence was, oddly, consoling. With the French girl Ritchie was more himself than at any other time, in any other company.

Madelaine had been born under a Gemini sign; heavenly twins – Art and Money. Her father, Claude, and her Canadian uncle, André, were more influenced by the former but she, sole legatee of their talent for deception, made up for their unworldliness by concentrating on the latter. It was not the trappings of wealth that attracted the child; she was engrossed by the power that money could buy. Having been reared from infancy in basements and garret studios where the lines between genuine and false were too blurred to be recognisable, the one incorruptible truth for little Mademoiselle Cazotte had become hard cash. The value of a dollar, a mark, a franc or a British pound were not determined by the fantasies of wayward collectors; they were printed each day in newspapers, along with interest rates and the price of gold. One knew exactly where one stood with money; it never went out of fashion.

A motherless orphan, Madelaine had been well enough cared for by her papa, but the erratic motion of her childhood years – papa slipping quietly from one town to another, one country to another – had bred in her a deep need for security. She craved not love or affection but control, a mode of life that would be as safe as a bank vault and as changeless as the Pyramids; an unattainable preserve for which she would quest and strive all of her born days, until the questing and the striving became the mode, and the mode secure. In addition to his sexual attractiveness, in Ritchie Beckman Madelaine found a man who shared these unusual instincts, whose career had been similarly wired and who was willing to teach her all she needed to know to go him one better.

It was her character not her breasts or bottom that had first opened Ritchie's eyes to the treasure that sat in Cazotte's studio. The magnetism was, indeed, not physical at all. It was not until Ritchie had tested her out by giving her tricky little chores to perform – all of which she had done with ease – that the Englishman had finally decided she was the right material out of which to fashion a mistress and had taken her to bed.

Claude, a fatalist at heart, had put up no fight; better a rich and clever Englishman than an impoverished art student or a loutish artisan.

Only once, soon after her first experience, had Claude, with considerable embarrassment, referred to the relationship. He had shown just a trace of fatherly concern by asking, "Does he not make you afraid, Madelaine?"

To which the child-woman had replied, "Do not, Papa, be a goose."

She feared Ritchie no more than Ritchie feared her, which was to say just enough to add a dash of spice to the relationship, a whisper of *tartare*. She appreciated all that Monsieur Beckman had done and was doing for her, providing her with clothes, a comfortable place to live, facilities to travel in style and, most important of all, an occupation that suited her grand design! Her papa had seldom been happier. Left to himself to paint his fabrications, he explored the minutiae of the masterworks he loved more than bread, beef or coffee, more than he loved her even, though she had never tested him out in that manner.

The ornate enamelled stove glowed in a corner of the attic. The tapestries that Ritchie had brought her breathed on their frames. There was the smell of rain and tobacco and the brandy that Ritchie drank only when he was with her and in need of fortification, the warmth of the beaver fur quilt, the man's body beneath her, coupled to her own. The best loving was the long idle loving in the hour before the hour of the dawn – and the murmurous conversations they would have, like that, as close to each other as it was possible for a man and a woman to be.

"If we could discover who de Rais is trading with," Madelaine was saying, "I might arrange an accidental meeting with them and avoid the necessity of paying de Rais a great quantity of money for what is, after all, three miserable old canvases."

Ritchie adjusted position slightly.

"The Phantom is too crafty, and his run's too wide. We'd never winkle that kinda information outa him."

"It will be three months or longer before Papa completes the work."

"How soon before he decides on a style?"

"For days he will prowl around those canvases. It will come to him at the end of much contemplation. He has never worked to order, Ritchie, but he is quick when he gets started, as you know. Is there urgency?"

"Nope. Something else – de Rais; he's too useful to bilk."

"He is beyond it now, burned out. Why else would he trade in such small stuff, and with us?"

"Times change. He queered his pitch once too often," Ritchie said. "That's a mistake I don't intend for us to make."

"I won't let you."

"Easy," Ritchie groaned, "easy on me old bones, *chérie*."

"I worry because de Rais is careless."

"He did that job with the Holbein to perfection."

"His part was small; it was the miniature itself, and my provenance which made it perfection."

"Yer, I suppose it was. Easy, Madelaine."

"And using your sister as a front – impeccable."

"Well, that's the secret," said Ritchie. "We've got a top quality product coming off the easel, it would be pretty goddamned stupid to spoil it by shoddy dressing and careless distribution. When I really get things going, we'll have five or six outlets like the Dubriels to leak stuff through."

"And we will not need de Rais?"

"I don't know about that. I think you underestimate him. His contacts, connections . . ."

"But he is not *innocent*," Madelaine interrupted.

"I'll say he's not."

"Innocence is the best front of all, Ritchie."

"A middle man who doesn't know, doesn't even suspect that the articles are anything less than one hundred percent genuine; sure," said Ritchie. "That was the whole point of the exercise, *chérie*. That's how we fooled experts like Staedle and Waxman, the Ogden Hillises, Lenormant, and my bleedin' sister."

"And even Frasher."

"Yer; with an Auvercamp too. And him the Auvercamp big expert."

"I have heard Papa's painting will be the frontispiece in Frasher's new monograph on Auvercamp."

"Shows you how good we are," said Ritchie, chuckling.

"We are very, very good," said Madelaine. "Papa, you and me."

"Especially you and me."

"If we could only find out the name of de Rais' client."

"Hey, Maddy, not right now."

"But we could double your profit."

"Come here."

"I am here."

"You know what I mean."

"Now?"

"*S'il vous plaît.*" said Ritchie.

*　　*　　*

"Please," said Ruth Beckman, "Don't lock the door."

"Of course not," said Fletcher.

"I'm . . . I'm scared in case there's a fire."

"We'd have you out in a jiffy," said Eunice McKim.

"How do you feel now?" Fletcher asked.

"Better; a little better. I had . . . had a nightmare. I was sleep walking."

"Sure you were," said Eunice McKim.

"Is there anything further we can do to increase your comfort, Mrs. Beckman?" said Fletcher.

"Pour me one more whisky."

Fletcher glanced at McKim who nodded and held the crystal glass while her colleague plied the decanter.

"More," said Ruth from the bed.

"I think that'll be enough to knock you over," said McKim.

"I can sleep all day tomorrow. He won't be here."

"A long lie-in will do you good."

"Better?" Fletcher said, as McKim gave the glass to her mistress who accepted it in both hands and sipped the liquor as if it was Ovaltine.

"Fine now," said Ruth. "You won't lock the door, will you?"

"Of course not," said Fletcher again.

"Will I sit with you?" asked Eunice McKim.

"No, Eunice. Honestly, I'm okay."

"We will withdraw, in that case," said Fletcher.

"I'm so sleepy."

"Tomorrow afternoon we'll all have a nice walk in the park."

"Yes, Eunice."

"All right now?"

"Yes."

Decanter in hand, Fletcher led the older woman to the door of the bedroom. She switched off the ceiling fitment leaving soft lamplight to console her mistress. Somnolently Ruth watched the pair from the bed. She slouched down against the pillows, glass in two hands.

"Nightie-night," said McKim.

"Good-night, Madam," said Fletcher.

"Don't lock the door," said Ruth.

She listened and, after a moment, heard the key click in the lock. She nodded to herself; it was part of the plan, *her* plan. She had conned them into doing exactly what she wanted them to do. She was alone now, would not be disturbed. They thought she was a child, stupid, brainless, a nitwit, a jughead. She would show them. She laid the almost full glass of whisky on the bedside table, turned back the clothes and got out of bed. She crossed to the little white dressing table, ignored her reflection in the mirror in case she might find it reproachful, and opened the 'lace' drawer in the bottom left pedestal. She took out the tiny silver box, hardly larger than a half-crown, and beautifully engraved with vine leaves. She enclosed it in her fist. She closed the drawer with her knee and returned to the bed, got in and drew the bedclothes tightly around her. She opened the box and placed it very carefully in the hollow of her lap.

She lifted the whisky and swallowed a mouthful, hesitated for an instant and then, with a smug little smile, wetted her finger and dabbed it into the chaste silver pill box.

She would not be disturbed until noon.

By noon it would be too late.

Damn them, damn him; by noon on Saturday she would be gone.

* * *

Saturday morning was the busiest segment of the week in Maurice Beckman's office. The boss would arrive early and rip into all the extraneous paperwork that had accumulated during the preceding five days. Casually dressed in sports jackets, flowered dresses and fancy hats – and not seeming like themselves at all – the staff responded to Mr. B's enthusiasm, and the imminence of forty-five hours of freedom, by tearing in too in an attempt to clear their desks before twelve-thirty. On the stroke of the half-hour, Mr. Beckman would throw open the door of his private office and, like the starter of a race, personally sound the gun. Putting aside dignity for a moment or two he feigned the kind of eccentricity that his employees adored, vocalising the general excitement by shouting in his best big navvy's voice, "Down tools. Monday's another day. Everybody out. *Vite! Vite!*" Strolling the corridors, flinging open the doors of side offices, he barked at the tardy and, grinning, wished them all a pleasant weekend. Within minutes, nobody remained on the premises except Mrs. Frobisher and Miss Grubb, senior secretaries who would tidy up the correspondence, bring it to Mr. Beckman's office and often sit with him and drink a glass of sherry just to show that they were privileged and above the common ruck. Then they would leave too and Maury would have the place to himself, quiet and calm and strange, while he read and signed non-urgent mail or puttered among the desks and drawing boards, more like a janitor than a magnate, before going off for a late lunch and a stroll through the bookshops of the Charing Cross Road.

But not that particular Saturday.

Mrs. Frobisher and Miss Grubb were just leaving when Stan Nuttall arrived.

With pleasant courtesy Maury saw his 'invaluable ladies' to the office's main doors and had opened it for them when Stan Nuttall came quickly out of the elevator. With a shade more haste than was polite Maury got the secretaries away, brought Stan into the office and closed the door.

Stan did not beat about the bush.

"It's Ruth, your brother's wife."

"What about her?"

"Tried to do herself in."

"Tried?"

"I got a doctor friend round at the 'ouse now. Pills, she took; pills an' whisky."

"How bad is she?"

"I reckon she'll pull through okay."

"Thank God for that!"

"I want you to come round to Vallois Street."

"Did Ritchie send you?"

"Ritchie's in France; I dunno how to reach him."

"I assume your tame doctor will transfer Ruth to hospital."

"Not," said Stan, "a good idea. It was an accident, see."

"But you just said she took pills, tried to . . ."

"An accident, Maury; pills an' whisky; no hospital, no enquiries, no fuss an' bother."

"What the hell's going on here, Stan?"

"Your brother, he's doing his wife in, slowly, inch by inch."

"*Poisoning* her?"

"Nah, killing her by neglect. It ain't really a doctor she needs, Maury. It's a friendly face."

"I hardly know her. Why don't you send for her mother?"

"Her mother wants nothin' to do with her, and her father's a sick old man. He had a stroke last year, apparently."

"Holly then; Holly knew her, a little."

"I tried Holly; she's out of town. Not even her husband could say where," Stan explained. "Come on, Maury. Do the kid a kindness."

"I don't want to meddle, Stan."

"I've a car right outside. Twenty minutes, half an hour; just to show the kid somebody cares. Say you'll come."

"All right, damn it, all right."

*　　*　　*

"Who . . . who are you?"

"Maury Beckman. I'm Ritchie's brother."

"I . . . I remember. I met you once, in your uniform. You were a soldier."

"Too true," said Maury. "How do you feel now?"

"I fell asleep."

"What did you take, Ruth?"

"Nothing."

"I . . . we know it was a mistake. What was it?"

"You'll tell Ritchie."

"Not me. It'll be our secret. What was it?"

"Nembutal, to help me sleep. I drank some whisky too."

"Should be more careful," said Maury. "Got to be with sleeping pills. Promise me you won't do it . . . be so careless again."

"Ritchie . . ."

"Seems he's in Paris. He'll be home soon."

"You won't . . ."

"No, no."

"I just wanted to sleep, to have a nice long sleep."

"Well, Ruth, you were lucky," said Maury gently. "Nearly a very nasty accident. The doctor's been and he'll call again tonight but he seems to think you're well out of danger. Do you remember his visit?"

"Yes . . . I . . . think . . . so."

"You'll be all right now, Ruth."

"Don't go. Please don't go."

"You won't be alone. Your maid's here, the house-keeper; Stan, too."

"But they'll tell Ritchie."

"Ritchie'll have to be told."

"*You* tell him, Maury. Tell him the truth."

"I have to push along."

"No, no. Stay with me Maury."

She was tiny in the large bed, face pale above the coverlet. Her hair was damp with perspiration, her huge eyes swimming with panic and a reluctant sleepiness. She struggled to free an arm, reached out and sought blindly for his touch.

Maury covered her hand with his fist.

He was moved by her frailty and drawn to her through a fusion of pity and unexpected desire. In her vulnerability there was still a trace of enticement. Deliberate or innate, it made no matter. Maury was conscious of it. Her need of him was complete – and double-edged. She made him feel strong.

He squeezed her hand.

The girl sighed.

"What'll we talk about?" Maury asked.

"The old days," Ruth said, and closed her eyes again.

*　　*　　*

Inevitably the Beckman brothers met soon after Ritchie's return. Maury had stayed with Ruth until late on Saturday evening. He had called again on Sunday afternoon when he had persuaded her to eat a little chicken soup and, later that evening, a couple of crêpe suzettes that he personally whipped up in the gleaming kitchen. To enter the kitchen at all he had to trample over the housekeeper's vehement protests and let it be known, in no uncertain terms, that when he was around no bloody servant was going to set the ground rules. Though this situation was not of Ruth's making, not directly, she stood at the heart of it and Maury's masterful disregard for the rules of the house had a flamboyance that contrasted with his usual civilised manner; what was more, he found it refreshing, found that it stimulated him and made him feel youthful once more. When he returned to Ruth, he was rewarded by her admiration, touchingly and innocently displayed, a primitive female response to the protective male. Maury was not completely carried away; he knew more or less what was going on. He enjoyed the novelty, wistfully, ruefully, but with a pinch of self-deprecation that kept the knightly analogy from becoming, as yet, too serious.

Stan Nuttall hovered in the background. He confined himself to the living room, however, stationed there like a warden, straining his ears to hear what was going on in the bedroom, though he knew that it was nothing more corrupt than the drinking of chicken broth and the nibbling of crêpe suzettes. Stan's anxiety was palpable but he did not choose to explain how things stood between his employer and his employer's wife. Maury, he reckoned, had enough experience of the world to interpret things for himself. Maury asked Stan no questions, ignored the servants and spent hours alone with his sister-in-law. Clearly, Ruth was in desperate need of somebody, not only to talk to but to cling to. Who better than Maury? Never in a hundred years would he be Ritchie's man.

Leaving Sunday, Maury committed himself to a promise that he would come round again 'after work' on Monday. Being honourable, he kept his promise faithfully, though instinct told him that Ritchie would be back and he would be stepping into the very relationship he had sought to avoid.

Ritchie opened the door to him in person.

"Maury, Maury, me old son. When Ruth told me you said you'd come, I knew you would." Ritchie reached out for his brother and wrapped his arms around the passive bear-like man as if there had been no hostility between them and only circumstances had kept them apart for so long. "Maury, Maury! My God, do you look well. Affluent. The extra weight suits you. Come upstairs. Give Eunice your coat. Come on. Ruth's waiting. Kind of you to step in, give 'er moral support. You can always count on Maury, I told her."

"How is she?"

"Better, much better. She'll be joining us for dinner."

"I can't stay."

"Course you can. You've gotta. Ruth'll be so disappointed. She's been lookin' forward to it. She says you've only seen her at her worst. Tonight she's gonna look her very best."

"Should she be out of bed?"

"Talked with the doctor. Good feller; very understandin'. Nembutal tablets an' whisky are a bad mix, Maury. My fault. I blame myself for leaving her alone when she was below par. She hasn't been sleepin' well lately; has nightmares. That's how it happened. We figured it out. She'd had a nightcap – a drop too much, you know how it is – took pills, woke up, forgot what she'd taken, took more. I thank my lucky stars I had the active content in those prescribed tablets halved."

"You what?" said Maury.

"Changed the refill prescription. Hate those damned happy pills. I wouldn't 'ave them in the house, if Ruth didn't need them from time to time. Better safe than sorry, I thought. Halved the dosage."

"Just in case?" said Maury.

"In case of accidents," said Ritchie. "And right I was. Thank God I did take that wee precaution. Otherwise . . . it don't bear thinkin' about."

"Did Stan manage to contact you?"

"Couldn't. I was travellin'." The slovenly Lambeth accent dropped suddenly as if, now that he had made a link with their boyhood past, there was no need for it. "I had a lot of folk to see this weekend. Business, you know."

"Advertising? In France?"

"Advertising's only one of my interests," said Ritchie. "Say, you really *do* look well, Maury. Health okay? Fit?"

"Perfectly, thank you."

Ritchie had changed little. He was the same handsome, affable scoundrel that he had always been in spite of the tailoring and the smooth fleshiness that good living had imparted. In maturity he had learned to mask his inherent slyness so that his bonhomie seemed – almost – genuine. For a fleeting moment, however, as the Beckman brothers paused in the quiet carpeted alcove outside the dining area, Maury was possessed of hatred and rage; it welled up from hidden pools of uncertainty. Because of Ritchie, Holly had lost a husband, young Chris a father and they had all lost Grandpa Tal, bulwark of the Beckman family. Maury could not prove that Ritchie had deliberately evaded vengeance intended for him by thrusting it on to the family's shoulders. It may, after all, have been an accident.

For Ruth's sake, Maury was willing to give his brother the benefit of the doubt, something he would not have done a week ago. The anger waned and died.

Candles were lighted at the dining table, a plane of black glass floating on stainless steel legs. Fine plain Finnish china plates and cutlery were set round pretty painted cork place mats; simple, expensive, and a far cry from the kind of vulgar opulence that Maury might have expected from his gangster brother. Maury did not altogether care for the rigid, hard-edged geometry of 'modern' décor. Even the woman, standing by the little bar that flanked the dining area, lit by a hidden strip above her, seemed to have been pared down to

203

match Ritchie's ascetic concept of domestic elegance. Ruth was as pale as a candle in the classic chic of an Augusta-Bernard evening dress of black velvet, her short hair lustrous, her cheekbones brushed with rouge. It required only a spark of life to make her ravishingly beautiful and, when she saw Maury, that spark was struck. Her dark baleful eyes lit with delight.

"You came, you came."

"Of course he did. Our Maury never broke a promise in his born days," said Ritchie.

"Feeling better, Ruth?" said Maury.

"Much, much better."

He was conscious of Ritchie, behind him to his right, as he crossed the corner of the dining area to the bar and, as he would have done with any woman, took Ruth's hands in his and leaned to kiss her cheek in greeting.

"There now," Ritchie said. "Isn't that nice."

And Ruth, still smiling, whispered into Maury's ear, "Help me. Please help me."

Minutes later, armed with drinks, they seated themselves at the steel and glass table to eat dinner like any normal family.

*   *   *

Between the baked pork tenderloin and the coconut parfait, Eunice McKim's best dishes, Ruth fell asleep at the table.

"Shouldn't she be put to bed?" said Maury.

"No, she'll just have a bit of a nap and waken up in time for dessert," said Ritchie. "It's the wine; always makes her dozey."

"Ritchie, it's none of my business . . ."

"You're right, Maury; it isn't," said Ritchie. "How was the meat?"

"Just right," said Maury.

"More wine?"

"Not right now," said Maury. "You still haven't told me what you do in France?"

"Boring old import, export," said Ritchie. "Got something else to discuss with you, something a damned sight more

204

interesting than my business."

"You mean Leo; Pa."

"Hey, you know about it?"

"If you mean, do I know about his matrimonial intentions, the answer's yes."

"What do you think, Maury?"

"Won't do him any harm."

"Have you met the fancy woman?"

"Nope. Have you?"

"Nope."

"I assume, though, he's put the bite on you?" said Maury.

"It's too good an opportunity for the old scrounger to miss," said Ritchie.

Ruth sighed, settling her chin on her chest. She slept upright in the chair, hands on her lap. She looked, thought Maury, like one of Holly's finer examples of eighteenth century clockwork with the spring wound down. He brought his attention back to Ritchie. He could relax just a little when they talked of Leo, for Dad was a problem for both of them, one thing that they could share. Ritchie had never traded on his position as Leo's blue-eyed boy. He treated Leo with affectionate, almost whimsical scorn, an attitude that was unique to the father-son relationship.

Ritchie said, "What did he ask you for?"

"Shares."

"Holy Cow! What the hell does old Leo know about shares?"

"I think," said Maury, "that his light o'love's the motivating force behind the request."

"A golddigger?"

"Perhaps," said Maury. "Charitably, though, she may only be protecting herself – and you can't blame her for that."

"How did she meet him?"

"No idea."

"Sally Ann activities and Leo don't seem to go together."

"Hallelujah – and into bed," said Maury. "Don't laugh. I really do think the initial attraction was sex."

Ritchie laughed, wheezing. "The old cock sparrer's last fling?"

"Point is, we're paying for him anyhow," said Maury. "Holly and I have . . ."

"*You* have; so have I."

"Regularly?"

"Every six months."

"Why?"

"He's my old man. I thought, well, I figured you pair'd abandoned him. Can't say I blamed you. Hell, it was guilt," said Ritchie.

"Thicker than water?"

"Geeze, Leo must be living like a bleedin' lord."

"Steak and chips three times a day," said Maury. "The point is do we give him what he needs by way of a dowry?"

"Dad's dowry," Ritchie wheezed again. "Oh, God, that's rich."

"What did he ask *you* for, by the way?"

"A house, no less. Retirement-type bungalow in Bournemouth or Eastbourne. The locale don't matter, apparently."

"That's Cissie talking, for sure," said Maury.

"Will she, or won't she, still be around in five or six years when Pa's ready to be tucked into a wheelchair and trundled along the prom, fed his bleedin' booze with a warm spoon – that's the rub, Maury; right?"

"Right."

"You don't like the old bugger, do you?" Ritchie asked.

"No," Maury admitted. "I never did."

"Well, I suppose I do – kinda," said Ritchie. "I just don't want him hanging around me. Rather preserve my fond memories at a distance."

"Do we pay up?" said Maury.

"After we meet the bird, not before."

"Draw up terms, you mean."

"Let's see if she's willing to take him off our hands, permanently."

"It's a bit cold-blooded, Ritchie."

"Wasn't our idea, Maury. Pa cut the rope an' picked the tree himself, remember. Still, neither of us is short of a bob or two. What say we indulge him one more time?"

"Why not?" said Maury.

"Will our Holly chip in?"

"I doubt it."

Spite flickered in Ritchie's expression but he censored the acid remark that burned on his tongue; the bitterness he still harboured towards Holly was a remnant of petty jealousies that not even he could properly unravel now. He kept silent, smiling, but the mood of rapport between the brothers had been subtly dissipated and was not restored that night.

A moment later the cook brought in dessert and Ruth wakened from her nap.

She yawned and put her hand to her mouth. "Oh, God, Maury. How rude of me," she said.

"No need to apologise, sweetheart," said Ritchie. "Maury's family. He understands."

"Do you, Maury," the woman anxiously enquired. "Do you really?"

And Maury answered, "Yes."

*　　*　　*

November's first hoar frosts rimed London. Fog loitered all day along the flanks of the Thames, skulking in passageways and culs-de-sac and, when noon passed and morning yielded helplessly to early dusk, turned not Windsor brown but moleskin grey flecked with tiny grains. To Kennedy it seemed an age since he had returned from Torquay, but the calendar told him it was only a matter of weeks since he had basked in the late summer sun and watched Chris, lithe as an eel, bathe in the sea. Now summer had slipped away and the city held him like a dry memento in a casket of ebony and ivory.

The coal fire, gleaming brass and all the amiable clutter of Emma Chubb's parlour should have cheered him, but did not; it too was a seedy pavilion of memories. Even Emma, dishing out tea and buttered muffins, looked heavy and unhealthy as if she had indulged herself too often from the silver cake stand. Kennedy could not help but compare dear Emma with himself, noting how her buxomness had become obesity, her whirligig energy a kind of fussiness. She was bound by the friendly details of four o'clock tea, a victim of habit who responded to every tiny trivial deviation from the rite with peevish irritation; the butter was too creamy, the raspberry jam too thin, the chocolate not dark enough. Throughout she *tsked* and *tutted*, while Kennedy sat in a mustard-coloured wing chair, eating remorselessly and assuring her that everything tasted good.

At length, when Emma held out a bitten eclair and complained that the cream was 'off shade', even Kennedy could stand it no more and asked sharply, "Emma, what is wrong with you today?"

She placed the offending eclair in the centre of her tea plate and nudged it with her finger this way and that like the hand of a clock. Tears welled in her eyes.

"Is it Simon?" said Kennedy, embarrassed. "Is it because his wife's unwell and he's been out of circulation for so long?"

"His wife's been unwell for twenny years."Emma tugged a handkerchief from her sleeve and dabbed her nose with it. "She's a hypochondriac. Oh, I mustn't be catty. Whenever Lizzie thinks she's being given too short a stick she has a 'bit of a turn'." More work with the hanky helped Emma avoid Kennedy's puzzled stare. "It's supposed t' be her heart. I suppose it *is* her heart. Used to envy Lizzie, being Simon's legal wife, having his children, lookin' after his house. But I'm not sure any more. I think maybe I got the best of it after all. I saw as much of him as she ever did, maybe more. The shop's still where *his* heart lies."

"Emma, what's bothering you?"

Now she lifted her head. "Don't you know, Kennedy?"

"I . . . No, I don't know."

"Oh, *hell!*"

"Tell me, Perhaps I can help."

"You know me, Kennedy; old gossipy Emma. I love scandal. Allers have. Whissy-whissy-whisper. Something to talk about. But this time it's too close to home. Simon, you and Holly are my oldest friends; my family. I *hate* this. I *hate* havin' to be the one."

Kennedy sensed what was coming next. He put down the

teacup and saucer. Gossiping was a habit with Emma, as ingrained as the tea ritual. Generously she regarded herself as his friend. Had she weighed her loyalties before inviting him here today? Sympathetically he said, "Better you tell me than another, Emma."

"You do know?" she said.

Kennedy said, "I can't be sure until you tell me."

Resting his head against the chair wing, he regarded her cautiously.

Emma leaned forward, whispering in spite of herself; his hurt might hurt her too but it was still gossip. "I'd never have brought myself to say a blessed word, Kennedy, but it's the absolute God's truth, and it's serious. I mean, if I'd thought she was just flirtin'. . ."

"Holly isn't like that."

"No, no, you're right, she ain't. That's why I've gotter tell you. She's . . . she's, you know. With the dancer. The American."

"Freeman."

"Yer. You *did* know, didn't you? You had an idea?"

Kennedy nodded.

"You're her husband, Kennedy. Holly's my friend an' I hate to see this happen, but you've been my friend for – what – thirty years. I hadda tell you the truth."

"Is she sleeping with him?"

Kennedy's bluntness was almost too much for Emma. She started and drew back. "'Course she is."

Kennedy said, "How did you come by your information, Emma?"

"From Bobbie Oliver; you know him, don't yer?"

"The chap who collects Chinoiserie, the barrister?"

"That's him. He has a flat in that splendiferous new block in Holland Park Place. Freeman rents the flat next door."

"Who told you this?"

"Bobbie Oliver did. Holly's there often. Last Wednesday night, for instance, Holly wasn't home, was she?"

"She went to call on Lady Clare in Lincoln. She stayed overnight."

"Did she sell 'er Ladyship anythin'?"

"I really couldn't say."

"Did you ask?"

Kennedy answered, "No."

"But you 'ad suspicions?"

"I may have had."

"An' you didn't even ask her to explain?" Emma said. "Kennedy, she's your bleedin' *wife*. Don't you *care*?"

With great concentration, Kennedy extracted his cigar case from his vest, eased a cigar from its holster and lit it.

Emma ate the remaining half of her eclair, snapping it down in one mouthful, chewing angrily. She was mad at Kennedy's passivity. Why couldn't Holly King settle for what she had? God knows, if she, Emma, had ever pulled in the kind of billet that Holly King had she'd have offered up prayers every blessed night. Emma had not the wit to realise that she viewed Holly now across a chasm of years, through a distorting fog of age, that Holly was not yet old enough to 'settle' comfortably, to abrogate decisions, deny her right to change. Holly now was as Emma had been before the muffins and the port, the Dover sole and eclairs, before the pace of the years slowed her body and her mind.

Emma identified with Kennedy. She could no longer empathise with Holly Beckman King.

But Kennedy could; he had not forgotten, even in late middle age, what kindness was and compromise and how all that came to you, given or wrested, could not be denied to others. How unfair, how intrinsically selfish that would be.

He contemplated the coal of his cigar.

Comfortably.

Emma lost all patience. She tossed her handkerchief at him and thrust herself to her feet, crying. "What about what you done for 'er, takin' 'er on when she was strapped? You deserve better'n this, Kennedy. What about what you done for 'er?"

"I prefer to recall," said Kennedy, "what Holly has done for me."

"What – apart from makin' you money?"

"Made me happy."

"What'll you do, now she don't make you happy?"

"That hasn't changed, Emma," Kennedy said. "I'm in much the same position as Lizzie Black, I suppose."

"That's dif'rent."

"Not so different," said Kennedy. "I wish, of course, that it had never happened; that Holly and Freeman had never met. But Holly's no tart, Emma. She's in love with Freeman."

"An' love makes it all right?"

"I don't know. Perhaps it does. We know what obsession is, Emma, you and I? We've seen so much of it in our business. Desire. Need that quickly expires."

"But what d'you intend to do about it?"

"At all costs avoid a confrontation."

"You . . . you . . . you *coward*."

"I will not risk losing what I have," said Kennedy. "I'll accept what Holly is willing to give me and be grateful for that. If that's cowardice, very well, Emma, I admit that I am a coward. But what else can I do? Throw her out?"

"Why not, tell me?"

"Because what would I have left? Nothing. I'll take Holly on *any* terms. I'll share her with Freeman, because there's always a chance she'll get over him, and come back to me. Completely back to me."

"I never heard the like!"

"Perhaps that's because you've never spoken with Lizzie Black." Kennedy got to his feet. "I'm grateful to you for bringing the matter to my attention, Emma. I mean it sincerely. It must have been difficult for you. But it's my affair . . . I mean, my concern now."

Emma placed her hands behind her, palms flattened against her broad beam, like a washerwife.

"It's the boy, isn't it? You're afraid of losin' the boy?" she said.

"Very," Kennedy admitted.

"So that's the truth at last?"

"Yes," Kennedy told her. "Chris comes first."

"He ain't even yours."

"Oh, yes," said Kennedy. "No matter what happens, Chris will always be mine."

211

3

Madonna on the Rocks

Rehearsals had taken their toll of Peter Freeman. He had shed eight or ten pounds from his already lean frame during the arduous weeks in the Mayhew's basement and on its cold morning stage. Now he was nothing but sinew and bone, though he cheerfully claimed to be still a couple of pounds short of his 'fighting weight', excess ounces that the nervous strain of final run-throughs would remove. Unclad, Peter was a different person, his ethereal lightness and man-about-town dash replaced by earthy athleticism. He had a proud concern for his body. In the apartment in Holland Park Place he would sit crosslegged on the bed like a yogi and perform stretching exercises, unashamed of his nakedness. He was not showing off, merely 'working'. By neglecting to preserve his stage persona, the mystique of 'immaculate man', Peter had drawn Holly into his private world, a sphere so divorced from the gleam of theatre-land that Holly might have been the lover of two distinctly separate men. She was more comfortable with the Holland Park Peter whose vitality was not choreographed, whose charm was unforced, than with the public personality.

Deceit did not shadow their hours together; the secrecy was enjoyable. Holly did not flinch from weaving fabrications to explain her prolonged absences from the Gallery and her Chelsea home. What hurt her more than the lies was the ease with which Kennedy allowed himself to be deluded. It did not take her long to realise that Kennedy was aware that she was having an affair and, passively, condoned it. As winter deepened and she spent more and more time with Peter, Kennedy continued to swallow every excuse. He made no enquiries that might trap Holly in a lie, risked no conversations that might prove embarrassing. The tension that stretched their marriage close to breaking point was created not by guilt, suspicion and anger but by mutual fear of a final, irrevocable exposure of the truth.

Holly knew her husband so well. She could read into his brooding, courteous silences not so much concern about the present, unpleasant though it was, but fear of the future. He was too old, really, to cope with change. The loss of Holly at the core of his life would make his comfortable routines seem arid. For the business, and Holly's role in it, Kennedy spared hardly a thought. No more did Holly. Cavalierly, they dismissed the business as being capable of looking after itself. A similar attitude applied to Chris. Though Holly loved him deeply, he no longer occupied her thoughts. Since he had gone to St. Justin's his hold over her had slackened. Chris was a man's man, wrapped up in a young man's interests. In three years or four, he would hardly need her at all. She had done what was best for him, and could do no more. Through determination and self-sacrifice she had wrested her son from the poverty of a South London slum, given him all the advantages that money could buy, and a loving step-father. Could he expect more from her? Knowing Chris, he would be resilient enough to adapt. It disappointed her that he had betrayed no interest at all in art or antiques. Like his father, like David, he was obsessively wrapped up in sports.

She lay beside Peter in bed, watching him stretch his leg, his fingers kneading the hamstring muscles. He frowned, flexed, stretched again.

"Painful?" Holly asked.

"Tight. I guess I'm showing my age."

"Rubbish."

"Maybe I'll spray it again. It's only the right leg. I'm straining on the jumps, I reckon."

"It'll be all right, won't it?"

"Oh, sure." He abandoned the examination. "Howard arrives tomorrow. I had a cable this morning. He isn't exactly overjoyed at me being with you."

"How did he find out?"

"I told him."

"Does he think I'm taking your mind off your work, is that it?"

"You would believe, old Howard's a prude?"

"After all the girls he's pursued?"

"But not married ladies."

"Will he give you a hard time, Peter? Would you rather we stop seeing each other?"

"Hell, no. Howard's my manager, not my nursemaid."

"Doesn't he realise how discreet we've been?"

"No such thing as discreet in the theatre, Holly," he said. "Besides, I want you to come to opening night."

"Are you sure? I thought I'd just slip in quietly on Tuesday or Wednesday."

"Opening night – and the party afterwards."

"No, Peter,"

"All of you. Kennedy and your son, too. Will Chris be able to get time off from school?"

"I expect so, but . . . I don't know, Peter. I don't think I want to go through that kind of thing."

"I want you there."

"But Kennedy . . .?"

"Without your husband, it's going to look wrong."

"And with him, it looks . . . defiant."

"Please, Holly."

"What will Howard have to say to it?"

"I ask who I like," said Peter.

"Might be very awkward, though."

"It needn't be. Let me send you an invitation, a three seat special."

"Really, is that what you want?"

"Really."

*   *   *

Father and son kneeled together on the damp grass of the watermeadow by the banks of the river Quiddle, boundary of the school's sprawling grounds. There seemed to be nothing but space and air in the flat landscape, acres of grassland running to a line of stationed oaks that chopped up the vista of St. Justin's formidable towers. The most daunting aspect of St. Justin's was its architecture. Kennedy had chosen the school with care, eschewing reputation in favour of the relaxed atmosphere of a place where a boy's individuality was not trampled down by rigid discipline or slavish obedience to 'time-honoured' traditions; a far cry from the grey stone prison where Kennedy had spent three miserable years as a lad, smarting under philistine regimes, where parents were actively barred from visiting except in cases of emergency. St. Justin's had been a wise choice. Chris was happy here. His interests were encouraged, and, in consequence, his intelligence was not cramped by boredom. Chris was an excellent cricketer and a promising prop at rugby but was not as obsessed by them as he was by aeroplanes.

"You see," Chris explained. "The double strands delay the rate of uncoiling and feed power to the prop gradually. That's the trouble with rubber propulsion planes. They tend to go off with a swoosh and expend their drive in thirty seconds. Apart from which the strain on the wings is excessive. Wrecks them in no time. Do you know what this model is, Dad?"

"Frankly, old chap, I haven't a clue."

"It's a replica of a single-seater Albatross biplane. German."

"Is that what was in the kit I brought you last month?"

"Oh, no; that was a table model; the Schneider Trophy plane. It's up in my room. Didn't I show it to you?"

"I believe you did," said Kennedy. "Isn't that tight enough?"

"Almost." Chris held the model between finger and thumb of his left hand and stirred the balsa wood propeller with his forefinger. Chris's dexterity never ceased to amaze Kennedy who was almost devoid of manual skills. "There. Now I've got to hold it until launch. See."

Obediently Kennedy peered into the painted cockpit and saw the rubber bands curled taut below. "Who bought you this one, Chris?"

"Made it from scratch from plans in the B.O.P."

"*Boys' Own Paper*; must have been very detailed plans."

"They were. Not sound, though, really."

"Shall we try it?"

"It goes a treat."

"Careful of the river."

"Oh, she won't go near the river. She has a good directional stability, but a tendency to dip." He glanced round, neck craned, nostrils flared as if he could smell the breeze. "She should just about make it to the oaks – if we're lucky. Ready?"

"Fire away."

Gravely Chris positioned his body like that of a javelin thrower, glanced at Kennedy again to make sure he was watching, then, quite slowly, extended the plane forward through a rehearsed arc and, with a final thrust of the hand, released the propeller and steered the plane into the air. Rather to Kennedy's surprise, the Albatross performed no wild contortions but took off steadily enough in a straight line and climbed shallowly into the headwind. Stooped forward, hands on thighs, Chris watched the plane's flight, oblivious to everything else.

"She won't flip now," he said, nodding. "The wax tail-weight's steadied her up."

He straightened and, momentarily forgetful of Kennedy's presence, walked after the departing aeroplane jauntily while a companion, kite-flying several hundred yards away, waved and shouted to signify his appreciation of the successful weighting experiment. Chris waved back. Smiling, Kennedy followed his son at a respectful distance.

"Sorry," said Chris, stopping.

"That's all right," said Kennedy. "How will it land?"

"Badly," said Chris. "She always does. Ground landing's the only answer to that problem. Ground take-off, too. Need a petrol engine for that."

"A petrol engine?"

"We're not allowed to muck around with inflammable fuels, except under supervision at the Flying Class. Sensible rule, I suppose."

The plane had gone at last into a dithering curve that steepened as it lost thrust. It dipped abruptly and skidded wing first to the grass five or six yards short of the tree line.

"Not bad," said Chris.

"Looked excellent to me," said Kennedy. "I'd never have believed a rubber band would carry it so far."

"Two bands, that's the trick," said Chris.

They reached the plane together. A wing was broken, balsa shapes and painted paper destroyed, the stump crushed into the fuselage.

"What a shame," said Kennedy, with genuine concern.

"Happens all the time," said Chris. "Won't take long to repair. I should have brought down the Hanriot too and we could have had another go."

Tenderly the boy lifted the fragments of the Albatross and examined them while Kennedy resisted an impulse to put a consoling hand on the boy's shoulder. To him the partial destruction of the patiently-constructed craft was a disaster; to Chris, he realised, it was all part of the pleasure, a simple little hazard that could soon be put right, by glue and wire and paper; patience, knowledge and dexterity.

Then Chris said, "Why did you come down today, Dad?"

"Just to see you. Why?"

"You usually – you always – let me know in advance."

"Did it spoil your plans?"

"Heavens, no!"

"I felt like surprising you, that's all."

"I thought it had something to do with mother."

"What on earth gave you that impression?"

"Something I heard."

"Concerning your mother? You mustn't pay any attention to rumours, Chris. People can be unintentionally cruel when it comes to chit-chat."

"It isn't chit-chat, though," said Chris.

Kennedy changed position to obtain a better view of the boy's face, to see if there was hurt in his eyes. Thinking that his father intended to walk back to the school buildings Chris cradled the broken 'plane and set off. Kennedy fell into step by him. "What did you hear, Chris? What sort of thing?"

"Well," Chris appeared to be concerned with establishing facts, a recondite approach that reminded Kennedy of the boy's father, Deems. "Well, Frank Telfer's mother left his father. For a man in the wine trade, a sherry importer, I believe." Kennedy did not attempt to rush the boy to a conclusion. "Frank said it hardly affected him in the least. He sees both of them more often than he did before they parted. Has mother left you?"

"Of course not."

"But it's on the cards, isn't it?"

"Chris, will you be good enough to tell me . . ."

"Oh, yes, sorry. Telfer's sister lives with a chap. I don't think they're married, you know. It must be a very unstable sort of family, don't you think? Anyhow, the sister lives in Holland Park and she knows mother. Bought a Regency table from Kings'. I think it was Regency. Susan Telfer. You don't happen to remember her?"

"Not offhand."

"Telfer's sister says that mother often visits an American in a flat in Holland Park. I can't think of any reason why Telfer's sister would invent that kind of story, or why Telfer would pass it on if it wasn't true."

"Perhaps Telfer is jealous of you for some reason, and wants to hurt you. Could it be that, old chap?"

"Not Telfer. He's Upper School. Jolly decent sort. Quite concerned about it, actually," said Chris. "Is Mum . . . *has* she left you?"

"No."

"Do you know the American fellow; he's in the theatre? Freeman's his name. Telfer's sister knows quite a bit about it, really."

"I met Freeman last spring in Monte Carlo. He's in London to open in a musical show in the Mayhew; quite soon. He's a dancer."

"Yes, I . . . well, I looked him up in a *Playgoer*. One of the other chaps did, actually."

"What do you have here, Chris; a nest of budding detectives?"

"It is a small world," said the boy, "when you think of it. I suppose other friends of yours . . ." He cut off the question.

Kennedy saw how close they were coming to the long pavilion where a number of seniors were punting a rugby ball about, disgruntled because no match had been scheduled for that particular afternoon. He put his hand on Chris's shoulder now and held the boy back a little.

"Yes," Kennedy said. "Your mother has struck up a friendship with Freeman."

"Is she in love with him?" The question did not seem clichéd. Kennedy caught the taint of worldly inexperience there, the literary use of the word 'love', truth and euphemism innocently mingled.

"I suppose she might be," he answered.

"Hasn't she told you?"

"I'm sure your mother still loves us, Chris."

"Oh, yes!"

"Can you . . . do you understand that?"

"Being in love with somebody else; yes, Telfer explained."

Kennedy made a mental note to contrive a meeting with the Upper Schoolman, to assess his worth as a counsellor to young Chris. From what he could gather Telfer had not been salaciously taunting the boy but, as Chris had claimed, seemed genuinely concerned that the junior should not suffer too grievous a wound.

What surprised Kennedy was the equanimity with which his son accepted the news that his mother was involved with another man. In his days at school such a thing would have created an almighty stink and the poor abandoned wretch would have had to endure all kinds of torture, vicious slanders more wounding than knuckles in the neck. Obviously not all of Kennedy's fellow pupils had come from settled homes; not all parents were models of rectitude. But there had been such discretion, such reticence in those days that the child was always the last to find out.

Kennedy said, "I'm not altogether sure what your mother will decide to do, Chris. Whatever it is, she'll tell you in person."

"She mustn't worry about me."

"She probably will."

"No, Dad, you must tell her not to worry about me."

Kennedy said, "I'd rather not tell her anything about this conversation, Chris. I'd be most grateful if you didn't mention it to your mum, not in a letter or even by an inadvertent remark next time you're home."

"But haven't you talked about what's going to happen?"

"No."

"Oh!"

"You see, old chap, if I admit that I know what's going on, if I admit it, then I'll be expected to do something drastic about it."

"Kick Mum out of the house, you mean?"

"Yes, more or less."

"You wouldn't have to, though, if she didn't want to go, and you didn't want her to go. Would you?"

"It would create an impossible situation," said Kennedy. "It isn't easy as things stand, Chris, but under those circumstances it would become impossible."

"I understand. You can live together with the open secret. Is that it?"

"I must say, Chris, you're taking this very coolly."

"I expect I shall be all right. Telfer said he was."

"What . . . what will you do, have you thought?"

"Apply for a commission in the Air Force just as soon as I'm old enough."

The information had already been relayed to Kennedy and came as no surprise; Holly was disturbed by her son's unswervable dedication to flying machines but Kennedy saw how firmly rooted the enthusiasm was in Chris and tried to buy the boy a little peace by assuring his wife that the 'fancy' would pass in due course.

Kennedy said, "I didn't mean quite that, Chris."

"Ah, yes. Telfer told me that you might want to take me away from St. Jay's. Mother might want me to travel to America with her, if she goes off with Freeman. Would I have to do that, Dad? Would it be legal to take me away?"

"I don't know about the legal side of it, son. Perhaps – have you considered – perhaps you might enjoy living in America with your mum?"

"Unless I absolutely have to, I shall refuse to go. I don't want to live anywhere but here in England. With you."

"But if . . . what if your mother . . .?"

"It won't come to that, really, will it, Dad?"

For the first time a certain strain was apparent in the boy; a tremor in the voice, an uncertainty. Was it incurred at the prospect of losing his mother and the secure home that was built around her, or was it at the thought of being uprooted and packed off to a foreign country? Kennedy put his arm about his son's shoulder. He was thinking now of how Christopher Deems would have coped with this situation. Before the unimaginable stresses of trench warfare had sapped him of will, Christopher had been a fighter, a romantic warrior full of passion and pith – and he was young, would still be young, capable of satisfying that side of Holly's nature that had languished, that had not, after all, found lasting sublimation in running a gallery, in motherhood or in being wife to an ageing fuddy-duddy who, like one of his own antiques, had passed out of fashion.

"Will it, Dad?"

There was no ambivalence in the question. Chris needed reassurance, and devil take the squalid truth. Kennedy drew his son to him. The boy showed no embarrassment under the circumstances, even with his friends so close. He was too sensible to fear ridicule for demonstrating affection, father to son and – that too – son to father. He nudged Kennedy gently with his shoulder, as a pony will do, not to butt him away but to signal mutely that the gesture was welcome.

"It won't come to that, Chris," Kennedy said. "Not if I can help it."

"Am I old enough to choose?"

"I would think so, yes."

"Then I'd choose to stay with you."

"Are you sure?"

"We see eye to eye, Dad, don't we?"

"Chris, I'm not your real father, remember."

"To me you are. Yes, I'd want to stay with you. If you wanted me to. Would you – want me to?"

Only with a great exercise of will did Kennedy King hold

back his tears; it would have been too much, too expressively much to weep on this fourteen-year-old son's shoulder. He drew in a long breath through his nose and clamped his throat closed then, because he did not dare delay in giving his answer, and it was unequivocal, said. "Of course, old chap. Of course I'd want you to."

"That's settled then." Chris was relieved.

"Between us, at least."

"That's all that matters," said young Christopher Deems, man to man.

Damn it all, thought Kennedy with a stiffening of resolve, the boy's quite right; it is all that matters. If Chris is with me, I can stand up to a separation if I have to.

Much relieved by the talk, father and son put the awkward subject behind them and set off into school to find House-master Maitland who would give Chris permission to take tea with his Dad in the nearby town.

*　*　*

Maury preferred to think of his weekday call on Ruth as premeditated impulse. For four days, since the edgy dinner party, he had held his instincts in check. He was beginning to formulate a true, and rather astonishing, notion of why he was drawn into meddling in Ritchie's domestic arrangements. However much he pretended to be a dyed-in-the wool pragmatist, there was in him, as in most studied cynics, a streak of romance. He could not understand, however, why a girl like Ruth Beckman should attract him, in and of herself. Could it be nothing but pity? She was not quite so pathetic as she had at first appeared. It was surprising that she had survived the years with Ritchie at all, had managed to retain any vestige of individuality, however weak and selfish – for it was selfish – it had become. In the rich and pampered waif there endured a thin strand of the old toughness that Maury sentimentally identified with Lambeth and the girlfriends of his youth, girlfriends that ambition had left him no time to woo and that an unpleasant snobbery had finally sliced out of his thinking.

Though – obviously – he had liked, admired and enjoyed many women, he had never before found himself drawn to one with such irrational force. Magnetism? Or malice? How could he separate Ruth from Ritchie, unless by testing himself charitably against the latter in the cause of the former? What daunted him, and brought his intellectualising to a dead stop, was the suspicion that he would never have given a girl like Ruth a second glance if she had not been so entangled with his brother; in other words, that he was making of her a mere instrument of animosity. Beyond that nasty idea lay another, even more daunting; could it be that he was attracted to Ruth on simple terms of male-female desire?

To evade the issue, Maury mentally classified the call as a nice little bit of 'own back', the kind of petty needling that had made family gatherings in Lambeth so much fun, an abrasive sport that he missed out on in his present bachelor seclusion.

Besides there were wrongs to right. He had figured out the housekeeper and maid; it was not just loyalty and salary that made the pair so bloody good at their jobs. They wallowed in power. Their authority over Ruth was arrogant and cruel. It riled Maury more than any other factor. He began his preparations to surrender to 'impulse' as early as Tuesday morning when, casually, he set about clearing his calendar for Thursday, and, abetted by his secretaries, ensured that the day from noon on was 'free'.

Twelve twenty, he pulled the Humber up outside No. 44 Vallois Street and, mentally rolling up his sleeves, tramped up the path to the door. The housekeeper had not forgotten him. Like a duster passing over chalk, all expression wiped from her large square face.

Breezily, Maury said, "Good afternoon. I've called to see Mrs. Beckman."

"Mrs. Beckman's fine now, Sir."

"I'm delighted to hear it."

"Mr. Beckman isn't here."

"What's your name?"

"Pardon?"

"Your name, your name?"

"McKim."

"Very well, McKim, Tell Mrs. Beckman, that Maury's called to take her out to lunch."

"Out to . . ."

"I assume you *are* going to let me in?"

Icily, Eunice McKim said, "Step this way."

She kept him waiting in a downstairs lounge, a square room with a black carpet on the floor and a two-seater sofa in spotless white hide; nothing else, except four paintings, one on each wall, each lit by a spot. Maury recognised two of the artists instantly. A Gainsborough lady in a salmon pink dress stared into a Constable view of the Wye Valley. He got to his feet and examined the other canvases. Courbet? Strong, solid and awesomely Gallic, the nude looked as if she would have hair under her armpits and niff of garlic. And – surely not – a Rembrandt? a study of carcases hanging in an abbatoir, the texture so realistic that if you touched the surface suet would grease your fingertips. Ritchie's Paris connections fell into place. The sly little bugger was investing in art. Maury wondered if the paintings were genuine. Holly would know at a glance; Gainsborough, Constable, Courbet and Rembrandt – no rubbish for Ritchie.

The scrawny maid whisked open the door. Obviously she had been sent to calm him down. Not that he needed calming down.

"Madam has just arisen, Sir."

"You're Fletcher, right?"

"That is my name, Sir."

"Well, Fletcher, make sure Madam puts on her best togs; a nice fur, say, since it's nippy out."

"Madam doesn't feel up to luncheoning, Sir."

"Did Madam say that, Fletcher, or are you a mind reader?"

"Madam never feels too well first thing in the morning."

"A decent lunch in convivial company will soon set her up."

"Madam is . . ."

"Madam is going out, Fletcher. With me."

"But Mr. Ritchie's instructions . . ."

Maury changed tack. "Fletcher, old gal," he said; the

familiarity galled her more than insult, "do I look like an Arab slave trader, or the phantom rapist of Clapham Common? Your boss is my kid brother. Be a love, hop smartly upstairs and help Madam into her things. Got it?"

Fletcher gave a creaky bow; Maury could imagine enamel flaking off her backbone. She closed the door softly behind her. Maury sat on the white hide sofa, unbuttoned his overcoat, lit a cigarette, stared at the Wye Valley, and wondered why the devil his heart was beating so loudly.

Ten minutes later, the top gun arrived; Stan Nuttall, summoned from the Apex by McKim's urgent phone call.

"Hullo, Maury."

"Hullo, Stan."

"Fancy findin' you here."

"Fancy," Maury said. "What's next, the household cavalry?"

"She's better now, Maury. Leastwise Ritchie thinks she is."

"Meaning he doesn't want me calling on her?"

"Dunno about you," said Stan. "You might be okay."

"The prisoner has been returned to her cell," said Maury. "It was you who came to me, Stan, not the other way around. You told me – 'Not a doctor, Ruth needs; a friend.' Next time there's an 'accident' it might not be so easy to bury – or do I mean all too easy to bury."

"Listen, Maury," Stan said. "She's desperate. If you're kind to her, even with the nicest of intentions, it's a cert to get out of hand."

"Come off it, Stan. An occasional outing for lunch?"

"I'm the one Ritchie'll send to sort things out."

"Sort me out, that what you mean?"

"Walk away, Maury. You've done your bit for Ruth. You were there when she needed you. I'll keep you posted if you're concerned about her welfare. But right now, take my advice, toddle off."

"What if I don't?"

"Crossin' Ritchie can be risky."

"I know."

"Believe me, pal, you don't know the half of it."

"Tell that po-faced maid to help her mistress dress."

"Maury, I'm warnin' you . . ."

"I appreciate it, Stan. Now, unlock the poor bird's cage, will you?"

Stan grinned reluctantly. "So long as you know the score."

"Take it as read," said Maury.

Stan went out and Maury did not see him again that day.

Twenty minutes later, dressed like a bride in an all white ensemble and a hat with two little wings of feather above the ears, Ruth was brought to the room by Eunice McKim and sourly handed into Maury's care.

*　　*　　*

Seated in the tenth row of the stalls of the Mayhew Theatre, Holly felt like an interloper who had stumbled on the secret rites of an arcane society. Uncertain and conspicuous, she did not find the costume rehearsal of *Step Out Along the Strand* enjoyable.

Strained and fragmented, it seemed to reflect the current state of her life. If she hadn't known how much her presence meant to Peter, she would have slipped out and returned to work in the Chalfont Arcade. Half a dozen men and a couple of women were ranked in the rows ahead of her and off to one side sat Howard Crocker. Howard presented quite a different aspect of his character. No longer amiable and bumbling, he had greeted Holly with no more than a casual wave. His concern was for Peter, and the quality of the vehicle that he, Howard, had had built for his Broadway star. Sitting in the half dark, coat around her shoulders, Holly tried to fix her interest on the happenings on stage. Colourful costumes, clever make-up, ingenious sets; the music was, to her, thin and repetitive but – so Peter had told her – had four catchy numbers that would send the patrons away whistling. In spite of a natural apprehension about his own performance, Peter was confident that Ralph Brooks and Rosemary Case would 'on the night' exude the easy charm that would lift the mechanised production out of the rut and give it flow and sparkle. "That's what the reviewers will say," Peter predicted. "'Sparkles like vintage champagne.' I have to admit,

Brooks is some trouper." But Holly was not a fan of the elegant Englishman. She had eyes only for Peter. Even in the inhospitable atmosphere of his world, she experienced a soft slow yearning for him that was inexplicable in a clear-headed, twice-married business woman.

How far from the truth was the simple-minded story around which *Step Out Along the Strand* had been draped? Boy meets Girl? Peter in love did not really dance on the hammers of Big Ben or involve a gang of Irish roadmenders in a celebration of his happiness; Peter in love leased an apartment in Holland Park Place, went to bed naked, made love aggressively. What sort of people cherished the dream that the backers of *Step Out* had staked their money on? Most people, Holly supposed.

The massive curtain shivered. The orchestra conductor lashed his baton and cried, "*Crescendo, for Christ sake. Crescendo,*" audible even above the racket of the imperfectly dampened stage and the creaking of shifting scenery. The principals entered past a rabble of chorus boys and girls, too tightly packed for comfort. There was much unseemly pushing and shoving as Ralph, Rosemary and Peter got together for the last ebb and flow of the score. The curtain tumbled a half dozen bars too soon and, as if to correct its own error, promptly whisked up again to reveal the appalling disorder that, Holly gathered, was considered to be the essence of a full-dress run-through a week before opening night.

Roly-poly Hew Saracen stirred under his voluminous black overcoat and clapped ponderously, a laconic comment, while Benedict leaned over the rows and whispered with two younger men who, it transpired, were the authors of the book. Benedict got to his feet and hurried down the aisle to the rail of the orchestra pit. "Not bad, not bad, boys and girls. A trifle undignified, but we can rid it of the army barracks' look, I'm sure."

Ralph Brooks kneeled above the footlights. "Giles, let's do it again, please," he begged.

"No, I prefer to see the second act in sequence," said Benedict. "Twenty minutes to rest and change. The dressers are waiting for you."

"But it isn't *right*," said Brooks.

"I want sequence, Ralph," said Benedict. "Positions on stage in twenty minutes, please."

Ralph was overwrought and inclined to argue the point. Before he could make an ass of himself Rosemary and Peter engaged him in conversation, freeing Benedict to answer the orchestra conductor's urgent questions. The cast drifted off stage and stagehands in overalls attacked the set. Howard Crocker rose, stretched, ambled across the aisle and, to Holly's surprise, beckoned her to join him.

"There's . . . ah, tea upstairs," he said. "Shall we . . . hm?"

"Thank you," said Holly gratefully.

Hew Saracan's office was deserted. An oval beechwood table was surrounded by eight handsome beech chairs. A salver set with silver and china stood forlornly on it. Howard entered the room without hesitation but left the outer door open. Framed portraits and playbills covered the flock-papered walls. A pair of bronze busts on black marble pedestals flanked the empty fireplace. Plaques identified them as Emlyn Griffiths Saracen and Sir Andrew Dobbs Mayhew, partners in the founding of the theatre a century ago.

"Smell the history?" said Howard, pouring coffee.

"Don't I!" said Holly.

"Find it exciting?" He handed her a cup and saucer.

"Interesting rather than exciting."

"And the . . . ah, rehearsal?"

"It isn't what I expected it to be."

"Fair to middling," said Howard, "as these things go. You thought it tawdry, uh?"

"Mr. Crocker . . ."

"Call me Howard."

"Howard, what are you trying to say?"

"I . . . ah, uh . . . Peter's informed me of your . . . relationship."

"You don't approve, is that it?"

"Not up to me."

"I think I'm good for him."

"Don't doubt it."

Holly gave the man no help. He hardly seemed to need it.

Vagueness had been replaced by concentration. In Howard now Holly glimpsed the steely quality of the expert negotiator. He still spoke in a lazy drawl but there were no swallowed vowels, no bumbling pauses.

"May I be blunt?" Howard asked.

"Please, be as blunt as you like."

"You won't be insulted?"

"It's about Peter, isn't it?" said Holly.

"What do you want from him?"

"I'm not sure."

"Is Peter just an excuse to help you leave your husband?"

"No, he's more than that to me."

"Are you in love with him?"

"I'm . . . I'm not sure of that either."

"Holly, he'll hurt you in the long run."

"I'm aware of his reputation. It's hard to credit."

"Oh, no, Peter's not cruel, not deliberately cruel. But women expect so much of him, you see. I don't mean, *dans le boudoir.* I mean, they try to persuade him to belong to them."

"I'm not the possessive type," said Holly.

"That," said Howard, "is what worries me."

"Meaning?"

"Deep down, Peter's an honourable chap. Yes, yes, I know what the columnists have made of him but not all – very little – of the rubbish that's written is really true."

"Howard, are you 'advertising' Peter Freeman to me?"

Howard Crocker smiled wryly. "On the contrary."

"What are you trying to say?"

"Leave him. Now. Tonight. This week. Please."

"Are you jealous of my relationship with him? Perhaps you're the one who's possessive, Howard."

"I am, I am. Very possessive. Peter has a brilliant career ahead of him. Not to look past tomorrow, this particular show will run until doomsday – but not without Peter."

"I see," said Holly. "You're protecting your investment."

"Madam, that's not terribly nice," said Howard. "I care for Peter as much – more – than you do. But I'm in a better position than you are to know what's good for him; and, believe it or not, what's good for you too, Holly."

"And what's good for Howard Crocker."

Howard ignored the jibe.

He said, "Come summer, come hell or high water, Peter goes home to America."

"I know."

"It'll be over, then, anyhow. So decide now, Holly. Since you haven't done anything too drastic – squabbled with your hubby, that sort of thing – it isn't too late. You're not in love with Peter. You don't even wish to be in love with him – do you?"

"Perhaps not; I don't know."

"Break with him now, Holly. Pete's buoyed up and thoroughly occupied with the show right now. When he settles to the run, it won't be so easy on either of you."

"What if I don't want to break with Peter?"

"Then you must understand that you're risking the whole shootin' match; desertion, divorce, emigration . . ."

"Oh, hold on; it isn't that serious."

"Unless I've lost my judgment of character, Holly, this *is* serious. I don't pretend to understand how or why you two were attracted to each other . . . "

"That isn't hard to guess."

"Sure, all right; you're both . . . dynamic, but, Holly, Peter's falling in love with you."

"I doubt it."

"Believe me."

"How can you . . . Howard, surely I would know better than you?"

"Did you think you were safe with him, Holly? Is that it? Did you imagine you could safely have an affair with somebody who had no real feelings for women. Love 'em, leave 'em, damn 'em all, honey? All surface stuff? I think you're being more cold-blooded than any of the rich bitches that have chased after Peter."

"Because I loved him – without loving him? Is that just the prerogative of men?" said Holly.

"That," said Howard, "isn't worthy of you, Holly King. You don't mean it?"

Holly wetted her lips with the tip of her tongue. She could feel shame growing in her; Howard Crocker's candour, and his insight, had forced her to consider herself, to isolate herself from the situation that she had created and, at last, to examine what sort of woman she had become, and what endings that change would demand.

She was only too well aware that she had been wilful and self indulgent. She was not so swept away by Peter Freeman that she could not, at any point, have stopped it. But why should she? Because she was a married woman? Because Peter was a gadfly? What did the terms have to do with it? Condemnation was for others, for outsiders, those not included in the geometry of her life. How could others be expected to understand what she was and what forces had shaped her: David Aspinall's deceptions; Ritchie's ruthless and unmerited attacks upon her security; Christopher's love, Christopher's death? She had been hardened by these events and the tendons of her soul torn in ways that time could not heal and that the satisfaction of professional success could not soothe.

Now she saw how it was, how the affair had come about. Saw it as sharply defined as if Howard had turned a brilliant white spotlight upon her heart. *She had wanted to see if it was possible.*

No more, nothing more complex than that. She had wanted to discover if she had lost her capacity to attract, and be attractive to, a man who was not her husband. Peter was the ideal stranger; in all ways, he was not for her, nor she for him.

But now she had proved herself to herself, other possibilities had been opened up. An infinite number, a limitless variety. With sudden dread, she realised that she had perhaps begun to change into that which she had always been. Howard had been right. She had never believed Peter to be genuine. Howard, Maury, Emma, even Kennedy, how shabbily she had dismissed their disdain. She fell, in that instant, into a pit of dislike for herself, birched by all the uncertainties and fears that had haunted her girlhood. She had *pretended* to love Peter because he was himself a model of pretence, a romantic dream. In each of them the seeds of the lie had flowered and blossomed. Now – so Howard said – Peter was cheating again, deceiving her by falling truly in love.

Holly caught hold of herself.

She sounded icy, her words chilled by calculation. She despised herself for being unable to yield to Howard Crocker's honesty, to show him how much she regretted her rashness, that there was no ecstasy, only foolishness.

"Are you afraid that if I leave Kennedy for Peter, the scandal will harm his career?" she said.

"Lord, no. There's no scandal involved here, Holly. You're not a princess of the blood or anything wonderfully newsworthy. You won't do Peter much harm. Won't do yourself much good, though."

"Are you trying to warn me that there can be no half measures?"

"Pete's old-fashioned."

"What, Howard, if I were to tell you that there can be no half measures with me?"

"That means, ah, leaving everything."

"I'm aware of that."

Howard pursed his lips and made a series of small popping noises with his lips. "Holly, would you be happy, enough to make him happy?"

Holly understood Howard's anxiety. He was afraid that, cut off from England, in the brash society of the picture community, Holly would pine for all that she had sacrificed, and become a burden.

"I won't know until I try," she said.

Howard sighed. "In strict confidence, Holly, it's five months in the Mayhew then up and away to Hollywood. Six months at most."

Holly said, "I thought the show would run for at least a year."

"This show's only a springboard. I don't much care how long it runs."

"Does Peter know this?"

"Not yet awhile. In confidence, between you and me."

"When, Howard? When will Peter leave England?"

"Probably no later than June."

"If," said Holly, "I were to ask for your honest advice,

Howard, what would you recommend me to do?"

"Quit him right now."

"Peter wouldn't stand for it."

"Be adamant. You're tougher than he is, stronger."

"That's not true."

"'Fraid it is."

"What if I won't quit?"

"Let Peter marry you."

"I can't do that."

"You see?" said Howard. "You're creating your own, ah, dilemmas. You mean *won't*, not *can't*. Fundamentally, there's no problem. It's your choice. Leave Mr. King, let him divorce you, marry Peter and accompany him into realms of glory in sunny California, or wherever."

"Assuming that Peter wants me to."

"Peter will do what you wish, or rather what you give him an opportunity to do. When Peter finally departs these shores, I would prefer him to go clean."

"Clean?"

"With you as his lawful wedded wife; or with the whole, um, the thing over and done with. *Finito*. It is your decision, young lady. You must make up your mind soon. The legal process in England is as slow as a snail."

Holly placed the cup down on the salver. "If you're worried about Peter's reputation . . ."

"Fiddlesticks," said Howard. "I'm worried about his concentration, his performance, how he settles in Hollywood – which, Lord knows, is not the easiest place in the world for a talent to fulfil itself at the best of times – and about his, um, happiness"

"Do you think I would make him miserable?"

"If you were happy, he'd be happy. But *would* you be happy?"

"If I was with Peter I would be."

"Stardust, soft music and romance?" Howard said. "Marriage is the subject under discussion. Marriage to a man who will be a motion picture star. Guaranteed. Can you cope with it? Would it be too much, particularly when you remembered what you'd sacrificed?"

"Stop it, please," said Holly.

"Point made, uh?"

"Point taken," said Holly.

"You decide, young lady. Make up your mind. Peter will say . . ."

"What will Peter say?"

How long Peter Freeman had been in the doorway neither Howard nor Holly could be sure. He was no eavesdropper, however. His manner seemed to indicate no pique as surely it would have done if he had caught more than the final snatch of the conversation between his manager and his mistress. Costumed for his second act appearance in an ultra-smart golfing outfit, including a huge tweed cap, and already dabbed with pancake and greasepaint, Peter was amused by the fact that Howard and Holly had been discussing him. With a degree of curiosity, he asked, "What has Holly to make up her mind about?"

Quickly Howard said, "Whether to tell you that she didn't much care for the Big Ben sequence, or soap you."

"Is that all?" said Peter making for the tea pot. "The truth, darling; always tell me the truth."

"I found . . . I found the scene too contrived."

"Because you saw the mechanics of it," said Peter. "It'll work out fine by opening night. Howard, my rhythm, was it okay?"

"No flow," said Howard. "You *looked* as if you were dancing."

Peter absorbed the criticism soberly. He drank tea. "The length of the drops between the clock hammers is two, three inches too much for me."

"Well, tell Benedict that," said Howard. "Don't allow yourself to become a victim of the, um, set designer."

"I suppose I should mention it."

"I'll tell him."

Peter grinned. "I was hoping you'd say that."

"I'll tell him right, um, now."

Leaving Holly and Peter alone, Howard shambled out of the office.

"He likes you," Peter said.

"But he doesn't quite approve of 'what's going on'."

"He'll get over it. He's too used to having my undivided attention. 'T'aint right, Ma'am: T'ain't nat'ral.'"

"Some things are best left between a man and his manager," Holly said. "A mere wife should not intrude."

"Wife?"

"You know what I mean."

"Sure I do."

But she had found in his expression the answer, had evoked the truth with a single word. Howard had not lied. Peter *was* in love with her. He had slipped into it like a shadow, moving softly apart from himself. No longer could she shield her emotional aridity, water it with imaginative excuses. If Peter was falling in love with her, she was responsible for it and, with hurt in her heart, felt compassion for him. Why could it not have stopped with the pretence of love, with sex and compliments, perfume and champagne? With relief, Holly caught at another excuse – or was this the truth of it? – that she had not changed at all but had loved him all along, lacking not love's courage but only an explanation for it.

Peter laughed uncertainly.

"What's wrong with you?" he asked.

"Not a thing."

"Good. So, give me a buss on the boko, darling, but be careful not smear my make-up."

Carefully Holly put her arm about his shoulder and kissed him on the tip of his nose.

He held her, a little too tightly and a little too long.

"Well, darling?" he said1

"Yes," Holly said.

"I've got to get back now."

"I know."

"Is the Big Ben sequence really contrived?"

"A little," Holly answered.

"I'll work on it," said Peter, "first thing tomorrow."

"Not tonight?"

"No," Peter said. "Not tonight."

*   *   *

"Your trouble, Henry," said Ritchie Beckman, "is you got carried away by greed. I mean what the bloody hell did you think you could do with three religious panel paintings and a fifteenth-century statue? This gear isn't like Georgian plate. You can't boil it down on a gas stove. Look at it; inventory marks, catalogue numbers, Christ knows what, plastered all over."

Chastened and sheepish, Henry Loftus explained, "They was just a-layin' there in the room, 'andy size. Reckoned they was val'able."

"Well, Henry, I could lie to you and tell you it's junk. But I wouldn't do that to an old school pal," said Ritchie. "What you hoisted is fair quality. In Christie's you'd earn maybe five grand on it."

"Five grand!" Henry forgot to be embarrassed. He had a large ruddy face, a chin like a tombstone, and a chaplet of hair the colour of river sand. His glaucous blue eyes went slightly out of focus with excitement. "Five bleedin' grand!"

"But," Ritchie interrupted, "I suggest you take the loot out back, lash it with petrol and put a match to it."

"You just said it was val'able."

Henry was confused and his nether lip quivered as if he was about to dissolve in tears.

"I said you could sell it – them – at Christie's. You wanna do that, Henry?"

"Noah."

"What you're storin' here isn't five grand, pal, it's fifteen years in the pokey."

"The statue?" Henry pleaded.

"Silver parcel gilt."

"We could melt it."

"Drown it," said Ritchie. "Drop it off the bridge."

"What . . . what bridge?"

"Henry, for Gawd's sake," said Stan Nuttall. "Use yer loaf."

"Told me Ritchie could shift it."

"Yeah, who told you?" said Ritchie.

"Feller in the Feathers."

"What did he tell you, Henry?" said Ritchie.

"Ritchie was 'ome. Try Ritchie 'e says. Paintin's's Ritchie's meat, 'e says. I was a-asking', see, 'cause I knewed they was val'able but didn't want no hitch shiftin' 'em."

The old patois, the old smells of Lambeth, the umber air of damned-near a midwinter morning with a struggling sun caught behind webs of dust and dirt on the window frames; New Paradise Square, ground floor, the six-storey jailhouse quadrangle with its bricked-up ornamental fountain and the mainline to Waterloo earthquaking past so close to its southern flank you could lob soda pop bottles down the train stacks over the wall without getting out of bed; a hobby, come to think of it, that had had the local copper kicking on Henry's door pretty often in days of yore. And since those days things hadn't changed much in Loftus's Lambeth, just become more squalid and tougher, even though it was no longer Stan, Jeff, Henry and Ritchie that ran wild in the weedy court but Henry's kids. Henry's wife was a replica of Henry's ma, and Henry's middle son was the *real* Henry now, the way Ritchie saw him, an innocent, insolent marauder. Continuity struck no chords of sentiment in Ritchie's heart. He had no lingering love for Lambeth, for former mates like Loftus. Only the results of Stan's preliminary investigation of Loftus's offer, three smallish holy paintings on wood and a statue – plus the disquieting fact that a two-bit upper-storey man not only knew that he, Ritchie, was back in London but that he was into the art buying business too.

Ritchie did not want to confuse Henry. He came at the subject of Henry's source obliquely. "Where did you lift the stuff?"

"Posh flat in a mansion backin' Berkeley Street."

"Who put you in the way of the job; Vince Shotten?"

"Nah, Vince's retired, like. Geezer called Crowe. Yer won't know 'im. He's outa the East End. Does solo turns, mostly. I done jobs for Crowe for three, four years, like. Never 'ad no cause for complaint."

"Crowe's *kosher*," Stan put in.

"What were you after in Berkeley Street?" Ritchie enquired.

"Jools; small 'aul, old-style stuff; heavy ginger, though."

"You got them?"

"Yer, sure."

"And you hoisted the pictures on impulse."

"'Ouse was choc-a-bloc with holy junk."

"Did you let on to Crowe you'd taken art?"

"Wouldn't be Crowe's line. I kept 'ush about it. Asked round the 'ouses, like."

They were seated at a tiny table in the cramped kitchen of the Loftus house, the door closed. Pans simmered on the gas stove, burping out the odours of pea broth, cabbage and scrag. Against the pimpled orange distemper above the draining board sat the three paintings, quite at home, and a two-foot high statuette of a Madonna and Child on a throne of rocks. The art objects had a crude, primitive beauty and blended well with the peasant kitchen. Three or four centuries ago a guy like Henry Loftus would have eschewed the theft of such iconographic items. Even the twentieth-century Henry found the objects 'creepy'; he wanted rid of them as he might have wanted to disassociate himself from Egyptian artifacts drenched in ancient curses.

Ritchie reached into his overcoat pocket and brought out a wad of fresh banknotes bound with a rubber band. He unsnapped the band and began counting the notes, fivers, into piles of ten spread in front of him on the oilcloth of the tabletop. Henry's blue eyes followed the motion of every note.

Ritchie said, "Who was on the job with you, Henry?"

"The boy, just the boy."

"Your son?"

"'Arry, yer. Father 'n' son, like."

Ritchie recalled an early robbery in which the Beckmans, father and son, had worked together; the only thing was that Leo had been the apprentice, and a lousy one at that.

"Harry won't talk, will he?" said Ritchie.

"Not 'im. Can't getter word out of 'im, best of times."

Ritchie went on counting out five-pound notes. Four piles; two hundred quid. The sight of that new money, thus arranged, had distracted Henry's mind completely from

238

Ritchie's original estimate of the worth of the stolen goods. Ritchie put the wad away again and laid his gloved hands on the piles. Looking straight at Henry, he said, "I'm doing this because we're old mates, Henry. No other reason. I'm not in this business, whatever you've heard. You listenin'?"

"Yer, I'm listenin'."

"You got choices; you can sell the four items to me for cash, right now, or you can hawk them round the dealers and run the risk of getting nicked at it, or you can burn them, like you'd burn evidence. I take them, I take the risk."

"Gotyah, gotyah."

"I'm payin' you chickenfeed, Henry, because I gotta sell the paintings and the statue abroad. I have expenses, big expenses, in reworkin' them, shippin' them over, findin' the right buyers. Whatever, I have to hold them until they cool down, and that's capital tied up."

"Yah, yah, I gotyah."

"You made a decent draw in the jewels anyhow?"

"Fair."

"I'll give you two hundred," said Ritchie. "Stan and I wrap the stuff up and we carry it out to my car round in Mitre Street and you never see it again. You forget you ever heard of it, that we ever came here."

"Sure, Ritchie. Gotyah."

"But," said Ritchie, "I also want the name of the guy that put you on to me, so I can straighten him out on his facts. No name, no dough, Henry. You're stuck with the creepy pictures."

Henry stole a glance at the four faces of the Virgin on his draining board then, with yearning, at the fivers on his tabletop under Ritchie's steady fingers.

"Nice bloke," said Henry. "Met 'im round the Feathers. Knowed 'im for years'n'years, like."

"Who was it, Henry?"

"You really wanna know?"

"Sure I wanna know."

"Yer Pa," said Henry Loftus.

Ritchie gave the man the money.

*　*　*

Baggy-eyed and anything but spruce, Leo opened the door to the sound of the knocker. He had been asleep on the sofa and had heard nothing and if she hadn't called down to him he would have ignored the steady rapping even if he had heard it. He registered the fact that the tramp of the carpet-sweeper had ceased and tried to draw himself together as he made his way through the narrow hall to the door. He fastened the stud at his shirt collar, buttoned his flies and wiped his nose on his wrist. Tilting up his head, he opened the door.

Ritchie's black glove closed neatly over the rim of his collar and pulled him on to his tiptoes while the other black glove fastened round the nape of his neck. Without changing his hold, Ritchie scuttled Leo down the hallway while Stan Nuttall stepped into the house and softly closed the street door. Ritchie backed Leo against the wall so violently that a china duck, one of three, dropped from its hook and broke on the lino. Ritchie's tone was like a cat's purr, the voice of a tiger at its kill. "Now, Pa, what's this I hear about you advertisin' my business round the bloody public houses. The Feathers to name but one."

"Not," Leo gurgled, "me, slon."

"Name Henry Loftus mean anythin' to you?"

"Orr, yerr, Henly, slon. Old chlum. Ho halm'n tellin' Henly."

"Tellin' him what, Pa?"

"Easy, Ritchie," Stan murmured. "He can't breathe."

Ritchie slackened his hold on the collar and Leo smiled with all the warmth of a naphtha flare, a blind white smile.

"Henry 'ad somethin' in your line t'shift. Didn't do no more than tell 'im t' give you a buzz on the blower. All I done was put a bitta business . . ."

"Pa, Pa, what d'you take me for," said Ritchie. "I don't need the junk guys like Henry hook on to."

"Paintin's?"

"How did you know I was into art?"

"Yer letters."

Ritchie jerked his father from his guardsman's stance against the wall and pressed his forehead to Leo's brow, rubbed it, quite gently at first, saying "I should kick your ass

240

from hell to breakfast, Pa, really I should. I'm not into anythin' crooked. I run a respectable advertisin' service, is all. Right?" He rubbed a little harder. "Right?"

"Yer, yer."

"So you don't go braggin' about me, even raisin' my name. I don't need you to scout for me. I don't want you to scout for me. Right?"

More chafing, the hair abrasive on the bald brow.

"Right, Ritchie, right."

"Give folk the wrong ideas about me. Right?"

"Ri, ri . . ."

"TAKE YER BLEEDIN' 'ANDS OFF 'IM." The order boomed down the shadowy staircase and the leaves of the castor oil plant in its pot on the landing trembled. "HANDS OFF, THIS BLEEDIN' INSTANT."

Ritchie reacted involuntarily to the voice of authority by leaping back from Leo with his hands held low like a Dodge City marshall about to snatch for his guns. To protect his boss – to protect himself, perhaps – Stan stepped to Ritchie's shoulder. Both men stared in awe into the dim slot of the stairs from whence came that thunderous command.

"GET AWAY FROM 'IM, I TELL YER." *Basso profundo.* "HON-OUR THY FATHER THAT THY DAYS MAY BE LONG UPON THE LAND, SONNIE."

Cissie Moran descended the stairs one at a time, the Ewbank sweeper held by its handle hanging before her. She came down into the light step by step. A cotton pinafore printed with tulips, a brown wool dress that clung to her contours like a coat of shellac, 'a bloody dwarf' of four feet six, muscular as a Blackwall docker, with mahogany calfs and tiny feet in shiny brown shoes, like castors, breasts that overhung her torso like an eaves, an incongruously sharp featured face, and loose chestnut curls flecked with grey dangling from under a mopcap; Cissie Moran, the woman who was about to become a metaphor for the mummy he had never really known; Ritchie quailed.

"Don't yer know the Commandments, sonnie? Moses was a Jew." She stabbed the Ewbank down on the hall carpet with such force that another china duck died of fright and swung feet up on its wall hook.

Ritchie did not even have the wit to retreat.

She stalked up to him.

"So you're Ritchie, the great Ritchie?" she said, sizing him up and down. She stuck out one small muscular hand. Ritchie flinched. "I'm Cissie. You'll 'ave 'eard about me. I'm yer new mother."

She hoisted Ritchie's hand from his side and pumped it once, then turned her cheek to him so that he had no alternative but to bestow upon it a quick pecking kiss that signified submission rather than friendship.

Leo was still in the lofted position that he had been in when Cissie came to his rescue. He seemed as cowed as Ritchie by the woman's intervention, as if he was a collaborator in the breaking of God's ordinance concerning the behaviour of fathers and sons. Stan's mouth hung open.

"Who's this 'un. It ain't Maurice, is it?"

"S . . . Stan Nuttall; no relation," said Stan hastily.

"Thought not," said Cissie; she still had Ritchie by the hand. "Got good beef sausages. Very tasty, ain't they, m'love?"

"Very tasty," Leo agreed.

"Break bread?" said Cissie.

There was no reference to the bullying or the reason for it or to her own extraordinary introduction to her stepson-to-be. A lifetime in the service of the Salvation Army had trained Cissie Moran to react vigorously to wickedness but to go light on recriminations. Slum country was breeding ground of complexity and, unlike some of her colleagues, Cissie had long ago learned that simple black and white were no colours to fly under when it came to making war on sin.

"I . . . we've . . ." Ritchie began.

"'Ad dinner?" said Cissie. "Cuppa tea, then? Want a word with you anyhow. Leo, put kettle on. High gas."

Leo scuttled off and Cissie led Ritchie into the living room, gesturing to Stan to follow them.

"Coats off," she said. "You'll feel the need of them when you get out. Come by motor?"

"Yer," said Ritchie.

242

"I'll 'ang 'em up."

She was gone just long enough for Stan and Ritchie to exchange glassy-eyed stares. Leo stayed in the kitchen. Cissie was talking even before she came through the door from the hall again, minus the overcoats and hats. "Sit down." Stan and Ritchie perched on the edges of the sofa, side by side, like patients in a dentist's office. "Can we talk confidential in front of 'im? 'Course we can. Eh?"

"I'll . . . I'll wait in the . . ." Stan volunteered, eagerly.

"Sit," Cissie said. She took one of the chairs at the table and positioned herself like a docker in a public bar, elbows splayed. She had removed the pinafore. The wool dress was like a pelt, her bosom more intimidating than ever. "Ritchie don't mind his pal hearin' a little family talk."

Ritchie managed to nod. He was beginning to adjust, to settle, even to enjoy the challenge of the woman's belligerent self-assurance. He could see what old Leo saw in her, the didactic sexuality in back of her imperiousness. There was a kind of honesty to her, not naive but not grasping, that pleased Ritchie now that the first shock was wearing off. He listened with both ears.

"I'm gettin' on, sonnie," Cissie said, apologetically. "Me an' yer father, both. I know what you think. You think I gave up me principles for a meal ticket. Might 'ave thought so, too, if I'd been in your shoes. Sally Ann girl throws 'erself at well-to-do widower." Ritchie hadn't considered that aspect of it, the fact that there were principles involved; nor had it occurred to him that in the context of lowly Lambeth his father had become well-to-do, thanks to the generosity of his children. Cissie continued, "Got talked to by me Major, very stern. Sent ter Coventry when I wouldn't stop. But, well, I done all the good I can an' honoured me father while he was alive. God won't mind now."

"Sure He won't," said Ritchie.

"It's love, see," Cissie folded her arms. "Ain't it, Leo?"

"Right you are, dear," came Leo's obedient response from the kitchenette.

To Ritchie Cissie said, "Mutual. I never couldn't wed one of them dry devout ones. Be like bein' married to me own father."

Ritchie cleared his throat. "You don't have to explain, Miss Moran. None of us thought . . ."

"Be honest, none of you thought it was love."

"Well, Pa's been on his own so long . . ."

Cissie lowered her voice. "Yer Pa's a good man, sonnie. Deserves better'n a punch in the 'ead. Look at what we're savin' now I come ter live 'ere, now I give up the Army. Savin' on the costs of the cleanin' woman, my 'ouse, grub – and his lordship drinks less. Oh yer, he still likes 'is night out with the lads, but what man don't. I won't let 'im down. I won't take 'is money an' scarper. But it's no good blinkin' the fact that yer father's twenty years'n'more older'n me. If the Lord spares us both through the promised span, I'll be alone awhile at the end of the tunnel, like."

Ritchie was sensitive to such pragmatism, even to this fusion of love and money in the mouth of a woman of undoubted principle. His fears, and Maury's, were ill-founded; Cissie would never abandon Leo in senility. All she wanted was a modicum of security for her own declining years. It was on the tip of Ritchie's tongue to say 'Ask and it shall be given unto you,' but the quotation, though apt, was New Testament and he wasn't at all sure it would sound right coming from a descendant of Moses. He said, "A house by the sea, and an endowment."

"Don't trust finance companies," said Cissie. "Property an' a few shares."

"Shares in what?"

Leo had come to the kitchen door; he stood behind the curtain, only his nose and slippers visible.

"Maurice's company," said Cissie.

"Why not my company?" said Ritchie.

"Don't know nothin' about your business," said Cissie.

"It's legitimate," said Ritchie.

"But bricks an' mortar," said Cissie, "they endureth."

"Amen!" said Stan.

"What if Maury and I say 'no dice', what'll you do then?" Ritchie asked.

From the kitchenette the kettle sang but Leo did not move away.

Even Cissie was silent; clearly Leo had led her to believe that his sons would do anything for him. What poison he had spread about Holly and why her name had never been mentioned in connection with a settlement Ritchie neither knew nor cared; he had inherited much of his hostility towards his sister from his pa in the first instance. He gave Holly not so much as a passing thought; it was man's business, this marriage settlement.

"We'll wed, whatever," Cissie said. "If his children revileth him he will have more need of me, an' I of 'im. But it would be *nice* to be settled, like."

"No ultimatum?" Ritchie asked.

"Love needeth no ultimatum," said Cissie, without pomp. "You're a married man, you should know that."

Stan slid a sidelong glance at Ritchie to see if his boss found irony in Cissie's clumsy comment, but Ritchie was grinning. Leo's face appeared through the curtain, a wreath of steam around it.

"All right," Ritchie said. "I'll guarantee the house by the seaside, outta London. Maury'll come through with the shares in brick and mortar. We'll all meet soon to discuss the details."

In the kitchenette, out of sight, Leo Beckman performed a little jig all to himself while Ritchie, rising from the sofa, involuntarily sealed the pledge by kissing Cissie on both cheeks.

"I'm pleased," said Cissie, holding Ritchie close to her, a hand on his sleeve. "But there's one thing more."

"What's that?"

"Promise you'll never lay a finger on yer pa again."

"What?"

"You heard?" said Cissie quietly. "Now, sonnie, promise."

"I promise," Ritchie said.

Cissie Moran's eyes filled with unexpected tears and she drew Ritchie down and hugged him to her breasts.

"Ain't that a good boy!" she said.

*   *   *

Ritchie did the photographic work personally. He laboured throughout the evening and most of the night, alone in the Apex offices. He had taught himself how to use the equipment and obtaining sharp black-and-white reproductions of the paintings was comparatively easy. Lighting the statuette of the Madonna was tricky, however, and he spoiled the first batch of angles by over-exposure. It was after four a.m. before the batch of prints was dry enough to pack. He made coffee on the office gas-ring, rested for a few minutes, then seated himself at one of the Royals and pecked out a full description of each of the pieces followed by an unsigned letter to Madelaine. He cut protective card on the guillotine, leaved the photographs with tissue, taped the card around them and slotted the block into one of the large orange envelopes stencilled with the warning *Photographs*: *Do Not Bend*. He addressed a label, licked it and stuck it on the envelope, drank another mug of coffee then cleared the four art objects out of the studio. He packed them with considerable care into a large suitcase that he had brought with him for the purpose.

Around five, he put out the lights, locked the office and carried the suitcase downstairs. He had a key for the street door and had been instructed by Murgatroyd on how to switch off the alarm long enough to get the door open, how to set it so that it would come on automatically when the door was closed. In the dark foyer of echoing tile and shiny linoleum, Ritchie fumbled for his keyring. He almost jumped out of his skin when the lift gate rattled at the base of the shaft and the cables snapped behind the weights. He was inclined by instinct to fling open the door and dash out into the street, the suitcase cradled in his arms; to make a getaway. He controlled the impulse by breathing deeply. He waited.

Murgatroyd had thrown an overcoat over his pyjamas and stepped into a pair of green rubber galoshes. He looked ridiculous but Ritchie did not see the funny side of the caretaker's appearance. Murgatroyd stared at him through the grid.

"It's me," said Ritchie. "I told you I'd be working late."

"Didn't think you meant this late, Sir. Thought you'd be

long gone, Sir," growled Murgatroyd, who managed to sound obsequious and recriminatory at once. "I'll let yer out."

Ritchie didn't argue. "Thanks."

Murgatroyd emerged from the lift, shuffled to the door and did his business with keys and locks, stilling the burglar alarm.

Ritchie waited, suitcase in hand, a fiver handy in his coat pocket.

"Sorry to have bothered you," Ritchie said. "Urgent job."

"'S all right, Sir. Hadda be gettin' up soon anyhow."

Ritchie offered the five-pound note. Murgatroyd accepted it without gratitude, saying, as he closed his fist around the note, "No need for that, Sir, no need for that. Only doin' me duty."

"Good-night," Ritchie said, carrying the case out into the cold empty street.

"Night, Sir."

Ritchie walked quickly towards his motor car. Though he did not turn round, he was fully aware that the caretaker was still at the open door, watching his every move, wondering, perhaps, why Mr. Beckman was driving an inconspicuous Ford Eight and not his usual sleek limousine.

"Bugger him!" Ritchie said under his breath as he fired the engine and edged the car away from the kerb.

He drove through an almost deserted London at a steady pace, fiddling constantly with the lever that controlled the car's inadequate heater. He was cold, bone cold, and fatigued. He thought of home longingly; not of home, really, but of a soft bed and a warm, sleepy woman who would wrap her arms about him and calm his taut nerves, send him down quickly into sleep as day broke; Madelaine, not Ruth.

The flat was in the Pentonville Road, one up, above a dry-salters' shop. The reek of turpentine overlaid the musty odour of the sad Late Victorian furnishings that came with the lease. Lace curtains, browned by weather and soot, screened the windows, half-guards of printed cotton and side drapes of cheap velvet completed the process. Ritchie went up by the open stair from the street and let himself into the two-roomed hideaway with his key. He lit two bleary lamps, one in each room. Stepping past the mousetraps that he had scattered round the skirting, none of which had been sprung in the ten days since his last visit, he pushed the suitcase under the big double bed that packed the bedroom. He would return tomorrow or the next day and store away the stuff properly. Tonight, this morning, he was too weary to do more than go through his customary checking routine; opening the wardrobe, he cast his eye over the frames, canvases and wooden boxes stacked up inside, opened the drawers of the dressing chest one by one to scan the engravings, the drawings, the tray of miniatures, all the fine things that he had squirrelled away in this anonymous treasure house, leased and paid for by a man who did not exist.

Two minutes was all it took to unlock the fireproof safe that squatted under the table in the living room, to remove the red leather account book and enter the first record of the transaction there: *3 paintings, 1 statuette*; *bought H.L. £200.* He would leave the rest of the page blank so that he could fill in details of the objects once Madelaine had identified them. It would be months, maybe years, before he penned in a selling price against each one, with the initials of a buyer. But he could wait, wait until the heat was off, until he had something going that would give a safe route through to Paris, until market values climbed. He closed the account book with a snap.

A matter of a half hour later he was perched on a bar stool in the gleaming kitchen of his house in Vallois Street eating the waffles and bacon that Mrs. McKim had cooked for him. On the breakfast bar was the large orange envelope.

"Post it as soon as you can, Eunice; right?"

"Will do, Mr. Beckman."

Ritchie pushed away his plate, sipped tea and rolled from the stool stiffly. He was not as young as he had been; a twenty-four hour day definitely took its toll. He stretched, arching his back like a cat.

"Call me at ten, Eunice."

"Yes, Mr. Beckman. Oh, Mr. Beckman?"

"Yep."

"The other Mr. Beckman was here again last evening."

"Was he now?"

"Do I . . . what . . . ?"

Ritchie was too tired to care. He smiled and winked at the housekeeper. "Doesn't matter, Eunice. Let her have her head with Maury. She'll bore him pretty soon."

"But, sir?"

"Maury's my brother. A stuffed shirt. She's safe enough with him."

Mrs. McKim kept her doubts to herself.

Ritchie went to bed, alone, pleased with the day's events.

*   *   *

In spite of Peter's generous offer Holly did not invite Maury to the show's opening night. It was, she felt, none of Maury's concern; she was wary of Maury's bluntness. She preferred to attend with her family, with her husband and son, as if that unit would protect her against the magical influences of dazzle and razzmatazz and brake her long slide into love. It did not occur to her that she was asking just too much from Chris and Kennedy until Chris telephoned from school to explain – in what was patently a rehearsed speech – that he was too busy preparing for term examinations to make the trip to London midweek. Holly told her son that she quite understood, and hid her disappointment. But at the last moment Kennedy too begged off and her disappointment turned to dismay. Unjustifiably she felt that *they* had let *her* down.

Kennedy appeared at breakfast with a scarf wrapped round his neck.

"Strep throat by the feel of it," he croaked. "Shouldn't risk spreading it on to the songbirds. Best go along without me."

Angrily, suspecting a deception, Holly packed her husband back to bed. She removed all his cigars and sent up the maid with a glass of warm barley water in lieu of breakfast.

When she returned from the Gallery around five thirty, she found Kennedy at work in the library. When challenged he declared that he was feeling a little better.

"Well enough to come to the theatre with me?"

"No, m'dear. It wouldn't be wise."

"Tell me the truth, Kennedy. You just don't want to go tonight, do you?"

"Not madly."

"Why not?"

"Oh, you know me, Holly. I don't much care for late nights and silly chatter."

"Is that the . . . the only reason?"

"Of course."

She found Kennedy's evasiveness irksome. It was almost as if he had decided to abandon her. How could he fail to see what was happening to her, to realise that she was in process of falling in love with another, younger man. Over-emphasising the importance of Kennedy's support – his presence at her side would have been enough – she illogically edged the blame in his direction.

"I shan't go either then," she said.

"Nonsense. Didn't you promise?"

"Yes, but . . ."

"Wouldn't be terribly polite not to turn up, would it?"

"If you're ill . . ."

"I'm not *that* ill."

"All right, Kennedy. I'll attend the performance. But I'll come home again as soon as it's over."

"And pass up a gala supper at the Savoy?"

"I can hardly trot into the Savoy on my own."

"If that's the way of it," said Kennedy, "I'll put on my bib and tucker."

"And risk making your throat worse. No."

"I didn't mean to spoil it for you, Holly."

Holly did not bend. It was the simplest ruse of all, and Kennedy had collaborated in it; she found that she could delude herself into smothering guilt with anger, believe that Kennedy did not care, that his indifference had finally been unmasked. She skimmed the surface of reason and emotion, speaking rapidly.

"It's spoiled already."

"I'm sorry."

"Oh, don't apologise."

Kennedy got to his feet.

He said, "Don't you have a hairdresser's appointment?"

"In twenty minutes."

"Go, then, What is it they say – knock 'em dead."

"I can't go unescorted, don't you see?"

Kennedy said, "But you won't be unescorted."

"What do you mean?"

"You're Peter Freeman's guest."

"Are you suggesting . . ."

"One of Peter Freeman's party. One of dozens, I expect."

"Kennedy, Peter and I . . ."

"Howard Crocker's a nice chap. Perhaps he'll give you his arm."

What did it mean, Holly wondered. She was twisted by guilt as well as anger. Commonsense told her that it would be fatal to accept Kennedy's gracious stand-down at its face value, that he was only being kind to her again, indulging her. Only *she* knew how the thing had changed, had become not a gadfly folly but a dilemma that reason could not solve. It was another of the many small decisions, each of which, when made, seemed less than conscious, almost as if she, Holly Beckman King, had had no part in them, no choice at all.

"Do you want to go?" asked Kennedy hoarsely.

"Yes. Yes, I do."

"Then go. I don't mind."

"All right."

Her husband had released her, had cooperated, had nudged her yet again into Peter's arms. At that instant she hated Kennedy for his charity. His understanding lay so close to weakness that she felt no sympathy for him and no drop of shame.

Shrilly, she said, "I may be very late."

"I understand."

"Do you, Kennedy?"

He tugged the scarf tighter as if to restrain himself from shouting at her. "Yes, of course; theatre parties always sprawl into the wee small hours, do they not? Wait up for the first newspaper reviews, that sort of thing. Tradition, and all that."

It was as if he was saying good-bye.

He kissed her on the cheekbone, holding his hand to his throat.

"I'll see you in the morning, Holly."

"Sometime," Holly said and, without another word of comfort or reassurance, left her husband alone in the library.

*   *   *

From the hairdressing salon, Holly called Peter and told him of her predicament. Fifteen minutes later he called her back. She spoke with him on the extension while the helmet of the drier droned over her head. He had solved the problem. Bring her evening clothes to the Savoy; she could change in his room. He wouldn't be there, of course. Howard was leaving for the theatre from the hotel; Howard would be her escort. All settled, all solved; no arguments.

At seven forty that evening Holly was conducted from Peter's room by Howard Crocker. During pre-theatre drinks in the cocktail bar, Holly discovered that Peter had become 'rather a hermit' since his arrival eight weeks before, refusing all invitations to parties and weekends. It had, of course, leaked out that Peter's withdrawal from society was due to 'a young lady', and speculation had been rife as to what the lucky female was really like. Holly found the questions that she was asked – in a seemingly casual manner – difficult to parry. She had built no bunker against snipers, no disarming lie large enough to cover her from innuendo. On the other hand, several of the couples were genuinely concerned for Peter's happiness and one or two of the women confided in Holly that they were relieved he had found a 'companion' at last. The fact that she was married did not cloud the more relative issue, that Peter Freeman was 'on cloud nine', which was where the chap deserved to be. Seated in a row of Peter's friends, Howard on one side of her and Constance Lock on the other, Holly tried to give herself up to uncritical enjoyment of the musical. It had everything now that critics and

252

public expected; gone the jerkiness, uncertainty and confusion. Opening night nerves accounted for a couple of minor mishaps but the sheer verve of the production created an infectious gaiety that swept the audience through the acts to the final triumphant curtain.

Peter was superb. Even his most energetic routines seemed effortless, his acting so relaxed that the great charmer and pastmaster of throw-away, Brooks, seemed a trifle wooden by comparison. In the third act a song-dance duet between Gwen Flowers and Peter proved to be a poignant showstopper, a perfect set-up for Peter's bold 'capture' of the Rosemary Case character and the final parade along the Strand.

Even Howard *ah-ummed* an opinion that his protégé had never been in better form and that the show would be the hit of the West End season. The streamlined express train of 'publicity' would have a clear track come Tuesday morning. Backers and contractors would surely be rewarded for their acumen and faith. Sheet music prints of 'Tip-Top Top o'the Mornin', 'Waiting for my Girl', 'Another Time, We Two', and the Rosemary Case up-beat solo 'He Comes from the Land of the Indian Brave' would be in the shops by the weekend. Recordings of the vocal numbers, plus the catchy melody from Peter's special 'Hickory Dickory Dance' would be pressed and issued within a fortnight. Dance band leaders would clamour for arrangements and, by Christmas, *Step Out Along the Strand* would be coining money for everyone concerned, including its stars.

For all that, the opening night party in the small ballroom of the Savoy had a defensive atmosphere that Holly found most strange. Amid the glitter and glamour there was tension. Few of the guests seemed willing to indulge in truthful circumspection; their mouths declared something extravagant while their eyes held something envious and certainly strained. Brooks was going through an act. Rosemary Case was using all her wiles to extract oodles of flattery from anyone in pants as a balm to her anxiety and only Gwen Flowers had leisure and inclination to assure Holly that Peter was 'the real thing'. At ten minutes to four the morning newspapers were wheeled in on trollies by hotel staff, and the guests, drunk, sober and poised between, fell like vultures on the copies and dragged them off to their tables. Holly had been infected by the general neurosis. Even Peter gnawed his lip as he flanked Howard and stared at the review page of the *Mail* that Howard had filleted from the paper's bulk.

"Stupendous production. Brooks at his best."

"What about me?" Peter asked, peering. "What does it say about me?"

Howard shielded the paper, frowning. "Not a word, Pete," he said. "Not a single word."

"*What*?"

Chuckling, Howard clapped Peter on the back and thrust the page at him. "Not a word, m'boy, an entire paragraph devoted to singing your praises. Here, see for yourself."

Peter grabbed the paper and, drawing Holly close to him, held it while they read the glowing review together.

All around the ballroom, members of the cast were shouting, whooping and declaiming the best of the critics' unanimous hyperboles. Celebration lost its inhibitions. Even Benedict executed three mighty leaps and skated over to kiss Gwen Flowers. The redoubtable Ralph Brooks, his stomach complaint miraculously cured, was for a few fleeting minutes the man his worshippers supposed him to be. Grabbing the hands of two chorines he led a dancing snake between the tables, picking up all those who had endured the rigours of the long wait. Threading round and round the floor to the strains of the orchestra's rendering of *Step Out Along the Strand*, the snake devoured everyone, including Rosemary's grandmother, an ex-Karno girl, who skipped and shimmied with the best of them. It was all so smooth and spontaneous, Holly thought. She wondered at the egotism of professional people who could set store by critics' flattery. But the sudden release of tension, the sloughing off of doubt, was more than infectious now; it was explosive, a great gay cracker of happiness bursting in all directions. When everyone was on the floor, Ralph raised his arms and called for silence. The orchestra gave him a chord and a drum roll.

"It would seem," Ralph announced, "that we have entered

the sacred place. Trumpets proclaim our triumph and the pillars of the Pantheon shake with the din of our success." He paused. "Hannen Swaffer laughed." A bellow of delight greeted this announcement. Hands in pockets, swaying on the balls of his feet, a modest smile upon his lips, Ralph rode it out. "Encumbent upon me as the *youngest* member of the cast is the privilege of offering the thanks of all us 'umble players to the director of '*Step Out Along the Strand*.' To Giles Benedict, our father confessor and the Simon Legree of Shaftesbury Avenue. To Bob Harman our muscular musicologist, the man with the loudest voice and the biggest stick, shall we say, in show-business. To Mr. Hew Saracen who risked a small part of his all in daring to stage such a show, and, personally, my own thanks and congratulations to my co-stars – and stars they are, brighter by far and more luminous than I can ever hope to be." Cries of 'Shame; never; twaddle' greeted this piece of rhetoric.

"The lovely, the adorable, the utterly cuddlesome Rosemary." Whistles, heavy breathing and applause. "And, of course, our kissin' cousin from the land of the free-lunch, that Yankee Doodle who has made us all so welcome." Laughter, laughter. "Peter Freeman."

With his arm still about Holly's waist, Peter took his bow while the ballroom rocked with the ovation. He straightened and, with the smile still upon his face, murmured into Holly's ear, "He sure does go on, old Ralphie."

"You deserve it," Holly whispered.

Ralph was eloquently but briskly running through the catalogue of other persons connected with the production, acknowledging them one by one.

"I don't care about the notices, Holly, not tonight."

"I'm sure you do, Peter, really."

"All I can think about is you."

"Come on, you can't put me in a scrapbook to console you in your declining years," said Holly, trying to make light of it.

"I don't want you in a scrapbook. But I'd rather have you with me, Holly, in my declining years than all the glowing notices there ever were."

It was no longer banter, the crosstalk of likeable lovers. In the Savoy ballroom they were alone suddenly, caught in a brief ebb in the carnival air. Indifferent to friends and enemies alike, Peter put his arms about her shoulders and drew her to him. She sensed his sincerity; he might lie to her still with his mouth and make the trite phrases of the romantic lover, but there was no lie in the touch of his hands or the pain that lay exposed in his eyes.

The flippant retort stayed on her tongue. She was mute with a dry and shaking passion, made vulnerable by Peter's hurt. He was so prepared to lose her that he could not hide behind the inevitable banalities of flattery.

"Oh, Peter, Peter," she murmured.

"I need you, Holly."

"For how long, though?"

"For ever."

The orchestra struck up with 'Another Time, We Two'. The lights dimmed. Peter lifted her lightly into position and they danced. They had no need to speak.

It was tulle and lace, the silk facings of evening dress, diamonds, celebrities and breakfast champagne, the effortless dance. Peter held her so lightly that she seemed dispossessed, as if he had somehow removed the burdens that the years had laid upon her. She was the Lambeth girl, as innocent and trusting as Cinderella, unencumbered by responsibility to anyone or anything, freed of selfishness and of material desires. In Peter's arms, on the floor of the ballroom of the Savoy, Holly was liberated from all the cares and woes that had shaped her up to that hour. She supposed it was love of the very best kind and forgot Kennedy and Chris completely. They were elsewhere, in another life, on another plane.

Later, in the hotel's third-floor suite, Peter undressed her and, tipsy and sated with excitement, lay naked in bed by her side. He touched her breasts with his lips, gently, and the feverish need in both man and woman was transformed into a constant satisfaction, each with the other, that their love-making only increased. Like a butterfly escaping from its caul Holly welcomed the sweet free floating feeling that illusion had become reality and that romance was, after all, no chimera. Peter had made it so, and with Peter it would always be so.

"Holly, I don't want you to leave me."

"How can I now?"

"I want to take you with me, wherever I go."

"Yes, Peter."

"Do you mean you'll come with me?"

"Yes."

"And Kennedy, your husband?"

Holly had a split-second vision of Kennedy, the grey woollen scarf wrapped around his throat and the jacket, like a shawl, hung around his stooped shoulders, weeping into a handkerchief; an image so faithful to her present view of her husband that she had no hesitation in giving Peter her answer.

"I'll leave him."

"When?"

"Soon."

"Tomorrow?"

"Yes, yes, yes, Peter. Tomorrow, if you wish."

Dazed with the discovery of love, Holly had no notion what that impetuous promise would really mean to Kennedy, to Peter and to Chris.

*　　*　　*

Wharton's, in Gerrard Street, was an old fashioned restaurant that catered to the Englishman's addiction to meat and custard and to his need for privacy. Acres of emptiness seemed to surround each square table; for those who had earth-shaking secrets to discuss over the oxtails there were a half-dozen booths sealed off by partitions. It was more Kennedy's sort of eating house than Maury's but it seemed to offer a degree of sobriety that fitted in with Holly's purpose and she chose it without hesitation as a suitable spot in which to break the news to Maury.

She lunched her brother at Wharton's on the Wednesday after Peter's opening night. She chose her wardrobe as carefully as she had selected the restaurant, a swagger-style suit in chocolate brown wool and a caramel shirt with a tie, smart and business-like but not mannish.

As soon as they were seated in seclusion and had ordered from the menu, Maury said, "I take it you want the gory details about dear old Dad?"

Holly's mind was on other things.

"Pa? What about him? He's not sick, is he?"

"Only love sick," said Maury. "He's getting spliced again. In February. All cut and dried. I didn't bother to consult you. I realise the old buzzard's welfare isn't a subject close to your heart."

Diffidently Holly said, "Have you met the bride?"

"Once," said Maury. "I like her. She'll keep Leo in line and cherish him as he dodders into senility. To be frank, she's better than he deserves."

"I suppose I should send him something. Not a peace offering, a gift."

"Suit yourself," said Maury. "He's screwing enough out of Ritchie and me, God knows."

"Ritchie? You've been . . . you've seen Ritchie?"

"Several times," said Maury. "Mainly because Pa kinda pushed us together." He shrugged. "Our Ritch hasn't changed much. Anyhow, we discussed it and decided not to ask you for a contribution to the Out-of-Sight, Out-of-Mind Fund."

"Is that what it is?"

"Ah, Leo'll love it by the sea. Cissie, his intended, will see that he does. I'm keeping an eye open for a bungalow for them on the south coast. Out of London. That's part of the deal. Ritchie'll foot the bill for the house purchase. I'm giving the happy couple a block of shares in Beckman Buildings. Mumford's handling the legal details. Pa hasn't a clue about them really, but the lady has a head on her shoulders."

"Good, that's good," said Holly.

"Point is," said Maury, "do you want to be asked to the wedding breakfast, or luncheon, or whatever? Won't be a big do, just a handful, family mostly."

"Pa wouldn't thank you for inviting me."

"No, but he'd be pleased enough to have Chris along, I'm sure."

The elderly waiter placed soup before her, a dish of pâté in front of Maury. Fuss with bread, slivers of toast, the butter plate, covered Holly's silence.

"The wine's on me," said Maury. "What're you on? Fish?"

"Chicken."

Maury ordered a bottle of the *vin blanc*. He plastered pâté on a curl of toast and popped it into his mouth.

"Well?"

"Well what?" said Holly.

"Pa's nuptials, are you coming?"

"I think not," said Holly. "Especially under the circumstances."

"Come on, love. Bury the hatchet, let byegones be byegones and all that," Maury wheedled. "Cissie's a gem. Odd, but a gem. The circumstances aren't all that cuckoo, you know."

"I meant my circumstances, not Pa's." Holly hesitated. "Maury, I'm about to ask Kennedy to give me a divorce."

"What did you say?"

"I'm leaving Kennedy."

Maury rocked back in the chair. "Ey-yah!" Colour fled from his cheeks and he appeared stricken. "Holly, Holly; not you!"

"It happens," said Holly.

"That's not good enough." Maury sat forward. "What's the reason?"

"Another man. I've fallen in love with somebody else."

Anger and disgust; Maury tossed the knife to his plate, swept crumbs from his napkin and tossed the cloth after the knife. "A bloody infatuation, that's all."

"I don't think so."

"Don't bloody *think* so; aren't you even sure?"

"Yes, I'm sure. Sure enough."

"Holly, God, Holly! You're the last person I'd have expected to carry on like an idiot schoolkid."

"I suppose you should hear the rest of it, Maury. I've been having an affair. Still am, come to that."

"An affair? You mean . . . bed, and all?"

"Maury, don't be so damned obtuse."

"All right, all right. But look, love, an affair's one thing, divorce is quite another. Let this, this affair take its course. It's bound to taper off. Affairs do, you know."

"Not this one."

Though she spoke emphatically, her assurance was no more than a response to Maury's patronising tone. She had not expected sympathy from her brother but she had expected him to treat her like an adult, not to talk down to her as if she was a witless girl. It was typical of the male attitude to suppose that a woman who fell in love could not be serious about it, could not suffer guilt and doubt, could not quite know what she was doing. She had expected more from her brother. Perceiving this, perhaps, Maury suddenly drew himself together and hid his bitter disappointment behind a practical question.

"What about Chris?"

"Chris will come to America with me."

"America? The guy . . . he's an American?"

Holly delivered information in pre-wrapped packages. She had prepared for her meeting with Maury thoroughly. Luncheon was served about the couple but the waiters, sensing the charged nature of the conversation, worked rapidly and without courtesies.

When Holly had told him of Peter, Maury said, "Why didn't you talk it out with me first?"

"You're not my keeper, Maury. Anyhow what would you have done? Treated me to a fit of moral indignation." Holly stabbed a piece of chicken breast from the sauce and ate it. "What do you know about marriage, you can be so free with good advice?"

"I know it shouldn't be entered lightly. Marriage, I mean."

"I've never done *anything* lightly, Maury. Including falling in love with Peter."

"You're right. You're right. What do I know about marriage? I mean, what the hell do I know about women? But let me ask you this, Holly; how far have you thought this through?"

Holly pushed away her plate.

"I want nothing from Kennedy, if that's what you mean."

"No, that's not what I meant; not quite." Maury shook his head. "Here we sit, calmly scoffing lunch, carving up your future. Takes me back to the bad old days when you were carrying Aspinall's child."

"Maury, nobody else knows about Chris, who his father really is."

"Sure, sure, and I'm not about to tell. Don't panic. I'm not that nasty. But remember how it was? You were willing to do anything to ensure that Chris had a decent life, that he wasn't dragged up in Lambeth like we were."

"I remember you were all for kicking David Aspinall's head in," said Holly. "I solve my own problems, Maury."

"You solved that mess pretty damned well. Until now."

"Oh, God, Maury, you don't think I married Kennedy on the rebound, do you?"

"I'm not talking about Kennedy."

"Christopher?" Holly endeavoured to sound bewildered but she took his meaning clearly, and all the implications behind it. He was accusing her of arrant selfishness. But the addition of those two words, "Until now," told her much about Maury, hinting that he had masked his disapproval of her actions all these many years, that he saw her now as fulfilling a destiny, trapped by her own calculation, her cunning. The revelation hurt her. If he had been a woman, a sister instead of a brother, perhaps he would more readily have understood that she was driven by responses that could not be explained, that her life had not been planned and engineered as his had been. For a moment she was tempted to dismiss Maury but then she recalled the warmth, the affection that had held them together and she sought to transform his rebuke into understanding.

"Christopher was unique," Holly said. "It's true I didn't love him when I married him but it grew, Maury. Yes, it grew. Since the day Chris died . . ."

"Go on." He was waiting for her to lie to him, to pretend that she had loved no man since her first husband's death.

Holly said, "The French have a phrase for it."

"They usually have," said Maury sardonically.

"*Maladie d'amour*," said Holly.

"The sickness of love."

"It doesn't mean that, really. It's untranslatable. *Maladie d'amour*. Christopher – now Peter."

"Are you trying to tell me you're actually in love with this American?"

"I'm trying to make you understand, Maury."

"It's Kennedy you'll have trouble with; not me."

"Kennedy knows."

"You told him?" Maury said.

"No, but he's aware of it."

"Why hasn't he put his foot down then?"

"I wish he had. He's allowing it to happen, giving me all the rope I need. I resent it. Yes, I do. I really resent it. Kennedy devalues himself."

"Meaning, he doesn't know how to cope with you."

"He's willing to love me, knowing I don't love him any more."

"That's strength, Holly; not bloody weakness. Anyhow, I don't believe you've stopped loving Kennedy."

"Perhaps you're right, Maury. But, God, how things have changed. How my feelings have changed; my feelings for Chris, for Kennedy, for . . ."

"For me?"

"Yes, for you too. Everything seems so shabby now, so grey. I don't expect you to understand."

"Sure, I understand. You're bored."

"That's what I thought too. I thought I was just plain bored. But it was something more serious than that. Maury, tell me, where did the colour go?"

"I haven't a clue," Maury said.

"Peter – being with Peter; it makes everything vivid again. Oh, this is such nonsense."

"No," said Maury, sadly. "I know what you mean, love. Really I do."

"How can you?"

Maury shrugged.

How could he tell his sister that Ruth – Ruth as Ritchie's wife – had changed the shading of his existence, altered the browns and ochres to simple primaries, to red and fiery yellow and rich green? He *did* understand what Holly was going through, because he was going through a similar experience himself. The certainty of purpose that had sustained them both for twenty years had been challenged. He – though he would not openly admit it – was as confused as she was. He realised what she expected from him and gave way to the deep fraternal love that had always been a bedrock of his character. "Look, never mind the moral issues. The hell with them. How can I help? What do you need?"

"Nothing," said Holly. "That's it – nothing."

"What about money?"

"I told you already; Kennedy can have the business – intact."

"You're a full partner, Holly. Why don't you sell him your share?"

"I'm not that mercenary. Besides, where could Kennedy find the capital?" Holly said. "Kennedy will need the business to keep him going."

"Stay in as a partner then."

"Yes, if he'll have me. Oh, he probably will. Things are so stretched right now."

"Stretched? Kings'? You're kidding me."

"It's true. We're dependent on rapid profits, quick turnover. We buy, say, a couple of paintings, sell them, divide the profit on the sale and instantly reinvest it."

"The old, old story; just the way you used to run Aspinall's."

"More or less," said Holly. "Only now I do my sums in hundreds of pounds, not shillings and pence."

"But I was always under the impression that Kennedy had scads of money?"

"Kennedy was never rich. Most of it was show. The motor car, the fine suits – a little bit spendthrift. Postwar inflation hit his investments which is why we've had to slave at the business so unremittingly ever since. If Kings' slips, Kennedy will be hard up. And I don't want that to happen to him. I want him to be as comfortable as possible."

"He'll never be comfortable without you, Holly."

"He . . . he must learn."

"And he'll miss Chris. He loves the boy."

Holly's eyes misted; it was the one great hurdle that she had to overcome, Kennedy's love for his stepson. She had encouraged it, welcomed it, and now she must bring it to an end.

Sternly, she said, "California's a wonderful place. Chris will love it there. Sunshine, sports, anything he wants."

"Kennedy will fight you, Holly."

"If he insists, Kennedy may have Chris over here for the summer, for the cricket season. Them and their damned cricket."

"Are you crying?"

"No, of course not."

"Second thoughts?"

"No. It's just that now I've made my decision I wish it was all over and done with."

"It's a long way from over and done with. If you ask me Kennedy isn't going to surrender without a fight."

"Yes, he will," said Holly.

"What makes you so sure?"

"He's never fought for anything in his life," Holly said. "No, Maury, Kennedy will do what I ask."

"Including giving you a divorce?"

"Even that," Holly said.

*　　*　　*

"No divorce," said Kennedy.

"I'm leaving you, Kennedy; don't you understand?"

"I'm afraid I do understand. You must do as you see fit, Holly. But I will *not* sue for divorce."

"I intend to live openly with Peter Freeman."

"Perhaps that's better than living with him in secret."

"Kennedy, please."

"I suppose," Kennedy said, "that we will be separated, in the legal sense of that word, whatever it means; Mumford will enlighten us."

"Peter wishes to marry me, not just live with me."

"Peter may wish all he wants to, m'dear."

"Kennedy, why are you doing this?"

"I'm doing nothing, Holly. Isn't it apparent that I am, and will, do nothing. Nothing to prevent you. Nothing to abet your plan."

"The Gallery . . ."

"I assume you mean that you no longer wish to be an active partner?"

"How can I, darling? An arrangement like that would never work."

"The Gallery's the very least of my concerns," Kennedy said. "I managed a business capably enough before we met; no doubt I can do so again."

"Kennedy, I don't want to hurt you."

"It's too late to avoid it, Holly."

"You knew, didn't you?"

"Yes."

"Why won't you divorce me? It's what I want."

"I'll tell Chris that we've decided to live apart."

"No," Holly said. "No, Kennedy. I'm not that much of a coward. I'll tell him myself. On Sunday. I'll go up to St. Justin's on Sunday."

"Alone I trust."

"I'm not that crass," said Holly. "Yes, alone."

"Chris . . ." For the first time in the course of the conversation Kennedy seemed at a loss for words. "Chris has an inkling of what's in the wind. I think you may find him prepared."

"Prepared?"

"Rumours filtered up to St. Justin's," Kennedy explained. "He fished, quizzed me. I told him a little of the truth."

"What did you say? Kennedy? What did you tell him?"

"Only what he needed to know for his own peace of mind."

"How did he react?"

"Like a brick," said Kennedy.

"That's it, that's the reason you won't consider a divorce." Holly said. "Because of Chris. Isn't it?"

"It has nothing endemically to do with Chris."

"Unless I'm married to Peter, it would be very difficult,

perhaps impossible, for me to obtain custody of Chris, to take him to live with us in America."

"Believe it or not, Holly, that thought hadn't occurred to me."

"They won't, you know; the authorities won't grant him a visa or whatever it is," said Holly. "Don't lie to me, Kennedy; *that's* the reason for your refusal."

"Have you considered," said Kennedy, "that Chris may not want to live with you and Peter Freeman?"

"I'm his mother."

"In a few months, Holly, he will be fourteen."

"He's still a child."

"No, he's almost – very nearly – a young man. I'm aware that you don't value my opinion, Holly, but for what it's worth I don't think it would be beneficial to remove Chris from St. Justin's, and uproot him from England at this stage in his life."

"Shouldn't he be the judge of that, Kennedy?"

"Yes, I believe he should."

"If Chris . . . if he tells us that he wishes to live with me in the United States, will you give me a divorce?"

"Then, and only then," Kennedy answered.

* * *

Maury was too long in the tooth to confuse ingenuousness with innocence. He recognised the irony of what was happening and found the parallels between Holly's situation and his own uncomfortable. For that reason he was reluctant to condone her infidelity. He even tried to convince himself that she was selfish and cold-blooded – the Beckman genes taking over at last – but he could not brush aside affection so easily. He was pained by the collapse of her marriage and nervous about his nephew's future, sorry too for old Kennedy, but he kept his distance and did not rush in with solicitous advice. Thinking it over, Maury saw that his sister had not behaved in the classic manner of a spoiled wife; she was not using her affair with Freeman to escape from Kennedy. She had fallen – positively – in love with Freeman. It was quite against the grain of Holly's character. Clearly she had not chosen to have it happen any more than he had chosen to enter a relationship with Ruth.

My God, if you want a helping of nastiness and duplicity, Maury told himself, try that for flavour; my brother's wife! At what particular moment, he wondered, did it become too late to walk out of it. For sure, it was too late now. For Holly. And for Ruth.

Ruth was the unlikeliest sort of woman for him. During his career as an eligible bachelor he had kept company with women of character and intellect so that even the sexual side of the affairs had a certain tone. There appeared to be no such depths to Ruth and yet, Maury told himself, what she is now is only what Ritchie made of her. To stop the inexorable erosions of time Ritchie had tried to keep Ruth as she had been during the fast, mad days of their underground courtship. And, damn it, Ritchie had very nearly succeeded.

Travel had not broadened Ruth's mind. To her Toronto had been the same as Vancouver, Chicago no different from Paris, just a series of hotel suites and rented rooms. Ritchie had never encouraged her to take an interest in reading, music or painting; she collected nothing except dresses, furs and jewelry, the baubles of affluence. She did not much care for them, either, Maury had discovered, though she had sufficient guile to look sexy and pretty to please her husband as best she could. She was, it seemed, much her father's daughter; Maury had heard that Mendel Erbach had been compliant to a fault. On the other hand, beneath stultified emotions and rusted intelligence, Ruth gave evidence of a power of endurance that Maury found admirable, considering all that she had been through. What Ritchie's treatment had sapped from Ruth was not wit but will. A dozen years dwelling under the thumbs of domestic gorgons had turned her confidence and optimism to stone. Hope, Maury thought, was the most valuable gift he could give to her and, with it, the confidence to grow. Such a process would not take place overnight. Ruth would not simply wake like the Sleeping Beauty as fresh and forthcoming as if the years of trauma had never occurred. He would painstakingly nurture her back to mental health. In the meantime he must excuse her drinking, her play-acting, her weeping fits, even her moonstruck adulation. For a while he had to be strong enough for both of them. He must make no false moves, do nothing precipitately to damage their friendship. And, against his personal desires, he must hold Ruth at arm's length until he figured out how to wrest her away from his brother.

Ritchie's role in the triangular relationship was almost non-existent. He had virtually lost interest in it, as if Maury had been appointed a 'guardian' in the same category as Fletcher, McKim or Stan. He did not taunt Ruth about the afternoon jaunts but referred to them in a casual manner, shrugging them off as inconsequential.

"What did you do today?"

"Went out."

"Who with?"

"Maury took me to the pictures, up town."

"What did you see?"

"*Smilin' Through.*"

"Like it?"

"It made me cry."

"Maury too?"

"No, he laughed."

The brothers rarely met. When chance did fling them together they talked mainly of Leo and Cissie and the progress of the search for a suitable seaside bungalow; safe subjects. Things could have gone on for long enough in that desultory fashion but, as Stan had warned, Ruth's reaction to Maury's 'kindness' was inevitable.

When Ruth took Maury's arm and rubbed herself against him, Maury did not push her away; he detached her without remonstrance. When she kissed him by way of greeting, he was careful to offer his cheek and not his mouth. When she sought his hand in darkened cinemas or in public restaurants Maury found something else to do with his fingers. It wasn't indifference to Ruth as a woman that prevented Maury taking all that she offered, and it certainly wasn't fear of Ritchie's reprisals. It was a futile attempt to maintain the *status quo*, to preserve decorum in the relationship.

For this reason Maury was careful never to take Ruth to his house, not even when he knew that the servants would be there. He was not even sure that Ruth knew where he lived. It came as quite a shock, therefore, when he arrived home around six thirty one Friday evening in early December, to find Mrs. O'Connel still on the premises and in a state of some agitation.

"There's a lady," said Mrs. O'Connel. "Came about an hour ago. She says she's your sister-in-law. She's a bit the worse for the drink, Sir. I didn't know what to do. Tried to telephone you at your office . . ."

"I was in Finsbury, on a site," said Maury. "Where is she?"

Mrs. O'Connel's mouth pursed; she did not answer.

"In the bedroom?"

"Sir, she is."

"That's all right, Mrs. O'Connel. She is my sister-in-law and probably is the worse for drink."

"Would you be wantin' me to stay, Sir?"

"It's not necessary. I'll call my brother to come and collect her."

"She's been in there the devil's own time, Sir."

Maury divested himself of his overcoat and hat. He behaved calmly, though the memory of Ruth as he had first seen her, suffering from an overdose of nembutal, slid into his mind and set his pulse thumping with apprehension.

"Can you hold on a moment, Mrs. O'Connel?" Maury smiled. "Maybe I should make sure it really is my sister-in-law, hm?"

"Right you are, Sir."

Maury went to the master bedroom and opened the door a matter of six inches.

Ruth was on the bed. She glanced up, radiantly. "Hi, Maury!"

"Be right back," Maury closed the bedroom door and hurried back to the hallway where he lied to Mrs. O'Connel, assuring her that everything was fine and that his sister-in-law was having a nap. Pleasantly he bid the servant good-night, locked the main door behind her and switched on the burglar alarms. He detoured to the drinks table, poured himself a whisky and carried it back to the bedroom.

To Ruth he said, "Well, this is a surprise."

"I've been here for ages'n'ages."

A bottle of Beefeater and a glass were on the bedside table. Maury tried to recall how much gin had been in the bottle which was almost empty now. He did not approach the bed. He did not dare.

Ruth had come prepared. Coat and dress had been tossed over a chair and she had put on a pair of pure silk pyjamas and a silk 'night turban' with a mock ruby set in a circlet of sequins sewn to it. It was obvious that she wore nothing beneath the pyjamas.

Cross-legged on the moss green spread with pillows packed around her, she had spread the contents of her handbag between her knees and, to pass the time, doctored her toenails with a pair of manicure scissors from her reticule. In the calm, dignified surroundings of the man's bedroom with its muted shades, cherrywood, rosewood and knurled beech furniture, its books and framed dry-points of memorable architectural achievements, Ruth looked as out of place as a wedge of cream gateaux.

Maury said, "Does Ritchie know where you are?"

Ruth giggled and shrugged. "Him gone. Big Chief No-count done gone."

"Where?"

"On big bird. Him gone on huntin' trail. To Paris."

"How did you esc . . . get away from McKim and Co.?"

"Planned it." She glanced down at her body. "You don't think I walked through the streets in this outfit? Hey, Maury, aren't you pleased to see me?"

"Of course I am."

"Give me a kiss then; a nice friendly smacker. C'm'on."

"I think," said Maury carefully, "you're just a wee bit tipsy, Ruth."

"Sobe . . . sober'r than you think, Mister."

That was no lie, Maury realised. She twirled the manicure scissors around her index finger and gave him a steady unwavering stare, her eyes full of invitation. She had control of herself. What was more, she had found the will to elude

Fletcher and McKim. It probably hadn't been difficult but the important thing was that she had done it off her own bat. Maury did not wish to bruise the tender shoots of self-reliance. On the other hand he had to get her out of here and home again damned quick. Very damned quick. He swallowed whisky, coughed and put the empty glass on the dressing table. Deliberately he kept away from the area of the bed.

"You don't like me?" No uncertainty, no quaver; she was completely sure of her attraction for him. "Maury, he's gone for the night. He won't be home 'til tomorrow, earliest. I've been waiting for this chance, this chance to pay you back for all you've done for me."

"I haven't done a thing."

"You've been nice to me. You do love me, don't you?"

"Listen, they'll miss you. They'll worry."

"Let them worry."

"They'll tell Ritchie."

"The hell with Ritchie."

He could see her nipples through the silk, the curve of her belly. She lifted her right hand, hooked the band of the turban, took the thing off and tossed it to the floor.

"I don't like it either. Bought it months ago. Never wore it before. Ritchie's never seen it. Paid the bill, didn't even ask what it was. Doesn't even know I've got it. Maury, hold me." She straightened her spine, then arched backwards, more supple than he would have imagined her to be. "What do you think, Maury, he still loves me? Yeah, I'm fortunate. I'm in a class above his goddamned Bentley motorcar, in the same ball park as a painting by Rembrandt – a real one."

"Listen, Ruth, I must take you home."

"You're not scared of him?"

"No."

"What's to stop you, Maury?"

How could he tell her? Honour, decency and the preservation of trust were not qualities that Ritchie would have taught her about. Maury was more afraid of Ruth than of her husband. In about equal measure, he was also afraid of the fact that he wanted her so badly. His desire for Ruth

271

Beckman went far beyond the pleasurable stimulation that he had felt for most of the other women he had known.

"Why should you feel guilty, Maury? Ritchie's got a fancy-piece in Paris."

Maury was not surprised by the information, only that Ruth had ever managed to find out about it.

He said, "You're only guessing, Ruth. Besides, what Ritchie does, how he chooses to behave, that's his business. We're not the same, my brother and me. You wouldn't be here now, would you, if we were the same?"

She considered the implications, her intelligence roused.

"Ritchie trusts you?" she asked.

"That's it!" said Maury. "I want to go on seeing you, Ruth, but if we . . . if just once. *I* couldn't hide it from him. *You* couldn't hide it from him. If Ritchie thought, even for a moment, that you and I . . . It would be over between us. He'd whisk you out of England in a flash."

"Why don't you take me from him." she said. "You can, you know."

Maury said, "Why don't you dress now? I'll call McKim, tell her you're safe and that I'm bringing you home."

"I'm not scared of him," Ruth said.

"I'll tell the old cow to make dinner. We'll eat at Vallois Street. That'll be all right."

"I'm not scared of anything now, Maury." To his astonishment she twirled the glittering little manicure scissors and stabbed the sharp points down into her forearm. "See. When you're around, I don't mind how it hurts."

Involuntarily he stepped to her. She plucked the scissors from her forearm and raised them again. He caught her wrist. She yielded without struggle, lolling back, drawing him against her.

"I love you, Maury."

He kissed her mouth, eyes closed. She had the scissors in her right hand, behind his neck, her left arm flung back against the pillows. He kissed her lingeringly, bent awkwardly across her, still in his vested handcut semi-formal business suit that smelled of brick-dust, cement and tobacco. He drew himself back and opened his eyes. On the pillow six or eight little spots of blood stained the Irish linen slip. He closed his fist around the puncture wound on her arm and clenched it tight to stop the bleeding, then swivelled into a sitting position and, holding her, brushed her forehead with his lips.

He said, "You're mine, Ruth, aren't you?"

"Yes."

"I don't have to; you don't have to. You're mine anyway."

"Maury, I wanna . . ."

"*Shh*, now *shh*! Don't you see, Ruth; it isn't *necessary*."

"Love me, Maury."

"I do," Maury said. "I love you but I won't *make* love to you. That way we'd have to lie, and I'd become no better than Ritchie. You want me to be me, don't you; not just another Ritchie?"

The argument held no water but it was all he could come up with. Oddly, its illogicality appealed to her. She sat up, kissed him, and, with a brightness that disturbed him more than anger would have done, said, "I can be with you, you can be with me – and we don't have to lie?"

"Sure," said Maury. "But if we do . . . this, then we become liars and cheats. Ritchie's got us then, hasn't he?"

"You *do* want me, don't you?"

"Yes, I want you."

It was enough for her. The act was less valuable than the plain statement. She needed to be wanted, not taken. She had been taken too often. Maury had not counted on her understanding. She was faster to the punch than he was when it came to it.

"We go on as we are; our secret?" she said.

"That's it."

"I see you?"

"Frequently." He had detached the scissors and laid them on the quilt. He fished a handkerchief from his pocket, lowered her forearm and inspected the puncture. It wasn't serious or as deep as he had expected it to be. He brought it to his mouth and kissed it, tasting the saltiness of the blood. A tiny droplet lay on the lip of the wound. "As often as I can get away. Just you and me. No Ritchie." He gave her arm a cat-lick – she giggled – then he put the handkerchief around it and bound it. "There!"

"You know why I came?" she said, her arms about his neck. "I figured you were the same as him. I did it to keep you."

"You can keep me without that." said Maury.

"What about your other girls?"

"There are no other girls," said Maury.

"I don't believe you."

"Kid," he said solemnly, "I never lie."

She slithered her legs to the floor and stood up.

"Call McKim," she said. "Tell her I got drunk. Tell her we'll be back in a half-hour."

Thankfully, Maury felt her arms go from about him. He got to his feet too. "You're all right, Ruth, aren't you?"

"Never better, darling. I mean it. I'm all right now I know where we stand." She laughed. "Now I've got you."

An hour later they were sitting down to cold cuts in the dining room in Vallois Street, under the watchful eyes of Fletcher and McKim.

*   *   *

Excluded by her sex from participation in the Old Boys' mystique and sentimental attachment to 'School', Holly prepared the way for her talk with Chris with clinical brusqueness. Though she would not surrender her right to tell the boy of the impending upheaval in his life, she consulted Kennedy on the most effective way to break the news. She accepted her husband's advice that it was best to leave Chris in the detached, familiar background of St. Justin's rather than hold off until he returned home for the Christmas vacation.

"What will we do with him then?" Holly had asked.

"Share him," Kennedy had answered.

Holly drove to St. Justin's alone. She had telephoned ahead and requested an interview with Maitland, Chris's housemaster, to whom she explained the situation. Maitland had been through it all before. He assured the woman that he 'would

274

keep an eye on the boy' during the remainder of term and administer comfort should it prove necessary. Maitland offered the use of his room but Holly chose an alternative.

In the middle period of a cold blustery December afternoon Chris was brought from class to meet with his mother in his cluttered three-bed dormitory study. There, amid the treasures that three young men had hoarded – model aircraft, model trains and pictures of sporting heroes – Holly straightforwardly informed her son that she was leaving their Chelsea home to live with another man, adding that she hoped soon to marry him. Never before had she seen so much of his father in Chris; that closed, almost sly Aspinall look, the arrogant contained assurance of Andrea, the aunt he had never met, and the lofty petulant invulnerability of David, the father he did not know existed. She wondered at his reaction, at his curt nods, the dry eyes, wondered what pattern of behaviour he modelled his responses on, that hostile nobility; Christopher, perhaps? Or was it some half-baked notion of how Lindbergh or St. Exuperay would behave under stress, a brave face that would crumple as soon as she had gone?

"Do you . . . have you anything you would like to ask me?"

"I don't think so, mother."

"It won't change anything for you, Chris."

"Oh, mother, of course it will."

The cliché had been too quick to her tongue; her banality finally roused a spark of annoyance in him.

She said, "Not immediately. You'll still be here, and during the holidays you'll stay with your father, and visit with me."

"What if I don't want to 'visit' with you?"

"Surely, I mean . . . you will want to see me?"

"Yes, mother – but only you; not the . . . your . . . the fellow."

"I'm sure you'd like him, Chris. He's not an ogre."

"I'll stay with Dad, if you don't mind. I can visit you at the Gallery; or you can come to Chelsea, can't you?"

"I won't be at the Gallery, Chris, and it might be awkward if I were to come ho . . . to Chelsea."

Chris said, "When you marry this Mr. Freeman, you'll

leave England, won't you? He's an American, so you'll go to America?"

"Perhaps; yes, probably."

"I think you should know, mother, that I would prefer to remain in England."

The boy's formality was more wearing on Holly than tears. The gulf between them seemed, suddenly, enormous. Was she reaping a harvest of neglect? She had never consciously neglected him but had she been too careful, these last three years, not to smother him? She retreated, saying, "We'll talk about all that later, Chris."

"Why not now?"

"It's unfair to discuss such . . . such important matters behind your father's back."

"It's not all that's gone on behind Dad's back."

"Chris!"

"Well, is it?"

"I didn't *try* to fall in love with somebody else, you know."

"Did you try not to, Mother?"

He was not being profound or precocious; the barb of the question lay in its obviousness.

"When you're older . . ." Holly said.

"When I'm older, I won't care."

She tried to put her arm about him but he moved away.

Bleakly, Holly said, "You care now, don't you? You do care now?"

"Not much, if you must know." He lied effortlessly. His strength at that moment was formidable. "You mustn't worry about me."

"Chris, I'm your mother. I *love* you," she blurted out. "Haven't we been happy, the three of us?"

"Why did you marry Kennedy?"

"Because I . . ."

"Was it only to suit yourself."

"Is that what you think of me?"

"For me, then? To give me – this?"

"Who put that idea into your head?"

"Nobody. Certainly not Dad. He never said a word. But I believe you did it for me."

"And if I did?"

"It's . . . awful."

"To want something nice for my son, for you?"

"It's fraudulent, Mother."

Memories of her bargain with Christopher, the manner in which Kennedy had pursued her after Christopher's death, recollections too of the hideous night in Pimlico when Christopher had been burned to death and she had thought that she had lost not only her husband but her son; rhyme and reason fled, now as then. Her love for Peter was tainted by the same portentous circumstance that had once before brought her toppling down. In the boy she saw the mark of penitence, signal of a punishment of which he would be but the instrument, as Ritchie, those many years ago, had been only the tool of a greater destiny. Baptised in fire, Chris would cause her all the suffering that was needed to redress her guilt.

She said, "Your father wouldn't agree with you."

"What d'you know about Dad's real feelings?"

"Chris, that's enough?"

"I know why you came, Mother; you thought I was still a little boy, and that I'd do what you said was right? Well, I won't do what you want. I have a choice, don't I?"

Holly nodded, fearful of him, of the completeness of his powers of deception.

Chris said, "I don't *want* to go with you and Freeman to the United States. I'll stay with Dad in England."

"Perhaps you'll . . ."

"I shan't change my mind."

"Chris, oh, Chris!"

She had given him up too soon. Son of three fathers, he was destined to be lost to her. He had drifted away from her into impenetrable masculinity, a quality against which she had no defence.

"Classes will soon be over, Mother," Chris said. "My friends will be coming in. I'd rather they didn't find you here, please, it'll only lead to awkward questions, you see."

"We'll . . . we'll see each other at Christmas."

"If you wish."

"Chris, will you give me a kiss?"

Dutifully he kissed her brow, stepped back and opened the study door. She could detain him no longer.

"Good-bye, darling," Holly said.

"Good-bye, Mother."

*   *   *

Only when she reached the outskirts of London did Holly begin to cry. The tears were soft and she did not dare stop driving the car in case grief took over and possessed her completely. She continued to steer through the night hour traffic, sniffing and dabbing at her eyes. There was no one to whom she could turn for comfort. Peter would be at the theatre and she was too uncertain of Maury to trust herself to him. Even Emma had become an enemy, alienated from affection. Until Peter returned to the apartment between eleven thirty and midnight, she would find no welcome anywhere. In the end she headed for Chelsea, for the house she still thought of as her home.

She ate dinner with Kennedy and afterwards packed her clothes and personal items. There was precious little comfort in the act. As the moment of departure approached, she felt as if she was in limbo, suspended between desire to stay and anxiety to be away, to be with Peter and begin her new life.

Kennedy helped her with her luggage. He saw to it that the large trunk was put in the hall ready for the Gallery van to pick up in the morning. He was not, on the surface, restrained; he chatted on about clients and sales as if nothing out of the ordinary was taking place.

"Do you think I should buy those Bohemian glasses from Martineaux?"

"What's his price again?"

"Three hundred. We're getting thirty-six pieces for that, of course."

"I would take them, if I were you," said Holly.

"I'll write him first thing tomorrow," said Kennedy. "Now, is the Christie's sale on the ninth worth attending, do you think?"

"It's a mixed bag but the prices should be rock bottom."

"I assume you'll be there, Holly?"

"No, Kennedy; no, I won't."

"Not even to the viewing?"

"No."

"But Arbuthnot expects you to bid on . . ."

"Arbuthnot expects Kings' to bid, Kennedy. He'll give you a note of his top bids on the canvases he wants. You don't need me for that."

"But what if the paintings . . ."

"I wouldn't dabble in paintings, Kennedy. Concentrate on what you know best."

"Yes, I suppose you're right, Holly."

"If any major snags crop up, you know where I can be reached?"

"Yes, I have the address."

"I expect I'll be in touch quite often."

"When shall I see you next? Christmas, when Chris is home?"

"Oh, yes. Christmas. Definitely."

At length she could endure it no longer. She would have preferred the honesty of anger and recrimination, even embittered silence. She felt as if Kennedy was intentionally wounding her with his lack of demonstrable emotion. She had seen him more visibly upset when bidding good-bye to Chris at a weekend. She left earlier than she had intended before the urge to stir up a quarrel could get the better of her. Kennedy escorted her to the car. He closed the door carefully, wished her a safe journey and stood at the kerb with a mackintosh draped over his shoulders waving good-bye. Out of habit, sheer persistent habit, she tooted the horn in farewell as she rounded the corner out of Tite Street.

This time she could not drive. The crying fit assailed her violently and she parked, only yards from the corner, to weep sorely for ten minutes or more in the darkened car. She dried her tears at length, lit and smoked a cigarette then drove on to the theatre.

When Peter came off stage at final curtain Holly was waiting in his dressing room. He took her eagerly in his arms.

"All right?" he asked.

"Yes." She sighed and smiled. "Everything's fine."

That night Peter and Holly went to a party at the Ritz in honour of Gwen Flowers' 'umpteenth' birthday, thus acknowledging their relationship in public.

Peter danced with Holly and the trials of the day slipped from her and she found what she was looking for: for a time she was happy to be someone other than herself: for a time she was relieved to be free of Maury, Kennedy and of Chris: for a time.

* * *

"Are you blubbing, Deems?"

"'Course I'm not blubbing."

"Does he miss his mamma, then?"

"Shut up, Edgars."

"I'm *not* blubbing."

"Edgars, you're a tactless boor."

"Mater's gone off with a Yank, lor'lummie."

"Edgars, I'm warning you; leave Chris alone."

"Oh, let him say what he likes, Paul. I'm not fussed."

"Perhaps he'll get her into pictures and we'll all be able to gooze at Deems's mater in her scants. Lubberly, lubberly!"

"There's a limit, Edgars, and you're reaching it."

"Shut the row, both of you. Matey'll hear you."

"More liable to hear you fiddlin' with that damned wireless."

"Hold the noise, Edgars. I'm getting something, a foreign station."

"Frying tonight!"

"What have you raised, Paul?"

"Not sure. Listen. What do'you think, Chris?"

"It sounds like ocean waves."

"It's a wireless set not a damned seashell, Deems. Let the old maestro have· a lugful. Twiddle your knob, Williams, there's a dear fellow."

"Not so loud, not so loud."

"What is it, Edgars?"

"Something in German. Here, Williams, you try to decode."

"Yes, it's a speech, somebody making a speech, in German."

"What's he jawing about?"

"I'm not sure. I can hardly hear it, it's so faint."

"What's the roaring noise, Paul? Atmospherics?"

"Would you believe it, that's the crowd cheering."

"It's a footer match, must be, a Teutonic footer match."

"Don't act the fool, Edgars. Listen. Paul?"

"It's clearer now. Ah, the chap's name's Hitler. Adolf Hitler."

"Who the devil's he?" asked young Christopher Deems.

ooooooo
ooooo
ooo
o

PART THREE

PARIS EXPRESS

1

Vision of Venus

None of the Beckmans ever discovered the name of the law officer who manipulated their destinies in the course of the wild wet spring of 1933. It is doubtful if many coppers within the walls of New Scotland Yard could have identified Sergeant Kelloway and his position in the Detective Division was a mystery to all but a handful of his superiors. A casual observer might have surmised that Kelloway had no business to be on the Force at all, for he was deceptively weedy in appearance. Bert, however, had served his apprenticeship on the streets, had cracked his share of skulls with his truncheon and had even had the honour of being shot at by Mad Frank Philp during a rooftop pursuit in Bethnal Green. There were better men than Bert at that sort of caper, though, as Bert would be the first to admit. It had taken eight years for Sergeant Kelloway to find his niche as a silent contributor to the war against crime.

Kelloway worked without glory, without the satisfaction of knowing that he had truly 'nailed his man'. He seldom gave evidence in courts of law. His name appeared in the newspapers only once, a footnote to the celebrated Courtney Necklace case which, if truth be known, Bert had virtually solved on his own. Even in the enclaves of the art market Bert Kelloway was practically faceless; thus he retained the confidence of the narks, grasses and squealers upon whom he depended for his leads.

The Sergeant had the patience of a pole-squatter and the

stoicism of a blind Greek. He had learned long ago that only one in ten of his investigations, in a good year, would lead to criminal charges and one in twenty to a successful prosecution. Bearing the odds in mind Bert was not above 'squiring it' somewhere down the line by acting as a magistrate off his own bat and dishing out 'advice' to those who were 'at it'; he tended to follow this unorthodox, *ex-officio* routine when he knew there was no possibility of making a case stand up in court. As irritant and deterrent, Detective Sergeant Kelloway was worth his weight in wooden threepennies and his boss, being aware of the lad's virtues, let him get on with it unhampered by administrative pressures and demands.

Experts were fallible when it came to identifying works of art of questionable origin. Those sold *intentionally* to deceive, merited criminal proceedings. While dealers, collectors and curators chuntered on about varnishes, glazes and pigments Bert concentrated his attention on discovering just *how* the piece had been sold, a task made almost impossible by the unwillingness of said dealers, collectors and curators to admit to anything that might lower the tone of the trade and damage their reputations. Many victims of the forger's craft would rather lose money than face these consequences. 'Mitigating circumstances' arose like dragon's teeth in poor Bert's path as he strove to follow the trail of an obvious forgery back to its begetter. Paintings would 'vanish', taken suddenly 'off the market'. Collectors would 'withdraw' their complaints at the behest of internationally famous dealers and the questionable object, so it was claimed, would be 'destroyed'. Several of these 'destroyed' works seemed to be sprinkled with Phoenix dust for they rose again and again to flap about Sergeant Kelloway's head, until he learned the dodge of insisting that they were burned in his presence, which got rid of a few of them. The majority of the items that Bert Kelloway 'rumbled', however, changed into migrants and winged their way across the seas to France, Holland, Italy or to the United States of America where, in Bert's humble opinion, nobody could tell 'their arts from their elbow anyway'. Bert's brief did not stretch to long-range pursuits or to anything that smacked of 'cooperation' with foreign coppers. He had quite enough bother at home, thank you.

Let it here be said that Ritchie Beckman was too smart for any solo 'tec to entrap. Sergeant Kelloway barely got within sighting distance of Ritchie. The reason that the Beckmans – and the Kings – never discovered who was after them was that Bert Kelloway designed it that way. It suited the detective's purpose to throw a scare into men and women he had little hope of confronting face to face, to have them enlarge and exaggerate his power until he, a mild little Sergeant, became The Yard, poised to raid at dawn. Guilt, in a word, was Bert's principal weapon against the criminal elements that infested the wonderful world of antique art. Many a nice little racket did Bert scupper just by 'making his presence known'.

Detective Sergeant Kelloway's report on his investigation of a complaint made by Mr. Angus Robinson of Durham Grove, Kensington, in respect of the authenticity of a large landscape painting by the artist Hobbema purchased in good faith from Kings' Gallery, Chalfont Arcade, Bond Street, was, to say the least of it, scant in factual details. It made no mention of the 'chat' that Sergeant Kelloway had with Mr. Robinson, in the course of which the detective explained a few of the harsher facts of life to the collector; or that it was Mr. Robinson, not Sergeant Kelloway, who confronted the Gallery owner with his discovery regarding the origin of the landscape; or that Mr. Robinson received 'satisfaction' from the owner of the said gallery who took the painting back; or that later in the month of April Sergeant Kelloway, purporting to be a collector, visited the said gallery and professed interest in works by the artist Hobbema, and was informed that the only canvas in stock was 'unreliable and not for sale'. Collector Kelloway begged for sight of the landscape, to be the judge of its unreliability, but the portly owner of Kings' would not play ball. Adamantly he refused even to bring it out of the basement which, as far as Policeman Kelloway was concerned, was a very good thing indeed.

The Sergeant's handwritten report summarised all of this with the phrase 'Seller acknowledged error and made full retribution', and ended there, without so much as a hint that the detective's instincts had been sufficiently roused to push him into a discreet investigation of the impeccable Kings'.

Thanks to a wink and a nod from a nark, the investigation led to a certain Mr. Richard Beckman of the Apex Advertising Company who did quite a bit of business in Paris, who was related to the wife and former partner of Kennedy King and who, it transpired, had served time in Brixton.

Stubbornness kept Kelloway going. Experience told him that the 'case' would probably fizzle out at the door of the Apex offices. Evidence that Ritchie Beckman was dabbling in works of art of dubious origin and authenticity was abundant. The boardrooms of certain firms that dealt with Apex sported fine works that had the same 'flavour' to them as the forged Hobbema now residing in Kings' basement. A search warrant would have solved a lot of problems in short order but Sergeant Kelloway was leery of taking up the court's time with applications.

It occurred to Kelloway that he might apply pressure by fixing on to other members of the family. He had no doubt that Ritchie Beckman was up to some sort of dirty work, possibly also Maurice and the sister who was sleeping with an American theatrical who was not her husband in a posh flat in Holland Park. There was too much money floating about for it to have been honestly gained. The father, Leopold, had recently slipped off to live in Hastings with a new wife which seemed, to Bert Kelloway, to indicate that perhaps things had got too hot for the old man in Lambeth.

Sketchy though it was, Kelloway's private dossier on Ritchie Beckman presented the portrait of a villain who would not be liable to leave 'clues' lying around London, not when he was running a French end to his business. It is probable that the diligent Sergeant would have continued his spade work in the Beckman midden if another, more pressing matter concerning the awkward 'discovery' of a number of spurious Chinese bronzes in the Blackwall Museum had not demanded his attention.

Thorough and patient to the end, however, Sergeant Kelloway recorded the data he had gathered on the Beckmans in his personal notebook and prepared to tidy up as best he could by throwing a fright into Mr. Richard Beckman in the hope that it might upset the applecart, or at least tilt it sideways.

Bert's methods were strictly *infra dig*. He started with his informant, Murgatroyd, caretaker of the Apex building and a habitué of a cosy smokepot pub called the Moor's Head which had a skittle alley in the back. The clumping Murgatroyd was much addicted to this sport since hurling wooden balls at wooden pins was a splenetic activity and, as Murgatroyd played it, somewhat akin to war.

Kelloway had been leaning on the rail of the spectators' gallery for ten minutes before Murgatroyd noticed him.

"Mr. Kelloway, you been 'ere long?" Murgatroyd was respectful to anyone who paid him money; he clipped the Sergeant for the odd quid from time to time. He wiped his hands on his rump, leaving a dusting of French chalk on his trousers, and limped round the back of the rail, picking up his pint on the way. "Never saw yer there."

There were seven other men in the narrow room. A deformed boy at the alley's end was setting up pins and hefting balls out of the trench. Two of the men were known to Kelloway, though he had had no personal dealings with them and doubted if they would recognise him. He turned his back on the room and leaned his hips on the railing. He was more direct than usual. He had no need to foxtrot with Murgatroyd who was not a member of the criminal classes and therefore had nothing to lose by doing the law a favour.

"Apropos," said Kelloway softly, "of the matter which we discussed last month . . ."

"I'm with yer."

". . . the manager, Mitchell, you're on noddin' terms with him?"

"Known 'im for years."

"Want you to have a private word with him," said Kelloway. "Can you manage it?"

"Easy as pie."

"Tell Mitchell a gentleman was askin' about what goes on in the Apex. Want you to say the gentleman was 'asking

289

searching questions'."

"An' what did I tell this gentleman in answer to 'is searchin' questions'?" said Murgatroyd.

"You clammed up."

"Don't I know the gent's name?"

"No, but you suspect he's from Scotland Yard."

Muscles around Murgatroyd's mouth twitched in a grim lopsided leer. "Say no more."

"Cig?" Kelloway offered a crumpled packet of Player's Weights.

"Don't mind if I do," said Murgatroyd.

"Keep the packet."

Murgatroyd put the packet into his vest pocket. Inside, replacing the cigarettes, would be two or three pound notes, perhaps even a fiver if his cooperation with Kelloway had been valuable. He clumped alongside the detective to the mouth of the corridor to the public bar. "Still interested in this matter, Sir?"

"Still interested. You know how to keep in touch?"

"Ain't forgot, Sir."

Kelloway nodded and, surprised to find the glass still in his hand, passed the half-pint to Murgatroyd. "Polish this off for me."

"Can do," said Murgatroyd, obediently accepting the glass.

And the meet was over.

Armed with a pocketful of pennies and his notebook, trench coat collar turned up against the cold rain that drenched the city, Sergeant Kelloway proceeded from the Moor's Head to a public telephone box by the stage door of the Scala Theatre. Here he temporarily wound up his involvement with the Beckmans with three carefully rehearsed telephone calls.

"Mr. Beckman? Mr. Maurice Beckman?"

"Yes."

"Sorry to trouble you at home, Sir. This is New Scotland Yard."

"What branch?" No flies on Maurice; Kelloway ignored the question.

"I'm callin' in connection with a line of enquiries regarding your brother Richard."

"What's your name and rank, please?"

"About certain objects of artistic interest, Mr. Beckman. Can you help me, I wonder?"

"I doubt it," said the deep, grave, circumspect voice.

"Can't, or won't, Mr. Beckman?"

"New Scotland Yard, I'll talk to; an unidentified voice on the public line, I won't."

"I assure you, Mr. Beckman . . ."

"You want to talk to me – about anything at all – send an officer with an identification card and I'll be only too pleased. You still haven't told me your name?"

"You'll hear from us shortly, Mr. Beckman."

"Yeah?"

"Thank you for your cooperation." Sergeant Kelloway replaced the receiver.

Fair enough; he dialled a second number.

"Mr. Beckman's residence." The woman's voice was prim and formal.

"May I speak with Mr. Richard Beckman, please."

"Who is calling?"

"Mr. Oliver of Oliver's Stores," said Kelloway.

"Are you a client of Mr. Beckman's?"

"Of course I am, I'm Oliver of Oliver's Stores. Who the devil are you?"

"Fletcher, Sir. Mr. Beckman's domestic assistant." the woman said. "Mr. Beckman is not presently at home, Sir. May I have him telephone you from his business premises in the morning?"

"Where is he?"

"I cannot divulge where Mr. Beckman is this evening."

"In Paris, eh?"

"No, Sir."

"Well, it's about that painting he gave me."

"I really could not say about that, Sir."

"It's a blasted fake and not worth the canvas it's painted on."

"Perhaps, Sir, you would prefer Mr. Beckman to call you

later tonight."

"A miserable rotten forgery. He told me it was a genuine Pissarro. Turns out to be nothing of the kind."

"I will impart your dissatisfaction to Mr. Beckman, Sir."

"He hasn't heard the last of this, not by a long chalk."

"Mr. Beckman will be most distressed, Mr. Oliver. I have no doubt that he will have an explanation."

"It had better be a bloody good one."

Kelloway crashed down the receiver, smiling. He paused, sloughed off his feigned anger and dialled for the third and last time.

It took the man three or four minutes to answer. His voice was sleepy and yet lugubrious, and he sounded just a little tipsy, though Kelloway would not swear to it.

"King."

"Ah, yes, Mr. King," said Kelloway with drawling affability. "Perhaps you remember me. I called at your gallery couple of weeks back."

"In what connection, Mister . . .?"

"Concerning a landscape painting by Hobbema. Do you still have it?"

King wheezed slightly. "I thought I'd make it abundantly clear, that the landscape we have was not by Hobbema but was only a copy."

"I'd like to see it."

"There's no point, I'm afraid."

"You still have it?"

"Yes, but it's emphatically not for sale."

"How good a copy is it, Mr. King?"

"It's an excellent copy."

"Couldn't you be wrong about it then?"

"Regrettably not. It is not a work by Hobbema."

"I might be willin' to buy it, nonetheless."

"We would not be willing to sell."

"Where did you get the painting, Mr. King?"

"Who are you, may I ask?"

"Did you buy it from somebody in England?"

"As a matter of fact, it came from France, from a collection in France."

"In Paris?"

"Near Paris. Really, Sir, I must ask again to whom I'm speaking?"

"You wouldn't know my name, Mr. King. Listen, was it Mrs. King bought the painting?"

"That's none of your business." King hesitated. "In any case, my wife's no longer active in the business."

"I heard a whisper that Mrs. King's brother can supply paintings to order; any truth in that rumour?"

"Mrs. King's brother? I don't know what you mean. Do you mean Mr. Ritchie Beckman? He isn't a *bona fide* dealer. I don't know where you got your information. Look, my wife isn't here. She isn't . . . connected with the firm any longer. The paintings were her side of it. I don't know too much about that side of it." King checked himself. "If, however, you are interested in works by Hobbema, I'll keep my eye open. Now, your name?"

"I'm interested, Mr. King, but I want them urgently. Are you a *good* source – if you know what I mean?"

"I *don't* know what you mean."

"I'm sure your wife would."

"Sir, I don't like your tone, or your remarks about my wife."

"Put it this way, I'll pay top price for good copies, really *good* copies of works by Hobbema or other Flemish painters of his century."

"We have nothing of that nature for sale."

"Can you put me in touch with somebody then, somebody who has?"

"No, I cannot. What's more, we – I – don't deal in doubtful stuff. As a matter of fact, my wife is considerably concerned about being landed with a dud and is making her own enquiries."

"In London or in France?"

"In France. Now, Sir, I really do not wish to continue this conversation."

"I heard that Mrs. King's brother had a line in paintings?"

"Then you've heard more than I have, Sir. Good-night to you."

"Think it over, Mr. King."

"There's nothing to think over. Now, again, good-night."

At his end of the line King replaced the receiver.

Kelloway was disappointed. He should have made more of it. He had had the old duffer off guard. All sorts of nefarious plots were imaginable, collusion between Holly King and her brother Richard for instance. Sister and brother could be operating a laundry for forgeries in the Chalfont Arcade right under King's nose. King finds out, kicks wife out, wife takes up with wealthy fancy-man? Possible!

Pity about the Paris connection. Sergeant Kelloway could not be bothered with the administrative palaver necessary to enlist the help of the Sûreté. The French were prickly and not helpful unless national art treasures had been stolen. Then there was the strange coincidence of Leo Beckman, Lambeth born and bred as far as Kelloway could make out, suddenly taking a new wife and decamping for Hastings. Was the old man's house in Hastings a link in the chain too? Could it be the repository of art work of doubtful origins or a springboard in a smuggling operation? At least Bert Kelloway had settled one thing in his mind; whatever the rest of them were up to, he was willing to bet his best brown boots that Kennedy King was an honest man or, at worst, an innocent bystander.

It was still raining hard.

Bert Kelloway left the telephone box and struck out for the underground to catch a tube home to Dagenham where his dear old mum would be waiting for him with a hot supper in the oven. For the time being there was no more he could do apropos the Beckman gang. He hoped, however, that he had put a spoke in their wheel, put the wind up them good and proper. Perhaps there would be enough guilt among them to cause them to curtail operations until The Yard, in the shape of one dedicated copper, could find the time to expose their secrets and, with luck, bring one or more of the gang to the dock.

*   *   *

Conscience, like caviar, was not particularly sustaining to a serious-minded man. Maury had never acquired a taste for self-examination any more than he had for the black fish eggs served in such awful abundance by the waiters behind the buffet tables at the top of the long morning room. Although he had adhered to capitalist principles for most of his life, the latent revolutionary that lurked in every slum-born kid was roused by the sight of so much waste. Maury was overtaken by a queasy feeling that perhaps Holly wasn't the only one who had been corrupted by an excess of material comfort and who really belonged here among the charming spendthrifts who had become, by proxy, 'her crowd'.

It was not Holly, however, who highlighted the universal attractiveness of pretty people doing trivial things in the sunny glare of publicity. Maury had been floored by Jane Tatton Swale's eager acceptance of his invitation to be his partner at a supper party given – thrown was a better word – by Peter Freeman to celebrate the one hundred and fiftieth performance of *Step Out Along the Strand*. Maury could see no valid reason why a five and a half month's run of an obvious box-office winner should merit an expensive milestone but he reckoned that theatricals thrived on endless incestuous beanos and needed them as addicts need cocaine. Slightly jaundiced, yet caring enough of Holly despite everything, Maury had gone for support to the one woman he supposed he could trust not to be impressed by the glamour of the West End mob, Miss Jane Tatton Swale. Apologetically he had requested her company, more or less as a favour. But Maury's knowledge of the spinster scholar was incomplete. Jane had a secret. At the very mention of the name Peter Freeman, Jane Tatton Swale, shedding twenty-five years of disciplined restraint, was transformed into a bubble-brained girl again, a side of her that Maury had never seen before.

"Peter Freeman! My God, Maury! Of course, of course, I'll come."

"Jane, it's . . ."

"I wanted to ask you to ask your sister to introduce me to Peter sometime but I didn't know quite how to broach the subject without seeming like a chump. And now this, a supper party, in *his* house. Who else will be there? Will Ralph be there?"

"Ralph? Do you know Ralph Brooks?"

"No, no, we've never met."

"I take it," said Maury drily, "that you are willing to 'waste an evening', Jane?"

"How can one waste an evening in which one meets with Peter Freeman and Ralph Brooks? Maury, you can be so crass sometimes."

"Crass – because I don't rave about Saracen revues?"

"It isn't a revue; it's a musical comedy. Enormously entertaining." Jane defended *Step Out Along the Strand* with more passion than she had ever defended the theories of Adam Smith or the world-view of August Strindberg. "One has the feeling that you haven't even seen it, Maury?"

"Well, that's true. I haven't."

"In that case, I'll try to obtain seats for an evening next month."

"How many times have you been, Jane?"

"Four, if you must know."

"Shakespeare, Chekov, even Shaw, you go to more than once, but what do you get from a second viewing of a Saracen revue, Jane?"

"Pleasure."

The explanation silenced Maury.

Pleasure was not something with which he was terribly familiar these days. It had become associated with Ruth and consequently all tangled up with guilt and revenge. Ruth hardly seemed to need his protection any longer. She was happy to defy her husband and Maury had become the focus of her existence. What was even more disturbing, Maury too was becoming addicted to defying Ritchie and found the stubborn daring quite heady. He had even considered taking Ruth to the Freeman party. That, however, would have been too revealing and would have put him in an awkward position with Holly.

It was the first occasion on which Maury had visited Holly in her new environment. The changes in his sister were not at all to his liking. She had lost her calmness and her grace and had been infected by the edgy anxiety of the performers around her. She seemed frantically keen to be noticed. She had learned to use her hands in the making of large gestures and was constantly touching people, Freeman in particular. But she did not do any of these things naturally and could not, Maury thought, rid herself of the reserve that been the bedrock of her character since girlhood.

Freeman's affection for Holly was, however, apparent. He did not chide her for laughing too loudly or for trying to steal his thunder. Perhaps he hoped that Holly would 'calm down' when they became man and wife.

Maury had been in the Holland Park flat for twenty minutes before he had a chance to talk with his sister.

She spoke to him in the same breathless, distracted manner as she conversed with the outrageously theatrical guests.

"And Dad, how is Dad, tell me, Maury?"

"Settling down."

"Hastings, isn't it?"

"Wemlock Bridge, just on the outskirts."

"Is he happy with his new life?"

"Seems to be."

"Do you visit them?"

"I've been down once. Had tea with them."

"Will she be good for him, the new wife, do you think?"

"I think so. She has him pretty well under her thumb."

"It's hard to imagine Dad under anyone's thumb."

She laughed; it was all Maury could do to stop himself wincing.

He said, "You seem to have settled down too, Holly."

"Oh, I have, I have. Peter's such a nice man, and his friends make me so welcome."

"Don't you miss . . . the business?"

"Hardly at all; well, just a tiny bit."

Holly did not enquire after Kennedy and Maury did not offer any information concerning her husband or son. He had parked Jane – who looked ravishing in a brand new black evening dress – with Peter Freeman. Without doubt Jane would be negotiating an introduction to Ralph Brooks who having slept all day – it being a Sunday – was stoking up at the buffet and calculating just who was who in the forty-strong crowd that packed the apartment and spilled out into the hallway.

"What do you do with yourself?" Maury asked.

Holly answered, "We sleep in the morning. In the afternoons, unless there's a matinée, we shop or visit galleries; Peter's become very interested in paintings. Now the racing season's coming in no doubt we'll slip out to Ascot or Goodwood."

"Sounds . . . pleasurable."

"It is, oh, it is."

Holly's anxious-to-impress gaze had become unblinking, almost furtive, though she smiled all the while and stirred the air with her hands. Was she like this when she was alone with Freeman? Maury doubted it. Surely it was an act designed to show the world, such as it was, that she had been 'right' to give up everything for darling Peter.

Maury supposed that he had better make some show of friendship towards the man who might eventually become his brother-in-law. It was not difficult, Maury imagined, to like Freeman. Communicating with him might be less easy. He watched Freeman take Jane's arm and lead her across the room to waylay Brooks who, with brimming glass and a laden plate, was trying to find a place to eat his first meal of the day in peace.

Maury nodded to Holly. "Excuse me, Holly. I must look after my partner. Besides I'm curious as to what she'll actually say to Ralph Brooks."

Holly snatched his hand. For an instant Maury thought that the charade was about to collapse, that his sister was about to draw him into some awful confidence, confess that she had made a mistake, beg for his help.

Maury was wrong. Even her confidences were trivial. The intimate touch, the whisper; "Maury, darling, you *must* try the quiche. Speciality of Francini's, the caterers. It's *divine!*"

"Divine?" Maury was unable to disguise his reaction to this incredible banality.

For a moment the Holly of old was exposed. She did not apologise or recant, however, but briefly acknowledged the silliness of her remark.

Affecting the most appalling accent, Holly repeated, "*Dee*-vinah. Abso-bloomin-lutely *dee*-vinah."

Maury chuckled. All was not lost.

Holly patted his hand. "Call me, Maury, will you? We haven't had a chin-wag in ages."

"Lunch?"

"Make it dinner; just the two of us."

"Next week?"

"Perfect."

"It's a date."

Encouraged, Maury left his sister and headed towards Freeman and Jane in a corner behind the white hide couch. Here Ralph Brooks had found not only peace but a place upon which to park his plate, having deposed a potted plant from its circular table. Maury approached in time to catch the expression of dismay that flickered over the actor's handsome features as Peter Freeman buttonholed him. Maury paused, loitered, lit a cigarette. He did not join the trio. He had no wish to dissipate Jane's moment of glory. The don's austere beauty was burnished by excitement. She looked much the better for it, less regal, more human; a parlourmaid had replaced the queen.

"Ralph, I'd like you to meet a close friend of Holly's brother," Peter was saying. "Jane Swale; Ralph Brooks."

"What a pleasure it is to meet you, Mr. Brooks. I've . . . I've revelled in all of your performances."

Ralph did not open his pores to flattery nor did he stifle his boredom with fans' praise. He squinted at Jane oddly then, with a wag of his fork, interrupted her anthem to his talents. "Your name: Jane Swale?"

"Yes?"

"Jane *Tatton* Swale?"

"Yes."

"My God! *The* Jane Tatton Swale?" Brooks slid the fork into his breast pocket and caught the startled woman's arm, lifting her hand to his lips. "I'm delighted, thrilled, over-whelmed to meet you, Miss Swale."

"But . . ."

"When you wrote *Equal Endeavour*, what age were you, twenty? Twenty-one?"

"Very young, it's not much of a . . ."

"It's a *wonderful* book. I was weaned on it. *Wonderful* book."

"But how did an actor . . .?"

"Actor-schmactor!" said Brooks. "Da war a miner, a Durham lad. I war a miner an' all, lass. Nowt abaht t'coahl trade you'm can be a-teachin' owd Brooksie. I *devoured* your book. It opened my eyes to so many things. How strange that we should finally meet in such a gathering as this, on such a night as this."

Blushing, Jane allowed her hand to remain in Ralph's.

She stammered, "B . . . but I'm the one who . . . I mean . . . It's *my* pleasure to meet *you*."

"A jaded old hoofer, a painted doll?" said Brooks; he was serious in his self-deprecation. "Dust under the feet of someone of your calibre, Miss Swale."

"Oh, really, Mr. Brooks!"

"Please call me Ralph. Look, I ha'n't hadda bite o'snap all t'bleedin' day, lass. Say thee an' me spark off an' eat while we natter? Peter, where can we hide?"

"The guest bedroom," said Peter. "There's nothing in there but coats. I'll find you a table, though."

Brooks' desire to be alone with Jane was too strong to be denied; it swept away the woman's hero-worship on a flood of rapport. Poor Jane, Maury thought, she had lost an idol in the very moment that she had found a friend. He watched Ralph Brooks, talking nineteen to the dozen, lead Jane away, the Durham miner's son and the tally-clerk's daughter. Even he, Maury, hadn't read that first book, a work that Jane disowned as being far too subjective to stand the test of time.

Peter said, "It looks like you've been ditched."

Maury said, "I don't mind."

Peter said, "I'm glad you could join us tonight, Maury."

They seated themselves on the white hide couch, a piece of furniture almost identical to the one in Ritchie's lounge. Davenports, Maury thought, inconsequentially, must be in this year. He offered Freeman a cigarette, lit it for the dancer and settled into an uncomfortable pause, a silence that neither man could break just at first. There was no common ground between them, except Holly, and the awkwardness of that relationship had to be avoided.

"Do you go to the races, Maury?" said Peter at last.

"No. I believe you do, though."

"I love 'em."

"Are you an owner?"

"Not yet. I'd probably buy a share in a throroughbred if I thought I was going to be in England for long. When I get back to California – maybe then."

"When are you leaving England?"

"Mid-summer."

"For good?"

"That depends on how things go with me in the movie business."

"Will Holly travel with you?"

"I sure hope so."

A sense of impending loss came on Maury then, the realisation of just how much his sister meant to him, coupled with a fear for her future and, oddly, for his own future without her.

In the last four or five years they had not seen much of each other, yet they had become closer than ever before – until Freeman had intruded. Maury felt a sudden surge of anger towards the American. A nonsensical emotion; Freeman wasn't to blame for what had happened. He could not entirely blame Freeman for wanting his sister. But how long would it take for them to become bonded, welded into the sort of unit that Holly and Kennedy had made? How much opportunity for that sort of maturity would there be in the alien hills of Los Angeles?

Another awkward pause; Peter beat a little swinging tune with his polished evening shoe, one knee crossed over the other. In apposition to the dancer Maury felt as heavy as suet pudding.

Selfishly Maury wanted all to be as it was, Holly, Kennedy, Chris to come together again, to provide him with the surrogate family he had never had time to build for himself.

And then, in that modernistic flat, amid the chattering of the party-goers, Maury was filled with need of Ruth. His sense of loss over Holly transferred itself to dainty Ruth Beckman, to the children she had never had. Grief over the wasted years that had turned yellow like the pages of a cheap novelette troubled him. He imagined himself with Ruth, as Freeman was with Holly.

For weeks now the poor imprisoned unflowered child-woman had laid fully claim on him. If she had been wife to any man other than his brother he would have jettisoned all scruple and would have run off with her. Honour was only skin-deep. At forty-two the benevolence in him needed an outlet, a realisation. He had missed out on the delicate pleasures of love; it had become little more than an adjunct of conversation in which he gave nothing of himself. Now he knew what was wrong with the prospect of Peter married to Holly. There would be so little privacy in the years to come; that would be as damaging to his sister as Ritchie's unnatural imprisonment of his wife had been to Ruth.

Peter's voice intruded on his brooding. "Can I get you something, Maury? Champagne?"

"I'd like a whisky," Maury said.

Change, novelty and flux; his fear of them was testimony to his need. Holly, he saw now, had got there before him. But she had not found what she sought.

Freeman brought him the drink. Maury did not notice the dancer's embarrassment. He sipped the whisky gladly, wrapped up in his own problem.

"Maury?"

"Hm?"

"Maury, I could use your advice," Peter said.

Maury conducted his attention to the American; the stranger who shared his sister.

"Sure," Maury said. "What's up?"

From his pocket Peter Freeman removed a letter. He unfolded it carefully and hid the envelope in his pocket again. He stared at the letter. It was written in small fast-flowing characters in mauve ink on a quality paper.

"I got this a couple of days ago, addressed to me at the

theatre." For an instant Peter appeared ungainly, knees angular, shoulders hunched, the sharp chin poked out uncomfortably. "I don't know what to do about it. I figured you might . . . Hell, if we can't trust you, Maury, who can we trust?"

"Who's the letter from?"

"Woman called Marion Ogden Hillis."

"The American millionairess? Didn't Holly sell her something, last year in Monte Carlo?"

"That's where Holly and I met."

"So?"

Peter drew in a deep breath and passed the letter to Maury.

"The miniature's a forgery," Peter said. "It was examined at Columbia University. It's a dud. It's all in the letter. Marion wants her money back. If she doesn't get it – she'll sue."

Maury scanned the text; the woman's vengeful intentions were apparent.

"How did Holly react when you showed it to her?" Maury asked.

"I . . . I haven't shown it to her yet."

"Why not?"

"I . . . I don't rightly know."

Maury waved the letter back at Freeman.

"Show it to Holly," he advised.

"Listen, I don't want Holly upset," Peter said. "I'll pay the Hillis bitch her money. Hopefully that's all she wants, her goddamned fifty thousand back. I can do it. I can manage it."

Maury got to his feet.

"No, Peter," he told the dancer. "Like it or lump it, Holly must be told."

"Why?"

"Because it's her reputation that's at stake, Peter, not yours."

"Yeah," Peter Freeman said. "I guess that's what worries me."

For once Maury was not charitable; he did not sympathise with the man's predicament. He too understood what the letter would mean. Now Holly would be drawn back to

Kennedy, angered by an error that she could not bury.

"You will show it to her, won't you?" Maury said.

Freeman slapped his hand on his lean thigh, and got to his feet too. "Tomorrow," he said. "First thing."

Three evenings later, on Wednesday of that week, Maury received a phone-call from an anonymous person purporting to be an officer of New Scotland Yard.

By the week's end, the Beckmans were once more at war.

*　　*　　*

It startled Holly to be confronted by her son. She had seen Chris only three times – arranged visits during the Christmas holiday – since her departure from Chelsea and retirement from active participation in the antique business. That drizzling April morning she had been prepared to deal with Kennedy – particularly as she had such a demanding reason for seeking the meeting – but to find Chris there too was upsetting. Standing tall and rather aloof by Kennedy's chair in the gallery's office, Chris stole away the attitude she had decided, quite consciously, to adopt – a familiar brusque commercial tone. They waited, however, like a tableau, man and boy, welded by light from the ever-burning lamp in the windowless alcove at the rear of the shop. To Holly's discomfiture, they presented a deliberate unity, masculine solidarity, as if they had agreed to cooperate in thwarting her wishes or so Holly – nervous and disadvantaged – supposed.

She flung herself at once into a posture of dashing 'modernity', all gaiety and flutter, defence against a solemnity that she interpreted as disapproval.

Nobody – and certainly not her husband – had an inkling as to her true feelings. How could they guess that in heart and mind she was much less certain than she had been five months ago that a legal severance from Kennedy would solve her problems and bring her lasting happiness?

Holly tried to pretend that she was not becoming disenchanted with her new life style. The pattern of endless outings and parties coupled with lonely evenings had not assuaged her restless longing. Sharing Peter's bed and his affection was all that was left of the ill-considered dream. While love was worth any price, love was not so easy to define. Holly saw now that what she wanted was Peter as an element in her life, not she in his. What she had exchanged for love was independence and she could no more thrive without it than a lily can without moisture. Peter was not to blame, except in that he had come to love her, to need her; she had never bargained for that, not at the outset at any rate.

The stubborn pride that had pushed her into the affair seemed ugly to Holly now that the first ecstasy had dwindled and the continuity of her decisions and her actions became so dreadfully apparent. Pride, however, mitigated against her and would be its own punishment perhaps. She could not bring herself to admit to Peter that she had made a wrong choice. She had determined that she would stick by her decision in the hope that when she reached Los Angeles and the last connections with England were snapped she would become herself again and not a stateless person, a ghost caught between two worlds. But she was no longer sure and, in her heart, she was desperately afraid that Howard Crocker's predictions would come true, that her malaise would in due course infect Peter and that they would become victims of impetuosity not of love.

In the four or five seconds that it took Holly to sail from the shop door to the office, past the assembled members of Kings' staff who had come to stare at her, Holly was possessed of the most awful sense of failure. Why had she been so foolish as to protect the remnants of girlish illusions about romance, to chase not love but the mirage of a constant, intense passion created, and paradoxically destroyed, by the hazy white light of her lover's public persona? She did not feel wicked, only stupid and put on a strident act to hide it from the people who had once respected her.

"Mrs. Mazollo," she cried. "How *are* you?"

"Fine, Mum."

"Mr. Caldwell. I trust your rheumatics aren't bad?"

"Damp weather don't do them no good, Ma'am."

"And Wilf, dear Wilf, how are you?"

Wilf scowled at her adoringly and backed off down the

basement stairs without reply, innocently rebuking her for having changed so much that she would address him as "dear Wilf" even if he was and always had been 'dear' to her.

Nonplussed, Holly went on into the office.

"Chris, how wonderful to see you! What a surprise!" she declared.

"Mother." Chris was man enough not to shrink from the kiss she planted on his cheek, disciplined enough not to wipe away the crescent of lipstick in her presence. "Are you well?"

"Wonderful, darling, thank you."

She seated herself in the wing chair that Kennedy had placed for her so that her back would be to the light; *her* chair, re-covered in silk velvet, *her* Queen Anne desk with the recessed cupboard in which Day Book and Sales and Purchase ledgers had been housed, together with that most valuable of all volumes, the Client Book. Clearly Kennedy had been expecting her to arrive on time. Punctuality was one thing she had not sacrificed in the name of liberation.

The kettle boiled on its electric plate, the Georgian service and Worcester cups shared a tray with a plate of ginger biscuits. Holly felt the shop close around her. She would have given anything to be able to relax, to let its atmosphere envelop her again, to sip tea, chat with Kennedy about the state of the art market and browse over the arithmetic.

It would all have been so fine if only he had not invited Chris to the meeting, and, more importantly, if she had not had Marion Ogden Hillis's scathing letter folded in her purse.

"You look well, Holly, a little thi . . . more slender, perhaps," said Kennedy guardedly.

Chris perched on top of a heavy Tudor chest within which, unless things had changed, dumpy bundles of cash receipts, bound in sequence year by year, reposed. It had been Chris's 'throne' when he was a child, Holly remembered; he would tuck his knees up to disguise the fact that his feet did not reach the floor. She had not brought him to the gallery often. On the whole, it was a dull place for an active lad. An occasional trophy that turned up with job lots, a helmet, sword or flintlock pistol, amused him briefly but these ancient weapons had, for Chris, no life; in the context of his mother's trade they were mere items of barter concerning which the boy had but two standard questions to ask, the litany of dealers he had learned by rote: "How old, Mum? How much?" Now Chris was close to being a man. Tall for his age and in long trousers for the Easter holiday, at fourteen he could pass for a budding gentleman in Kennedy's club or one of the fusty restaurants that Kennedy favoured.

"I'm perfectly fine, Kennedy," said Holly. "How are you?"

"Not bad; a trifle wheezy. I wish the spring would come. This rain, you know."

Holly addressed Chris next. For a few minutes mother and son exchanged stilted questions and answers about school and examinations.

She turned her attention again to Kennedy. "Selling much?"

"This and that."

"The half yearly figures to December were excellent."

"Not bad."

"And the first quarter?"

"Down somewhat."

"Oh?"

"Superior stock's difficult to find these days."

"According to the *Times* the art market's beginning to pick up a little."

"Paintings and drawings, as you rightly pointed out, aren't my province," said Kennedy. "Fact is, I haven't been buying very much at all."

"But you have been selling?"

"This and that," Kennedy repeated.

Kennedy's reticence did not disguise the true meaning of the phrase. Business was bad. Sales were down and quality stock was low and the turnover and profit records would show it. Her husband had no need to be explicit; she had been far too long in the retail trade to need more than a hint. The knowledge made it difficult for her to broach the subject of the Ogden Hillis letter. A man of less courtesy than Kennedy would have asked her outright what her purpose was in calling at the shop and might have accused her of coming to gloat. But Kennedy was not one to harbour grudges or show bitterness. Holly was suddenly disgusted by her synthetic approach, the strained breathless eagerness of manner that she had consciously adopted to cope with Peter's colleagues. She took a deep breath, snapped open her purse and extracted Marion Hillis's letter.

"We have," she said, "a problem."

Kennedy took the letter, fitted on his spectacles and scanned the first page impassively.

Chris watched with a certain tenseness. Perhaps he suspected that the letter was part of a plot to lever him from the security of St. Justin's and chain him, under law, to his mother's keeping.

"Chris," said Holly, quietly, "it's a business letter, that's all. Nothing to do with you."

Kennedy read the second page, lips pursed.

"That's a bit thick," Kennedy murmured. "Accusing you of unscrupulously exploiting their friendship."

"Do you want to know what's going on, Chris?" said Holly.

"I wouldn't mind."

"Last year I sold a miniature painting to a couple of Americans. It seems the thing's a forgery."

"How on earth were *you* taken in, mother?" Chris perked up; his aloofness too had been only skin deep.

"The painting's history seemed so authentic."

"Who was the artist?"

"Holbein. The workmanship was brilliant. In addition I made the fatal mistake of trusting the dealer who sold it me."

"Somebody we know?" said Chris.

"He's not English. He lives in Marseilles."

"You mean Hugues de Rais? Isn't he a rogue?"

"Yes, he is. But, damn it, I took his word for it on this occasion."

"The letter Dad's reading, who's it from?"

"The clients who bought the item. They're howling blue murder."

"Are they sure it isn't right?"

"Apparently," said Holly, glancing at Kennedy, "Ray

Ogden Hillis, who fancies himself as an expert in period miniatures, was bragging about his find. Another collector, out of pique probably, challenged the painting's authenticity. He may only have been trying it on, trying to steal some of Ray's thunder. The Ogden Hillises got into an argument by correspondence in the New York *Journal of Art*. They were challenged to subject the miniature to scientific tests conducted by experts at Columbia University. They did. The scientific evidence *appears* to prove that the watercolour pigments and the prepared bases of the card on which they were laid down could not have been applied more than three or four years ago."

"Do you believe the scientists?"

"Copies of the reports, the client says, are available if I doubt their word." Holly went on.

"Do you doubt, mother?"

"Chemists," said Holly, "are not often wrong. Besides, an X-ray photograph of the painting was compared with an X-ray photograph of a proven Holbein watercolour – I shudder to think what all this cost the Ogden Hillises – and the application of the paint is completely different."

"X-rays don't lie," said Chris. "I've read a lot about their use in detection."

Kennedy had finished the letter. He took off his spectacles and let them hang on the cord about his neck. He seemed slightly stunned.

Holly said, "No forger, no matter how skilful, can exactly duplicate the master's stroke. Even in wash drawings and watercolours X-rays will show up major differences."

"Why aren't X-rays more widely used in our business?" said Chris.

"It's expensive," said Holly. "Besides, it takes the fun out of the collecting game. It robs art experts of authority and puts judgment into the hands of philistine scientists."

"I see," said Chris. "Nonetheless, somebody sold you a pup, Mum."

"Yes. A bow-wow without a bark."

Kennedy spoke. "Did Hugues de Rais know it was a forgery?"

Holly said, "Of course."

Kennedy said, "Can we prove that he intended to defraud us?"

Holly said, "Possibly not. What we can do is wring the bloody little Frog's neck – and get our money back."

"I hope so," said Kennedy. "If for any reason we are obliged to write off the whole fifty thousand dollars . . ."

"Kennedy, what's wrong?"

"We're in trouble, m'dear. Quite serious trouble. "I paid Robinson fifteen thousand pounds only last month."

"Robinson? But why?"

"The Hobbema," said Kennedy, "was also a forgery."

"Oh, God, no. I don't believe it!"

"Robinson had three depositions to prove it. I paid him back his money in full. What else could I do? It was either that or court."

"But the Hobbema came from an impeccable source, from the Dubriel collection."

"Robinson is adamant; it's an outright forgery down to the signature."

"Where's the Hobbema now?"

"In the basement."

"Two paintings," Holly said. "Two paintings purchased in good faith in France. Both forgeries."

"Coincidence?" said Kennedy.

Colour flushed Holly's cheeks. She had shed all traces of the flighty woman who had entered the gallery a quarter of an hour ago; she was as Kennedy first remembered her, radiating palpable determination.

"It's no damned coincidence," she declared.

"What d'you mean, Mum?"

"I mean, son we've been cold-bloodedly sharked."

"What can we do about it?" Chris asked.

"Find out who's behind it," Holly said. "Kennedy, are you game?"

"But, Holly, it isn't . . . I mean, you're not involved with the gallery now. Really, it's my affair."

"I *am* involved, Kennedy. I got Kings' into this mess. It's up to me to get Kings' out of it."

"But . . . Freeman? I mean, dear, do you actually have any time to devote to . . .?"

"All the time it takes." Holly got to her feet. "Now, show me the landscape and Robinson's depositions. Chris, telephone Croydon aeroplane departures. Reserve two seats on the midday aero-ferry to Paris tomorrow."

"Two seats?"

"Kennedy, you will accompany me?"

"Of course, my dear."

"Mum, please take me too."

Holly glanced at Kennedy; for once her husband seemed willing to abrogate his authority in decisions involving the boy.

Holly said, "When does school begin?"

"Not for another ten days."

"Three seats," said Holly, "Paris, express."

* * *

The frisky winds of March and April's pattering rains had delayed spring's final arrival. In Richmond Park the trees and shrubs had only just struggled into bud. Only Ruth's delight in walking and her belief that the sun was bound to shine on such a handsome couple persuaded Maury to steer the Humber over the Thames and drive to Richmond through an uncompromising drizzle. Maury did not object too much; he was generous when it came to yielding to Ruth's wishes in every small thing as if to compensate for his inability to give her that which she most needed, the assurance of happy times ahead, a future unmarred by trauma and neurosis. It was, he knew, only fear and uncertainty that occasionaly made Ruth seem unkind; her hardness was understandable. He did not suppose that it went far into her character, as it did with his brother. There was too much fancy in Ruth, too many unfulfilled dreams for cynicism to take firm root. Her fondness for Richmond Park was an example. Richmond – of all places – had become the Spanish plain upon which Ruth built her castles. The ease with which he could gratify her desire for hope salved Maury's conscience somewhat.

311

Richmond was not far out of London, yet far enough from Vallois Street to represent escape, a place of sweet rural air with spacious views over the Petersham meadows. Hardly had Maury parked the Humber by the gate at the old Star and Garter hotel than the rain ceased.

"See, I told you so," said Ruth smugly, her pagan optimism justified.

A broad wash of lemon tinted the clouds over Twickenham and, within minutes, enriched what colours there were in the cultivated landscape. It picked out struggling clumps of daffodils, conifers and laurels and gilded the expanses of the Thames that wound away west below the Terrace Gardens, found too the coats of the deer herds that roamed along the hay mangers in the winter enclosures, the dainty palette of roan and fallow, invigorated by the unexpected sun, even as Ruth and Maury watched.

Playing hookey twice a week had had no discernible effect on Maury's business. He had a fleeting suspicion that he had all but organised himself out of a job, so astute had he been in selecting executive staff. Work-mad Maury, acolyte of honest toil, strolled in the weekday park without a qualm of conscience. He was still half convinced that squiring his brother's wife was just another duty, a charitable chore that he had got landed with somehow.

Inevitably and insidiously he was acquiring the habit of leisure, learning what Jane Swale meant by 'pleasure'; a hint of blue sky, a passing phase of sunlight on grass, paths glistening like silver bands, deer moving in a leggy mass into the watery dell by the aspen wood and birch tree brake. Ruth hugged his arm, her small face bright and sharp within the black fur collar of her all-black coat. She smelled nicely of Coty, cognac and cocktail cigarettes.

"If," she said suddenly, "we were married, we could live in Richmond and come here after lunch every day."

"I'd be at the office," said Maury promptly.

"Before dinner, then, every day. Richmond's nice."

"Some fair properties around too," said Maury.

They walked in silence on a descending path, mounted steps and kept to a regular course along the crest of the hill.

"If something happened to Ritchie," Ruth said, "what would you do, Maury?"

"What do you mean?"

"Would you marry me?"

"Nothing'll happen to Ritchie."

"Suppose it did."

Maury strove to be flippant. "You wouldn't want *me*, would you?"

"I wouldn't want anyone else."

"Nothing will happen to Ritchie," Maury repeated liturgically.

"It might."

She turned on the heel of her shoe slightly and hugged his arm very tightly for support. "Oops," she said, then peeped round the black fur collar at her escort. "Well, Maury?"

For the third time, Maury said, "Nothing'll happen to Ritchie."

"It could be made to happen."

"Ruth, for God's sake."

She smiled and chuckled; she seldom giggled now. There was no silliness in her. Her mind had become active again. She had chosen to use it as Ritchie had taught her to.

"Oh, I didn't mean *that*," she said. "I may hate him but I wouldn't wish him dead – just removed."

"Ruth, you shouldn't talk that way."

"You sound just like my pappa, Maury. Not *really* stern."

"Ritchie's my brother, Ruth."

"So what? He'd stab you in the back if it suited him."

"I've told you before . . ."

"I know, you're not tarred with the same brush."

"Nor are you."

"Maybe I am now. Maybe I always was."

"*No.*"

She gave a hunch of her shoulders. "You know, Maury, you've never really asked me about life with Ritchie, what it was like before you came along."

"We should get back to the car, Ruth."

"Don't run away, Maury," she said. "It's a nice day for a serious conversation."

"I'd prefer to have you back home before Ritchie arrives."

"He's in Paris or somewhere."

"You didn't tell me."

"What difference would it have made? You'd have me home by five o'clock even if Ritchie was locked up in Dartmoor, wouldn't you?"

Maury could not concentrate while walking. He stopped by a wet park bench and drew Ruth gently round. He put one foot on the bench and held her by the wrist.

"Yes, I would," he told her. "It's the way I am. I can't help it. And I don't particularly want to change."

"That's why my dear husband trusts you. Ritchie thinks you're a mug, Maury."

"I don't give a hoot what Ritchie thinks of me."

"If you weren't 'good, old, dependable Maury' he wouldn't let you within a mile of me. It ain't trust, old son, it's scorn." There was no trace of neurotic anxiety in her expression, not even in her eyes which were calm and rather calculating. "Maury, I'm only thirty years old. I want a home, a husband . . ."

"You've got . . ."

". . . and children."

"Ritchie told me you can't have a child."

"The lying bastard. *He's* the one. He doesn't want a child to steel his thunder. It's not that he can't, medically, physically can't. He just *won't*. But I tricked him. While we were still living in Toronto, I got pregnant."

"Ruth, it isn't my . . ."

"Listen, Maury, please. I got pregnant. I thought when it happened, when it became a fact, Ritchie would change. Not him, not our Ritchie. I got sick. Nothing much really, just the usual sort of thing, plus the effects of strain, I suppose. But I got sick, and that was the only goddamned excuse he needed. He shoved me in a clinic and the baby was 'removed'. It was all very clean, very healthy, you know. It didn't do me any harm. I can still have babies, I mean. But not to him. Never to him. Even if he begged me, which he won't."

Maury found her gloved hand. Six months ago the pain of her confession would have shattered her, brought on weeping and hysterics. Not now, though. For that reason he did not doubt her account of the abortion or consider that she might have distorted the reason for it. He knew Ritchie to be capable of anything, knew too that Ruth would not lie to him about such a thing. His throat thickened, became gruff with sympathy and anger. He let her speak without protest or interruption.

"I want your baby Maury, I want you. Sure, it's hopeless. Ritchie'll never let me go. You're right, I wouldn't go on the run with you. Not with that bastard on my trail. But there are other ways, Maury."

"What ways?"

She seated herself on the curved metal arm of the bench even though it was rain wet. "I could have him 'removed'. Easy as pickin' cotton. I could find a man who'd do it for fifty quid, maybe even twenty."

"Ruth, how can you talk that way?"

"It's the way I was brought up," the woman replied. "It's true, though, isn't it? Old Vince Shotten, the Lambeth gangster, would be delighted to arrange an accident to Ritchie if we asked him nice."

"Probably," Maury agreed.

"Don't fret, darling. I'm no murderer, not even by proxy. I meant what I said. I don't wish him dead. But there are other ways to be rid of him."

"For instance?"

"I may have been forced to spend the last ten dreary years locked up, Maury, but I was never the dumb-bell Ritchie thought I was. I've got enough inside dope on my husband to send him up the river for life."

"Shop him? Could you bring yourself to do that, Ruth?"

"I never had a reason before," she answered. "I have now."

"Under criminal law, a wife can't give evidence . . ."

"I wouldn't have to appear in court. I know where most of the bodies are buried. All I'd have to do would be give the cops enough clues. They'd do the rest."

"Don't underestimate Ritchie. He's bloody clever."

"Don't I know it!"

"But is Ritchie really up to anything illegal here in England?"

"Sure. The Apex is a front. It makes money for him but it's just a front. He passes money into it, money he makes from other activities."

Maury was tempted to tell Ruth about the mysterious call from New Scotland Yard and the letter from Marion Ogden Hillis but he was wary of the vengeful streak in her. It did not dismay him. It was a sign of strength and volition, changes that the past months had wrought in her and for which he was, in part at least, responsible.

"Listen, Maury, the cops are already on to him."

"How do you know?"

"There was a phone call. Fletcher took it. It was supposed to be from a man called Oliver, a big wheel, about a forged painting Ritchie had given him."

"Given or sold to?"

"Given, a gift, a sort of bribe."

"Go on,"

"The call wasn't from Oliver at all." Ruth continued. "Oliver knew nothing about it."

"How did Ritchie react?"

"Oh, he kidded he was cool – but it riled him. It shook him up. Stan was summoned to the house right away. Seems the queer phone call wasn't the only thing that'd been happening. Somebody'd been sniffin' round the Apex building."

"The police?"

"Ritchie doesn't think so – but he can't be sure. He told Stan to put his ear to the ground then packed a bag and went straight back to Paris."

Maury watched the vanguard of the deer herd wander into sight over the lip of the hollow, six or eight beasts, calmer now but still alert. The puddle of sunlight had drained away and the sky was darkening once more. Puffs of wind shook droplets from the branches over the bench.

Maury turned up his topcoat collar.

"It's going to rain. Let's walk back to the car."

Obediently she took his arm.

She said, "If something did happen to Ritchie, if he landed a long stretch, I'd divorce him, Maury. I would. No question. He'd try to stop me, but I figure if he was inside he wouldn't have much hold over me. I've been thinkin' about it a lot."

Maury said, "Don't jump to false conclusions, Ruth."

"Imprisonment would be no more than he deserves."

"All right," said Maury. "Tell me, since you brought it up, what does he actually do that's illegal?"

"Deals in fake paintings." Ruth seemed surprised that Maury had not already grasped the point. "He's been at it for years. It's how he made his pile. All those years in Chicago he was selling fakes to men who didn't know any better."

"Why fakes, Ruth? Why not genuine art works?"

"There just wasn't enough genuine stuff around. Anyhow, it's cheaper to forge masterpieces than to buy them. He mixes in a few authentic pieces now and again, especially if he reckons the buyer knows what he's doing."

"The paintings in the room in Vallois Street, are they fakes?"

"No, they're the real thing. Investments."

"God, they *look* like fakes."

"Ritchie has records to prove their validity. He had them specially cleaned. I think he wants people to think they're duds. They're just window dressing, Maury. There's nothing in the house to connect Ritchie with the racket."

"Does he trade in Paris?"

"Paris is where the forgers live."

"Forgers – in the plural?"

"Our Ritch don't do things by halves. He had a specialist in Canada, name of Cazotte. Cazotte's brother runs the production side in Paris: that's what Ritchie calls it – the production side. In case you're wondering how come I know so much, I used to listen in from the bedroom in Paris when he would talk to this tart he keeps over there. Madeleine. She's Cazotte's daughter. She handles the faking details, the history and provenances."

Maury shook his head. "If Ritchie knew you were telling me these things . . . Hell!"

Ruth chuckled. "It's comforting to have something over him at last."

The rain began again, no drizzle now but a heavy plopping

shower. Maury and Ruth ran the last few yards to the Humber outside the park.

The car was a haven, leather-smelling, comfortable, sealed against the unexpected dash of rain that came loud across the windscreen. Maury took off his hat and gloves, lit two cigarettes and gave one to Ruth. She too had removed her hat. She shook her hair out, fluffing it. Her cheeks were pink with the exertion. She looked well, Maury thought. He wondered at the restoration. How much of it was really due to him and how much to her new-found purpose – the ruining of Ritchie?

Ruth inhaled smoke deeply and sat back against the corner of the seat, knees crossed. Maury switched on the ignition and the engine roared. He let it idle while he finished his cigarette. His mind was occupied not with Ruth but with Holly.

The relevance of all that Ruth had divulged was not lost on him. Coincidence did not stretch that far. For the first time in her career Holly had been landed with a dud, a very expensive, carefully-planted forgery. And Ritchie was up to his neck in fake art! Maury tried to knit the threads together, to comprehend the pattern his brother might have evolved and find the motive behind it.

Ruth's fingers stroked his cheek.

Involuntarily he jerked his head away.

"You still haven't answered my question, Maury."

"What question?"

"If something did happen to Ritchie, what would you do?"

Maury stubbed out the cigarette in the ashtray and released the Humber's handbrake.

He laughed to indicate that he was too wily to be caught in a promise he might not be able to keep.

"I'd cheer," he said.

Ruth laughed too.

"That's good enough," she said.

*　　*　　*

"Peter," Holly said. "You do understand, don't you?"

"Sure."

"It's not as if you could come with me."

"Can't let the public down."

"If it was only for myself . . . Kennedy needs help, Peter."

"Darling, I understand, I really understand."

"And Chris is an adult now. He won't be a bother."

"Do you know where you'll be staying?"

"The Regina – at least for a day or two."

"Will you tackle the Dubriels face to face?"

"Yes."

"Do you figure they diddled you?"

"I'm not sure. Mr. Robinson was kind enough to let me have the experts' reports. The Hobbema failed an X-ray test. The brushwork's all wrong. But the rest of it, the pigments, the canvas – marvellous; I mean, almost a perfect match for a genuine Hobbema, seventeenth century to a tee."

"It excites you, Holly, doesn't it; all this intrigue?"

"It makes me furious."

"But it is intriguing, right?"

"You know me too well, Peter. Yes, I'm intrigued."

"It's months since I've seen you so . . . I don't know."

"Kennedy can't afford to pay out two large sums. He's rather let things slide, Peter. I feel responsible for that."

"Is he in hock?"

"Oh, no, he's a long way from the debtors' court. He just hasn't been exerting himself. Frankly, he's lost interest."

"Is that why you're pitching in, Holly? To help him regain his interest in the business – or is there another reason?"

"I owe Kennedy . . . something, Peter. My relationship with him didn't come to an abrupt end. I thought, I hoped it would but, no, it didn't."

"He's still your husband, Holly, is that what you mean?"

"If you must know – yes, I still think of him as my husband."

"How do you think of me?"

"As . . . as someone I love very deeply."

"Compartments?"

"What?"

"Nothing."

"Are you annoyed at me for rushing off to France?"

"Hell, no."

"Are you sure?"

"Sure I'm sure."

"Well, I must dash. Will you be all right on your own?"

"I won't be on my own. Howard's due to arrive this afternoon. He called from New York. He has news."

"Good news?"

"Depends. He didn't elaborate."

"Tell me all when I get back. I'll be three or four days at the most. If de Rais won't be persuaded to come to Paris, we'll have to beard him in Marsailles."

"De Rais' really played you for a sucker, Holly."

"Absolutely. But I don't intend to let him get away with it."

"Good luck, Holly."

"I'll probably need it."

They kissed.

Holly left the flat in Holland Park.

Peter returned from the door to the bed. He lay on his back on the coverlet and stared at the ceiling. For a while he did not think of Holly, of the loss of Holly. He remembered Lakey who, in dying when she did, became fixed and, thus, steadfast. The loyalty of dead lovers was inviolable and impermeable, the one sort of love that the mischevious world could not twist out of shape. What he felt for Holly was an echo of what he felt, still, for the memory of Lakey. Maybe that was how Holly felt about Deems; but he doubted it. She had had Kennedy to erase the traces.

How would he feel, though, when Holly left him, as leave him she would? Would it be a magnification of the sadness that engulfed him now or would he contrive to part from her in anger, with bitterness to protect him against grief? It was that quality, bitterness, that Kennedy King had kept firmly at bay during the months of separation. The man was not weak but smart, real smart. Kennedy had made it easy for Holly to take up their relationship exactly where she had left it down. He had preserved it carefully like he would a piece of fragile and precious glass, with dexterity, with love. King's forte was that he had learned to balance one sort of need with another in a way that he could never hope to emulate.

Lying there on the empty bed, Peter saw now how he figured in the Kings' marriage, how his need had never been for Holly, just Holly, but for the union, the community of a kind of marriage that he could never enjoy.

With infinite sadness he admitted to himself that he gave Holly very little, nothing compared to that which Kennedy offered. And the irony of it all was that he had fallen truly in love with this woman who, without being aware of it, would break a corner of his heart in punishment for all the heartless affairs and casual romances he had begun and ended over the past decade.

But there was this in compensation; from Holly he had learned that loving became tenuous only when there is a fear of giving love.

Ten minutes out of the apartment and he missed her already.

Peter sighed, rose and performed a double programme of stretching excercises to keep his unwise body supple and in trim.

Ten minutes gone and he had lost her.

Howard's good news, delivered later that same night, seemed, inevitably, like bad timing.

*　　*　　*

Ritchie did not, after all, have to hang on to the nice little items that Loftus had pinched for months or years. The 'London Madonnas' were soon identified by the industrious Madelaine, aided by reports of the theft from the English press. Bellini, Lorenzo di Croce and Isaac Van Ostade: painters in demand. Madelaine fitted up the hot numbers with histories, bending the facts just enough to loose them from stigma.

Ritchie too was circumspect when it came to selecting buyers for the products of common theft. He could be pretty sure of jawing his way out of accusations of trading in fakes, even forgeries, but flogging stolen masterpieces was pretty damned hard to explain in any language and on any reasonable terms.

The Bellini, the di Croce and the Van Ostade were smuggled out of Dover wrapped in oilskins, strung to the underside of Ritchie's Bentley. From Paris two of them went south to Rome where Hugues de Rais, at a charge of only thirty percent, found a contact who pushed them on to a villa near Florence, a very 'secure' villa that contained more stolen art treasures than the Vatican itself, where they would be worshipped in secret by a mad female magpie who kept no records of her purchases. The Isaac Van Ostade, *Woman and Holy Child*, went to a collector in Oslo, a young man with more money than morals, who probably knew that the canvas was at least warm but whose only concern was that it was authentic. Contact with the Oslo chappie was made in Paris. Ritchie left it to Madelaine to do the convincing; after all the damned thing *was* authentic. Only the fourteenth-century silver gilt statuette remained in Ritchie's hideaway in the Pentonville Road. Madelaine had supplied it with a suitably vague provenance but it was too unique an article to shift in haste and Ritchie did not want to 'give it away for a song'. Having secured almost five thousand pounds on the paintings he could well afford to hang on to the statuette for a while – or so he supposed.

The peculiar telephone call that Fletcher parried did not set Ritchie's gyro off balance, not even when he discovered that Oliver of Oliver's Stores knew nothing about the complaint and was quite happy with his beautiful Pissarro. But that odd incident fitted just too neatly with Titus Mitchell's news that 'somebody' had been quizzing the caretaker about what went on in the Apex. After deliberation, Ritchie buttonholed Murgatroyd.

"What did he look like, this inquisitive guy?"

"Like a copper, Mr. Beckman."

"How, like a copper?"

"Shabby. Tall feller, 'bout your age. Sly, like."

"Have you seen him before?"

"Yer, saw 'im 'anging round for three or four days before he come near me."

"And since he talked to you?"

"Haven't seen 'im since; which don't mean ter say 'e ain't there, Sir."

"Exactly what did he ask you?"

"Just like I told Mr. Mitchell; asked me what went on on the top floor, inside Apex. Acted like he expected there was funny business. I told 'im it was none o' my concern. Asked me if Mr. Mitchell did any late night work."

"He only mentioned Mr. Mitchell, did he?"

"You an' Mr. Nuttall too, Sir. Seems he was familiar with all your names."

"What did you tell him?"

"I never made no mention of you bein' 'ere late at night, Mr. Beckman," said Murgatroyd "I mean, bloody hell, the bloke might be a burglar, all I know."

"I thought you said he was a copper."

"I said he *smelled* like a copper, Mr. Beckman. Any roads, I was takin' no chances. I told 'im nothin'. He chipped away for a while then I got sick of it an' suggested 'e shove off sharpish. I done right, Mr. Beckman, didn't I?"

"Apex has nothin' to hide," said Ritchie. "If this guy *is* a dick, he's free to apply for a warrant and search the offices any time. Let me know if he comes sniffin' round again, though, will you, Murgatroyd."

"Will do, Mr. Beckman."

"Here, take this for your trouble."

"No need, Mr. Beckman. Just doin' my job – but thanks."

There was no panache in the bribe; the tenner was un-varnished hush-money. Murgatroyd received it with stony gratitude, though inwardly exultant. Next time he saw Bert Kelloway he would have something to sell him too.

The caretaker would have been less delighted if he had known that Mr. Ritchie Beckman had swallowed only half the bait and did not for a moment believe that Murgatroyd had been loyal, suspecting that the inquisitive stranger had been liberally plied with information and charged for it. But Murgatroyd and anything that the snoop might have un-covered about the inner workings of the Apex Advertising Company, whose transactions were strictly on the level, were the least of Ritchie's worries.

Instinct told him that the watertight operation had cracked at some point on its circumference and was leaking like a Holland dyke.

He asked questions here, there and everywhere; of Stan, of Titus, of his dewy artists and copywriters, of McKim, Fletcher, even of Ruth. He despatched Stan to Lambeth to grill Loftus again. He even made a special trip down to Hastings to enquire of Pa and Cissie if everything was okay?

The problem was that Ritchie was too cautious. Unsure of quite what he was searching for, and not wishing to tip his hand, his interrogations were not demanding. They were, rather, invitations to confide in him. Lacking point, Ritchie's conversations seemed vague in the extreme and he derived little or no benefit from his efforts. All that he came up with in the course of that busy week was a bad case of galloping uncertainty.

In London Ritchie's only close associate was Stan. Ritchie had begun to harbour doubts about his loyal mate, to wonder if Stan had gotten so greedy he was dripping secrets to the Yard. Brooding on the problem, he concluded that it was best not to take Stan into his confidence more than he had done already.

That left only one person with whom Ritchie could freely discuss his problem – Madelaine. On the pretext of inspecting Claude's work on the de Rais' canvases, all of which were in the final stages of 'ageing', he took off for Paris yet again. Really, though, the purpose of the trip was to share his misgivings with his mistress and extract from her an assurance that he was making a mountain out of a bleedin' molehill.

Madelaine performed beautifully. That nimble young brain of hers quickly assimilated Ritchie's assessment of the situation and, between anchovy salad and pear Fresco, she devised a solution.

"It is this." Madelaine adroitly dismembered a round of Brie. "There is suspicion but there is no one place where a *flic* has put his finger. As you say, Ritchie, it may not be policemen but you have the hunch it is."

"There's a lot of stuff in circulation, Madelaine."

"But in England you have sold nothing?"

"I've given away a dozen paintings, mostly Claude's work. Been careful not to *sell* anything. Didn't even claim the canvases were *absolutely* authentic; nobody looks a gift horse that close in the mouth."

"So they cannot touch you."

"Unless they trace back some of the stuff I sold out of France."

"The danger for you, Ritchie, is that Scotland Yard have something you do not know about. From the Dubriels, perhaps? The Hobbema?"

"Maybe the Holbein. I wonder if my sister is behind this ruckus?

"There is nothing happening here in Paris. I would have heard if that had been so."

"What about our friend in Marseilles?"

"It is not impossible."

"But what could be in it for de Rais?"

"He is worth more to the Sûreté than you are, Ritchie. But if they cannot catch him, I think they might use him in other ways."

"He's a treacherous little rat," said Ritchie without heat. "Just the one to shop me – if the investigation's hot enough to threaten him."

"Then we must protect ourselves." said Madelaine.

"How?"

"Monsieur Black Hat, he has not seen what my Pappa will do on the old canvases. He does not know what the subjects will be. I am right?"

"Right."

"So we will give de Rais a *real* masterpiece, *not* a forgery."

"Just one?" said Ritchie.

"Unless you are feeling generous."

"Not that generous," said Ritchie. "Where do we find a genuine masterpiece without paying through the nose for it?"

"In the collection in the house of the Dubriels of course."

"I like it, Madelaine," said Ritchie. "Yes, I love it."

"Monsieur de Rais is given a real work of art. He is not aware of it. If he sells it, we take our profit and have three fakes to dispose of to cover loss incurred in the purchase from the Dubriels," said Madelaine. "If de Rais tries to trap us, we have done no wrong."

"Great," said Ritchie. "I'll go put pressure on the Count and Countess first thing tomorrow. What do you reckon?

Something Flemish, say seventeenth century? Do the Dubriels have such a painting? Remember how many 'copies' we've already placed there, Madelaine."

"There is the back room, is there not?"

"They won't let me near the back room."

"It is time to use 'influence', Ritchie. You have much power over the Comte and Comtesse now. You are their source of revenue – and you can put them into prison if you choose."

"Well, I couldn't," said Ritchie. "But they can be made to believe I can."

"Pappa will complete the three canvases. We will keep them hidden until we see what de Rais is up to. If he behaves correctly we will sell him two of the three." Madelaine finished the Brie and helped herself to grapes from the bunch in the bowl on the table. She ate quickly, her elbows upon the cloth, pinching the grapes from the stalk with her fingernail and lobbing them into her mouth. Her lips were moist, and Ritchie watched her tongue at work. She continued, "What have you hidden in London?"

"Not too much – the Perronneau, you know that sickly portrait, and Maes' girl's head, and about a dozen other oddments I've picked up, including the statuette."

"Can they be moved?"

"Sure, but is it necessary?"

"Do you wish, Ritchie, to risk imprisonment?"

"Listen, you think it's that serious?"

"Smokes do not happen without fires," said Madelaine. "My Pappa, he could give you a lesson, chéri, on how to panic and survive."

"He moves on."

"One breath of hot water," said Madelaine, "and Pappa packs his colours and runs like a hare. So he has never been in police trouble in all of his career."

"I see what you're driving at."

"Find a new hiding place. Make sure you are not seen when you transport the stocks to there. Trust nobody, Ritchie. If it becomes too difficult for you in England then you come back to me here for good."

"I'd like that," said Ritchie. "But my wife . . ."

"I will share you, *chéri*, if that is how you wish it. Why do you not shed this little wife. You are so seldom with her, what can she mean to you?"

"Enough of that kinda talk, Madelaine."

"You love her more than you love me?"

"It's different. I'm not unloading Ruth. And that's flat. Where I go, Ruth goes."

"Not true. She has never been in the attic in . . ."

"Cut it out!"

Slanted eyes, wide ungenerous mouth slitted, Madelaine said, "I have been of use to you, Ritchie?"

"Yeah, yeah, of course you have."

"Pay me."

"I pay you . . ."

"No, I mean take me home now, *chéri*, home to bed."

Ritchie studied her, trying to resist.

Minutes later he settled the bill and the couple set off, arm in arm, walking briskly, for the Cazotte studio three blocks away from the restaurant.

*   *   *

"This one," said Ritchie. "This is the one I want."

The Comtesse Dubriel reeled. Only her husband's arm about her dumpy waist prevented her tumbling to the carpet with the shock of it all.

It was not yet eight o'clock. Over the years the Dubriels' hour of rising had become later and later so that the monotonous daily round of the household never got underway until nine-thirty or ten. Roused from sleep by the Englishman's persistence, dragged into an audience with him before breakfast, before she had even had her first cup of *café noir*, forced – yes, forced – to admit him to the Italian Room and to be subjected to his threats, however charmingly delivered, the strain was almost too much for the poor Comtesse Dubriel's fatty little heart to bear. She would have opted out of the conclusion of the dismal scene by fainting but in peignoir, carpet slippers and with her hair stuffed untidily into a turban, there was no way in which she could swoon decorously. Instead she allowed her husband to support her while the vulgar Englishman ravished their collection.

In an ankle-length dressing gown of pearl silk, the Comte was a bastion of fatalistic strength. Former banker and man of the world, he was realistic enough to acknowledge that Beckman was a force that could not be denied. Soon after their first minor transaction with the English dealer, the Comte had resigned himself to the fact that one day they would have to pay for his indiscretion, the error of taking money from such a person; pay not just with francs or pictures but in loss of face. Indifference had calcified the Comte's possessive core. He loved nothing now, apart from his wife, with sufficient intensity to grieve or rage over its loss. The collection that he had built upon and cherished was nothing to him now but paint on canvas, all beauty gone.

The Comte said, "It is a very fine example of the work of Jacob Jordaens, the middle period, *circa* sixteen hundred and forty-two. It is said, with some verity, that this is one of the paintings that Jordaens produced to persuade King Charles to grant him the commission to decorate Greenwich Palace in England. It has been in the Dubriel family for a hundred years. It was the first painting my great-grandfather ever purchased, which is why it has a place here in our Italian Room, though, of course, it is Flemish."

"Fine," said Ritchie Beckman. "When was it last cleaned?"

"Three or four years ago."

"Fresh as a daisy," Ritchie said. "Yep, the Jordaens will do very nicely."

"It is worth," said the Comtesse in a croaking voice, "at least two million francs."

"Is it, now?" said Ritchie. "Well, we'll see what we can get for it."

The Comte held the Comtesse tightly. "It is a sale on commission?"

"Right," said Ritchie.

"The person desires a Jordaens?"

"Nope, but it's a superb work – and, more important, it's the right size."

"Size?"

"Are you in need of ready cash?" Ritchie reached into his overcoat pocket and brought out a wallet. "I can let you have something now; the balance, less my percentage, when the deal's concluded. Probably couple of months."

"Size!" the Comtesse cried. "He sells Jordaens by the metre!"

The Comte said, "How much will you pay us now, Monsieur Beckman?"

"Say fifty thousand – francs."

"It . . . is . . . *insulting*." The Comtesse twisted her neck to stare up into her husband's face. Perhaps she expected some explosion, a last suppuration of power from the dry depths of the volcano, for her husband to behave as he would have behaved twenty years ago. She was doomed to disappointment.

"Fifty thousand will be acceptable, Monsieur Beckman," the Comte said.

"Good. It's all I've got on me." Ritchie counted the banknotes into the Comte's left hand. "Right, I need the painting now."

"It will be packed for collection by this evening," said the Comte.

"No, no," the Comtesse shouted. "He is a robber, a brigand. He shall not have our *Vision of Venus*. Size, size! He talks only of size!"

Ritchie ignored the woman; he kept his eyes on the Comte's face, which betrayed no expression at all.

"Sorry, Dubriel," Ritchie said, "Now means *right* now. Bring me a stepladder and a half dozen bath towels; I'm sure you can spare them."

Then the woman was on him, her bird-like face poked forward, her claws reaching up for his eyes, reduced by the outrage to a common creature, like the trull that this Englishman had been spawned by.

"You cannot make us do this selling. Thief. *Thief*."

Ritchie held her off, trying not to laugh at the ridiculous sight the woman presented, defending himself with his forearms. Quite roughly, the Comte snatched his wife back and

329

pinned her with his hands, drawing her against his body.

"Tell her, Count," said Ritchie.

"My dear, we are Monsieur Beckman's partners."

"Never, never, never, never."

"It's true, Countess. Partners. We sold those fakes together. Do you reckon cheating becomes honest just because you're involved in it?"

"Enough, please," said the Comte.

"All right," said Ritchie. "Just let me ask you this, though: do you think the police are gonna be so impressed by your name they'll turn a blind eye to the fact that you're fronting for forgers? The cops would just love to have the Dubriels on the hook. Everybody would love it. Aren't I right, Count?"

"Monsieur Beckman speaks the truth, my dearest."

The Comtesse drew back her lips and hissed, "*Socialiste.*"

"You're not wrong, Countess," said Ritchie. "In this trade it's all for one and one for all – especially where you and me are concerned."

The Comte said, "Is it to protect us that you require the painting in such an urgency?"

"Very sharp, Count. You're on the ball."

"Is it that you . . . we are under suspicion?"

"Nope, I'm just protecting our interests."

"*Bâtard! Bâtard!*" The Countess would not be pacified by reason.

"With your permission, Monsieur Beckman," said the Comte. "I will withdraw to instruct my servant to bring you a stepladder and wrapping materials."

"Most kind," said Ritchie.

Holding his wife against him, the Comte edged towards the gallery door, opened it and sidled out. They looked, Ritchie thought, like a pair of arthritic tango dancers. Smiling, he bowed as the couple withdrew, the old cow's voice echoing even after she'd passed out of sight: "*Bâtard, bâtard, socialiste, bâtard.*"

Ritchie was not offended. He had enjoyed humiliating the Dubriels. Chuckling, he tipped back his hat and swung on his heel to survey the small gallery at his leisure.

Seventeen authentic masterpieces, covering the finest

flowering of four centuries of mainly Italian art; Fra Angelico, Botticelli, Titian, Veronese, Tintoretto, Tiepolo and Canaletto among others. The finest examples, adoringly preserved, a magnificent private collection that, once the business with de Rais was settled, Ritchie would patiently pick clean. He did not want one or two; he wanted them all. And he would have them, whether the bloody Comtesse approved or not.

An hour later, *Vision of Venus*, wrapped and snug, was stowed in the back seat of the hired Renault that, with Madelaine at the wheel, headed south out of Paris on the long haul to Marseilles.

*　*　*

The thrill of flying in a cross-Channel aeroplane kept Chris charged throughout his first afternoon and evening in Paris. He was by no means impervious to the charms of the finest city in Europe and the curtain-raising flight swept away his imposed sobriety and he chattered and chuckled with an infectious animation that his mother and step-father could not help but share and which made the purpose of their trip seem less than deadly serious.

In spite of rain-wetted streets and blustery winds Paris conspired to woo young Christopher Deems by exhibiting its eccentric face. The taxi-driver who whisked them in from Le Bourget, for instance, was as mad as a hatter and kept up a running commentary on traffic tactics in hilariously fractured English. When the Kings approached the Regina, they were treated to a sight of the annual parade of seamstresses, girls and women, decked in gay costumes, protected by hussars and a troop of desert legionaries on skittish Arab stallions. And at late luncheon in the quiet dining room of the Regina there occurred one of those little accidents that happen even in the best regulated hotels; a skewered kebab burst into a sheet of lambent flame and was promptly and coolly extinguished not three yards from the Kings' table by a head waiter armed with a newly-opened bottle of champagne.

After lunch, tired though he was, Kennedy took Chris out

to show him the sights while Holly set off for a prearranged meeting with Monsieur Lenormant at the Gallerie Voltaire.

For Holly the events of the past couple of days had been revitalising. She had no anxiety about the outcome of her meetings, no concern about the direction in which her stubborn pursuit of retribution would lead her, nor was she confused by the fact that there were two forgeries to contend with. She was convinced that Kings' had been the victim of deliberate fraud and that she had fallen foul of a plot to harm her reputation. It did not occur to her that she had forsaken the profession and that, in the matter of good will and good name, she no longer had anything to lose. After all every firm of art and antique dealers had a skeleton or two hidden in the basement closet. Rationalisation did not entirely console Holly. She had swung back into the business with such force that her determination seemed almost violent, evincing a hunger for involvement that would have confirmed Peter's suspicion that her heart had never really left the solemn galleries and musty salerooms. Holly knew it too. She behaved now as she had done five or six years ago, the *ennui* of the previous spring sloughed off and forgotten.

Apart from Kennedy – who could not be deluded – Monsieur Lenormant was the first person to detect the changes in Madame King. After twenty minutes of technical talk, Monsieur Lenormant would have staked his reputation that Holly King was enjoying herself. Business had once more become pleasure and the unusual gravity of the situation was an offspring of pride not profit.

Monsieur Lenormant did not question Madame King's assurance that the Hobbema landscape, purchased honestly from the Comte and Comtesse Dubriel, was a forgery. Monsieur Lenormant was also aware of the strides that had been made in the detection of forgeries by the use of X-ray photography. Though it saddened him a trifle, a glance at the three photographs that Holly had brought showed clearly that the brushwork was quite different, one against two. Such scientific devices robbed the art dealer of subjectivity and patiently acquired expertise. Nobody liked that. But once the thing was done, had become a *fait accompli*, only a fool would deny the value of the technique.

So Madame King and the Gallerie Voltaire had been peddled a dud, lulled by the reputation of the Dubriels who, on the face of it, were culpable. According to Madame King, however, the Dubriels may also have been the instruments of an expert forger. Monsieur Lenormant listened with keen interest to her account of the Holbein miniature. He made a lemon-drop mouth at the first mention of the name of Hugues de Rais and shook his head when Holly admitted that she had trusted the Phantom.

Two factors were involved: the rich historical detail of the Holbein's provenance had allayed doubt in Holly's mind that the miniature might have been forged; and the Dubriels' pedigree, which neither Holly nor Auguste Lenormant had seen fit to question. It was, Monsieur Lenormant agreed, an unlikely coincidence.

Immediately the Frenchman offered to return his negotiator's fee, including the five percentage he had received from the Comte and Comtesse. Brusquely Holly declined the generous gesture.

"No, Monsieur Lenormant," she declared. "We'll both get our money back."

"How will that be done?"

"By threatening the Dubriels," said Holly.

"With the weight of the law?"

"With scandal," said Holly.

It was at a more civilised hour than her brother that Holly called at the Dubriels' cloistered mansion the following forenoon. She did not give the couple advance warning, however, and rather expected to be turned away or to be kept waiting. Not so. Indeed she was greeted deferentially by the Comte in the arid drawing room.

"Madame King, how good it is to see you. My wife sends her apologies for not welcoming you today. She is indisposed."

"I'm sorry to hear that," said Holly.

"It is to purchase a painting that you have come?"

"Unfortunately," said Holly, "it's about our last transaction that I've come."

Holly wasted no time in long-winded explanations. She opened her portfolio of documents and put the three X-ray prints upon the table top, turning them to face the Comte. He bent from the waist, hands on knees, and studied the prints in solemn silence. At length he said, "It is an astonishing device, the camera that may do such a thing."

"You understand, Comte," said Holly, "that these prints prove beyond doubt that you sold me a forgery."

"You, Madame, selected that painting from among many."

Holly paused. She had talked over the approach with Monsieur Lenormant, but had agreed to allow the Parisian to opt out of the distasteful meeting, in the course of which she would be obliged to bully a couple for whom Lenormant still had a sneaking regard and a good deal of sympathy.

At length Holly said, "Are you implying, Comte, that I am responsible and that you are not?"

"Is it the same painting, Madame King?"

"Monsieur Lenormant will vouch for it – in court, if necessary."

"Court? You would take us to court?"

"With regret, Comte."

"But, Madame," the Comte repeated, "it was you who picked the Hobbema, not I who put it to your attention."

"Are all your paintings forgeries?"

"Madame!"

"The Sûreté have experts who would examine all your paintings, Comte. In spite of your position, the police would be obliged to search and examine."

"You have little authority in France, Madame King."

"But Monsieur Lenormant has authority and he too has been deceived."

"Not by the intention of the Dubriels."

"But with the collusion of the Dubriels; that is enough."

"Do you wish us to make recompense?"

"Yes, Comte, I do. In full."

"It is not possible."

Holly got to her feet. She gathered the documents and photographs. At that moment she recognised the vulnerability of the man and his angry desperation. But there was another quality in him too – bewilderment. For an instant she wondered if the Dubriels were innocent parties in a more complex deception than she had imagined. However, she did not relent. The threat of official police inspection of the contents of the gallery was her trump card. It would get her what she wanted; not justice or revenge but the Kings' money back – and information about the perpetrator of the scheme.

"Come, Comte, nine hundred thousand francs cannot be beyond your means," Holly said. "You could always sell another painting?"

"To you?"

"Oh, no! Not to me – and not to Monsieur Lenormant; not even a genuine, authenticated painting. Not from this house."

"From the Italian Room, perhaps? You have heard what is in the Italian Room. You want something from there? A Guardi? A Tiepolo?"

Mystified, Holly said nothing.

She had not heard the door opening and did not know how long the owlish little countess had been standing there or what interpretation she had put on the fragments of conversation she had picked up.

"*He* told you what was there," said the Comtesse. "You are alike; two cabbages, alike. Sister, brother. It is all a ruse to bleed us dry." The woman advanced into the drawing room, shouting. "It has been always a trick of confidence from the first. You and the *socialiste* in it together. We will give you no more."

"Kati," said the Comte soothingly. "Kati, you are not well enough for this excitement."

"I am well." She looked manifestly ill, wrinkled lids empurpled, tiny hands trembling, her ungroomed hair hanging limp about her shoulders. "You would not *dare* to summon the police, Madame. If you do, we will tell all, all concerning you and your brother and the manner in which you have corrupted us."

"My brother!" It did not have the accent of a question; Holly nodded, repeated. "My brother!"

"I told the Comte yesterday, your brother will want more than the *Venus*, our lovely Jordaens that has belonged to the

Dubriels for a century and that he purchased by its size, for fifty thousand francs only. He will not be appeased until he has taken everything. We are not the robbers Madame Beckman."

Holly sat down again.

"Ritchie?" she said. "Bloody Ritchie!"

"Do not pretend that you did not collaborate with him upon this plan to steal our paintings." Hands on hips, the Comtesse projected her face towards Holly as if she intended to peck her. "It is transparent. *You* are his partner in this crime, not us."

Holly addressed herself to the Comte. Between her and the elderly man there was a degree of rapport, a shared bewilderment that made both uncertain as to the common ground of truth.

"It's not true, Sir. Not a word of it. I haven't seen or spoken with my brother in thirteen years. I certainly didn't plan to cheat you. On the contrary, my brother has cheated me – twice over."

"She lies," the Comtesse hissed. "It is transparent how the English put their heads together to ruin us. *He* persuades us to show and sell doubtful works. *She* buys one such work so that he may extort our real treasures from us."

"Kati, wait," said the Comte. "Let Madame King have her speech."

"Let her *lie*."

"Madame King, do you deny that the man who calls himself Richard Beckman is, in fact, your brother?"

"Oh, he's my brother all right," said Holly.

"Yet he cheats you too?"

"He's cheated me of many things," said Holly. "Things more valuable than paintings."

"But the blood, it is thicker than . . ." The Comte could not recall the English phrase; he gestured.

"My brother," said Holly, in French, "has no heart."

The Comtesse started into another harangue but the Comte silenced her. Even in her wrath she did his bidding. She plumped herself down on an Egyptian divan, scowling furiously. The Comte seated himself beside his wife and took her hand to soothe her.

"Even if, as you claim, you also are a victim, Madame King," the Comte said, "you do dare to call upon the Prefecture to expose your brother?"

"That's typical of Ritchie," said Holly. "Ritchie's implicated us all. He gets off free with the profits. You're right, Monsieur le Comte; the police in France and in England would not believe that I was not in partnership with Ritchie at some stage. Ritchie was well aware of that when he dragged me into it. In your case what he wanted was an impeccable outlet for his forgeries, one that would not be questioned. Was it Ritchie who told you to insist that the Hobbema was sold outside France?"

"It was he," the Comte answered.

Holly went on, "What we say here, Comte, is in strict confidence. There are certain things I must know if I'm to bring my brother to book."

"You?"

"I'm not letting him off with it. At the very least I want my money back. Not just on the Hobbema but on another object as well. My second reason for coming to France. I see now what he intended for me. In a year or two, when I'd unwittingly sold three or four more of his forgeries, I'd be in too deep to pull out and he would have me in his power, just as he has you in his power."

"He is a man who loves power, is that not so?"

"Power and money," said Holly. "But he also loves deviousness for its own sake."

"Do you wish to know how it was that we first encountered your brother?" The Comtesse appeared calm enough now to take an active part in the conversation. "He came to us with no introduction but at a period when we contemplated selling one of our treasures. He put to us a proposition."

"Very charmingly," said the Comte.

"It could not be resisted. It seemed so small a thing to do, not much dishonest."

"A Rembrandt of doubtful origins," said the Comte. "He persuaded us we could sell this Rembrandt instead of one of our own. He had a person who came here, an American. The

337

Rembrandt was hung upon our wall. Beckman furnished it with a lineage. The history was not necessary. It was on *our* wall, do you see?"

"He gave you a percentage of the profit, of course?"

Abashed, the Comtesse averted her eyes.

The Comte said, "He was very generous. That first time."

"How many items did you sell for him?"

"Eight paintings."

"How many of the paintings in the long gallery are genuine?"

Without hesitation, the Comte answered, "Only three."

"My God! He must be running a factory," Holly blurted out.

"Eight paintings, we have sold as true," said the Comtesse. "Just as we sold the Hobbema to you, Madame. It is a lucrative business for your brother, do you see?"

Holly was not crass enough to remark that it was also a lucrative business for the House of Dubriel. The Comte was not without honour, however. He said, "The Comtesse and I have benefited also for three years. But I understood how it would end, how he would finally come to rob us."

"What will you do with us, Madame King?" asked the Comtesse.

"With you?" said Holly. "It is not up to me what happens to you. I can't involve the police even if I wanted to. Not here and not in England. What I can and will do is stop him."

"How may we assist?" the Comte asked.

"Take down all the forgeries. Don't destroy them. Hide them away. On no account sell any more, no matter what sort of threats you might receive from my brother or his agents. That's all I ask of you, Comte Dubriel."

"Yesterday," said the Comte, "Beckman took from us a genuine work by Jacob Jordaens, a magnificent example, from the middle period."

"*Vision of Venus*," said the Comtesse. "It was the size he liked; the *size*!"

"It was an urgent need," said the Comte.

"And the size was important?" said Holly.

"It appeared to be so."

"He transported it with him in a motor car," said the Comtesse.

"What's the painting worth?"

"A million francs or more."

"He paid us fifty," added the Comtesse. "Fifty thousand francs – only six hundred pounds."

"Put away the forgeries. Sell no more to my brother. If he comes here, no matter what he says or what threats he uses on you," said Holly, "have no more to do with him. He's caught in his own web, you see. He daren't summon in the law or create a scandal by exposure."

"We are all deceivers," said the Comte.

"Will you do as I ask, Comte Dubriel?"

It was the Comtesse who answered.

"With pleasure," she said.

*   *   *

Hugues de Rais switched on the overhead light and drew the protective cloth from the easel upon which he had set the Jordaens. The room, on the third floor of de Rais' house in Marseilles, seemed to be haunted that damp spring night by the spirits of whispering novices and disapproving nuns who sighed and gasped at the sight of so much robust flesh in this place of sanctuary and contemplation. There were no furnishings in the chamber, apart from the easel and a single Salem rocker into which de Rais lowered himself with peculiar gentleness as if afraid that he might scare away the Muse of Inspiration upon whom he hoped to call for help now that all the pros and cons had been weighed and he had been bullied by Beckman into parting with three hundred thousand francs after an hour of indecisive haggling. For the life of him old Black Hat could not fathom the reason for his unease. After all *he* had instigated the transaction and, if Beckman was to be believed, would take delivery of two more superb forgeries in the course of the next month or so. And yet there were things, odd things that rubbed his fur the wrong way and made him very wary.

Hugues de Rais lit a Caporal and tipped the rocker into

motion with his toes.

Vision of Venus was an exact match to one of the canvases he had sold to Beckman, minus four inches which, Beckman claimed, had been too rotted along the stretcher to take fresh oil and had been trimmed away. Trimmed away so neatly that there was no sign of roughness in the fibres? What, of course, was the point of commissioning work from an expert forger if one could detect anomalies in the finished product with the naked eye? The composition itself was immaculate, the colours intoxicating. The central female figure, with arm outstretched and torso twisted, was so honestly pictorial that it could only have been done by Jordaens – or a master of the forger's craft. Beckman's history was ingenious. He claimed that the *Venus* was one of the missing Greenwich pictures, charged by King Charles, that had been languishing in the private collection of a banker – Dubriel, of course – in a Paris suburb for three generations. The early part of the tale of ownership was blank; all the more convincing for that.

De Rais puffed on his cigarette.

But, but, but, but? He was not satisfied – why?

Hard times had not made the Phantom rash. Rather, his impecunity and dwindling credibility in the circles of the rich had rendered him ever more cautious. But three hundred thousand francs had diminished his capital to a dangerously low level. He had placed a nice little Hubert Robert landscape with the purchasing curator of the Louvre, slipped in, as it were, through the back door. He had an indifferent Willem van de Velde marine painting under consideration at the Toulouse museum. Not much profit in either sale. He was depending upon the three Dutch works to boost his flagging trading account and had clients in his sights. Herr Perleberg of Munich might take all three. If not, Curvetto, in Rome, would agent for him since there was much money in Italy under *Il Duce*. Theoretically there was nothing to prevent him carting the *Venus* to Munich and selling it to Perleberg on the spot. Great God, if it completely fooled him even when he *knew* it wasn't genuine, there was no danger that Perleberg would spot it for a forgery.

De Rais rocked forth and back.

That was it. Yes. That was the reason for his disquiet. The forgery was *too* good, *too* perfect. Whoever Beckman had on contract that could duplicate not only the appearance but the 'feeling' of a Jacob Jordaens, not to mention Hans Holbein and half a dozen others, must be a genius. What use he, Hugues de Rais, might have made of such a man in the green and happy days of his prime! But it was Beckman who really bothered him, not just the canvas that he had delivered in such an unprofessional manner that late afternoon. There was so much difference between them; Beckman did not care about the works, only about the profits. Alas, the world belonged to the Beckmans these days. The old legends, the Phantoms, were being rubbed out of existence. He suspected Beckman and, by inference, suspected the painting. Why in God's name should he suspect a work he knew to be a forgery? What was there to suspect?

Beckman was up to something.

"I am the Phantom, the Black Hat," de Rais said aloud. "I am reputed to be so cunning that I can steal your gloves while I shake your hand. I robbed the Hermitage, cheated the Russians. Six million dollars in a single trade. Why cannot I solve the puzzle of what is wrong with the Jordaens and what it is that Riccardo is trying to put over on me?"

The ghosts of the novices sighed along with the wind from the harbour and the invisible nuns grunted an accompaniment to the night trains in the Gare St. Charles.

De Rais tilted the rocker and slid his feet to the floor. He padded to the easel.

Venus seemed to beckon him. The passionate young man with muscular thighs and eyes like a stunned bull's might have been gaping at a clue hidden on the edge of the frame. But de Rais had already checked every inch, back and front. There was no answer to his questions. If anything, ten minutes' contemplation of the *Venus* had served only to increase his confusion and add to his doubts.

Only too vividly did he recall how random Ritchie Beckman's maliciousness could be. The business with the Holbein miniature, for instance, had been superbly engineered. Great God, if Beckman would dupe his own flesh and blood, his

341

delightful sister, for a few thousand dollars there was no saying to what lengths he would go to squash a competitor.

But how? That was the catch. How?

Hugues de Rais tormented himself no more. Like a cagey old fox he elected to obey his instincts. He would *not* attempt to sell the Jordaens to Perleberg or Curvetto or to anyone – at least not for some time.

Whimsically he placed his finger tips on the canvas and asked, "What do you say, Jacob? Am I a fool?"

But Jacob did not answer him and even the nuns were silent now that the breeze from the bay had skittled away into the back streets and the last train into the Gare St. Charles had been berthed for the night.

It was the following morning before the Phantom had an answer. It did not come from Jacob or some fanciful Muse but, amazingly, from Holly Beckman King.

* * *

In trains Chris felt confined, never more so than during the long night ride across France stuffed into an airless slot in the side of the corridor of the Paris to Marseilles express. He had hoped that his mother's business would be so urgent that she would elect to take another aeroplane but, so Holly told him, cost had to be considered; while a cross-Channel fare was not exactly cheap it was reasonable compared to the exorbitant charges levied by French aeroplane companies for internal flights. So it was a couchette and an interminable uncomfortable night during which the young man had an opportunity to dwell on questions that, in the normal course of events, he would have pushed out of his mind.

He was aware that his mother and father had shared a bedroom in the Regina. Less ill-informed on sexual matters than fourteen-year-old boys were supposed to be, he wrestled guiltily with his curiosity as to whether they had 'gone to bed' as man and wife, which they were still, or if they had behaved, as he would surely have done, with modesty. He had not had an opportunity to see into the Regina's double bedroom and did not know if there were two beds or only one. If his parents had been obliged to sleep side by side had his father done 'that sort of thing' ?

Chris wasn't *exactly* sure how it was between adults, though dormitory talk, to which he listened without contributing, had furnished him with the principles of 'that sort of thing'. He had been excited, and made ashamed, by ribald braggarts who claimed to have 'done it' to girl cousins, servants or even to 'fillies' picked up casually in the street. Youthful misconceptions rather than misinformation clouded the more important issues that the trip to France raised. Chris's dwelling on the sexual mysteries was neither morbid nor unhealthy, just difficult for him.

In a strange way Chris understood the nature of the attraction that his mother and the American shared, though he had never even seen Peter Freeman. He had resisted a meeting in spite of his mother's attempts to bring them together. Chris was curious about Peter Freeman and only devotion to Kennedy caused him to reject his mother's pleas. The enormous popular success of *Step Out Along the Strand* had made Freeman quite famous and had kept gossip fluid in the halls of St. Justin's. To defend his mother's reputation Chris had developed a series of withering answers to the leering questions that were slung at him, and a *hauteur* that hinted that retribution might be swift and sudden and decidedly painful if the ass didn't 'stow it, p.d.q.'. In fact Chris had fought only three times, with a ferocity that smacked more of his nominal father than of Kennedy King. So bloody had the battles become that he had made even the nastiest fourth form bully leery of 'insulting' his mother. Still, it was tempting, for the sake of his stock in school, to go the whole hog, to be 'sophisticated' enough to join Peter Freeman and his mother for dinner at the Savoy, to go 'back stage' to meet the glittering West End stars; tempting but impossible. Chris had not one drop of rake's blood in him. His heroes were men of singular dedication and high ideals. How he performed the trick of continuing to regard his mother with respect as well as love remained an enigma even to Chris.

In Marseilles on that muggy April morning after a restless night even Chris's mercurial energies were sufficiently reduced, however, to force him to concentrate on the situation into which his mother had drawn him and to enable him to comprehend some of the qualities that made her rather special.

While Chris and Kennedy were bleary at the breakfast table in the restaurant of the Gare St. Charles, Holly was full of pep. She was dressed in a bright red wool coat with a large fur collar and a dramatic wide-brimmed hat and, Chris noticed, her eyes shone darkly. He pitied the old fellow who waited, all unsuspecting, in the fish-smelling town. He had formed a mental picture of an inadequate provincial junk dealer, akin to those in the dirty little shops he had visited with his mother when he was younger. Surely de Rais would be no match for his sophisticated mum, in spite of the tales that Kennedy had told him of de Rais' reputation and the string of comic-paper nicknames he had acquired. Chris did not expect to be admitted to the show. He assumed that he would be given a few francs to spend and packed off to stroll the streets of the seaport for two or three hours while his mother crossed swords with the Phantom. But Holly had other ideas.

Husband and son accompanied her to the doorway of the drab shop in the backstreet near the station, then Chris realised that far from lessening impact the arrival of the whole Kingly clan would surely disconcert de Rais a little. At last he had been incorporated into the business that buttered his bread. Chris had never felt so much pride, so much closeness to Holly as he did at that moment.

"Knock on the door," Holly said.

"Me?"

"Yes, darling. A good, loud knock."

Chris clenched his fist and rapped on the fly-blown glass.

"Louder."

Chris hammered, making the glass shudder.

"Keep it up, son."

Willingly he did until at length a heavy-set woman swam out of the brown depths and with ill grace unlocked the shop door.

"Madame Sempach," said Holly, "I have come to talk with Monsieur de Rais."

Madame Sempach, who looked as if she ate little boys on toast for breakfast every morning, glared at Chris as if he was some mischievous street arab who had rattled the house awake for devilment. Oddly, Chris felt no embarrassment. Adopting his mother's attitude, he defied the woman's intimidating stare.

"Who knocked on my door?" said the woman in gutteral French.

"The King family," said Holly, also in French.

"Monsieur de Rais is not expecting you," the woman said. "He is not at home this morning, Madame."

"Be kind enough to inform Monsieur de Rais that we are waiting in the shop." Boldly Holly stepped into the interior followed by Chris and Kennedy.

The odour of the place reminded Chris of school chapel. He could smell fish very strongly and the pungent aroma of garlic. At the rear of the shop was a short broad staircase which led to a wooden deck from which corridors spread to left and right. Madame Sempach had hardly put a foot upon the stairs before Holly called out, *"Monsieur de Rais. It is Holly King. You know why I'm here. It is of no use hiding."*

De Rais appeared immediately. The unexpected visit did not seem to dismay him. He was dressed for the day in an old-fashioned vested suit with a stiff little collar to the jacket and wore buttoned ankle boots. He was not at all as Chris had imagined him. His affability, his warmth was engaging and contained no trace of nervous unctuousness.

"Come up, come up, Madame. And your family, is it? What a surprise! Madame Sempach, coffee if you please. And a cake for the young man."

Chris smiled in response to the Phantom's beam as introductions were made at the top of the staircase. With much good will on de Rais' part the Kings were shown into a handsome front room, found seats, made comfortable and, very quickly, served with coffee by the whiskered brown woman.

Appetising though it looked, Chris did not eat the cake.

It was only nine thirty in the morning; he was too aware of his newfound stature as a man of the world to succumb to boyish greed for sweet and sticky things. Taking his cue from Kennedy he sat still and quiet, sipping strong coffee, while Holly, in an abrasive tone, told Hugues de Rais why they had come and what she wanted from him.

At first the Frenchman appeared mystified, then hurt, as if Holly had slandered his reputation. He did not, Chris noticed, pay much attention to the sheaf of documents that Holly handed over to substantiate the clients' claim that the Holbein miniature was a recent forgery. Nor did he, when challenged, dispute the Ogden Hillis exposure.

Rather peevishly, de Rais said, "Ah-hah, Americans are too clever for their own good," as if the buyers were to blame for the whole affair. "Such science is too much for an old fellow like me."

"I assume," said Holly, "that you purchased the Holbein in all good faith, Monsieur de Rais, and sold it to me as a genuine article?"

The question was astute; Chris wondered how de Rais would wriggle out of giving a direct answer.

The Frenchman said, "The history was so vivid, Madame King. It was difficult for us not to be deceived, was it not?"

"Did you or did you not sell me the miniature as a Hans Holbein?" said Holly. "The history too was a clever piece of fakery and adds to the felony. The miniature was sold as a Holbein, without equivocation, without demur. I bought it as such and sold it as such."

"I provided you with opportunity to examine and decide," said de Rais. "You judged it to be authentic."

"That isn't good enough," Holly snapped.

"We are all human, Madame King. To err is human, is it not?"

"Error's one thing; fraud is another," said Holly. "You gave me your word, Monsieur de Rais, that you would take the miniature back if it proved to be a dud. Do you intend to break your promise?"

"But I too had it examined. It is the word of my expert against the American technocrats."

"Come bloody off it, de Rais!"

Chris was startled by a glimpse of the Lambeth street trader under the layers of sophistication that his mother had acquired. Something appealed to him – if not to de Rais – in the tough no-nonsense phrase; it reminded him of his Uncle Maury and, covertly, of the red-eyed little man in Abraham's Terrace, his grandfather.

"Copies are so hard to detect," said de Rais.

"This Holbein isn't a sixteenth-century copy. It's modern. That makes it a calculated forgery. Even you, de Rais, admit that."

"I am not inclined to admit anything, Madame, so angry are you."

"Admit it to me, then," said Kennedy softly. "I'm not in the least angry."

Kennedy's unexpected intervention caught de Rais off guard. Chris was enjoying himself; it was like watching a West End play. His mother, he thought, would have looked very well on the stage and Monsieur de Rais was a character that any playwright would have been happy to have created.

To give himself a moment's respite, Hugues de Rais lit a cigarette. Smoke, thick and acrid, hung above the little man's chair in a slow-dispersing cloud.

Kennedy said, "The rules of the game, English or French, have always been perfectly clear, Sir; proven duds are returnable. Fakes and forgeries are the responsibility of the seller and the buyer is entitled to full restitution."

"Re-stee . . . hm?"

"Money back," said Holly, in French. "Is that plain enough?"

"But," de Rais gestured with the cigarette, scrawling smoke in the pale air, "but *I* do not have the money back."

"It's up to you to wring it from the person from whom you purchased the Holbein. It's patently obvious, Monsieur de Rais, that you have also been deceived," said Kennedy. "That does not alter the fact that Kings of London are obliged to repay the whole of the purchase price to the Ogden Hillises – and make grovelling apology. Such 'mishaps' do occur but two or three of them can erode a firm's reputation very swiftly."

"Yes, *oui-oui-oui*," said de Rais taking only what he

wanted to hear from Kennedy's contribution. "I too was deceived."

"Then you'll repay our thirty-eight thousand dollars?" said Holly.

"Where is the miniature now?"

"In transit from America," said Holly.

"I will pay you when I have received the alleged forgery."

"Ordinarily, Monsieur de Rais," said Kennedy, "that would be the order of things but under the circumstances we must ask *you* to trust *us*. We want our money now. Today."

"Never," said de Rais. "It is not how it is done."

"Then the Holbein will be sent directly to the French police," said Holly.

De Rais had anticipated the threat. His reply was ready. "I do not have thirty-eight thousand dollars, Madame."

"Monsieur de Rais," said Kennedy, "do you expect us to allow you time to raise the sum?"

"I will raise it." De Rais seemed to be admitting defeat.

Holly said, "Don't give me that, de Rais. If we leave Marseilles today on the strength of your promise, we'll never see you again, will we?"

"This is my home, Madame."

"For how long?" said Holly. "Regrettably, you're being caught by your own reputation. *Le Fantôme*: the great vanishing ghost. Here today and gone tomorrow. *La Bota de Clavos*? Would the Nailed Boot hesitate to change into his running shoes? No, Monsieur de Rais: you'll have your black hat on your head and a wallet full of dollars and francs and be off like a shot. Thirty-eight thousand used to be nothing to you. But I've heard that times are hard. You confessed as much. You'd vanish before you'd pay – and we'd be left holding a dud miniature."

"It could be sold. It is very fine . . ."

"For Gawd sake!" Holly cried, giving an excellent impersonation of a woman at the end of her tether.

"Sell it 'After the manner of Hans . . .'" de Rais suggested.

Holly cut him short. "For peanuts? All a doubtful miniature would fetch is twenty or thirty pounds. The price all down the line is overblown, because the damned

348

miniature was so fine and so unique."

De Rais nodded: he hadn't expected to get away with it.

"I cannot pay you now," he said. "There is no help for it. I wish it was possible for me to pay you now. But – no. I cannot."

"Do you trust me?" Holly asked: she did not wait for an answer. "You have no choice but to trust me. We will return the fake miniature to you. What you do with it is your business. But we're not leaving Marseilles, not leaving this house, without our money."

"*Impasse.*" De Rais shrugged.

"Perhaps not," said Kennedy.

De Rais lifted one eyebrow very high, while the other remained squinched. "What is it you say, Monsieur King?"

"If it's impossible to have money perhaps we might take goods instead."

"No, Kennedy," said Holly. "Once bitten, twice shy."

To Holly, Kennedy said, "All the objects can't be fakes, my dear."

To de Rais, Holly said, "Well, are they – fakes, I mean?"

"Madame King, I do not trade in works of doubtful origin."

"Only Holbein miniatures," Holly stated. "What *do* you have on the premises that we might take in exchange for the money that you owe to us?"

Hugues de Rais' expression did not alter.

He said, "In settlement?"

"Exactly," said Holly. "Something we can sell quickly."

"I . . . I have . . . nothing."

"Oh, stop fabricating, de Rais. You're bound to have something in stock. What about ceramics, silver, something?"

Hugues de Rais' eyes closed then opened again. His head shifted on the stalk of his neck, levering involuntarily to the right so that he squinted at the Kings, each in turn, including the boy.

"*Alors!*" he mumbled. "There is a painting. But you see, my friends, you will not trust me when I say I have a painting. Is that not so?"

"Try us," Holly said.

Later Holly assured Chris that she had had no prior knowledge that Ritchie – the legendary uncle whom Chris had never met – had brought the Dubriels' Jordaens to Marseilles. She had done nothing more clever than spread a wide net for de Rais and, by proxy, for her brother. Chris found it hard to believe that such a neat piece of irony could not have been calculated. His wonderment was not diminished by his mother's modest denial, the reiteration that she had been 'very lucky'. The art market, was, after all, a small world. Ritchie's machinations had made it even smaller.

However it came about, the mordant quality of the barter delighted Chris. He took pains to act out all the parts for his friend and confidante at St. Justin's so that Paul might share the comic overtones and the nuances of word and gesture. He made it sound as if it had gone on for hours. In reality the transaction had been quickly effected. On de Rais' part there was protestation; insistence by Madame King; a threat tossed away as casually as a cigar band by Kennedy; then all three were climbing stairs behind the Phantom whose air of dejection was quite superficial and did not fool Chris.

The bare room, with rocking chair and easel; the painting unveiled; its colours were so strong that it resembled a gigantic postcard. Chris did not care for it at all though his ribald friend Tweaker would have drooled over the female nude and drivelled about what he would do to a woman like that behind those rocks. But the subject of the study hardly impressed itself on Chris who, having tuned in on his parents' conversations, knew that this was the Jordaens, the *Vision of Venus* from the collection in the House of Dubriel. He saw instantly how it would all end.

French and English phrases were chopped back and forth like ping-pong balls. Doubts were expressed, eagerness was masked by ire. Kennedy remained inscrutable, saying only that, with apologies, he did not trust Monsieur de Rais awfully much but that he would be guided by his wife's judgement provided it didn't cost him anything.

Party to the secret, Chris, kept his mouth firmly shut.

"What of its provenance – though I suppose that hardly

counts for anything in the light of recent experience – but you may as well tell me where it came from?" Holly sighed.

"It has no history."

"You mean you won't tell me."

"Madame King, I *cannot* tell you."

"Gawd, it's stolen!" Lambeth again, a shrillness.

"No, no, no, no. I swear solemnly on . . . on . . . on my sacred oath that it is not stolen."

"I think it's a dud," said Kennedy.

"Really, Monsieur King, would I be so foolish as to risk releasing to you a second unauthenticated work?"

"Oh, I think you might."

"It is not so! It is a *genuine* Jordaens. My honour, my *word* on it."

"It isn't worth thirty-eight thousand."

Pain clutched at the Phantom's heart; he pressed his fingers to the spot. "It is worth *twice* that amount."

"How could I sell it with confidence?" said Holly.

"Because it is *genuine*."

"Genuine – but without a history."

"It does not *require* a history."

"I suppose a label saying, 'Vouched for by Hugues de Rais' is going to bump up the asking price?" said Holly.

"I let it go to you in payment of a debt of *honeur*, Madame. For no other reason I give it to you at all. How can you deny it? Even if you do not wish to present it as a Jordaens, the quality – *ah-aha* – it is *so* fine it would bring forty thousand as a wall decoration."

Holly seated herself on the rocker and scowled at the *Venus* for another five minutes. At an increasingly rapid tempo the pair argued. De Rais tried to persuade the Kings to pay him fifty percentage of the difference between thirty-eight thousand dollars and the fetch-price of the painting. Holly laughed and accused him of 'trying it on' again. She admitted that his argument about the piece being worth 'close to' thirty thousand dollars just as a bit of wall paper was valid. But Kings had to be careful – thanks to certain recent events. De Rais skated expertly away from the sore subject of the Holbein then abruptly, lost patience.

Slapping his thigh, tossing his head, he cried, "Madame, I have *nothing* else. I have not the money. And *you* will not wait. It is *this* painting, or it is *nothing*. I do not even have the Holbein. I *trust* you for it. Can you not trust *me* to make you a deal with the Jordaens?" He bent close to Holly who sat motionless as a waxwork on the motionless rocking chair. In a soft seething voice he begged her to see reason, to understand the predicament he had fallen into through no fault of his own. "It is *all* I have. It is my *one* investment. I give it to you because I *cannot* have trouble with police at this time. *Please*, Madame King, please."

"Kennedy, what do you think?"

"Well, I think it's risky."

"Still, we don't have much option, do we?"

"I suppose not. Bird in the hand and all that."

"Write me a transfer of ownership," said Holly.

"Is it necessary between us, Mada . . .?"

"And think yourself fortunate, Monsieur de Rais, not to be in the hands of the law."

"Can we carry it with us?" Kennedy sized up the painting.

"I could carry it," said Chris.

De Rais shook his head. "A letter of transfer? And packeting"

"Please."

"We will go downstairs to do the business."

"In that case, we'll take the painting with us."

"Madame, Madame, I have *robbed* myself and *still* you do not *trust* me."

"Kennedy, Chris, bring the thing downstairs."

"You are returning to England today?"

"To Paris," said Holly, consulting her wristwatch. "In one hour and forty-two minutes."

"Thank God!" said de Rais and, now that the battle was over, grinned.

*　　*　　*

They ate like wolves, working through the varied menu offered on the daylight express to Paris. All three were excited, and amused. Chris drank two glasses of the champagne that Kennedy had bought to celebrate and laughed so loudly that Holly had to hush him up.

"But what's it worth, really worth, mother?"

"At auction, about sixty thousand dollars, twelve thousand pounds."

"Holly, are you absolutely certain it's the same painting that Ritchie extracted from the Dubriels?"

"Absolutely," said Holly. "In any case, we won't firmly ascribe it. We'll list it as purchased in France, sell it under our name and let the big boys make up their own minds about it."

"In what auction room?"

"The first that can take it," said Holly.

"How soon will that be, Mother?"

"Two or three weeks."

"But the papers – the export thing?" said Kennedy.

"Monsieur Lenormant will attend to the details. I'll sell the painting to the Gallerie Voltaire for ten francs and repurchase it for twenty. We'll do it first thing tomorrow. The sale will be recorded as between Voltaire and Kings and the estimated value, in this case a formality, will be based on the assumption that the painting is not an authentic Jordaens. I doubt if there will be a problem with red tape. Monsieur Lenormant will ship it to us within a week and we'll have it at the auctioneers just as soon as we can after that."

"Can I come down for the sale?" said Chris. "Can I take a day from school? Will you pick me up, Dad? Will you arrange it with the beak?"

Holly and Kennedy smiled at their son's enthusiasm.

"We'll see," Kennedy said.

"Will you?" Chris's excitement waned into doubt. "Will you be there? I mean – together?"

It was Holly who answered.

"Of course we will," she said.

ooooooo
ooooo
ooo
o

2

Nine Points of the Law

"Peter, I can't. I'm sorry. Tomorrow perhaps but not today."

"Tomorrow's Wednesday. I've a matinée."

"Thursday then? No. Wait! I can't."

"You've a previous engagement, right?"

"Darling, I'm sorry."

"That's all I hear from you these days, Holly."

He sulked; a surprising trait. Holly could not know that his silences covered despondency. Male pride had become part of it too now. Peter would not show her how much he needed her, how fear of losing her distressed him.

Still in pyjamas and bathrobe he scanned the sporting newspaper that was delivered to the flat every morning. He held the pages as a barrier between them.

Already dressed for the day, Holly finished kippers and toast and poured tea.

"Peter?"

He glanced over the newspaper as if surprised to find her there.

"Tea?"

"No," he said. "Thanks."

"Look, darling, I'll be free about four. We could have cocktails together," Holly offered.

Peter ruffled the newspaper. "You know, I think I'll call Ralph. See if he feels like a day at the track."

"What a good idea!"

354

"Okay!"

Peter retired behind the racing form once more.

In the week since Holly's return from France the relationship had changed drastically. She was exhilarated at being back at work, though she assured Peter that it was a temporary return and she would 'retire' again, this time for ever, as soon as things in the Gallery were restored to order. What she did not tell Peter was that she found the evenings becoming increasingly dull in contrast to the activity of the day.

She suspected that Peter resented her association with Kennedy. Perhaps Peter was afraid he would be stranded without a daytime companion, would lose touch with her. He had given up pretending that he was in the slightest interested in what went on at the Gallery and was dismissive of Holly's manoeuvres with the Jordaens' painting. Holly could not seem to make him understand that it was professional pride that drove her to see the deal to its conclusion.

She was aware that it was a difficult time for Peter.

Step Out Along the Strand had done wonders for his reputation.

It was, however, grindingly hard work to maintain freshness night after night. Performing had become a chore; as Peter put it, "monotony's the bottom line in every dancer's contract."

In addition Howard had negotiated many endorsement deals for his protégé, the sort of commercial exposure necessary to sustain star image. Holly had grown blasé about seeing Peter's face on hoardings or smiling at her from magazine advertisements. Jokes about the products he was paid to advertise – hair tonic, shirts, a cocktail mix, cigarettes – had become stale with over use and Peter had forbidden her to say one more word about them. Press interviews and photographic sessions were fitted into the week by Howard's London secretary, a slender woman of Holly's age who kept Peter up to the mark on his appointments with a daily call backed by neatly typed memoranda. The Holland Park apartment, however, was Peter's castle and he jealously guarded his domestic privacy. Short of making Holly a total slave to Peter's whirlwind schedule, the couple were separated by forces that seemed increasingly hostile.

The theatrical world, Peter's natural habitat, had become unfriendly in Holly's eyes, a market place where talent was traded with picayune recklessness and most commodities were branded transitory. When stage lights darkened and the curtain fell, what was left of Peter's art but memories and the promise of another show tomorrow? Peter's view of Holly's profession was equally misinformed. He professed to see no point in preserving so much 'old junk'. He accused the art dealers of pumping up prices by peddling greed. Challenged, he refused to define his argument and lapsed into another sulk.

Only in bed did the relationship flare. When caring was soured by possessiveness the sexual element took on enormous importance for both of them. The heat, the intense selfish intimacy of love-making stripped them of apology and excuse. It made Holly ashamed, that demanding need, and saddened her to realise that the climax of romantic attraction must, of necessity, be expressed in an act so physically satisfying. She did not dare ask herself if it was enough to bind her to Peter for the rest of her life. She was afraid that the answer might be yes. In all other respects, however, the shape of her future appealed to her less than the shape of her past.

In exasperation Peter tossed the racing form to the floor.

"Just what *are* you doing today that's so darned important you can't call it off?" he demanded.

"The Jordaens' painting is due to arrive at the Gallery this morning."

"So what! Can't Kennedy see to it?"

"To the unpacking – of course. But I want to have a close look at the thing and make an estimate of its value."

"Do it tomorrow, when I'm at the matinée."

"Peter, I would. Really. But the painting's due to be delivered to Partington's later this afternoon. We must give their valuators and cataloguers a crack at it."

"What's the rush? This guy Jordaens isn't waiting on the cash, is he?"

Holly ignored the jibe. "The painting's due to be sold in

eleven days. It doesn't give me long to drum up interest in the sale."

"I still don't see what the crazy rush is about?"

"Money, darling, plain old-fashioned money," said Holly. "Kennedy paid off Marion Hillis and recompensed the chap who bought the dud Hobbema. Outgoings that left an exceedingly large hole in our trading account."

"Come on, Holly! I don't believe it's all or nothing on this Venus painting?"

"Not quite. But almost."

"He really messed things up, that husband of yours."

"That's not fair, Peter. Kennedy didn't mess things up. I did."

"Meaning me too, right?"

"Kennedy was tired and dispirited, that's all I meant."

"Hell, I reckon you've been carrying him for years."

"Peter, I've neither the time nor the inclination to discuss Kennedy with you right now."

"How about discussing your divorce with him? How about that?"

"I will," Holly tried to sound sincere and enthusiastic, to assure Peter that she had not retreated from a final commitment. "But let's get this sale over first."

Peter deliberately relaxed.

He smiled at her, nodding. "Sure."

"You do understand, Peter, don't you?"

"I wouldn't love you if I didn't admire your loyalty."

"I love you too, darling," said Holly.

He reached for her, drew her to him and kissed her on the mouth. She let her lips linger against his.

"Hey, listen. I've had an idea," Peter said brightly. "This big sale, the auction. Why don't we make a special thing out of it? Give a lunch at the Ritz. How about it? My treat."

"Peter, the sale's on a Wednesday afternoon; the matinée."

"Ask them to change it."

"Peter, I can't."

"Goddamn it, Holly, you could try."

"Peter, it . . . Oh, never mind, never mind!"

She sensed that he was striving to break out of his mood

and restore communion between them but the relationship had developed so many sharp edges that the fibres of rapport had been frayed.

Peter looked lean and strained. He could not hide his melancholy in anger. Holly felt a pang of guilt directed not towards Kennedy and Chris now but towards Peter. "Once the painting's sold, we'll celebrate."

"Celebrate what? You giving up Kings' – or you going back to it?"

"Giving up: once and for all."

"No more dabbling?"

"No more. I promise."

She was lying to placate him, devising tiny lies only to circumvent a quarrel. They, the lies, were too loosely woven to be classed as deceit. Neither Peter nor she believed them; the reassurances were untrue but served to keep the spirit of despair at a distance.

"I don't know why I begrudge you your work, Holly," Peter said. "But I do. I want you around me all the time."

"It'll soon be over," Holly told him.

"What'll soon be over?"

"The sale. After that, I'll stop."

"You mean it?"

"Honestly. Work isn't a drug, Peter; not for me."

She kissed him once more on the mouth.

"Call Ralph," she said. "He'll groan about the early hour but he'll probably be delighted to run off to the races with you."

"Sure, I'll call Ralph."

"I'll see you tonight," said Holly.

"For cocktails?"

"You're going to the races, remember."

"Sure, sure."

"After the performance," said Holly.

"Your performance or mine?"

"Peter, don't be so sharp. I'll be here when you get back."

"I hope so."

"I'll probably be in bed . . . with a good book."

Peter grinned. "Not too good a book!"

Holly experienced anticipation of the night hour when all the duties of the day would be behind them, the shadows of tomorrow low and unestablished and they would be alone in the candlelit room, in the oceanic double bed.

Her warmth was genuine. "Look for me there, darling."

"What happens when I find you?"

"You can spend the day guessing," Holly said.

"And if I guess right?"

"You get a special prize, " said Holly.

She was relieved to hear Peter laugh. But she was also relieved that she was leaving to spend the day with Kennedy, working hard at the Gallery. It suited her to be two separate women, true to her separate roles.

"Bye, darling," Peter said.

"Bye, love," said Holly.

*　　*　　*

Knowing a good thing when they saw it, and hungry for the publicity that a record price would attract, Partington's laid on a splendid show. Young Trevor Partington, fresh down from Oxford with a glowing First in History, was smooth, shrewd, arrogant and stiff with ambition. He made a personal crusade out of the selling of the Jordaens. The catalogue entry was discreet, promising a 'bargain'. Distribution, however, was extensive and many little rumours were planted, by Holly as well as T.P., to ensure that important collectors got wind of the sale. The premises were tarted up with swathes of dark blue velvet and a standard range of chairs, albeit in brown rexinette, helped to give the second league rooms some sort of class.

It was Trevor who had first cast an expert eye over *Vision of Venus* on its arrival from the Gallerie Voltaire. To Holly's relief the young man had gone into raptures about its quality and had unequivocally declared it to be 'the finest example of Jordaens' work to come on the market this century'. Consequently Trevor had bullied his father and uncles into spending a bob or two on presentation. The provenance, or lack of it, did not disturb T.P. one bit. He made a virtue of it by cloaking the origins of the painting in mystery, building up the notion that here was an 'undiscovered' masterpiece that could be had for a snip. The scheme was enhanced by the fact that the *Venus* was being sold on behalf of Kings' Gallery. It was unusual for a commercial dealer to sell through an auction house; the general assumption was that Kings' were acting agents for a 'famous personage' who wished to remain anonymous.

The sale was not large; one hundred and forty lots of paintings, engravings, etchings and drawings. The Jordaens' was slated to come up last of all. The 'supporting cast' was carefully selected from Partington's 'on hand' stock, enriched by a small but exquisite collection of Old Master drawings that Trevor had persuaded one of his Oxford tutors to part with on the promise of a really top notch price. Radiant in a handsome gilded frame that Kings' had paid for, the Jordaens' canvas was the star of the show, bait for posh dealers, collectors and purchasing curators who would not normally be found dead in a dump like Partington's.

Though the general mood was guarded, bidding was uninhibited even in the early stages. Those curators who had come down from the provinces in the hope of picking up the Jordaens for a song spent their allocations on other items, probably to justify a trip that they knew in their bones would be fruitless. It was a highly satisfactory build-up for a 'quickie' sale. Holly – seated near the front with Kennedy, Chris, Maury and Emma Chubb – had seldom experienced such exhilarating excitement. It was important to Kings' to sell the Jordaens for a high price, but other factors were involved, not least of which would be the effect of the sale on Ritchie. It would not have surprised Holly to see her brother lurking in the rear rows but Maury told her that, to the best of his knowledge, Ritchie was too preoccupied to pay much attention to sale catalogues.

"But he will find out afterwards, won't he?"

"Damned right he will," said Maury.

To convince their colleagues that they were still two-way traders and that the reason for selling the *Venus* was not insolvency, Holly purchased four of the Old Master drawings, including a wonderfully free ink and sepia cartoon of brawling soldiers by Urs Graf. Chris had been instructed to bid for the Graf to add spice to the adventure of his holiday from school. The young man, who looked almost as mature as T.P., spoke out confidently and made no slips. He put his prices vocally, which was bold of him, with chin cocked and his eye fixed on Trevor, an attitude so confident that he seemed to defy anyone to bid against him. Only Kennedy and Holly noticed how his fingers trembled during the two minutes it took for the Graf to be knocked down to Kings'.

"Name, sir?" asked Trevor Partington.

"Kings' account," Chris replied.

Pride in her son warmed Holly. With difficulty she restrained herself from reaching over to squeeze his still shaking hand; Chris would not have appreciated such matronly behaviour.

"Good lad, good lad," said Emma who, being a sort of aunt, had no constraints placed upon her when it came to showing pride and who could even get away with nudging Chris with her hefty shoulder.

"Thank you, Emma," Chris murmured politely.

At twenty minutes to three o'clock Mr. Trevor Partington, in that slow haughty tone he had developed, announced the final lot, Jordaens' *Vision of Venus*.

Six minutes later the painting was knocked down to Mr. Greuber, London end of the international art house of Maston-Greuber-Perles. He had spent a solid hour poring over the canvas early that morning with an enlarging glass screwed into his beady eye. He had a client in Amsterdam panting for the item and, consequently, a blank cheque in his pocket. Mr. Greuber honestly believed that he had stolen a march on his competitors and found a bargain in spite of the record price he had paid. Everybody else in Partington's that afternoon thought that Greuber had gone bonkers. Writers from *Apollo* and *Connoisseur* and specialist journalists from quality dailies buzzed round Greuber like bees or clamoured with Trevor for permission to photograph the painting for reproduction, requests that the smart young auctioneer referred to 'the new owner'.

The Kings were not exempt from attention.

"But where did it come from, Mrs. King?"

"An impeccable source."

"Come on, Holly! Is it out of a Royal household?"

"No."

"It must have come from somewhere in Britain?"

"No names, no pack drill," said Holly. "My colleague, Mr. Greuber, has been furnished with certain confidential details. What he divulges is up to him."

Exodus – barring one sly elder statesman from Fleet Street who sidled up to Holly and, in jargon more suited to a crime reporter than a saleroom expert, enquired, "Not selling it for your boyfriend, then?"

"My boyfriend?"

"Twinkle-toes; you know, Pete Freeman?"

Holly remained calm. "No, sir, I'm not."

"That's enough." Maury put an arm about Holly and steered her through the crowd.

The incident dampened Holly's elation. It was all that Kennedy and Maury, and Chris too, could do to restore her high spirits over a celebratory tea in Claridge's.

"Eighteen thousand pounds," said Kennedy. "Amazing!"

"A record for Jordaens," said Emma. "You'll have your name in the annual volume."

"And the drawings too, Mum; they aren't bad, are they?" said Chris.

"No, they'll look well in a catalogue."

"Don't be so glum, Holly," said Kennedy. "We're out of the woods, thanks to you."

"And Chris won't 'ave to become a sweep's apprentice after all," said Emma.

Holly drank a second cup of tea.

How could she explain that she was ashamed? The business with the forgeries, the trip to France, all the fuss of arranging the sale had been like a sedative, numbing her anxiety at the approach of the hour when she must choose once and for all to give up her business and her friends. With each passing day the choice became more difficult. It was no longer a matter of Love versus Duty. She was snared by her own bloody-minded pride, unable to admit that she had been wrong, selfishly wrong.

"Remember, it's only half over," said Maury.

"What? What is?"

"Ritchie still has to be told that his dear sister got the better of him."

Malice cheered Holly a little. "Oh, yes. I'd love to see Ritchie's face when he realises how he bungled."

"It wasn't even dishonest, was it?" said Kennedy. "All those people, the Dubriels, de Rais – they were all at it."

"Everyone's at it," said Holly.

"Except us," said Chris cheerfully.

Maury opened his lips to correct his nephew, then thought better of it. In the past six months Maury had learned too much about brother Ritchie to be sure that Ritchie *would* admit defeat. It might yet be necessary to fight fire with fire, a confrontation that Maury, like champions of old, would undertake unwillingly but with all the determination he could muster. He could do nothing for Holly, Kennedy or Chris, however.

He must look, alas, to himself.

*   *   *

Ruth was dreaming of Maury when Ritchie returned. There was no coincidence in the fact that she was dreaming of Maury. She often dreamed of Maury in the soft morning hours. Even if Ritchie had had sex with her the previous night, chaste images were easy to conjure up out of wishes and yearnings.

Ruth had wakened early that morning. She had rolled over to peer at the drapes to see if it was sunny enough to tempt Maury to drive her to Richmond in the afternoon, found that it was and settled languorously to pick up the threads of the story she was writing in her head. In her picturebook story Maury pushed a silver baby carriage along a riverside path while deer and white swans followed him and pink doves crooned and fluttered overhead.

Almost asleep again Ruth drifted back to the beginning of

her tale; she imagined herself seated in the steep-roofed parlour of her father's house, baby carriage and a suitcase by the chair, her tummy stuck out before her like a sail in the wind. She smiled to herself, not dismayed by the vision; she was waiting for Maury to come for her; Maury, not Ritchie. In her fantasy she had never heard of anyone called Ritchie Beckman. It made her incredibly happy to be back at the beginning, a girl on the threshold of life. She smiled and purred and sighed and hugged the sheets, visualised the door of the parlour in her father's house opening and thought how she would hold out her hand and laugh and Maury would come in.

Shouts snapped her rudely back to reality.

It was not Maury who came through the door but Ritchie. Ritchie, shouting.

She had no idea what time it was or how long since Ritchie had left the bed.

It occurred to her that perhaps she had slept all day and had missed an afternoon in Richmond with Maury; she felt bereft, cheated and angry with herself. But he would have wakened her, Maury would, and she hadn't lost a whole day for months now, not since Maury had come into her life and she had quit trying to drink herself to death.

Ritchie shouted again. He threw himself against the side of the bed, shaking her awake. He gripped her shoulders and yanked her upright from the pillows.

For some reason a crumpled newspaper was spread across the quilt.

Ritchie shook her like a rag doll.

"You treacherous bitch. Why did you tell him?"

"Ritchie, what . . .?"

"You cow, how did *you* find out?"

"Find out . . . what?"

"That it was real?"

"What . . . was . . . real?"

Releasing her, Ritchie swept up the newspaper and thrust it in her face. "Look at it. Go ahead, take a bloody good look. Never heard a dicky-bird, uh, you crafty bitch. Maury and you cooked it up good between you."

Ruth stared at the half-page article. Facts were printed under a photograph of a painting, a blurred copy of some old religious work.

"Ritchie, I don't know what . . ."

"Don't *lie*, you cow, don't make it *worse*."

She scanned the printed text – and began to understand.

"Paintings, Ritchie, what do I know about paintings?"

"Maury put you up to it, di'n't he?"

"Maury? No, he never . . ."

"You told *Maury* and Maury told *her*."

"Who?"

"My bloody *sister*, that's who!"

"Holly, what's she got . . . ?"

"She got a bloody *fortune* for it, you hear me? *A bloody fortune*," Ritchie cried. "*She* conned de Rais. My *sister* conned *de Rais*. She must've *known* the painting was bloody genuine. *She must've been tipped off*."

Ruth had experienced her husband's rages too often to be frightened by them. They were seldom directed against her; not since her affair with Cole back in Evanston had fizzled out. Until six months ago, however, she would have wept and cowered and accepted the blame for anything.

But she had changed; Maury had changed her.

"So Holly got a fortune for an old painting?" Ruth said. "What's it to you?"

"You *spied* for Maury."

"Like hell I did."

"Maury's the *only* one could've figured it out. And *he* had to be *tipped*. And *you* had to be the one who tipped him."

"Why does it have to be Maury and me?"

"Nobody *else* could've known, stupid."

"Not even your French tart?"

"Madelaine?" Ritchie blurted out the name involuntarily. Fury had made him incautious. He tried to retract, but it was too late. "What . . . what French . . . what you talkin' about?"

"Why couldn't Madelaine have peached on you?"

"Don't gimme that, it was you and Maury. I never should've trusted you with him."

"It wasn't us," said Ruth. "It was Madelaine."

Ritchie swung in reflex. His fist caught Ruth on the cheek, dragging at her flesh and crushing her lips. A tooth pricked the tissues inside her mouth and she felt a sudden wet swelling heat. The unexpectedness of the blow was more shocking than the pain.

She did not cry out or recoil.

In that brief moment of violence Ritchie's power over her vanished like an exploding gas.

Thunderstruck, Ritchie stared at her. He was smitten by the enormity of the outrage he had committed against his beautiful wife and by a realisation that he had just knocked away the last prop in their relationship. His hand brushed the livid bruise on her cheek. He uttered an odd grunting sob at the sight of the blood on her lower lip.

Ritchie disintegrated before Ruth's eyes, his rage blown back against him like a sheet of flame in a shifting wind.

"Christ, what've I done? Ruth, Ruth! I didn't mean it, Ruth!"

She allowed him to caress her, tentatively touching her cheeks, her lips, her throat as if he had been struck suddenly blind and sought recognition in the darkness. His arms snaked about her body and drew her to him. He did not seek to possess her; there was no demand in him. What he sought was the reassurance that after all the insults, all the injuries, that one final blow would be forgiven too.

Ruth remained limp in his arms.

His hard chin dug into her collarbone.

It would not have surprised her if he had wanted sex with her there and then. But he wanted only comforting, patting, petting and consolation like a spoiled child.

Ruth did not respond.

"I didn't mean it, you know I didn't mean it, darling."

"Ritchie, you're hurting me."

He let her go at once.

Panic was written all over him; a kind of horror.

"I've been workin' too hard, under a strain. I didn't mean it, Ruth, honest to God, I didn't *mean* to hurt you."

"I didn't do anything to deserve it, Ritchie."

"No, no, I know you didn't, Ruthie. *You* wouldn't do that to *me*. I don't know what came over me. Christ, how could I . . . ?"

"What did you think I'd done?"

"Told Maury that the Jordaens' painting was the real thing."

"I've never even heard of the Jordaens' painting."

"So Maury could tell Holly so she could get back at me for, for what happened all those years ago, bloody years an' years ago."

"Holly ain't like that," said Ruth.

"She is. She *hates* me. She thinks I did in her husband, Deems, and old Grandpa Tal an' all. I never. How'd I know what was gonna happen? I was out the country, remember? You an' me. We were up in Scotland waitin' for the passports, remember, when her shop burned down."

"Yes, love, yes," said Ruth.

She could not help herself. She knew that she was being cynical and cunning in exploiting his collapse but she could not resist such a rare opportunity to wield power over him and to obtain information for Maury. Even if she had paused to take tally she would have found no score for her husband, not matched against the debt she owed to Maury.

"Tell me about it, love," Ruth said.

And because Madelaine was far away and Ritchie was weakened by a need for forgiveness, Ruth became his confessor – and learned all.

*   *   *

Pancake make-up and a discreet little hat with a veil hid the bruises. The Humber was well clear of Vallois Street before Ruth unfolded the strange story to Maury and, to convince him that she had not exaggerated, showed him her broken lip and puffy cheekbone. Maury promptly stopped the car by the kerb, took her in his arms and kissed her. She wept a little, though not too much; she was too full of the rest of the story to need an excess of comforting.

Maury lit cigarettes.

Ruth talked and Maury listened.

"Ruth, I certainly didn't tip Holly off."

"I know you didn't."

"My God, he's cracking up."

"You bet he is."

"Ruth, be careful, please."

"You know what he'll do, Maury; he'll hit the trail."

"Run, you mean?"

"Run for cover to France, to Paris, I expect."

"But what's he actually running from?" said Maury.

Ruth shrugged. "Himself?"

"When?"

"Whenever it gets too much for him. I've been through it umpteen times, Maury. One morning, or late one night, he'll come get me, pack me up like a piece of the baggage and whisk me away."

"You won't go with him," Maury said.

"What is that, Maury – a question or a statement?"

"A statement," said Maury.

"Maury?" Ruth held her breath.

"Frankly," Maury said, "I won't let him take you, not now, not ever. You don't mind me being blunt, do you?"

"Mind? Are you kidding?" Ruth said. "I love it."

*   *   *

The end was inevitable. Peter had lost faith in his ability to hold both the woman and his career together. Holly had gone from him long before he was willing to release her. If she had been one of his rich bitches he would have been relieved but the grief that was in him allowed no hope of a compromise. He had tried and failed to find the grail of an unambiguous love. He saw now that he would never be able to hold a woman like Holly in spite of the wistful longing that remained in her for the dreams he offered and the undiminished passion that had ousted them; a longing impossible to fulfil without complete sharing. Separately, perhaps, they loved each other still. Together they were slipping down through love into rancour. Peter preserved what was left by

368

avoiding conversation, Holly by matter-of-fact breeziness. They were, together, lonely in the discovery that their completeness did not depend each on the other's company.

The determination that had stamped their character had marred the affair from the first. It was that quality that Peter masked by gaiety and charm, that Holly veiled with calm efficiency. There could be no illusions on the plane of ambition only the one last chimerical hope that love would change everything. Now that chimera too had faded Peter felt empty. If he let Holly go, if he released her from the tacit promises she had made to love and cherish him, he would lose forever the dreamer's last refuge; he would be alone with the character he had made for himself, unaltered and unalterable. And Holly – would she settle for being the woman she had fashioned, week by week and year by year, wife and mother, running her business skilfully, the Holly that she was and not the Holly that she wished she could become? Peter figured that she would.

The end was inevitable because he would make it so.

Their affair had been scored and scripted long before they met. It had never occurred to Peter, in years of womanising, that he would come close to finding what he sought. It had never occurred to him that the love of mature people was a composite of lost ideals and deprivations, a sequence of steps so complicated that no man or woman could hope to do more than stumble through it and reach for the curtain still on their feet. He had learned that it was possible, though, just possible; the lesson came from Kennedy, not his wife. Had Holly learned that lesson too?

He would find out soon enough.

On the third Monday in May at a secret parley in a suite in the Dorchester Hotel, Howard Crocker and Peter Freeman met with the Deputy Head of the R.K.O. Picture Corporation and three high-powered lawyers. After a couple of hours of final negotiations a series of impressive contracts were signed; three years, a five picture guarantee, a fortune per week, a starting date for the shooting of *Dance, My Darling Daughter* assigned to a top director and boosted by a healthy budget. Small print contained codes and restrictions, the assurances that 'paternal' studios demanded of potential stars. Howard and the lawyers had settled the details in advance and Peter was a passive pawn in the final stages of the game. He asked few questions and, when instructed, signed the contracts while Howard hummed happily at his shoulder.

Later, when the agent and his client were alone, Howard asked, "Will you take her with you?"

Peter answered, "I can't be sure."

Howard said, "You – ah – better be quick in making up your mind."

"When do I sail?"

"Six weeks, ah, Thursday."

"My God! Does Saracen know?"

"Your contract for the run's up then."

"But does he know I won't be signing again?"

"Ah, no."

"He won't like it. None of them will like it. Ralph, Rosemary, Gwen, they're dug in for a long, long run."

"You'll be replaced."

"Sure, nobody's indispensable."

"Does that include your, ah, Mrs. Beckman King?"

"She isn't *my* missus, Howard. Kennedy won't divorce her. He refuses point blank."

"Obliging of him, don't you think?"

"What the hell's that supposed to mean?"

"Figure it out for yourself, Pete," Howard Crocker said.

Hew Saracen had been through it all before. He was not unduly surprised to learn that Freeman was not renewing his contract and intended to pull out in the middle of June. Saracen was not so steeped in egotism that he did not wish the dancer well in his Hollywood career. Press announcements would have to be prepared. The cast would have to be informed. A replacement for Peter would have to be found. Could Howard help? What would it cost for Astaire if he was free? How about a newcomer to London? Who was twinkling on Broadway these days?

Peter hardly listened. For a man who had just penned his signature to a contract that would earn him close to a million dollars he was far from happy. He wanted Holly to belong to him in the same way he belonged to the studio, on a long term body-and-soul contract with all the points of service set out and every eventuality covered.

Peter did not tell Holly of his meeting with R.K.O's executive or of its outcome. In a couple of days the press would bray the news to the breathless world; he had forty-eight hours to examine what success meant to him, to push the surface of his future to see how much or how little it would yield. Would it accommodate Holly too? Peter had always been aware that he dwelled in the shadow of inconsequentiality but never more so than during that week in London in the May month.

Kennedy held the key. To Kennedy King, Peter abrogated a once-and-for-all decision.

He telephoned Kennedy at home during the second intermission at the Mayhew and, after assuring the man that Holly was okay, asked for a private meeting the following forenoon.

Husband and lover met in civilised fashion for a pre-lunch drink in Kennedy's club. There, seated face to face in the gloomy lounge, they discussed the one and only thing that they had in common, their love for Holly.

The meeting was short. Neither man was sure of his ground, but Kennedy was the more positive.

"If you still wish it, " he said, "I'll sue Holly for divorce."

"That isn't why I asked for this meeting, Kennedy."

"Oh. No matter. It may save embarrassment to come straight to the point."

Peter sipped an unpalatable sherry. He was perched on the very edge of the club armchair as if he might decide to flee at any moment.

"It's up to Holly," Peter said.

"What's wrong? Aren't you sure you want her any longer?"

"It isn't that. I guess I'm not sure that Holly wants me."

"Leave Holly out of it," Kennedy said. "Do *you* wish her to be your wife?"

"Of course I do. But I'm not like you, I'm afraid. I want her on my terms."

Peter searched the antique dealer's aging features in search of derision but found only sympathy.

Kennedy said, "She's not the sort of woman with whom one can easily fall out of love, is she?"

"She's still your wife, though."

"Holly chose you, not me."

"If I . . . if she won't go with me to Hollywood . . . ?"

"Go on."

"What can she do here in London?"

"Are you tactfully enquiring if I'll take her back?"

"Right," said Peter. "Will you?"

"Of course I will," said Kennedy.

"Have you told her as much?"

"I don't have to tell Holly. She's always known she could depend on me."

"Lucky girl," said Peter.

"Lucky me," said Kennedy.

"What about the boy, your son?"

"What about him?"

"How will he feel about you when he finds his mother's come on home again?"

"Chris will be delighted."

"Won't he figure you for a weakling?"

"You don't know Chris, or you wouldn't have to ask. No, he'll be happy."

"Seems I'm the only villain in the piece," said Peter.

"There are no villains, Peter; that's the unfortunate part of it," said Kennedy. "If I divorce Holly it won't solve anything; not for you, not for her. Divorce is not a means to a discernible end, you see. My wife, however she appears, is quite an ordinary person."

"Meaning I'm not?"

"We're all 'ordinary' people, Peter – sorry, I don't mean to lollop on like a Dutch uncle – but there's no theory to fit us all. No solutions to the problems of reconciling what we want and what we can feasibly have."

"You reckon I misled her, uh?"

"I suspect that Holly misled herself. It was nice for her not to be responsible for a while."

"For a while?"

"She's too much of a realist to be loved in the manner in

which you love her. Unconditional acceptance, isn't that what you're striving for, Peter? Isn't that what you hope to find in California?"

"Dancing's just a job, Kennedy. Don't exaggerate its mystique."

"That isn't my intention," Kennedy said. "Let me put it another way. You want perfection in your life as well as your career."

"Maybe," said Peter. "What do you want?"

"My wife back," said Kennedy King.

"You want me to walk out on her?"

"I want you to give Holly an opportunity to return."

"And give her up?"

"She was never yours, Peter. I think you know that now," Kennedy said. "Give her a chance, Peter, to leave you with grace."

"What if she doesn't take that chance?"

"She'll be your wife, then, not mine."

* * *

Crises in families have the nasty habit of coming in pairs. Neither Holly nor Maury was aware of the parallel courses that circumstances had mapped out for them or that they were moving rapidly towards resolution.

Once, thirteen years ago, Ritchie had provoked suffering for his sister and brother. Now, with less malice and more justification, Holly and Maury united to reshape Ritchie's future.

Ritchie's cocksure cunning had always been vulnerable to delusion and guilt. Now Holly had bested him and he could not figure out how. Suspicion flared into rage and rage, fanned by neurotic anxieties and desires, ignited again his violent proclivities. England was no longer a haven. Judases were everywhere, eager to sell him to the highest bidder. Holly knew all about his business; how else could she have tracked the Jordaens' painting through the Dubriels to de Rais? Maury had sucked Ruth dry of secrets. He could trust nobody, depend on no one. Not Fletcher, not McKim, not Titus Mitchell or Stan, not even his brother Maury or his beautiful child-wife Ruth. While he remained in London he must cut himself off, make himself invisible, become a phantom like Hugues de Rais.

But bloody de Rais was lucky. Bloody de Rais didn't have an advertising firm to run. Bloody de Rais didn't have a wife that couldn't be trusted.

In Ritchie's twisted imagination Paris became the only possible sanctuary. He cancelled the threat of de Rais with thoughts of Madelaine. During his sojourn in Paris he had been confident and comfortable, flying high. He cursed himself for ever wanting to come home to London. Paris was the place for him, the only place for him. He set about closing his London deals.

Planning how he would slip away to Paris, when the time was ripe, he regained some of his confidence. He would buy a nice house to put Ruth in, out in the suburbs, in Enghien-les-Bains, maybe, or Montmorency. He would get rid of Fletcher and McKim who had begun to give him the creeps; Maddy would find a couple of reliable servants to attend to Ruth. Apex? He would retain his interest for a while now that it was ticking over. Mitchell and Stan could run it in his absence. Maury would sell the house in his name. Hell, no. Maury wasn't to be trusted. Any good estate agent would shift the goddamned place. He had never felt comfortable in the house, anyhow. In fact he hated it. It had been foisted on him by Maury who'd probably guessed that he'd hate it. He would arrange a gradual transfer of funds through a Swiss bank, like he'd done when he quit America. One afternoon when all was ready, he would shove his belongings into a couple of cabin trunks, load the Bentley and, without giving anyone warning, he would take his wife by the arm and blow. No tears, no regrets. He would put England behind him for good and all. Paris was the place. Paris – with Ruth and Madelaine to keep him happy.

It took time to close the repository in Pentonville Road, however, and to find a custodian for the half-dozen items that he had not dared sell. Time to find buyers for the stuff that wasn't too hot to handle. Time to tie up the Apex's more lucrative accounts and secure the two chainstore contracts that were in the pipeline. Too much time.

During the weeks of preparation, Ritchie's paranoia increased. He was plagued by fears that Scotland Yard had marshalled damning evidence and were on the verge of arresting him. He had tasted prison life and wanted no more of it. He couldn't take it now, not even a year, locked up in a bleak British prison, away from Ruth, cut off from Madelaine.

As a defence against that possibility and to calm all sorts of dreads, on the fifteenth of May, in the back yard of a shady public house in Wapping, Mr. Ritchie Beckman bought himself a gun.

* * *

"Listen, Maury," Stan said. "Maybe it ain't none of my business, but your brother is sailin' round the bend."

"You heard about Holly?"

"Only tales," Stan interrupted. "The whole truth, I can live without. It's more'n that, though. Ritchie's behavin' like a bleedin' caged wolf."

Stan's analogy was surprisingly apt. Maury could easily imagine his brother as a trapped animal, skulking round and round in a cage of his own making, gnawed at by hungers that he could not satisfy.

"What can I do about it?" Maury said.

"It ain't Ritchie that worries me. Hell's bells, you think I care about that creep? It's you an' Ruth what have to be looked out for."

"Come on, Stan, we're not in any danger."

"Who knows with Ritchie? Remember how violent he used to be. I don't reckon he's changed much. Except to get more nutty. You've seen him?"

"Not for a month. I keep well out of his way," said Maury. "Anyhow, he's hardly ever home."

"I know. He's up to something."

"Something criminal?"

"Probably."

"Is Apex involved?"

"It's possible. He is workin' like a troll on building up the big accounts. I've got the feelin', Maury, he's about to pull out of the advertising business."

"So why's he building it up? To sell as a going concern?"

"That's what Titus Mitchell reckons. My guess is Ritchie hopes to keep a majority shareholding in Apex and use it as a revenue source."

"How could he keep it quiet, and get the dividends out of the country undetected?"

"Easy," said Stan.

"What makes you so sure he is about to scarper?"

"Because he's so scared. Scared of every damned thing. He kids on he's cool but he's runnin' scared, Maury."

"Of the law?"

"The law, the gangsters; everything."

"Why are you telling me all this?" said Maury.

"'Cos I'm all heart."

"Because of Ruth?"

"Yer," Stan admitted. "If Ritchie whips her off to some foreign country again she's as good as wiped. Next time, without you around, she'll make a proper job of doing herself in."

"Stan, what do you want from me?" said Maury.

"Take the bird away from him."

"He'll go mad."

"Right you are."

"What's in this for you, Stan? The Apex, is that what you want? Are you hoping you'll inherit the Apex if Ritchie gets jugged?"

"I can live without the Apex," said Stan. "Sure, I'd like to stick there but – what the hell."

"You haven't answered my question."

"What question?"

"If I scupper Ritchie, what do you get out of it?"

Stan grinned and raised his bunched fist in a Roman solute.

"Freedom," he said. "I get to be free of bloody Ritchie."

"You'd be out of a job."

"I can find another job."

"In the big money?"

"Big money, who needs it? I tell you, Maury, I'd rather sleep nights. Listen, my girls are near grown up. I don't much care how I live."

"It's all very well saying that now."

"Yer, I admit Ritchie's done well by me but I don't like how he done it. What's more, he's in over his head. Least, he thinks he is."

"And that's enough."

"Listen to me, old mate. Get Ruth out of there before Ritchie pops his bleedin' cork," said Stan. "Don't you want her?"

The thought of being separated from Ruth filled Maury with dismay. He had grown used to being needed. He would miss the luncheons, the afternoons in Richmond, the undemanding pattern she had created for him. He would miss her childish dreams and the optimism that went hand in glove with her toughness. She had taught him that he had sailed alone too long. He had come to need her. There was no longer free choice in the matter. And that, Maury supposed, was love.

"I want her all right," Maury said.

"Then you'd better do somethin' about getting her."

"I intend to."

"Shop him, will you?"

"No, Stan, that's not my style."

"What then?"

"I'll take Ruth away."

"When?"

"Tomorrow night."

"Behind his back, you mean?"

"No, Stan. Right under his nose."

"Bloody hell," said Stan, admiringly. "Rather you than me, old mate."

*   *   *

Some instinct told Holly that the night had unusual significance and attuned her senses to take heed of every impression and store it in her memory. Peter had given her that, like a boxed orchid, an awareness of how poignant life's happiest moments were now that she was no longer quite young enough to see the years as rich in unlimited pleasure and the prospects of the heart as infinite. In retrospect she believed she knew all along that she would never again be a midnight dancer in tulle and lace, that the Starlight Dome and the orchestra strings were for lovers of a different sort.

The gilded butterflies of yesterday, the Bright Young Things, the flappers had been replaced by softer and less frenetic people no longer jolted by the shock of change. The evidence of change itself had changed as the twentieth century became accustomed to its novelties.

While she danced with Peter, Holly was held in the patient *ennui* of the times. Behind and around her, anxiety pricked the couples hardly at all. They had adjusted to hunger marches and the threat of economic collapse, had learned the trick of not letting depression spoil their fun. Uncertainty was an institution that only the privileged few enjoyed. Holly did not wish to join the privileged few. In glitter and glamour she had found no satisfaction. The rich would always be with us; the young would not. It was a fact that Holly had come to terms with during her months with Peter.

But in the Starlight Dome in the hour after midnight, she could almost believe that the world was as she had made it and that she was in control of her destiny, that everything was of no consequence except the pleasant languid prattle and shuffling steps.

Lady Evelyn did the quickstep with Tinker Powell.

Miss Rosabelle waltzed with the son of Lord Jepps.

Poor Mrs. Calder-Lloyd was obliged to dance with her husband.

C'est la guerre, darling. C'est la guerre.

Bobbed hair and tiara bandeaux were definitely in, and without them you were nothing. Holly had finally caught up with the youth she had missed only to find that she had passed it by.

Sincerely she danced to 'Rainy Day' and 'Body and Soul', defiantly to 'Lucky Seven'. She scanned the tables and the floor for stars and scandal, for Jack Buchanan and Ralph

Brooks and, that midweek night in spring, saw – only herself. Me, Holly thought, smiling softly against Peter's shoulder, I am looking for me out there. I'm the dark-haired woman in Peter Freeman's arms.

When that begins to happen it is time to stop.

'We Two, Alone' summed it up nicely.

What would they say of her when Peter signed with Hollywood and chucked her over? They would say she could have expected no more of such a notorious cad.

C'est la guerre, darling. C'est la guerre.

But she had been there, once.

And that was enough, more perhaps than she deserved, to be loved by Peter.

And by Kennedy.

Peter," she whispered, "Let's go home."

*   *   *

Peter drove the raffish red Alvis, hired from a Knightsbridge firm, with less than his usual verve. It was pushing four a.m. and the streets were deserted, the buildings cut in planes of dry shadow from faint moist dabs of light. In the Green Park the birds were barely awake. Holly sat close to her lover, her head against the leather seat, and watched the unfamiliar, handsome emptiness of London roll past. She had left the dance floor for this, to be with him in motion, not in the tumbled bed. Peter seemed almost indifferent to her presence. She preferred it that way. It was as if they had detached themselves from the picture they made together, a tipsy couple prowling home through the dawn light.

The Alvis was half way down Sloane Street before Holly realised it.

"Peter?"

"Hm?"

"You've taken a wrong turning."

"No, I thought we'd go this way tonight."

"It's a long road to Holland Park."

"There's no hurry, Holly, is there?"

Sensing his sadness, she sat up. "You're not driving to

Holland Park, are you?"

"No, darling."

"You're taking me home, aren't you? To Chelsea?"

"Yes."

"Why, Peter?"

Peter tapped his foot upon the accelerator and the Alvis picked up speed. Holly drew in a breath of the fresh morning air. She felt calm, incredibly calm. She studied her companion; the lean, youthful American, stripped now of the relaxation that was the hallmark of his appeal, fingers clenched on the rim of the wheel, the line of his jaw taut, his lips compressed.

"Are you angry with me, Peter?"

"No."

"Tired of me then?"

"Yesterday I signed a contract with R.K.O.; three years, five pictures."

"I see."

"Go ahead, Holly." He glanced at her. "Tell me that's wonderful."

"It's what you want, isn't it?"

"Sure it is. Howard finally pulled it off. I go into shooting in ten weeks."

"And the London show?"

"As far as I'm concerned, *finito*. Howard will break the news the day after tomorrow. Ralph and Rosemary will be howling mad."

"They won't begrudge you your success."

"In the middle of a settled run, sure they will."

"Hew Saracen will find somebody to replace you."

He glanced at her again.

"I want to make a clean break with England. And with you."

"I see," Holly said. "Did Howard issue an ultimatum?"

"Howard had nothing to do with it."

Peter sounded so different, almost shrewish. Holly suffered a moment's guilt; had she disappointed him so much that he could not be bothered to sustain a pretence of affection for just a few minutes longer?

Peter said, "Look, we had fun, right? It's time to quit before either of us gets hurt."

"That," said Holly, "sounds like a line from one of your shows."

"Maybe it is. I can't separate them out any more."

"When did you decide it was over?"

"When I signed on the bottom line. You wouldn't be happy in Hollywood. It's no place for you. It's my Shangri La, Holly, and I can't share it with you."

"What if I'm willing to try, Peter?"

"I don't want you any more."

She could smell the soft salty odour of the river and, blinking, realised that they were already in Chelsea.

"Yes," she said. "That's a valid reason."

"Holly . . ." He twisted towards her, the Alvis slewing on the cobbled street. He caught the slide and braked and shook his head. He had been on the point of taking back the lie, of recanting. The love in him could not be repressed by denial. It cost him every ounce of will power to let the harsh rejection stand. "Holly, it's over."

"What if Kennedy won't take me in?"

"He will."

"You sound very sure of that, Peter."

"Sure I'm sure. He never let you go in the first place. You were never really mine, Holly."

"Yes, Peter. Yes, I was, if only for a little while."

The Alvis eased against the kerb outside the Kings' house which stood asleep behind its high brick wall. Gulls mewed on the railings of the embankment and the river rippled like silk under a mist that lay like breath upon the water.

Holly noticed that the boughs of the trees that stooped over the wall had come into blossom again.

In the morning light the old house seemed quite new.

"What do I do now, Peter?" she asked. "Get out of the car and just watch you drive off?"

"I guess so."

Holly nodded and slipped from the Alvis and walked around the bonnet. Her eyes never left Peter's face behind the windshield. She reached the pavement's edge and leaned to the car's open window.

"Don't pretend, darling," she said. "You're doing this for me, aren't you?"

"For both of us."

"To preserve what there was between us?"

"Preservation's the name of the game."

"I'd never have left you, Peter."

"I know that," he said. "But isn't this what you really want, to go back to what you had in the first place?"

"No, darling," said Holly with a self-deprecating smile. "What I really want is – everything."

Peter smiled too.

She saw the change in him, the sum of all the changes. He could not bring himself to leave her, his courage running out at last.

Holly kissed him awkwardly upon the lips.

He grabbed for the door handle but she pressed her hips against the door.

"Let me go, Peter. Please."

"Go then, for God's sake."

She swung away and hurried to the iron gate and unlatched it. She stepped through and paused. Beneath the hanging boughs of the crab-apple tree the grass was beaded with dew. She moved into the screen of the boughs and put her hands to her cheeks, fingers pressed against her flesh. Behind her, over the high wall, the Alvis roared. Echoes surged from the face of the house and bellied away across the expanse of the river. Startled, the gulls rose in a heavy flock, squealing and mewing. The sound of the car's engine dwindled into quietness.

Tears ran unchecked down Holly's face.

She wept for Peter, for the poignancy of her discovery that he had loved her enough to give her back to a man who loved her more.

In time she dried her tears and, still in the dress of tulle and lace, let herself into Kennedy's house with the key she had never relinquished.

*   *   *

"Holly? Holly, is that you?"

"Yes, Kennedy. I brought you some tea and toast."

"What time is it?"

"About six."

"Good God! What on earth are you doing here at this ungodly hour? What's wrong?"

"Nothing's wrong. Here, sit up."

"You've been up all night, haven't you?"

"Yes, dancing at the Starlight Dome.

"You still haven't told me what you're doing here."

"Kennedy, I'd like to come home. For good, I mean. Permanently."

"Ah! I see."

"Don't . . . don't give me an answer now. Wait until you're properly awake."

"I'm quite awake, Holly."

"May I sit beside you?"

"Of course."

"I know it sounds like an excuse, but I'm not leaving Peter; I'm coming back to you. To you, to Chris . . ."

"Bit sudden, isn't it?"

"Peter's definitely going to California. I don't want to go with him."

"But do you really want to come back here, to Chelsea, to me?"

"More than anything."

"Holly, you must understand that I can't be a dashing young chap again."

"I like you as you are."

"Is that marmalade?"

"Yes. Want some?"

"Please." Kennedy chuckled and shook his head. "Matter-of-factness; the curse of the English. Reconciliation and toast."

"It'll never happen again, Kennedy. I promise you."

"How can you be sure?"

"I won't let it."

"It might prove easier a second time."

so relieved to have you back. To the devil with terms. I just want you to stay, to stay and be happy."

"I will, Kennedy. I will."

"Holly, I must ask you one question. Please answer me truthfully."

"If I can."

"Do you still love him?"

"Yes, Kennedy. I suppose part of me always will."

"Then why are you letting him go?" he said.

"Kennedy, don't you see?" said Holly. "You're my life. Peter could never be that, not in France or London or California. He could never replace you."

"Are you going to bed for a while?"

"No, I'm not sleepy."

"Have breakfast with me then, in the kitchen, like we used to."

"May I . . . may I stay, Kennedy?"

"As long as you want to, darling," said Kennedy.

She kissed him. He smelled of marmalade.

"Thank you," said Holly.

"For what?"

"Forgiving me."

Kennedy looked surprised. "I'd be a damned fool if I didn't."

A half-hour later, bathed and sensibly dressed for the day, Mr. and Mrs. King ate breakfast at the big kitchen table and, an hour after that, left together for a day's work at their gallery.

* * *

Cissie's house was tucked behind the shoulder of Castle Hill, out of sight of the Regency front that made Hastings such a pretty town. It was early in the season for holidaymakers and, in spite of the fine weather, the highroad from London had been very quiet. The Humber had eaten up the miles with gratifying rapidity and Maury reached Hastings around eleven thirty. He wasted no time in sniffing the sea breezes or in sampling the pleasures of the sands. He was here for a purpose, a deadly serious purpose and the thought that his hunch might be wrong nagged him constantly. Tonight he would have a showdown with Ritchie. He needed ammunition.

All that he had gleaned from Ruth and Stan about Ritchie's dealings in fake and stolen art pointed to there being a storehouse of incriminating evidence. Zoning in on Hastings was not quite such a long shot as it might seem. Long term planning was Ritchie's *forte*. He had taken too friendly an interest in Leo and Cissie and in helping them establish their new home. If Ritchie needed a store in which to leave hot items while he resided out of Britain, the innocuous bungalow in Hastings would be an ideal place.

If Maury was wrong, however, he would be obliged to confront Ritchie without weapons and his chances of besting his brother would be slender. If he had been a different kind of man, slyer and less scrupulous, Maury might have slipped Ruth out of Ritchie's clutches easily enough. But that would have settled nothing. Ruth and he would have been dogged by Ritchie's shadow all the rest of their lives.

The trim little bungalow with its privet hedge and lace curtains was a far cry from the terrace house in Abraham's Box. It had a peculiar quality of appearing both individual and anonymous, a characteristic of much of the estate building of the period. What the neighbours thought of his father and stepmother, Maury could not imagine.

There was no doubt at all that Cissie's influence on the old man had been beneficial. Spruce and tanned, Leo admitted his son with expressions of welcome and none of the uncouthness that had been his usual attitude to unexpected callers back in Lambeth. Maury wondered how Cissie had managed to mellow the old devil and teach him manners in such a short space of time.

"Good t'see yer, son. Good t'see yer." Leo shook his hand.

"Maury, is it?" Cissie emerged from the kitchen, forearms dusted with flour. "What a nice surprise."

"Come int' the . . ."

"The front room for Maury," said Cissie.

"Oh, yer, the front room."

"I'm no guest, Cissie," Maury protested.

"'Course you are, son," said Leo, unprompted.

"Front room's the place for mornin' tea," said Cissie.

"In that case," said Maury, "lead on, Pa."

Display cabinets in mock mahogany were filled with Cissie's collection of china and brass ornaments. A huge overstuffed suite in uncut moquette crowded the room. Print curtains hung from a curved pelmet and the atmosphere was redolent of polish and pine air freshener. In the hearth a bow-bellied gas fire purred and May sunlight, cleaving through the windows, showed hardly a mote of dust.

"May I smoke?" asked Maury.

"In 'ere?" said Leo uncertainly.

From outside the room Cissie's voice gave an answer. "Maury can smoke wherever 'e likes. Give 'im an ashtray, Leo."

Leo obliged.

"Ask Maurice if 'e's stayin' for lunch."

Leo asked Maurice if he was staying for lunch. Maurice regretted that he had business that required his attention elsewhere. He could not stay for long.

Maury looked at Leo. Leo looked at Maury.

Father and son, with little to say, smiled uncertainly each at the other and waited for Cissie, the interpreter, to appear with the tea-trolley to enable them to communicate in a manner that befitted the surroundings.

"Comfortable here, Pa?"

"Fine, it's fine."

"What're the pubs like?"

"Pubs?" Leo found the question puzzling. "Oh, we don't go ter no *pubs*. Cocktail bar down the County Hotel." He patted his son's knee and confided in a low voice, as if it was a fearful secret, "Ciss likes a little snifter now'n'again."

It was becoming more difficult by the minute for Maury to tackle his father about Ritchie. The ancient involvements seemed far away, as remote as Abraham's Box. Was this what money could do? Money, security and the attention of a good woman? Would it have been like this all along if Leo had not been widowed? More likely it was a feature of the aging process, nothing more significant. Strangely Maury mourned, just a little, for the outrageous Leo of yesterday, for the crude old bull who was gone for good.

Cissie wheeled in the trolley. She had changed into a floral-print dress. On tea cups and plates were sepia vignettes of famous Sussex landmarks. The freshly-baked scones with clotted cream and Co-op strawberry jam were delicious. Maury made a pig of himself. Leo was permitted to relax the diet that Cissie had put him on 'to save his 'eart'.

They talked of the weather, the price of foodstufs, the Depression, of the trivial engagements that the Beckmans had made with the seacoast town, the best kind of grass seed to sprinkle on the rug-sized front lawn and how quickly, in Maury's opinion, it might take to establish a rockery. All three partook of second cups of tea from the mighty china pot with its frieze of Brighton's Royal Pavilion.

Ritchie and crime became even more remote.

At length Maury roused himself from pervasive lethargy and raised the subject of Leo's second son. Had Ritchie dropped in here lately? Only ten days ago, in fact. Had Ritchie brought anything? Brought Ciss a Hart-Dekko lamp for the bedside table, in fact.

"Anything else, Pa?"

Maury sensed that he was on to something.

Leo had never been a glib liar and had lost the brass neck that had enabled him to hide secrets. The old man glanced at his wife. She was sharp enough to be cautious yet too much of a novice to the machinations of the Beckman clan to appreciate the seriousness of the situation.

"Nothin' else." Leo defied Cissie to correct him.

Ritchie had no doubt warned his father not to tell anyone, not even Maury, about the stout wooden box stowed in the bungalow's vee-shaped attic. Had he warned Cissie too?

Cissie was staring at her lap.

Maury took a chance. "Ritchie told me all about it."

Cissie sighed and smiled. Maury felt rotten at having to deceive the woman.

"That's all right then," Cissie said. "Don't like secrets in families."

Leo was not so easily taken in.

"Told yer what, Maury?"

"About the stuff."

"What stuff?" Leo was losing the battle.

"Stuff Ritchie put in the attic," said Cissie.

Maury was reminded of the night the coppers raided the Beckman house in Abraham's Box; Grandpa Tal had told him about it. Ritchie was on remand in the local nick. The loot from several robberies was stashed under the boards of a shed in the back yard. Ritchie had been fortunate; Grandpa Tal had managed to talk the coppers out of completing their search and had saved Ritchie an extra three or four years in prison.

The domestic downfall of thieves was legendary yet seemed out of kilter with a smart fellow like Ritchie. For all his international experience and connections would Ritchie founder on a box of stolen stuff tucked away in the attic of a Hastings bungalow?

Aware that he might be estranging himself from his father for ever, Maury got to his feet.

"Leo, I want it," he said.

"Ritchie *don't* know yer 'ere?"

"Nope."

"What's wrong, love?" said Cissie.

"Maury." Finding strength, Leo jerked himself to his feet to defend his beloved son Ritchie against wicked honesty. "Maury, get outta my 'ouse."

"Your house? That's a hoot," said Maury.

Cissie was disturbed. "What's wrong, Maury?"

"*Don't tell 'er.*"

"Too late, Pa."

"Leo, what's in that flamin' box upstairs?" Cissie demanded.

"Nothin', dear, nothin'."

"Ritchie couldn't even let you live here in peace, Pa," said Maury. "He's using you again. You know damned well what'll happen if the police come rootin' round. *You'll* carry the can."

"Police?" Cissie's tone was one of strident outrage.

"What've *we* gotter do with the police?"

"Nothin', nothin', dear."

"What've you been up to, Leo Beckman?" Cissie demanded.

"*Now see what you've been 'n' done, Maury*," Leo shouted.

Much as he wished to, Maury could not back down now. What distressed him most was the fact that he had finally stooped to using Ritchie's tactics.

"Stolen goods Ritchie's got us hidin' for 'im, ain't it?" said Cissie thinly.

"Cissie, look, I didn't mean to . . ." Maury began.

She cut him off. "You knew they was stolen goods when Ritchie brought them 'ere, didn't you, Leo Beckman?"

"Never knew nothin' of the sort," Leo mumbled.

"But they are, ain't they? Stolen goods?"

"Yer, might be," Leo, in shame, admitted.

"Ritchie – a bleedin' common thief! My Gawd, I landed a son who's a thief. I'm livin' under a roof bought with dirty money." To Maury, Cissie said, "What has 'e got stowed in our attic?"

"I don't know," said Maury.

"You another 'un? Another thief?"

"Nah, Maury's straight as a die." Leo's unprompted defence of his character touched Maury. He felt worse than ever.

"But not yer precious Ritchie?" Relentlessly Cissie chased the truth. "He ain't straight, is 'e?"

"Ritchie didn't say what was in the box," said Leo. "I never asked."

"*But you knew*?"

Maury intervened. "Maybe Pa didn't know, Cissie."

Leo opened his mouth to endorse the diplomatic statement that Maury had come up with, then thought better of it and hung his head penitently. It was unclear whether he was ashamed of being an over-indulgent father, of having a son who was a criminal, or was frankly embarrassed at being caught out.

Cissie paused. "What's your angle, Maury?"

"I'm here to take the box away."

Cissie scowled. "For what?"

"T' save my bleedin' hide," said Leo. "Ain't that it, Maury?"

"That's it, Pa."

Slowly Cissie nodded her blunt head. She could accept Leo's foolishness and forgive it. It was a more palatable truth than any other. Once again Leo had struck it lucky, no thanks to Ritchie.

"Fetch the box down, Leo," Cissie said.

"I'll give you a hand," said Maury.

A folding ladder had been fitted within the attic. One tug on a stout drawcord released a trap above the hallway and dropped the ladder's weighted sections to the floor. Maury peered up into the gloom. It did not smell musty but had the pleasant odour of raw timber and tarred lagging that he knew so well.

"Where is it exactly?" Maury asked.

"Behind the chimney, under a blanket."

A couple of minutes later the box stood in the hallway and the Beckmans' attic was sealed up again.

The box was of inch plywood bound with nailed tin stripping. Maury and Leo had lifted it easily down the ladder.

"Is that it?" said Maury. "Just one?"

"Just one," Leo said. "You want an 'ammer."

"I'll take it as it stands; unopened."

From the doorway of the front room, Cissie said, "You're right, it's better not to know what sins we 'ave 'arboured."

Leo took Maury by the arm. "Listen, you ain't gonna cart that box to the police, are yer?"

"What do you think, Pa?"

"Gawd, Maury! He's yer brother, yer own flesh 'n' blood! Please, son, please – for yer old man – one favour – don't shop 'im. Please."

Deliberately Maury turned to the woman. "Cissie?"

She folded her arms over her bosom. "I was taught forgiveness, Maury. Give the beggar one more chance."

"All right," said Maury. "No coppers. I promise."

"Tell Ritchie this, though," said Cissie." Tell 'im never to come 'ere again. Never. Right, Leo?"

"Yer, tell 'im that, Maury."

Maury lowered himself to one knee, put his arms around the box and lifted it. It did not tax his strength. He held it high against his chest. Cissie came forward and put his hat upon his head.

"What about me?" Maury said. "Am I no longer welcome?"

"You're always welcome," said Cissie. "But tell me something, Maurice, what do you intend t'do with that box?"

"Drop it on Ritchie."

Cissie looked at him long and hard. "Cain or Abel – which one are you, Maurice Beckman?"

"Neither," Maury said. "I think it's my turn to be Adam."

*   *   *

It was after eleven before Ritchie returned to Vallois Street after a long, exhausting day in the course of which he had buttered-up no less than six Apex clients plus one decidedly shady art dealer. In all he had secured five advertising contracts. In the evening, over dinner in a Soho restaurant, he concluded a personal transaction by coming to terms with a nit-picking homosexual, agent for the Earl of Caldwater, chairman of the board of trustees of a national picture collection. Agent and Earl were in cahoots to skim what they could from the transaction. It was no exaggeration to say that the nation paid for the room, board and lingerie of the Earl's London mistress. What Ritchie sold – via the agent – to the Earl's committee was a package of six genuine masterpieces. After much haggling over division of the spoils, Ritchie was persuaded to let the six paintings slide for a total of fifty-one thousand pounds. The paintings would be offered to the gallery's trustees as individual items over the course of the next couple of years and the fifty-one thousand pounds would be leaked into Ritchie's Swiss bank account in five equal parts. In addition to ensuring a supply of capital for the re-establishment of his business in Paris, Ritchie had brushed over some of his tracks as a forger and resetter. If any smart 'tec pounced on him now Ritchie could be sure that the Earl of Caldwater would be on his side.

For all that Ritchie was satisfied with his day's work – and had pushed closer to the moment when he could take himself out of London and out of danger – he remained tight as piano wire. Somehow he had gotten it into his head that the queer was setting him up for the Yard; he had kept the Colt automatic in the waistband of his trousers all during the meal.

Ritchie was seldom without the gun these days. The nearer he came to 'escaping' from London the more he needed its lumpy comfort against his gut. It assured him that, as a last resort, he might choose to go out in a blaze of glory, like the suckers in the Chicago mobs whose brawling bloody deaths he had once so despised. Now Ritchie understood how gratifying it must be to pull off that ultimate con, to cheat the 'tecs of prey, the law of its victim. There was something appealingly pure in an act of self-destruction.

Naturally Ritchie did not want to become a martyr to revenge; he would not, however, permit himself to be arrested. So inflamed had his imagination become that he suffered recurring nightmares in which all of his many victims were packed into a witness box to testify against him; Vince Shotten, dead Jack Renzo, back even to Steiner, an old Jew he had almost beaten to death in a cavernous apartment off the Shadwell Road many years ago. They would expose him for what he really was, no smart, sophisticated crook but a dirty slum-bred hoodlum. He could not bear humiliation or the shameful weight of so many petty sins. He carried the gun as a guard against it.

The Colt automatic was still in his belt when he eased his car into the garage and cut the motor and the lights. He felt totally empty, scalded and raw on the outside but inside, hollow.

"Mr. Beckman, Sir."

Ritchie ducked and grabbed down through his overcoat for the gun. Fortunately for Fletcher her master was wearing a belted garment or she might have collected a bullet between the eyes.

"It's only me, Mr. Beckman. It's only Fletcher."

"*Geeze!*" Ritchie sagged against the wing of the car and screamed, "*Don't ever sneak up on me, you cow!*"

Fletcher blinked but stood her ground. Reaching behind her, she cautiously cocked the handle of the door that led into the house.

"It is a matter of some concern, Mr. Beckman."

"*What the hell is it now?*"

"It is the other Mr. Beckman, Sir; your brother."

"Maury? What about Maury?"

"He's upstairs." Fletcher pushed open the door and stood to one side. "He has been there for hours. With Mrs. Beckman."

The servant's frizzy hair seemed to glow like a coal under the light bulb. Her features were stiff as starched linen.

In Ritchie's belly a cold tumorous swelling grew. Fingers working involuntarily, he unbuckled his coat, unbuttoned his jacket.

Softly he enquired, "What'd you mean, *with* Mrs. Beckman?

"They are waiting for you, Sir."

"He's brought the cops, hasn't he?"

"No, no, Mr. Beckman. It's just your brother and your wife. Awaiting your arrival." Fletcher was human after all. Her pale throat bobbed, her eyes stretched wide, the corners of her mouth twitched. She swallowed then blurted out, "He-has-come-to-take-her-away-with-him."

"Say that again – slowly."

The woman's eyes closed, as if she could not bear to look at Ritchie while she enunciated the words more clearly.

"Your brother's come to take Mrs. Beckman away with him. They are all ready to leave, Sir. Now, Sir. Upstairs. Packed. Ready. Waiting."

"Waiting," said Ritchie, "for what?"

Fletcher's eyes opened again. She blinked in bewilderment then gave a tiny wooden shrug. "To rub it in, Sir, I suppose."

Ritchie stepped past her into the house.

*　　*　　*

Two suitcases, one winter overcoat and a Harrods' shoe box were stacked beside the davenport upon which, side by side like travellers in a railway rest room, Maury and Ruth waited.

Ruth was dressed in a light cream wool coat, far from the most expensive garment in her wardrobe. She wore a slouch hat, fine kidskin gloves and cross-strap shoes, carried her purse in one hand and a cigarette in the fingers of the other. When Ritchie entered the room, she leaped to her feet and dabbed the cigarette into an ashtray on the coffee table by her side. On the table were cups and plates, a silver coffee pot, the remains of a snack supper. All the lights in the huge room blazed. The scene looked naked, over-exposed.

Maury got to his feet too, broad-fitting tweed coat and fur-felt soft hat too run-of-the-mill for such a late night drama.

Ruth clasped Maury's hand.

"Hey!" said Ritchie, from the doorway. "This *is* a surprise."

Ruth raised her head. "I'm leavin' you, Ritchie."

"Hey!" said Ritchie. "I don't like surprises."

"I've had enough," said Ruth.

She sounded, Ritchie thought, like his sister, with that same detestably positive quality in her voice.

"I don't like jokes neither."

"It's no joke," Maury told him.

"Maury, will you take the cases?" said Ruth.

Ritchie said, "I oughtta be angry with you, Ruthie. But I can take a joke. Go on, go to your bedroom. I'll stand Maury one for the road. We'll have a yack about it tomorrow, you an' me."

"Not tomorrow, not any time," said Ruth.

"It's a fact, then?"

"It's a fact, Ritchie," said Maury.

Ritchie found a chair, a steel and leather sling, close by the door. He seated himself unsteadily upon it, still – apparently – puzzled and uncertain.

"I don't get it," he said. "I mean, what's goin' on?"

"I thought I'd made it clear," said Ruth. "I'm haulin' out, Ritchie. I'm going with Maury, to live with Maury. I'm sick of you. I've been *sick* of you for years."

"Aw, Geeze, Ruth!"

"You want it plainer than that?"

"Why didn't you tell me? I mean, I could've done something. I know what it is; it's London. Once we get back to France – to Paris, I'm taking you back to Paris, Ruth – we'll be fine. It'll be like it was."

"Ritchie, I don't want it to be like it was."

Ritchie switched her off. To Maury he said, "*You* did this; *you* put the idea into her head."

"Maybe I did," said Maury.

"An' I trusted you!" Ritchie shouted. "That's what I get for trustin' my own bloody brother!"

"Maury, come on," said Ruth. "I can't take any more of it."

"You're not leavin', Ruth. Not tonight. Not tomorrow. Not with him. Not with anyone!" Ritchie yelled.

"You can't stop me, Ritchie. I'm not scared of you."

"Yeah, I can stop you," Ritchie said quietly. "Yeah, that I can do."

Releasing Ruth's hand, Maury shifted towards the long cocktail sideboard. Ritchie shot to his feet, hand on the protruding butt of the automatic at his waist.

"Easy, Ritchie," Maury advised. "I only want to show you something that might interest you."

Ritchie's anguish had not yet burned deep. He felt that he was still in command, that power would triumph over infatuation. Ruth had never bucked him, much, before. After all wasn't he the guy who'd shaped her, rescued her from the Erbachs' ragbag house when she was only a kid? Wasn't he the guy who had devoted himself to her welfare ever since? She couldn't survive without his protection. She couldn't *exist* without him.

"Show me what? he said.

From among the bottles on the sideboard Maury lifted the silver gilt statuette of the Madonna and Child. He held it tenderly in cupped palms and extended it to Ritchie like a votive offering.

"This."

"What's that supposed to be?"

"A token, Ritchie."

"Think you can *buy* my goddamned wife away from me? Think she's for *sale*?"

"He means the price ain't high enough, Maury," Ruth said. "He understands what's on. Please darling, let's get out of here."

Maury said, "Buying and selling people has always been your racket, Ritchie, not mine. Don't pretend you don't know where this statue came from."

"Never clapped eyes on it before."

"I've a signed statement to go with it," Maury lied.

"I also have eight other art objects all of which are listed as stolen property on the New Scotland Yard register. All of which you secreted in Pa's house in Hastings."

"Lemme see that thing."

Maury handed the Madonna to his brother.

Ritchie turned it over and over then, with a ferocity that seemed to rip apart the membranes of his sanity, swung the Madonna and crashed it across the framework of the casual chair. The Virgin's head and that of the Christ child impacted, limbs crumpled and a fine storm of surface particles fell to the oatmeal carpet. Ritchie twisted the distorted statuette, grinding the likeness down – but it would not part, would not shatter, in spite of its great age and the malleability of its base materials. In fury he flung it from him. It thumped into the davenport, bounced and lay still, perched against a corner cushion.

"A cheap fake; a lousy cheap fake," Ritchie yelled. "You expect me to fall for that, Maury? What'd you take me for? Christ, that isn't evidence."

"It's evidence, Ritchie – that plus eight other items you hid in the box in Pa's house. I can rhyme them off for you. I can even tell you where you bought them or where they were stolen from. I can tell you – I can tell the police – about most of the forgeries you palmed off on clients."

"You got *nothin'*, Maury. You got *nothin'* on me."

"Oh, yer, Ritchie, I have. Believe me, I have."

"He's got me," said Ruth. "For starters."

Ritchie tugged the gun from his waistband and held it,

passively, in his hand. He had gone slack again, loose and grinning.

"I don't much care what you've done, Ritchie," said Maury, ignoring the gun. "But I love Ruth and I want her. I'm taking her out of here tonight. And that's that."

Ritchie shook his head at such wonderful faith in the power of love, at his brother's naivety.

"No chance, Maury."

"Yes, Ritchie," Maury said. "It's pretty damned crude, I admit, but what it comes down to is this – if you don't let us go, I'll hand the police a watertight case. I've more than enough evidence hidden away. Written statements. Dates. Names. Lots of names, Ritchie."

"You're lyin', Maury."

"Am I? Look at the couch. See the statue. Is that a lie? The box in Pa's attic wasn't a lie, was it?"

"You won't do it, you won't shop me."

"Right," said Maury. "I won't shop you, not if you let Ruth go. That's the price, Ritchie. I sit on the evidence and you get your chance to clear out of the country. But Ruth stays here with me.

"Maury, be careful," Ruth whispered.

"That's all I have to say, Ritchie. I'm going to pick up Ruth's cases now and we're clearing out, together, Ruth and I. Neither of us ever wants to see you again."

Maury stooped to lift the suitcases.

Apologetically Ritchie said, "Maury?"

Maury straightened, lifting his head.

Ritchie shot him in the chest.

*　　*　　*

The bullet struck Maury high on the chest wall. It scored laterally across the flange of muscle and gouged flesh from the crown of his left shoulder before plucking out through the sleeve of his overcoat. Initially it felt like a jet of freezing water, like the fine needle spray from a dentist's nozzle. There was no impact; Maury's grunted cry was one of astonishment, not of pain.

Fifteen years ago he had learned all there was to know about death by bullet wounds and his brain had not discarded one iota of that information. The ironic fact that the jerries hadn't managed to shoot him during interminable years of trench warfare, that he had to wait for his own brother to do it, glimmered in Maury's mind. His knee gave a little, touched the carpet. He grunted again as heat radiated in the wake of the bullet. Blood from the wound seeped swiftly through his clothing. It was nothing, though, nothing to write home about. His monitoring system assured him that he was not about to die, not from that first shot at any rate.

Ruth was screaming. There was that embodiment of death in the air too, the reek of cordite, the stench of the gun. Dark memories of suffering clouded Maury's senses for an instant. He braced his knee, shook his head, stretched out his right hand and hoisted up the larger of the two suitcases. Stubborn anger at the crudity of Ritchie's solution to frustrated greed filled him. He pushed himself to his feet and jammed the suitcase under his right arm. His left hand did not seem to be working very well. He juggled the second case into his right hand.

"Time to go, Ruth," he said.

Ruth stopped screaming.

Ritchie had her by the arm, pinning her. He cocked the Colt, aimed it at Maury's head.

Blood dripped from the pad of Maury's thumb on to the pale carpet. Carefully he adjusted the cases. He felt slightly nauseous.

"Let her go, Ritchie."

"Maury, I . . . I . . . I'll kill you next time."

"Tried to kill me last time, kid, but you hadn't the guts," said Maury. "Let her go."

Maury walked towards his brother, towards Ruth. She was the vulnerable one, the wounded one, the one who deserved a future.

Under the curled hat brim, her eyes were huge.

"Come over to me, darling," Maury said.

She seemed a long way off. Maybe he was asking too much of her. He felt as if he had walked miles already, and there were many miles more to go. *God, Maury, you're not so young as you were, are you, old son?* he thought. *You don't have much more of this sort of stuff left in the cupboard. Still, haul yourself together and make the most of it. One way or another it won't last long.*

Straightening his shoulders, he said, "Ruth, don't you want to come with me?"

"Yes," she cried – and began to fight.

That's it, Maury thought; *deny him an easy victory.*

He was close now, almost within touching distance of his brother.

Ruth tore free.

With a last wild snatch, Ritchie grabbed at her but she was gone, not running from the room but standing where Maury could protect her and she could protect him.

"You've lost her, Ritchie," Maury said. "If you reckon being rid of me'll bring her back, bring it all back, why don't you use the gun properly?"

Point blank range was reduced still further when Ritchie raised the weapon and, clasping right wrist with left fist, thrust the snout directly into Maury's face.

"Right between the eyes," said Maury. "That's it." He permitted no trace of uncertainty to leak into his eyes, no yielding. "Pull the trigger, Ritchie. That's all you've got to do. Pull the damned trigger."

But Ritchie was blown. The evil in him was dissipated, shown to be but chaff, without substance or worth, dry whispering stuff, the waste of years thrashed out by vanity and selfishness until no grain of nourishment remained to provide the strength he needed at that moment. He feared Maury. Fear was all he had to cling to. But he could not kill Maury, could not shear the iron link that fixed him to the reminiscence of his youth.

Slowly he lowered the gun.

Swaggering bravado, the familiar baseless charm could not hide the hurt in him.

"She isn't worth swinging for, Maury," Ritchie crossed the room, hoisted the telephone receiver from its cradle and, at the same time, flung the gun on to the davenport beside the crushed statuette.

"Stan? Ritchie. Get Klapper, Doc Klapper. I want him over at the house fast. You hear me – *fast*."

Deftly he replaced the receiver and, without another word, slipped through the door and hurried downstairs to the garage. Seconds later he left the wedding-cake house – and his wife – for ever.

Upstairs Ruth helped Maury to a chair.

Maury seated himself with great care, anxious not to disturb the ball of pain that clung to his shoulder and arm. Ruth wept. "Maury, Maury darling, you're bleeding so bad. Does it hurt?"

Maury rested his head on her shoulder to wait for the doctor to arrive. He squinted up at her and, with the last ounce of his strength, managed to wink.

"Not any more, love," he said.

oooooooo
ooooo
ooo
o

3

The Blue Evening Gone

If Maury and Ruth had hoped that Ritchie would vanish completely like an Indian boy at the top of a rope, they were doomed to disappointment. Once safe across the English Channel and settled in Paris with Madelaine, Ritchie's inflamed nerves soon healed and new challenges restored his exuberance. To give him his due, he did not boast about what he had done to his brother or wallow in self-pity as a wronged husband, victim of marital disaster. Only on rare occasions, when too much *vin rouge* had soured his disposition, would he rail against his family and mutter that he wished he'd done a proper job with the gun, popping off his damned sister and his faithless wife while he was at it.

"I do not believe that you mean it," Madelaine would say.

And Ritchie would answer, "I bloody well do."

Privately, however, he was rather glad to be free of his shop-worn obsession with Ruth Erbach, rid of the tiresome menage of servants and jail-like domiciles.

Superficially Ritchie's 'lousy year' in London changed him hardly at all. Beneath the chrome-plated exterior of the new Parisian, though, there was evidence of one vital change of which Madelaine was aware; Ritchie was no longer sure of himself.

For that reason, as the year of 1933 gave way to 1934, Ritchie gradually came not only to admire young Madelaine Cazotte but to depend on her. In bed and out of it, she dominated their relationship. Ritchie did not see that he had bartered the strength that comes from loneliness for something gentler but much more dangerous; that, by falling in love, he had become Madelaine's man.

All the best notions now were Madelaine's; the drive, the will to power, the clever little curlicues to various schemes and deals all stemmed from the French girl. She controlled Ritchie. She operated and exploited him – and Ritchie didn't mind one bit.

For instance, it was Madelaine who persuaded Ritchie that it would be much to his advantage to maintain some kind of a link with his brother.

"Come on, Maddy," Ritchie had protested. "I shot the guy. You think he's gonna forgive an' forget?"

"He stole your wife, did he not?"

"Maybe, but I can't ask him to do the donkey work."

"Do you not still trust him?"

"I trusted him with Ruth and look what happened."

"Now he has what he wanted, he will be a little guilty about it all, if he is the person you tell me. He will do what you ask, Ritchie!"

"What's the point, Maddy?"

"He will help to provide you with a clean sheet."

Hence Maury was again involved in Ritchie's affairs and flurries of letters between Paris and London forged a formal bond between the brothers. All Ruth and Maury wanted was to be rid of Ritchie once and for all. But Madelaine had been perceptive; there was a residue of guilt in Maury, a faint sediment of suspicion that he had acted shabbily.

"My God, Maury, he tried to kill you, didn't he?" Ruth would protest.

And Maury would answer, "I wonder if he did, really."

"He did, damn it! It was only by accident that he missed. You're lucky to be alive, Maury."

The shallow wound on Maury's chest had not even required a stitch and the underworld doctor, Klapper, had examined him and treated him with considerable skill. A month later a thready scar was the only reminder of that night. Naturally no report of the shooting had been made to the police. Stan had discreetly removed the gun and dropped it into the Thames.

"I'm lucky to have you," Maury would say.

But Ruth would not be sweet-talked. "Ritchie's up to something, Maury. Be careful."

"Well, he certainly has gall. Plugs me with a bullet, then expects me to act as unpaid executor and tidy up his affairs in England. Sell off Vallois Street, pay hush money to Fletcher and McKim, and take Apex under my wing."

"Don't do it, Maury."

"I'll see to it that the house is sold."

"And pay off those two bitches?"

"I've done that already. But I don't want to be mixed up with Apex. Too much fishy business went on there. I'm handing it over to Stan. He seems willing to keep it going. It's a thriving concern. With Ritchie out of the way, I'm sure Stan'll clean it up."

"I thought Ritchie wanted to stay on as a partner."

"That's up to Stan. I've suggested that he and Mitchell raise the capital needed to buy Ritchie out."

"Will Ritchie go for that, Maury?"

"Perhaps. It's worth a try."

After three months of negotiations, Ritchie accepted a generous offer for the major share hold in the Apex Advertising Company and his last connection with England, apart from one, was shorn.

Dining with Holly and Kennedy in Chelsea one bitter night the following November, Maury brought up the subject of Ritchie's motive for keeping in touch at all.

"I can't figure out what he wants from us now," Maury said.

It was Holly who supplied an answer.

She said, "I think he wants respectability."

"Ritchie couldn't be respectable to save his goddamned life," said Ruth.

"You're safe enough, Maury," said Kennedy, "provided you have that collection of stolen objects to threaten him with."

"I returned all that stuff months ago," said Maury. "I sent

it, anonymously, to Scotland Yard. The return wasn't made public, so Ritchie won't find out."

"And the forged paintings?" said Holly. "I wonder how many of Ritchie's fakes are across Europe?"

"Search me," said Ruth.

"I assume they'll turn up in salerooms for years to come," said Kennedy. "Fortunately the only two items we purchased are safe in our basement vault and will never see the light of day."

"The Holbein and the Hobbema; beautiful work," said Holly. "Forgeries, of course, but superbly well done."

"Is the forger still working? said Maury.

"Ritchie's not one to let a golden goose go loose," said Ruth.

"What about the Americans, Holly? Were they happy enough to be bought off?" asked Maury.

"We paid them in full," said Holly. "But . . . a friend called on them in New York and put in a good word for us. We've heard no more of the matter."

"A friend?" said Ruth.

"Peter Freeman," said Kennedy.

Quickly Maury changed the subject. "Holly, what did you mean when you said that Ritchie wants respectability?"

"You don't imagine he's going straight?" said Ruth.

"I doubt that," said Holly. "But the Dubriels and de Rais will have no more to do with him. He'll have to start afresh, work up new contacts. To live in France permanently he'll need all sorts of official documents. To obtain them, he'll have to convince the authorities that he's a decent, honest, upstanding character."

"He'll never make it," said Ruth.

"He might," said Maury.

"If he marries a French girl," said Holly.

"Marries Madelaine?" said Ruth. "He wouldn't marry a girl like that, would he?"

"If there's profit in it, he would," said Holly.

"Is that what it's all about?" asked Maury. "Divorce?"

"I thought it would please you two," said Holly.

"It does," said Ruth. "It does, it does."

"Not me," said Maury. "I love living in sin."

"You can't live in sin in Richmond," said Holly. "It's impossible."

"And you won't be so keen on sin, my boy," Ruth said, "when the babies come."

"Ruth, don't tell me you're pregnant?" said Holly.

"Not yet," said Ruth. "But we're working on it."

Divorce was indeed the crux of the matter.

Prompted by Madelaine, Ritchie invested his capital in a pleasant shop in the Boulevard St. Germain. He hired two venerable restorers and a framer to provide cover and spent six months buying middle-range works to grace the opening. Claude Cazotte was prised away from his easel and sent to Canada to visit his brother, to keep him safe off the scene for half a year. The shop was registered in Madelaine's name and from it the girl hoped to leap to bigger and better things. It was not love that dictated the shape of her immediate future but caution. Marriage to Ritchie was no more than a cornerstone in a façade of hypocrisy.

Maury did his bit in London and Madelaine Cazotte in Paris; within eighteen months the relevant business had been squared away. Monsieur Richard Beckman took Mademoiselle Madelaine Cazotte to be his bride. Ruth Erbach Beckman married Maury accompanied by a fleeting toot from gossips' trumpets that faded into indifferent silence almost faster than the petals of her bouquet.

By that time, towards the end of 1934, Cazotte's had acquired quite a startling reputation among discerning art collectors, not in Paris but in Munich and Hamburg, Dusseldorf and Berlin, centres of the new culture where power, wealth and greed went hand in hand and Madame Beckman and her spouse, in spite of their dubious origins, were made welcome and paid handsomely for the services they rendered to Art and Money.

It was then, and only then, that Maury, Ruth and Holly were left in peace, and ties with Ritchie finally severed.

Lord knows, Maury and Ruth Beckman had enough to occupy them, what with a fine new house in Royal Grove, Richmond, to lick into habitable shape and, in May, 1935, a brand new infant daughter who, Maury proudly declared, looked as if she had been licked into shape already.

Relatives and friends were delighted at the happiness that the arrival of young Laura – called after nobody but herself – bestowed upon Ruth and Maury.

Cissie dragged Leo up from Hastings once or twice a month and took charge of the nursery as a grandmother was entitled to do, as all-wise as if she had raised a dozen of her own. For once even Leo knew where he stood and was proud to be left in charge of the baby carriage all on his own, well warned by Cissie that if he dared leave the mite outside a public house, even for half a blessed minute, she would find out and would personally skin him alive.

Stan Nuttall brought his daughters round to Park Grove, with permission, to show them what motherhood looked like and to give them a hint that he believed marriage to be a more desirable objective than having a good time. But the tough, tender manner in which Ruth treated little Laura bamboozled the traditional Stan, though his daughters thought it hilarious and were obviously much impressed by Ruth and took to dropping in whenever their busy careers as girls-about-town allowed.

In the autumn of that year, when Laura was six months old and Ruth had become pregnant for a second time, Maury contrived a reconciliation of sorts between the ailing Mendel, Tilly and their daughter. It was a strained and difficult meeting. Mendel could not understand why Tilly had lied to him. He found it hard to believe that the pretty, self-confident woman with the baby in her arms was really his beloved daughter and not some *Doppelgänger* that Tilly had raised to haunt him in the winter of his days. But Maury was patient and gentle with the old man and the joy that it finally brought to Mendel made the pain worthwhile. When Mendel sat cushioned in his wheelchair, with Laura on his lap, his craftsman's hands secure about her, Ruth was so touched that she had to go out of the room to shed a few tears.

Mendel Erbach did not live to look on his second grand-child, however, and after that, ice caked Tilly's heart once more and mother and daughter remained enemies and apart.

All work and no play had made Maury rich; it had also come close to making him into an exceedingly dull dog. He took heed of Holly's warning that one's children grow up and grow away all in the winking of an eye and her suggestion that he had better make the most of these precious years of happiness.

Laura's illustrious godmother, Jane Tatton Swale, was more blunt about it. "Now, Maurice, what's going to come first; your family or your bank account?" Maury shed much of his work load, employed young men of flair and ambition to manage the more demanding parts of his empire and, within reason, gave them their head.

In fact Maury's income did not suffer by the delegation of authority and Beckman Enterprises went from strength to strength. Maury missed the daily grind of personal involvement hardly at all and revelled in a leisure that he had never known before. When his son, Charles Walter, was born he relinquished two more directorships to celebrate and purchased a large country cottage in the wilds of Kent where he and his brood could fill their lungs with fresh air and romp in the huge garden at weekends and holidays.

Though she disguised it well, Holly was a little envious of her sister-in-law. Her closeness to Maury had been lessened by his marriage and, if she was honest, by her affair with Peter. She missed being the sole object of her brother's affections and was ashamed of the manner of their alienation. At a deeper level, Holly was discomfited by Ruth's babies and the yearning that came on her to have her young womanhood returned, to experience an uncomplicated, devoted sort of motherhood that she had never quite known with Chris.

This too, Kennedy observed and understood. In spite of problems with his health, he gingered Holly to reshape Kings' business. To his surprise, Holly elected to contract rather than expand. In the course of a year she phased out trade in paintings, in spite of a bullish art market, and returned to dealing exclusively in fine antiques, particularly in porcelain and china which had always been her main field of interest. By the end of 1935 the vast floor space of the premises in the Chalfont Arcade had begun to seem super-fluous and the Kings spent many hours in amicable discussion of whether they should seek a smaller place, out of London perhaps. The matter dragged on, without resolution, but that, with other trade matters, kept the couple close and occupied.

Holly heard nothing from Peter Freeman, apart from one short note from New York soon after his return to America. She did not seek news of him but found that the dancer's fame brought her word of his progress and, if the columnists were to be believed, of his whirlwind personal life, a string of so-called 'romances' with Hollywood beauties.

Romance? Holly had found it, touched it, felt it separate and float away like thistledown. Perhaps the illusion was more substantial than the reality and more enduring; she would cherish it, intact and unsullied, all the rest of her days.

* * *

Fifth-former Chris was a man now. The assurance of youth had finally overcome the last vestiges of childish dependence. He was more of a pal to Holly than ever before and, apart from rebellious views on politics and a sense of purpose that more than matched Holly's own, mother and son found that they were, after all, compatible.

Holly was aware that Chris shared his deepest confidences with Kennedy, not with her, but she trusted her husband to steer the boy, the man, well. She suspected that Kennedy and Chris had had a long talk about her. It would be typical of Chris to seek answers to embarrassing questions about her behaviour. She had no notion what Kennedy had told Chris, how he had explained that kindness and forgiveness did not equate with weakness and that no man or woman was made without flaw. Perhaps he related it to honour, a quality that Chris admired more than any other as an illusion worthy of pursuit. How comfortable the Beckmans would have been if they had been born untainted by honour and by love. They might have thrived selfishly, without suffering – but they would never have known joy. Whatever Kennedy said – and perhaps there was no such conversation – Chris did not appear to harbour resentment for the grief and confusion that his mother had brought to his adolescent years.

Holly was sufficiently sure of her son's understanding to issue the invitation without hesitation.

It was two years and four months since Peter had gone out of her life. In that time she had not mentioned his name. With good reason, she felt that the time had come to put the seal on the episode.

Rain had washed out the late season cricket and the tag-end of the long summer vacation had become something of a bore to both Chris and his parents. The young man wanted to be on, to be at it, to finish his final year at school, cantering towards the moment when he would be old enough to enter Pilot Training with the Royal Air Force, when he might, literally, take wing.

In that drizzling, cloud-lagged autumn, on that dreary Tuesday afternoon, however, it was difficult to be patient. Chris was relieved when his mother returned unexpectedly from the gallery to lunch at home.

They ate together in the kitchen.

"Where's Dad?"

"Minding the shop."

"Glad you came, Mum. Are you staying or is there a sale somewhere?"

Holly cut up her lamb chop and asked her son to pass the sauce boat. Then she said, "No, I've nothing on this afternoon. I thought we might go to the pictures."

He did not ask; the advertisements had not escaped his notice.

"Chris, I want to go, but not on my own. Will you come with me?"

"The Odeon?"

"Yes, in Leicester Square."

Chris did not enquire whether or not Kennedy knew of her intention. Without hesitation, he said, "I'd love to."

"It's . . . it's a musical picture."

"I don't mind that."

"It's called *Dance, My Darling Daughters*."

"Yes, Mum." Chris nodded to indicate that he understood.

Holly made herself finish lunch. The maid served coffee in the upstairs lounge and mother and son talked with apparent casualness of other things for a quarter of an hour.

At length Chris put down his cup. "Well, I'm ready when you are."

"I'm ready," said Holly.

They drove through the rain in the Sunbeam, parked the motor car in Orange Street and hurried on foot round to the cinema.

The foyer was brightly lit and a surprising number of people, mostly women, waited in line at the ticket booths. From the walls the posters seemed to stare directly at Holly; Peter's face, Peter's eyes. She resented the other women there, his fans; they were free to admire his charm in innocence, moon over him, anticipate the pleasure he would give them for the next couple of hours. She noticed that Chris avoided looking directly at the advertisements.

Mother and son walked up the carpeted steps side by side, passing a life-sized plyboard model of the dancer in top hat and tails, his arm stretched stiff in welcome, the painted smile fixed, his painted eyes far, far too blue.

The door, the slanted plane of the screen, the usherette, carpet beneath their feet, sweeping rows of faces; they were minutes late for the beginning of the picture and pushed awkwardly past lumpy knees into tip seats in the centre stalls. Around them music flowed brashly. Holly settled, falling into a tense, attentive stillness while Chris, a habitual picture-goer, slouched down in the seat with his long legs cocked. For once Holly did not nudge him and tell him to sit up straight. The young man studied the images across steepled fingers and after a while Holly forgot that her son was there.

A winter's night, glittering snow, a huge black limousine canted into a drift by the side of a country road; Howard Crocker dressed in chauffeur's uniform, was playing his mumbling self. In the rear of the limousine, in top hat and black overcoat, was Peter. His voice, Holly noticed, was deeper than she recalled it, his features less sharp, his movements not quite so rapid. The relaxed charm seemed even more natural, as if he had been born with it. Then there was a mansion, brilliantly lighted across lawns, the strains of an orchestra; Peter and a complaining Howard argued by the mansion's gate. Impulsively Peter headed across a snow-covered lawn towards a terrace and a frieze of windows behind which a millionaire's party was in full swing. Lugging a couple of suitcases, Howard crunched through the artificial snow.

A girl: a girl more idealised, more elegant than Holly had ever been, stood on the terrace in defiance of the cold, quarrelling with a beefy young man who had somehow contrived to become her fiancé. Peter saw the girl. The music swelled in a sentimentasl crescendo. Love at first sight.

Holly's unexpected detachment increased.

She found the story silly and contrived. She searched in vain – out of vanity – for some sign, some signal that Peter might have made that would reach across the Atlantic and prove meaningful to her alone. It was a ridiculous conceit. Peter was nothing now but a figment of imagination. Only once, fleetingly, when he danced alone with the girl in a darkened ballroom did Holly know the painful pleasure of regret, identifying, for a handful of seconds only, the plain steps that preceded the elaborate waltz. The remembered touch, the lightness, the thistledown, she missed them for a moment.

She grew bored with the film and was relieved when it ended. She did not spontaneously applaud like many of the women in the audience.

Beside her Chris unfolded himself and stretched.

"What did you think of it?" she asked.

"It was all right."

She gave a little cough that turned into a chuckle. "I thought it was awful."

He sat up straight. "Really? Did you? But your . . . I mean, Mr. Freeman? Didn't you think he was good?"

Holly put her arm through her son's and squeezed. "I did once. But not in *Dance, My Darling Daughters*. Shall we go?"

"If you like."

Holly made to rise, then the curtains parted once more and she felt Chris stiffen beside her.

"Oh!" he exclaimed. "Do you mind if we stay for the short?"

"Of course not, dear."

Germany Today.

In a quarter of an hour the images of romance had been wiped from Holly's mind by the granular footage of a short documentary film presented beneath cheerful commentary.

Wakening from her dreams, her preoccupation with the world within herself, Holly saw for the first time what had been going on all around her.

If she had been alone she might have contrived to ignore its significance but, with Chris by her side, parading armies and rolling tanks brought back a flood of memories from an earlier period in her life, long before Peter. This was the incisive splendour that her first husband's poems had bitterly condemned. One poem in particular rang in her head while the military tattoo from the screen grew shockingly loud.

Young John Bull Strode Out One Noon.

Young John Bull?

She barely had the courage to watch the film to its end.

It was raining very hard in Leicester Square when Holly and Chris emerged from the cinema. The sky was lidded with cloud and theatre lights and shopfront displays cast glittering reflections on the pavements. Rush hour traffic glutted the streets. They ran down to Orange Street and clambered quickly into the Sunbeam.

She had gone out to taste the experiences of the past, to find Peter, but returned home filled with the future, with Chris.

Hastily Holly started the engine and nosed the motor car into the river of traffic that ebbed sluggishly down Haymarket. She felt hemmed in by the hordes of pedestrians, by the black umbrellas of London's businessmen as they marched in search of buses, taxi cabs and trains. She wanted to be home, home with Kennedy and Chris, secure again in the permanent warmth of Tite Street, Chelsea.

Unaware of his mother's mood, Chris was eager to talk.

"I say, wasn't that a sight?"

"What?" She knew perfectly well what had impressed him.

"The planes. Hundreds of them, thousands; the very latest. Did you ever see so many planes, Mum?"

"German planes?"

"The Luftwaffe; the finest air force in the world today."

The eagerness, the admiration in his voice and his total lack of fear chilled Holly's heart. She shivered. The military fly-past was etched deep in her mind too; endless formations of bombers, droning swarms of fighters wheeling over a massed gathering in a Berlin square, wheeling and turning, she imagined, to stream westward towards the coast.

A sudden wave of love and longing for Chris enveloped her, real and unstinting. Without speaking, without touching, giving no sign, Holly cherished her son passionately in her heart.

And carefully drove the Sunbeam home to Chelsea.